# BRITANNIA

Book three of the Veteran of Rome series

## By: William Kelso

Visit the author's website **http://www.williamkelso.co.uk/**

**William Kelso is the author of:**

*The Shield of Rome*
*The Fortune of Carthage*
*Devotio: The House of Mus*
*Caledonia – Book One of the Veteran of Rome Series*
*Hibernia – Book Two of the Veteran of Rome series*
*Britannia – Book Three of the Veteran of Rome series*
*Hyperborea – Book Four of the Veteran of Rome series*
*Germania – Book Five of the Veteran of Rome series*
*The Dacian War – Book Six of the Veteran of Rome series*
*Armenia Capta – Book Seven of the Veteran of Rome series*

D0611161

Britannia – Veteran of Rome Series

Published in 2015 by FeedARead.com Publishing – Arts Council funded

A CIP catalogue record for this title is available from the British Library.


**To: Sean, Katie, Ania, Jack and Robert, the millennials**

## Chapter One - Luguvalium

### Spring 89 AD

The horses hooves thundered across the wooden bridge that spanned the Eden river. It was late in the afternoon. Marcus, clad in his auxiliary chain mail armour and wearing his simple cap like Batavian cavalry helmet looked worried, as he led his patrol westwards along the Stanegate road and into the setting sun. He was a handsome young man of twenty six with red hair. The red hair, his Briton mother, had always reminded him, was a gift, so that he would remember the Celtic blood in his veins. Behind him the thirty Batavian horsemen were silent. The soldiers had slung their small cavalry shields over their backs and were holding their spears aloft. To their right the Eden was swollen with the melting winter snows and was winding its way northwards towards the sea and beyond the river the green lush fields and clumps of trees looked peaceful and beautiful. Marcus frowned. It had been four years since he and the Second Batavian Cohort had been posted to Luguvalium, Carlisle. The land around the fort was excellent farming country and the forests too were filled with game and the river had supplied a plentiful catch of fish to the garrison. But today he could not enjoy the scenery or the fresh western sea breeze. Irritably he adjusted the bronze phallic amulet that hung from a leather cord around his neck. The amulet had been a gift from his Roman father, Corbulo, a good luck charm. After all these years he still had it.

Up ahead the Stanegate looked deserted. The newly laid paving stones glinted in the sunlight. It had taken Agricola's engineers and Legionaries a whole winter to build the road and its construction was a marvel of Roman technology and engineering skill but Marcus hardly noticed the road as he struggled to contain his growing concern. They had not seen a single traveller on the road since they'd left Magnis and the lack of traffic on what was normally a busy strategic road, was beginning to fit a pattern. That morning everything had seemed normal as he'd taken his patrol the twenty-two miles up the

3

Stanegate towards the Roman fort at Magnea Carvetiorum, where the first Batavian Cohort were billeted. It was a routine patrol but whilst resting their horses at the fort, the Prefect of the First Batavians had given him alarming news. Several local men from the Carvetii tribe had come to him, the commander had said, and had warned him that the local tribes were planning to attack his fort. The men had been unable to offer much more information other than to say that the druids were going from village to village inciting the Britons to fight and drive the Romans from the land.

At the thought of the druids Marcus muttered a little prayer to warn away the evil spirits. His father Corbulo, a retired Legionary with the Twentieth, had told him about the druids and what they had done to captured Roman soldiers on Mona Insulis. His father's stories had been enough to put the fear of the gods into him and after his own capture and narrow escape from Caledonia, five years ago, Marcus had vowed never to show mercy to the Celtic priests. No, there could be no compromise between Rome and the druids. He snatched a glance northwards as he and his men thundered on along the road. The news he'd received at Magnis could be nothing more than false rumours spread by local men disgruntled with their own leaders or simply wishing to curry favour with the Batavian garrison. It was after all not the first time such claims had been made, but on his way back to Luguvalium, as a precaution, he'd passed through some of the local Briton villages and there he'd noticed that all the men of fighting age had vanished and that they had taken their cattle with them. Something was wrong he thought, something was going terribly wrong. The locals had never done that before.

Marcus's fingers tightened their grip on his horse's reins and a flush spread across his cheeks. He needed to warn Cotta, his commanding officer. If the Britons were about to rise up then Luguvalium could be attacked and his wife and young son were inside the fort. Marcus bit his lip. Cotta, the Prefect of the Second Batavians was an overweight fool who owed his position solely due to his Roman citizenship and political

4

connections. The officer had very little in common with the tough, simple Batavians or the smattering of local British replacement recruits he'd been appointed to lead. He did not speak their guttural Germanic language nor did he seem interested in their customs. Instead he remained aloof and relied on a few officers who possessed enough Latin to translate his orders. Often Marcus had overheard the Batavians discussing their commander and the comments were never complimentary. But as Beneficiarius, the second in command of the Cohort, Marcus had a sworn duty to support his commanding officer. Nor could he join the rank and file in their contempt for the Prefect's appointment, for he too owed his appointment as Beneficiarius solely to the patronage of Agricola, ex Governor of Britannia, which had been bestowed on him as a reward for his service during the invasion of Hibernia, three years ago now.

Marcus glanced at the riders following him. The men stank of horse but he no longer noticed the pong. He might still be young but it had been nearly ten years since he'd run away from his father's violent upbringing, to join the Second Batavian Cohort. He'd been the first non Batavian to join the unit and army service had turned him from a rebellious, lippy-youth into a battle-hardened veteran and he'd fought at the battle of Mons Graupius in Caledonia and had led the cavalry squadrons during the retreat from Tara in Hibernia. During this time he had come to love and admire these rugged, highly capable Batavian warriors from the lower Rhine delta, but balancing the respect of his men with his duty to the Prefect remained a delicate task.

As Luguvalium finally appeared across the fields, Marcus muttered a prayer of relief. The rectangular fort, sandwiched in between the Eden and a smaller tributary river, looked peaceful. As the patrol approached, Marcus' keen eye turned to inspect the earthen and turf rampart, along whose top ran a solid, seven foot high wooden wall. His men seemed alert. Sentries were strolling up and down along the parapet behind the wall and in the tall, roofed-watch towers, he could see that the Scorpion bolt thrower was armed and manned. He turned to glare at the deep V shaped ditch that ran along the earthen ramparts, but it had been cleared of debris and shrubs, just like he had ordered that morning.

Satisfied, he turned his gaze towards the small civilian settlement of huts and round houses that clustered around the southern gate. The settlement had grown since he'd first arrived at the fort and now stretched beyond the tributary river to the south. The intense smell of pig manure enveloped the village and from the smoke-holes in the houses smoke was drifting away to the east. Close by, a neglected cow was mooing loudly in a field and the dull metallic hammering of the blacksmith at work, echoed away into the thick forest that lined the northern bank of the Eden. Marcus eyed the Britons carefully as he and his patrol slowed to a walk and approached the main gate into the fort. The community made their living from the fort and there had never been any serious trouble bar the odd scrap over a woman or an unpaid debt. Amongst the round houses with their sturdy wooden wall posts, white wickerwork walls and conical thatched roofs, the locals were going about their business and few bothered to pay any attention to the patrol as it clattered passed.

The gates to the fort swung open as Marcus and the remainder of his troop approached and Marcus raised his hand in greeting as he caught sight of the officer of the watch, who was standing above the gateway.

"You are back early Sir," the officer cried with a smile.

"Everything alright?"

"Where is the Prefect?" Marcus called out, ignoring the officer's question.

"Old Cotta," the Batavian officer replied sheepishly, "I think he's having a bath in his quarters. Some of the lads have been asked to bring him wood and water. I think he's been in there for some time."

"Right," Marcus replied, lowering his gaze. Handling relations between the Prefect and his Batavian subordinates was a wearisome business. Sometimes the men's insolence towards the Prefect crossed the line, but many of the Batavian officers knew exactly how far to push matters, without earning themselves a rebuke.

"Get Lucius and Adalberht to meet me at the Prefect's quarters at once," Marcus called out, looking up at the officer of the watch. "No excuses, I have urgent news."

The smile faded from the Batavian's face.

"Urgent? Yes Sir," the officer nodded as he caught the look on Marcus's face. A moment later he hurried away along the parapet.

Marcus slid quickly from his horse and handed the reins to a slave, who led the beast towards the stables. Then he was stomping across the muddy ground towards the centre of the fort and a large wooden building. To his right and left the rows of simple wooden barracks blocks ran parallel to the walls of the fort. The men were preparing their evening meal and the smell of freshly baking bread and roasting meat competed with the smell of pig shit.

Cotta was lying in his bronze bath tub as Marcus stepped into the Prefect's quarters. Steam was rising from the water and Cotta was sweating. A slave, clad in a simple white tunic was hunched over him gently shaving the officer's cheeks with a little knife. As he caught sight of Marcus, the slave stopped what he was doing and retreated a few steps. Marcus saluted smartly as Cotta's nose twitched in disgust. The tub was not large enough to fit all of him in and the top of his belly protruded above the water.

"I am having a bath," Cotta growled as his nose twitched again, "Whatever you have to report can it not wait until I am done?"

7

"I'm afraid not Sir," Marcus said stiffly.

Inside his bath tub Cotta stirred irritably and sent some water splashing onto the floor. The Prefect was in his mid forties and had short, grey cut hair.

"If you must Marcus," he snapped, "I suppose you have come to discuss the news that we received this morning. I was going to tell you later today."

"I have been out on patrol since dawn," Marcus frowned, "What news?"

Cotta sighed and ran his hand over his forehead. "I thought you knew," he said looking confused. "A messenger arrived this morning from HQ at Deva. We have received orders. The whole Cohort is being redeployed. We are leaving Luguvalium at the end of this month for our new posting."

Marcus opened his mouth and closed it again without saying anything.

"Your woman and son can come with us of course," Cotta exclaimed. For a moment the Prefect was silent as he stared at Marcus, "I thought you would be happy," he continued. "At last we can leave this wretched, stinking shit hole behind. Personally I don't think I can stand another of these northern winters. Gods give me a bit of civilisation any day."

"Redeployed," Marcus muttered. "Where are they sending us?"

"Pannonia, apparently," Cotta replied with a serious look.

"Pannonia?" Marcus shook his head. He hadn't gotten a clue where that was.

Cotta, seeing the confusion on his second in command's face, shook his head in dismay.

"Oh for fuck's sake," Cotta hissed. "I forgot that you are an uneducated man. Look it up on a map of the world. It's the province north east of Italia and about two thousand miles from here, so we will need to discuss the preparations for our journey."

Marcus was just about to reply, when two officers quietly entered the room behind him and saluted. They were clad in chain mail and had tucked their helmets under their arms. It was Lucius and Adalberht. The two men gave Marcus a quick, questioning look.

"What the fuck are you doing here?" Cotta roared as he caught sight of the officers. "I am in the bath, I don't arrange meetings when I am in the bath."

"Sir," Marcus cleared his throat, "I called them here. I have some urgent news, which cannot wait."

He nodded at Lucius and Adalberht. The two Batavians were both old enough to be his father and as first Centurion and first Decurion respectively, they were the most senior officers in the Cohort after himself and the Prefect.

"I took a patrol up the Stanegate this morning," Marcus continued, "We went as far as Magnis. At the fort I spoke with Honorius the Prefect. He told me that a few of the locals had warned him that the tribes were preparing to attack his fort. Then on the way back I noticed that all the young men had left their villages. They have taken their cattle with them."

"They have taken their cattle. Are you sure?" Lucius said with a frown.

Marcus nodded.

Cotta glanced at his principal officers and then raised his hand in the air.

"So what are you saying Marcus?" he growled.

"I think there is going to be an uprising," Marcus replied. "Honorius told me that the druids are moving from village to village inciting rebellion. We should prepare ourselves Sir. We should order the garrison to remain under arms tonight. Then tomorrow we should send out patrols to find out what is going on out there."

The room fell silent. Cotta was looking down into the bath water as his fingers drummed the side of the tub.

"Ah," the Prefect said at last looking up, "Honorius is always seeing things that are not there and as for the locals and their cattle, maybe they have just decided to take them to new pastures. Who knows about these things. No, Marcus I don't think keeping the whole Cohort under arms throughout the night is a good idea. It's going to piss off the men just before we have to pack up and set out on a long journey."

"Sir, I believe the threat to be real," Marcus replied stubbornly. "It's just a precaution."

But Cotta shook his head.

"No, I have made my decision," he snapped. "I am not going to go chasing shadows and rumours. That will be all."

## Chapter Two - Shadows and Rumours

Outside Marcus turned to face Lucius and Adalberht. Lucius was a tall man, clean shaven with short grey hair and thoroughly Romanised to the point where he had taken a Roman name. His uniform, armour and helmet were immaculate. Marcus eyed him cautiously. Lucius, first Centurion of the Batavian infantry companies, which made up the bulk of the Cohort, was Bestia's younger brother, but in sharp contrast to Bestia, the violent bully whom Marcus had known, Lucius was a calm, quietly spoken, decent man and a loyal soldier. He had however, never gotten over his brother's desertion after the battle of Mons Graupius and Marcus had never had the courage to tell him that it was Corbulo, Marcus's own father who had killed Bestia in a tavern in Viroconium. Lucius still believed that his brother was alive somewhere and whenever he could, he would enquire about Bestia with passing merchants, travellers and messengers.

"Shadows and fucking rumours indeed," Adalberht broke the silence as he spoke in his native Batavian language. "Well that's settled then. Seems our illustrious leader doesn't give a shit about your concerns Marcus." Adalberht chuckled. "I am off to get my dinner, some of the boys are roasting a sheep in honour of my birthday. Fifty two today, boys, fifty fucking two."

Marcus sighed as he watched the two officers stride away. Adalberht was a bear of a man with a shock of unruly and unwashed white hair, a grey beard and piercing blue eyes. He had been with the Second Batavian Cohort for thirty-three years, making him by far the longest and oldest serving member of the unit. He'd fought for Rome, then against Rome during the Batavian rebellion, had been pardoned and then fought for Rome once more in Britannia and Hibernia and during all this time he'd refused to abandon his fierce loyalty to his native Batavian Gods, customs and traditions. The man was well passed retirement age but had simply refused to leave the unit and as commander of the cavalry squadrons of the Cohort, he was one of the most popular and respected officers in the unit. Marcus shook his head in weary resignation. Adalberht had never really accepted Marcus's promotion to Beneficiarius for it was a position he himself had craved and now and then the resentment showed.

Marcus blew the air from his mouth and glanced up at the sky. It would be dark soon. He had done what he could he thought. He turned in the direction of the barracks block that housed the slaves and where he had billeted his family. Fergus, his son was three years old now and liked to run around the camp carrying his small wooden sword that Marcus had made for him. The little' boy's infectious laughter and curiosity had already won him the affection of the Batavian soldiers.

From the corner of his eye, Marcus noticed a soldier approaching.

"Sir," the man saluted. "There is someone at the gate asking for you. One of the town's folk. He's insisting that he speaks with you at once."

Marcus raised his eyebrows and glanced in the direction of the southern gate. What was this? Another civilian trying to beg a favour or sell him something? With a nod to the soldier he set off towards the gate.

Outside the gate house waiting patiently was a humble looking, grey haired man of around forty, clad in a simple stained woollen tunic and as Marcus caught sight of him his heart sank. It was Brann, his father in law. Brann was a fisherman who supplied the fort with fresh fish. It was through this contact that Marcus had met his daughter. Marcus groaned inwardly as he stepped out through the gate and raised his hand in greeting. How was he going to tell this man that his daughter and grandson were about to leave on a two thousand mile journey across the empire to a new home? The news was not going to go down well.

"Marcus," Brann said, speaking in the Briton language, "thank you for coming to see me. I   know you are a busy man."

12

"What can I do for you Brann?" Marcus said in a tight voice.

Brann looked down at the ground and Marcus noticed a sudden tension in his father in law.

Brann looked up and there was something resolute in his eyes. "I would like my daughter and grandson to come and stay with me for a few days outside your fort. It will be good for them to spend some time with their kin."

Marcus was silent for a moment. Then he shook his head.

"No," he replied quietly, "after what happened to them three years ago when I was in Hibernia, I will not be parted from them. They are happy inside the fort and their place is at my side. I am sorry Brann."

For a moment Brann's face was unreadable as he stared at Marcus in silence.

"The fort is not safe Marcus," Brann hissed with a sudden hint of desperation in his voice, "trouble is coming for you Romans. Your family will be safer with me. I beg you Marcus, let them go whilst you still can."

Marcus eyes widened and suddenly he could feel his heart thumping in his chest. He took a step towards his father in law.

"What do you mean, the fort is not safe, what trouble?" he said quickly.

Brann glanced nervously over his shoulder at the Celtic round houses. Then he shook his head.

"Please Marcus," Brann was pleading now, "Let them out. I will take them to a safe place, no harm will come to your family, I swear it."

Marcus glanced over the man's shoulders at the civilian settlement and for a long moment he did not reply. Then slowly he turned to look at Brann.

"I will protect my family," he muttered, "You have my word and you will just have to trust me," and with that he turned round and strode back into the fort.

As the gate crashed shut behind him, Marcus felt a hot flush spread across his cheeks.

"Lucius, where the fuck are you?" he shouted as he strode across the open parade ground. To his right a group of Batavians were lounging about around the entrance to the officer's quarters. The men clad in their fur-lined helmets were singing a native Batavian song and, as Marcus caught the scent of roasting sheep, he veered towards the building. Inside, some of the off duty Decurion's were clustered around an open fire over which they were roasting a whole sheep. The men fell silent as they noticed Marcus. Then slowly Adalberht rose to his feet.

"What's going on Marcus? Have you come to join us?"

Adalberht grinned.

"Outside now," Marcus ordered as he turned away without waiting for an answer. As he stepped out of the barrack's block he saw Lucius hastening towards him across the muddy parade ground. Marcus waited for him as Adalberht emerged into the open air with a sullen look. Impatiently Marcus took a few paces away from the group of Batavians, who by now had fallen silent and were watching him curiously. Lucius frowned as he caught the look on Marcus's face.

"So what the fuck is going on?" Adalberht growled.

Marcus glanced at the two officers. Then he took a deep breath.

"Tonight the whole Cohort will remain under arms. I want every available man armed and wearing his armour and up on the ramparts. That includes your cavalrymen Adalberht."

The two senior officers looked surprised.

"But Cotta just ordered us to do no such thing," Adalberht blurted out. "You are disobeying a direct order Marcus. He's not going to like that."

"I will handle Cotta," Marcus said sternly, "just make sure your men do as instructed."

"Why?" Lucius interrupted with a concerned look, "Do you think the Britons are going to attack us tonight?"

Marcus nodded, "It's possible," he muttered. "I just received another warning."

"You are going to get into trouble for this," Adalberht snapped, "but fuck it Marcus, if you are convinced these Britons would be so stupid as to attack us then I'd rather be prepared than unprepared and dead."

"Good, then its settled. This is my decision and I shall take full responsibility," Marcus said, as he turned to look at the wooden ramparts.

"What about Cotta?" Lucius said, "He's bound to notice that the men are not in their barracks. Adalberht is right. This could end badly for you Marcus."

Marcus looked grim. "Maybe," he muttered, "but we are doing this none the less."

## Chapter Three - The Long Night

Marcus strode along the parapet with his hands clasped behind his back. Behind him came the Cohort's trumpeter, holding onto his conical brass trumpet and the standard-bearer, clasping aloft the unit banner. It was night and beyond the ramparts the darkness was silent and impenetrable. Marcus glanced up but there was no moon. The only light came from the torches that burned in the watch towers and around the southern gate. In the reddish devilish glow he could see the Batavian auxiliaries lining the walls. The men wearing their exotic feathered infantry helmets with the cheek and neck-guards removed, sat slumped on the parapet with their backs pressed up against the wooden palisade and their long flat oval shields leaning against their shoulders. Their long thrusting Hastae spears lay at their feet and in the faint light he could see the glint of their chain mail armour and hear the soft clink of equipment and the odd muffled cough.

Near the southern gate of the fort he turned to stare out into the dark night and mutter a short silent prayer. The darkness hid the look on his face and for that he was glad. If the decision he'd just taken proved wrong, his military career would be over and possibly his life too for the army took insubordination very seriously and there was no doubt he would be punished. He bit his lip. Long ago he had decided that he would never be like his father, Corbulo. For most of his life his father had led a debauched, violent life; he'd driven his first wife to suicide and he'd beaten Marcus more times than he cared to remember. No, he would never be like his father, so upon his return from Hibernia three years ago he'd made a solemn vow before the immortal gods that he would protect his family from all harm and that he would rather die than see them suffer. If the Britons were going to attack the fort they would slaughter everyone inside. There was no doubt about that. He sighed and rubbed his forehead. But if he was wrong and the authorities had him executed, how could he protect his family then? He shook his head. This was no time for doubts. He had made his decision and that was that.

"What are those men doing out of their barracks!" a loud annoyed sounding voice suddenly screamed in Latin. The noise seemed to come from the centre of the camp. Marcus closed his eyes. It was Cotta.

"What the fuck is going on? Cotta yelled.

The fort remained silent. Cotta was swearing now as he clambered up onto the parapets and began to pick his way down the line. He was coming towards the southern rampart and as he passed by, the Batavian auxiliaries turned to look at him.

"Adalberht," Marcus heard Cotta's voice cry out, "What are you doing? Who gave the order to move the men up onto the ramparts?"

For a moment the darkness remained silent.

"Marcus did, Sir," Marcus heard Adalberht reply. "He's over near the southern gate I think."

A storm of swear words spewed forth from Cotta's mouth.

"Marcus, get your arse over here right now," the Prefect roared.

Quietly Marcus turned and climbed down the ladder. On the ground he strode straight towards Cotta. The Prefect was holding a flaming torch in one hand and he was surrounded by a few men from his personal bodyguard. He glared as he caught sight of Marcus, his face flush with anger.

"What do you think you are doing?" Cotta hissed, as he shook his head, "You disobeyed a direct order, my order. What the fuck is wrong with you?"

Marcus glanced calmly towards the ramparts. "I believe we are in imminent danger of being attacked Sir, that's why I ordered the men up onto the walls. It was my decision alone Sir."

"You are fool and a disgrace," Cotta hissed his eyes flashing wildly. "There is going to be no attack. The Britons are not that stupid. There are a thousand armed men inside this fort." For a moment the Prefect was silent as angrily he examined Marcus. Then abruptly he turned to the men of his bodyguard.

"Take him," Cotta snarled, "and bind him to the lashing pole in the parade ground. At first light he's to receive twenty lashes and I want the whole camp to witness it. This man has surrendered any honour he ever had."

"What will you do with me?" Marcus cried out as the bodyguard closed in on him.

Cotta's lip curled in contempt. "I know about you and your father's friendship with Agricola but even he will not save you this time. I have witnesses. You disobeyed a direct order and I can have you executed for that."

\*\*\*

"Eighteen," the man holding the whip cried out.

The whip flew through the air and struck Marcus's back with a dull whacking noise. Marcus jerked forwards and cried out as an explosion of pain ripped through his body. It was dawn and he stood bare-chested tied to a wooden post in the centre of the parade ground inside the fort. Blood was welling up from the cuts made by the whip and his face was soaked in sweat. Around him, drawn up in neat straight lines as if they were about to charge into battle, rows upon rows of Batavians stood to attention, watching the spectacle in complete silence.

"Nineteen," the man behind Marcus called out and once more the whip came flying in and struck Marcus in the back sending his body jerking forwards. Marcus groaned and forced open his eyes as he waited for the final blow. His back was a streaky mess of blood and his legs shook as he tried to stay upright. From the corner of his eye he caught sight of Kyna, his wife. She was holding a hand to her mouth in horror and at her side Fergus, his three year old son clung to his mother's leg. Cotta had been adamant that they watch Marcus's disgrace.

"Twenty."

Marcus closed his eyes and cried out as the whip struck. For a moment he hung from the pole; the ropes that bound him, the only thing preventing him from falling to the ground.

"Soldiers! This is what becomes of men who disobey orders," he heard Cotta shout in a loud voice. "This man betrayed my trust; he betrayed the honour of this Cohort. He is a disgrace. He will stay where he is all day and all night. No one is permitted to give him food or water or speak with him. That will be all. Now get back to your duties. Move it."

The neat lines of soldiers dissolved as the men turned away and began to spread out through the camp. Marcus opened his eyes and looked down at the mud. The pain was intense. He groaned and a little bit of spittle slowly extended from his mouth. There had been no attack that night. He'd been wrong. He had thrown away his military career and possibly his life for nothing. The doubts came thick and fast threatening to tear him apart. With an effort he forced himself to look up. Cotta had gone but he caught sight of Lucius and Adalberht. The two officers were watching him with weary resigned expressions. Then they too turned away and joined the throng of men going about their morning routine. Marcus lowered his head as he suddenly thought of Corbulo, his father. His father had always been in trouble with his superior officers and had often been disciplined during his service with the Twentieth. Despite the pain and remorseless doubts Marcus raised his head and began to laugh.

And here he was believing that he was any different to his father.

\*\*\*

Marcus licked his cracked lips as he felt the glare of the sun on his head. It was late in the afternoon. He half hung from the wooden post. Around him the fort was going about its business, as if he did not exist. How long had he stood here? Wearily he closed his eyes. Cotta's punishment was proving brutally effective. Every man in the Second Batavian Cohort would know by now what happened to men who disobeyed orders. His mind began to drift once more. What would he give to touch Kyna's cheek or ruffle Fergus's hair.

Suddenly he heard someone coming towards him and a moment later a hand lifted up his chin and pressed a wooden bowl of water against his lips. Marcus opened his eyes and looked up at the man standing over him. It was Lucius. There was a stern look on the first centurion's face.

"Drink it, Marcus," Lucius said quietly.

Gratefully Marcus opened his mouth as Lucius emptied the bowl down his throat.

Around them a few soldiers had paused to stare.

"Thank you," Marcus whispered.

"Cotta has sent a messenger to Deva," Lucius said, eyeing Marcus carefully, "he is putting his case to the Legate of the Twentieth himself." Lucius sighed. "He intends to have you executed but he's wary of the patronage you enjoy with Agricola. It may be a few days before we receive a reply."

Marcus coughed and grimaced as his body shook in a spasm of pain.

"Lucius," he muttered at last, "Tonight, have the men arm themselves, have them ready to fight, but keep them inside their barracks. Do this, please."

For a moment Lucius remained silent as he examined Marcus sternly.

"You still think these rumours about an uprising are true?" he muttered. "There was no attack last night Marcus and some of the men are questioning your judgement."

"Just do it," Marcus said looking Lucius straight in the eye, "I am right about this, I know that I am right. They are coming for us."

"Alright," Lucius replied looking away, "I will think about it."

## Chapter Four - Rebellion

Marcus was woken by a sudden shriek. Startled he opened his eyes. He was still tied to the wooden post in the middle of the parade ground. It was night and the fort lay blanketed in darkness. To his right a flaming arrow arched gracefully into the sky and flew over the rampart before thudding into the mud not far from him. It was followed by another shout. Marcus blinked rapidly. What was going on? Ahead of him, along the north eastern rampart, one of the Batavian sentries suddenly staggered and toppled backwards into the camp clutching a spear, that had embedded itself in his chest. Marcus's eyes widened in horror as in the dim light he caught sight of silent men surging over the top of the palisade.

In one of the watch towers a Batavian yelled out and a moment later a hasty trumpet blast echoed away into the night.

"We're under attack, we're under attack!" someone screamed.

A dull bang suddenly erupted against the southern gate and one of the sentries cried out in alarm and fright.

"They are trying to break down the gate, help us, help!"

Suddenly the night erupted as all at once hundreds of voices cried out and screamed their battle cries. The noise sent a shiver of pure fear down Marcus's spine. The voices belonged to Britons. Along the north eastern rampart he caught sight of more ladders thudding up against the wooden palisade. The Britons were pouring over the wall and onto the parapet and some had already jumped down into the fort. The unlucky sentries along that stretch of the defences did not stand a chance, and as Marcus stared at the scene with growing horror another lifeless body tumbled from the parapet.

"What the fuck is going on?" a Batavian voice close by shouted. Marcus blinked. Had that been Lucius?

"Second Batavian Cohort, to arms, get out here and fight! They are coming over the wall!" the voice screamed a split moment later.

"Cut me free, cut me free, I am over here," Marcus yelled as desperation filled him with a surge of energy.

A figure loomed up out of the darkness. The man was holding a burning torch and he was clad in armour but Marcus could not tell who it was. Quickly and expertly the man sliced through the ropes that bound Marcus to the wooden post.

"You were right," the figure hissed, "you were right. Here take this," the man said flinging a Gladius onto the ground at Marcus's feet. Then he was gone shouting orders as he vanished.

From the barracks blocks the Batavian auxiliaries stumbled out into the fort. There was no time to form up into a body of men or execute any tactical manoeuvres. The Britons were already inside the fort and it was every man for himself. Marcus scrabbled wildly in the mud until his fingers closed around the hilt of the sword. Around him the night air was rent with screams, yells, shouts and curses as the Batavians ran straight into the attackers and the night descended into chaos. Clutching his sword Marcus crouched in the mud and wildly looked around him. The pain in his back was a dull throb but his long exposure had weakened him. There was no way he would stand any chance in the desperate, vicious, bloody melee, that was developing along the north eastern wall.

A loud bang echoed through the fort and another yell for help rose from the southern gate house.

"Get up on that parapet and clear those ladders from the wall," a Batavian voice boomed in the darkness.

Marcus rose to his feet and dashed across the parade ground towards the barracks block, where the slaves had their quarters.

In the darkness he collided with a figure running in the opposite direction and both of them tumbled to the ground with a startled terrified cry. There was however no time to find out if the man was friend or foe. Marcus groaned as he forced himself onto his feet and staggered off. He was in no state to fight, especially with no armour or shield. The barracks block, where Kyna and Fergus had their quarters, loomed up out of the darkness and Marcus crashed heavily into the wooden door, but it would not budge. He groaned as a wave of pain shot through him.

"Kyna, are you in there, Kyna, it's me Marcus!" he yelled, leaning his head against the door. Something was stopping it from opening.

There was no reply from inside. Marcus pressed his shoulder against the door but it would still not budge.

"We've barricaded the door, you won't get in," a frightened voice cried out.

Marcus groaned again. The man sounded like one of the slaves. Then a Batavian cry to his left made him groan in dismay.

"They are coming over the south western wall. Drive them back!"

Marcus stepped away from the barracks block. He would just have to hope that his wife and son were inside with the slaves. There was no time. All at once a yelling figure came charging out of the darkness to his left and instinctively Marcus thrust his sword forwards, catching the man neatly in his side. The man screamed and spun away into the darkness, taking Marcus' sword with him. To his left more men appeared, rushing along the sides of the barracks blocks towards the centre of the fort. Marcus pressed himself against the door of the slave quarters as the Britons rushed past yelling their battle cries. He was unarmed. A trumpet suddenly blasted away. It had come from close to the southern gate. Marcus snatched a glance in that direction. Then with a groan he was hobbling away into the darkness towards the gate. Figures rushed past him. A high-pitched scream rent the darkness. Then he heard a tremendous bang, followed by the splintering of wood. Then came a desperate shout.

"Hold them, hold them, don't let them get through," a Batavian voice screamed in the dark. Marcus stumbled over a corpse and tumbled to the ground. He cried out as a wave of pain crashed through his body. A shield and a discarded spear lay beside the corpse and wildly Marcus scrambled around in the darkness to get a grip. It was a useless idea for he just didn't have the strength to fight. Then he was on his feet and stumbling towards the gate and its flaming torches. As he approached he could see the defences were in a bad state. Corpses littered the parapet above and around the gate and the Batavians were locked in a fierce hand to hand fight with the Britons who were still coming over the wall. Down beside the gate the wooden doors had been battered until they were half off their hinges and the Britons were thrusting spears through the holes to drive the defenders back. A Decurion, clad in full armour, was trying to hack away at the spears with his long cavalry sword.

Marcus feeling his strength fading fast, staggered towards the officer, dropped his shield and grasped hold of one of the burning torches. Then with his last strength he hurled it into the confused mass of screaming and yelling attackers above him on the parapet before collapsing. As the pain and exhaustion became too much to bear, he felt himself sliding into a cool welcoming darkness. The last noise he heard before he lost consciousness was the sudden neighing of horses and the thud of hooves.

## Chapter Five - The Prefect of the Second Batavian Cohort

Slowly Marcus opened his eyes. He was lying on an army camp bed and someone had bound white bandages around his chest. The pain in his back was a dull throb and the smell of vinegar was overpowering. Slowly he realised he was lying in the Principia, the Prefect's quarters. The brass bath tub stood abandoned in a corner. Two men were sitting on the ground beside the bed. Quickly they scrambled to their feet as he stirred and groaned. As his eyes focussed, he saw that one of the men was a slave and the other was an exhausted-looking Batavian soldier, with long braided blond hair and an iron torque around his neck, implying that he had not yet killed a man. The soldier was clad in chain mail armour and a gladius short sword hung from his belt. In one hand he was holding his feathered helmet with the cheek and neck guard chiselled off. Dried blood was smeared across his right arm.

"You are awake. How are you feeling Sir?" the Batavian said, speaking in his native language.

Marcus stared up at the soldier.

"What happened?" he muttered. "Where am I?"

"The doctor and his staff are very busy," the Batavian replied, "They said that you should rest. We have so many wounded, but I will call him if you need him Sir."

"What happened?" Marcus groaned.

"We drove them out of fort Sir," the young man said quietly. "If it wasn't for your warning they would have caught us asleep and defenceless. You saved us Sir. You saved the fort and the entire Cohort."

Marcus closed his eyes. "I was beside the southern gate," he murmured. "They were trying    to break it down."

The young Batavian cleared his throat.

"Lucius took your advice Sir. He ordered us to remain armed and ready to fight. It would have been better if we were up on the ramparts but it was enough. We drove them out. It cost us Sir, but we drove them out. Adalberht even had his men sleep in the stables with their horses, so that they would be ready. It was he and his men who broke the Briton attack across the south west wall Sir."

Marcus groaned and his eyes flickered open.

"My wife and son?" he said with sudden alarm as he tried to rise from the bed.

"They are safe Sir," the young Batavian said with a triumphant grin, "They were with the slaves. They barricaded themselves into their barracks. They had no casualties. The doctor said that you were not to be disturbed Sir."

Marcus closed his eyes and lay back grunting in relief. A moment later he opened them again and stared up at the young Batavian soldier.

"Who are you?" he muttered. "Where are Lucius and Adalberht?"

"My name is Fridwald," the Batavian said proudly, "and Lucius has assigned me to be your bodyguard Sir. You are the Prefect of the Second Batavian Cohort now that Cotta is dead."

Marcus stared at Fridwald for a long moment in stunned silence.

"Cotta is dead?" he muttered at last. "How, what happened?"

Fridwald blushed and for a moment he looked away and Marcus saw that the young man could be no more than eighteen or nineteen.

"He died during the attack Sir," Fridwald said quietly. "You are in charge now. Lucius has ordered me to stay at your side at all times. You are the new Prefect and you will make a far better commander than Cotta ever was. The men think the same Sir."

"Enough," Marcus growled as he raised himself up onto his elbows. "I need to speak with Lucius at once."

Fridwald nodded at the slave and without a word the man turned and left the room.

"I have to stay at your side at all times," Fridwald explained with a cheeky grin. "Orders Sir, you understand, got to obey them, you see."

\*\*\*

Lucius looked exhausted as he stepped into the barracks room. Quietly he came up to the camp bed and saluted. His face was however clean and neatly shaven although his boots were caked in fresh mud. Marcus struggled up onto his feet and gingerly embraced the older man, watched over by Fridwald, who had remained behind guarding the door.

"Cotta is dead?" Marcus said, glancing at Lucius as he took a step back. "How did it happen?"

Lucius hesitated. "He was killed during the fighting Sir. That's all I can tell you."

Marcus examined the first Centurion carefully and for a long moment he didn't speak. Lucius looked calm and in control but Marcus had known him long enough to know when he was lying.

"Well I want to see his body," Marcus said in a slightly annoyed voice, "Were there any witnesses who saw him die?"

Lucius shook his head. "As you wish," he replied stiffly. "But the men he was with, they are all dead too." The First Centurion cleared his throat, "If I may say so Sir, it's damned fortunate for you and all of us that he's dead. The prick would have gotten us all slaughtered if it wasn't for you." Defiantly Lucius fixed his eyes on Marcus. "I will not mourn him Sir. He deserved what he got."

"Yes," Marcus muttered looking away, "It's fortunate." He sighed. There was more to Cotta's death than Lucius was willing to tell him but he did not have the moral right to reprimand the Centurion. Cotta's death may be suspicious but his death had also removed the threat of his own immediate execution. Marcus looked down at the floor and ran his fingers across his forehead.

"What is the Cohort's strength?" he muttered.

"As of this morning we have 683 men ready for duty, including the bulk of the eight cavalry squadrons," Lucius replied. "101 men were killed in the attack and we have 197 others who are wounded, sick or unaccounted for. The doctor and his staff are doing what they can but it's likely the death toll will rise."

Marcus looked up with a shocked expression. "They put a third of the Cohort out of action in a single assault," he exclaimed.

"Yes we took a beating," Lucius nodded. "Morale is low. The men realise how close to disaster they came. The barbarians really wanted to take this place. But we made them pay for it."

"I will speak with the men," Marcus said wearily. "What news is there from outside? Have we heard from the watch tower at Derventio? What about the neighbouring forts?"

Lucius shook his head. "Nothing, we have seen no one and our civilians seem to have fled. The houses are deserted and their animals are gone too. It's quiet out there." A faint smile appeared on his face. "At least we won't have to endure the smell of pig shit anymore Sir."

Marcus nodded. "What about the fort? What damage did we sustain?"

"I have set the men to work repairing our defences and buttressing the southern gate," Lucius replied, "but we've been waiting on you Sir, before we decide what to do next."

"Good man," Marcus said as he laid a hand on Lucius's shoulder. He groaned as he suddenly felt the wounds across his back. "What time is it?" he grimaced.

"Around noon."

"Alright," Marcus growled forcing the pain from his mind. "Tell Adalberht that I want three cavalry patrols ready to ride within the hour. One is to head east along the Stanegate to Magnis and make contact with the garrison. The second patrol is to head south to the Gallic Cohort at Brocavum and the third is to head north to see if they can make contact with men stationed at Birrens. If they spot the enemy they are not to engage them. They are to return at once. We need to find out what the fuck is going on out there, understood."

Lucius nodded.

"What about our food supplies?" Marcus snapped. "Were the granaries damaged during the attack?"

"They are intact," Lucius said, "We have enough supplies of grain to last a month, maybe more, and there is no shortage of water with the river so close by." Lucius paused and grunted derisively. "There is something else. Cotta's death has unsettled some of the men, Marcus. Losing their commander seems to be a bad omen. They fear it is a sign that the gods have turned against us."

Marcus turned towards the young Batavian guarding the door.

"Fridwald, make yourself useful and fetch me a new tunic, armour and a sword," he    bellowed.

\*\*\*

Slowly Marcus made his way across the parade ground as Fridwald and the Cohort standard bearer, clasping the unit banner, followed. It was raining but the drops were light and scattered. The Batavian dead had been laid out in straight lines in the mud. Some of the corpses had been covered with army blankets but others lay still clad in their armour and were staring up at the sky with lifeless eyes. A couple of men were crouching beside a corpse, and from their muttered words, Marcus saw that they were saying goodbye to a comrade. He strode on along the rows. From the direction of the southern gate he could hear men's curses and the noise of sawing and hammering and from the hospital the shrieks and cries of wounded men never ceased.

The enemy dead had been flung onto a great heap. The party of Batavians dragging the enemy corpses to the pile paused as they caught sight of him. They looked sullen, dirty and exhausted.

"Gather round, all of you, gather round!" Marcus shouted as he came to a halt. He turned and beckoned towards the men. Patiently he waited until a crowd of a few hundred had formed a large open and silent circle around him. The unwashed men with their feathered-helmets, pressed around him suddenly eager to hear what he had to say.

"Listen up, all of you," Marcus cried out, "You all know me. I was with you at Mons Graupius when I saw you hold the entire Caledonian army on the slopes of that hill. I was there in Hibernia when we defeated the Hibernian cavalry. It was our effort that day, which saved an entire battle group." Marcus fell silent as he turned to stare at the faces around him. "And I know this," he shouted. "Batavians love to fight. We love a fighter and we love to win. It's in our blood. That's why we are going to defeat our enemy, for battle brings out the best in us. The enemy are fierce and they pressed us hard last night. What did you expect? They fight for what they regard as their land. We

31

shall respect them, but we shall destroy them. They will try and scare us with their horns and painted faces, but a real man does not let fear overpower his honour, his manhood and his duty to his comrades."

Once more Marcus paused to glare at the faces around him. The soldiers remained silent as they eyed him.

"The bravest man I have ever met," Marcus cried out, "was a young cavalryman whose name I don't even know. He rode out with me during the breakout from Tara. We had orders to create a diversion so that the Legionaries and the rest of the battle group could escape and, as we crashed through the enemy line I saw this young trooper turn back to protect a wounded comrade, who'd fallen from his horse. Gods knows what became of him, for the enemy were all around us, but I know this: That man never wavered in his loyalty to his comrade. That man preferred to die rather than to leave his friend behind. That is the kind of men we are." Marcus paused. "So trust in the man beside you and do your duty for in the coming days I want our enemy to cry out in alarm as they see our approach; I want to hear them shout: Ah shit! Here come those damned Batavians again."

## Chapter Six - The Consequences of Rebellion

It was late afternoon when Marcus heard the sentry in the south eastern watch tower cry out a warning. A moment later the alarm bell rang out across the fort. Stiffly he strode towards the ramparts and clambered up the ladder that led onto the parapet. Fridwald, one hand resting on the pommel of his sword, followed on close behind. The Batavians manning the defences had turned to look at something beyond the wall. The men were clutching their long Hastae thrusting spears and their flat oval shields were leaning against the wooden palisade.

"Patrol returning Sir," the sentry in his watch tower called out.

Marcus joined the men along the wall. The rain had eased away and a fresh western breeze had picked up. To the east, the lush green fields and pastures were interspersed with copses of trees and along the Stanegate he suddenly caught sight of a troop of horsemen, as they flitted in and out of view. The sunlight reflected and gleamed on the men's armour.

"Looks like its Hedwig's patrol," Lucius said quietly as he joined Marcus on the rampart. "He's the first back and he's early."

Marcus did not reply as he studied the Batavian patrol. Then, as the horsemen approached the fort at a trot, he turned and made his way along the parapet towards the gate.

The cavalry patrol trotted wearily into the fort as the Batavians manning the gate called out to their comrades. The horses were covered in sweat and snorted and whinnied. Hedwig, the young Decurion in command of the patrol, had a white bandage wrapped around his forehead, which was partially covered by his helmet. With practiced ease he slid from his horse and handed the beast to one of the slaves, who led the beast away.

"Hedwig, what news?" Marcus called out from his position on the parapet.

The young Decurion turned as he caught sight of Marcus. He looked serious as he rapped out a quick salute. The strong smell of horse clung to the officer.

"I am sorry Sir. We couldn't get through to Magnis," he replied in a thick Germanic accent. "The Britons have destroyed the bridge across the Eden. They burnt it Sir. I thought about swimming the river but the water is high and we spotted an enemy war band on the opposite bank. The Britons didn't look like they were going anywhere."

"What about the villages? Did you speak with any of the locals?" Marcus snapped.

Hedwig shook his head. "The one settlement we ventured into was deserted Sir. Not a living soul to be seen. The Britons have taken their cattle and vanished."

"That makes sense," Lucius muttered at Marcus's side, "the Britons are not stupid. This is rebellion Marcus and everyone knows the consequences of defying Rome."

"Annihilation," Marcus murmured to himself. Then he turned to Hedwig.

"See to it that you and your men get some food and rest," he cried, "and Hedwig," Marcus paused, "lose that serious-looking face, you are frightening your men."

Hedwig frowned in embarrassed confusion. Then stiffly he saluted and turned away to snap orders at his men.

Marcus half turned towards Lucius and sighed.

"My father," he said, "told me stories about what Governor Paulinus did to the Iceni and Trinovantes after he'd crushed the rebellion of the Barbarian queen. It wasn't pretty. Paulinus was out for revenge. He would have burned every last Iceni village and killed the entire tribe down to the last child if the emperor

Nero had not intervened. The Britons will have remembered that."

"And still they rebel," Lucius replied sourly.

***

It was early evening when the sentries warning bell announced the return of the second patrol. Marcus thrust his helmet onto his head as he hastened from the infirmary block, where he'd been visiting the wounded and half ran towards the gate, with Fridwald at his side. The Batavian auxiliaries who lined the parapet, slumped up against the wooden palisade, paused from their evening meal of porridge, bread and sour wine and the low murmur amongst the men stopped as the alarm bell rang out once more. From beyond the ramparts a lone Batavian voice cried out and as Marcus reached the gate it swung open and the cavalrymen came surging into the fort. Along the walls a few Batavians rose to their feet in alarm.

"Where are the rest of your men?" Marcus cried as he grasped hold of the reins to the Decurion's horse.

The officer's face was covered in sweat and dust and he was bleeding from a cut to his leg.

"I lost eight men Sir," the Decurion replied sullenly, "the bastards ambushed us. I took the road north like you had ordered but we never reached Birrens. It's impossible. The Britons have blocked the road with felled trees and their war bands are everywhere. They are killing everyone they catch. We were lucky to escape Sir. The roads are impassable and not safe."

"What about the fort at Birrens?" Marcus exclaimed, "Did you see anything or hear anything; anything at all?"

The officer shook his head. "Smoke Sir. We saw black smoke on the horizon but it's impossible to say where it is coming from."

35

Marcus stared at the Decurion for a long moment. Then he turned away and clambered up onto the parapet. The Batavians slowly began to return to their dinner and he could hear the low murmur of their voices. Marcus turned to look northwards. The light was fading and all he could see was the great, dark green forest, that lined the banks of the Eden.

"The third patrol should have been back by now Sir," Fridwald said quietly, as he stood, beside his commander and gazed out across the land beyond the fort. "It will be dark soon."

Marcus did not reply as he stood lost in thought. Then at last with a grunt he stirred.

"Yes, they should have been back by now," he nodded. "The Britons have cut us off Fridwald," he said, trying to mask the worry in his voice, "they have us isolated. They have blocked the roads north and east. They are moving around in small war bands, that are strong enough to stop us from sending out patrols or foraging parties. They have moved their women, children and elders into hiding and they have taken their cattle with them. This rebellion Fridwald," Marcus said sharply, turning to his young bodyguard, "this isn't some spontaneous local uprising. This is co-ordinated; it's organized. Someone has planned this. Someone is leading this rebellion."

The expression on Fridwald's face did not change.

"How big do you think it is Sir?"

Marcus sighed. "Who knows," he muttered, "For all we know the whole province may have gone up in flames. The people around here are part of the Brigantian coalition but around Birrens they are Selgovae. That means that we are at war with at least two tribal groups."

"The Twentieth will push north from Deva and relieve us Sir," Fridwald said confidently, "I shall keep an eye on the road south. It's just a matter of time."

"Maybe," Marcus muttered.

***

It was night when a hand shook Marcus awake. Startled he looked up and saw Fridwald leaning over him. His unwashed bodyguard was holding a burning torch that crackled and spat.

"Sir," the young Batavian whispered, "the sentries report movement amongst the civilian huts around the southern gate. You should come at once."

Without a word Marcus rose from his camp bed, grabbed his fur-lined helmet and strode out of the Principia. The watch commander was waiting for him outside and rapped out a quick silent salute. Marcus ignored the officer as he started towards the ramparts. The muddy parade ground was quiet and deserted but from the infirmary the groans and occasional cries of the wounded rose and faded into the night. Carefully he picked his way passed the lines of Batavian dead. There had been no time to bury them and some of the corpses had begun to look bloated and disfigured and the stink of death was growing. He'd lost three more men who'd succumbed from their wounds since the second patrol had reported back. High above him the stars twinkled in the dark clear sky and along the parapets the moonlight gleamed on the men's armour and helmets. He'd kept the bulk of the Cohort on watch and the men had made the best of their situation and now lay asleep, wrapped in their winter cloaks with their weapons close by. The quiet movement of the sentries along the parapet was the only sign of activity. Then far away to the south he heard the mournful howl of a wolf. It was followed moments later, by another distant answering howl.

Quietly Marcus clambered up onto the parapet beside the gate and moved towards the sentry, who was peering into the darkness beyond the fortifications. The man half glanced round as he heard Marcus approach.

"Someone is out there Sir," the Batavian whispered. "They are moving in and out of the abandoned houses." With his finger the sentry motioned to his ear. "Listen Sir," he whispered.

Marcus peered out into the darkness. The night was quiet and there was no wind. It was too dark to see the huts of the civilian settlement. Then he heard it. The little clink of metal against metal and a muffled cough.

"I wasn't sure whether to sound the alarm Sir," the sentry whispered.

Marcus laid his hand on the man's shoulder. "You did well soldier," he said quietly.

For a long moment Marcus said nothing as he peered out into the darkness.

"You down there amongst the huts!" Marcus suddenly roared at the top of his voice, "What the fuck are you doing scuttling around here at night. Show yourself and give me today's password!"

The sentry beside Marcus froze in shock and behind him Marcus heard the watch commander grunt. Intently he peered into the darkness but there was no immediate reply.

"Well show yourself, damn you!" Marcus roared again.

The night remained silent, but along the parapet some of the Batavians were already reaching for their weapons. Marcus was about to signal the sentries to sound the general alarm, when from the darkness a voice replied.

"Who are you?" a tired and annoyed sounding voice snapped in Latin.

Marcus blinked in surprise. "Second Batavian Cohort. Who are you? What are you doing out there?" he roared switching to Latin.

There was a moment's hesitation in the darkness. Marcus strained to see but the night remained impenetrable.

"Batavians!" the voice cried out in relief, "Well thank Jupiter's cock for that. We weren't sure whether the fort was still ours. My name is Lollius, Centurion Lollius, lower your weapons and don't shoot, don't shoot, we're coming towards you."

With a creaking groan the gate swung open. Marcus stood in the centre of the gateway, with one hand holding up a burning torch and the other resting on the pommel of his sword, as he peered into the night. Behind him and along the parapet the Batavians clustered together, their shields and spears overlapping to form a solid shield wall, that blocked the entrance into the fort. Out beyond the ramparts nothing moved at first. Then in the moonlight a lone figure appeared. As he drew closer Marcus saw that the man was wearing legionary armour and a red plumed helmet and, that he was limping.

The Roman came to a halt a few paces from Marcus and silently glanced up at the Batavians on the walls. He was a big man of around forty with an ugly, unshaven face.

"Centurion Lollius, first Cohort, eighth company of the Twentieth. Are you in charge here?" the Roman said carefully.

Marcus nodded. "What are you doing out here Centurion?"

Lollius sighed and Marcus suddenly noticed how exhausted the officer looked.

"My men and I were building a road north of Birrens. One of the supply roads to the northern forts in Caledonia. They attacked us without warning. I lost half my men and all the fucking slaves ran away. We've been walking south ever since and my men are starving. We need to rest. The roads are not safe; the Briton war bands are swarming across the countryside…"

"Why did you not seek refuge at the fort at Birrens?" Marcus interrupted.

Lollius shook his head. "The fort was on fire when I last saw it. There was no way we were going to get through. The Caledonians were all over Birrens. I can't imagine that any of our boys were still alive inside."

Marcus lowered his gaze.

"Alright, you had better come in," Marcus said. "We will give you some food. How many of you are there?"

"Forty of us Sir," the Centurion said, as he half turned and whistled into the night.

For a few moments nothing happened. Then from the darkness men started to appear. The Legionaries looked utterly exhausted as they gathered around their Centurion. Some of them were supporting wounded comrades, whilst others were leaning on their throwing spears. Their fine segmented armour and helmets with wide cheek guards, were smeared with dried mud and all had discarded their shields. One man had lost his boots and was barefoot.

"We're grateful Sir," Lollius said humbly, as limping, he led his men into the camp.

## Chapter Seven - Marcus decides

Marcus hastily finished the last of his porridge, wiped his mouth on his sleeve and rose from his chair, as Lucius entered his command post. It was dawn. Lucius was as usual, impeccably dressed and clean shaven. His immaculate torso armour, greaves and helmet, glinted in the morning light and for a moment Marcus wondered how the man found the time to keep himself and his equipment in such perfect condition.

"Any news about our missing patrol?" Marcus asked as he reached for his helmet and replaced his Pugio knife in his belt.

Lucius shook his head.

"Nothing, the watch commander reports that it's quiet. The patrol should have been back last night Marcus. They are late, very late."

Marcus looked down at his helmet and with his finger scraped away a piece of dried mud.

"We must assume that the road south to Brocavum is blocked and that our patrol has been lost," he said heavily. "The Britons have us cut off. They may try and starve us out or they may attack us again. The men will have to sleep up on the ramparts for a while longer. See to it that they know our position, Lucius. We can't afford to be taken by surprise."

"I think another assault is unlikely," Lucius replied calmly, "After the bloody nose that we gave them they will think twice. We have a month's worth of food supplies. They will try and starve us out. That's what I would do if I were them."

Marcus grunted and glanced carefully at the first Centurion.

"It won't come to that," he said, "we will break out before I allow them to starve us."

41

A tight little smile appeared at the corner of Lucius's mouth. "Or the Twentieth will march north and come to our aid," he said.

"I would rather rely on ourselves than on any relief column," Marcus said sharply. "Waiting for the Twentieth to arrive is an excuse for inactivity and laziness and I intend to take action as soon as we can. These rebels attacked us Lucius. They tried to slaughter us in our beds. I am going to show them what it means to rebel against Rome! They are going to be shitting themselves with fear before I am done with them."

"Very good Sir," Lucius replied and his face showed his approval.

Marcus was about to say something else, when from the ramparts the alarm bell started clanging. Fridwald poked his head through the door as Marcus and Lucius hastened towards him.

"I know," Marcus growled as he caught the look on his young bodyguard's face, "I can hear it, I am not deaf."

Out in the parade ground the Batavian burial parties had paused in their work of loading the corpses of their comrades onto a wagon and were peering up at the sentries in their watch towers. The alarm bell continued to clang away. Marcus strode passed the long barrack blocks and towards the north-eastern wall and, as he did so, his trumpeter carrying his conical trumpet, hastened to join him. Along the ramparts the Batavian officers were shouting orders at their men as they rushed to get into position.

"What's going on?" Marcus roared, as he reached the rampart and clambered up the ladder leading to the parapet. The clanging abruptly stopped.

There was no need for the sentries to reply. Along the road leading north into Caledonia a small party of horsemen burst into view. The riders thundered across the wooden bridge spanning the Eden, their cloaks flying behind them, as they raced towards the fort. Close behind the fleeing men came a larger party of armed horsemen, mounted on small shaggy horses. The pursuers were shouting and as they closed the gap, the leading rebels flung their spears at their quarry.

"Get out there and drive those damned rebels off my road!" Marcus roared, turning in the direction of the men beside the eastern gate. Then his head jerked upwards at the watch tower. "Scorpion crew, shoot those bastards!"

The words had hardly left his lips when, with a taught twang, a yard long iron-tipped bolt, went accelerating towards the horsemen. On the road, a hundred paces from the fort, the projectile slammed into one of the pursuing horses, sending the beast tumbling and rolling to the ground and its rider hurtling and shrieking through the air. Marcus gripped the edge of the wooden palisade as he stared at the scene. The small party of fleeing men veered towards the eastern gate, just as it opened, and two columns of Batavian infantry charged out. On the road the enemy cavalry had come to a confused halt as they rode up and down aimlessly, their riders staring at the fort. Then one of the rebels slid from his horse, shouted something, turned and with a derisive gesture, pulled down his trousers to flash his naked arse at the fort. An angry mutter rose from the Batavians manning the wall and from the watchtower another Scorpion bolt streaked through the air and hammered into the ground close to the dismounted man. The rebels cried out to each other and the dismounted man leapt back onto his horse, as his comrades turned and trotted away towards the north.

Marcus did not stay to watch them go. The fleeing party of horsemen had reached the gate and the Batavian assault party clustered around, eying them curiously.

"Let them in," Marcus cried, as he approached the gate. As the assault party started to filter back into the camp, Marcus grunted in surprise as he caught sight of the five riders. The men were clad in civilian clothing and two of the riders were women. All of them were panting with exhaustion and their horses were lathered in sweat and dirt. The women were wearing long brown riding cloaks with hoods over their heads and the younger one was crying. Their cloaks were splattered with mud.

"Where have you come from?" Marcus called out turning to the older man. The rider was a balding man in his mid-thirties, clad in expensive looking clothes. He caught sight of Marcus and spread his arms open wide in a sign of gratitude.

"Thank you Sir, thank you and all the gods that protect us," he cried in a voice that cracked with emotion. For a moment he struggled to speak. Marcus folded his arms across his chest as he patiently he waited for the man to continue. The Batavian auxiliaries around him were staring at the new arrivals in silence.

"My name is Urbanus," the man gasped, "I am a merchant and these two young men here," he said, gesturing towards two lanky youths with identical long brown hair which they'd tied back into a ponytail, "are my sons. We were trading wine with the northern forts when the uprising began. I lost all my goods but we managed to escape. My sons are alive Sir, that's all that matters and, when I get back to Viroconium, I shall present Jupiter with the greatest offering I can afford. I make that promise."

Marcus nodded and his gaze shifted towards the two hooded women.

"And what about them?" he said.

Urbanus was about to speak when the older lady pulled back her hood revealing her long black hair. She looked about thirty-five, with an attractive face and there was a fiery, determined gleam in her eyes.

"Prefect," she said in a posh voice, fixing her eye on Marcus, "I am Claudia, wife of the Legate of the Ninth. My daughter and I were on our way north to Caledonia to visit my brother, the Prefect of the fort at Milton, when our party was attacked. These merchants found us. I am a soldier's wife, Prefect, and I know the routine of an army camp, so I trust that I and my daughter will be safe under your protection?"

Marcus blinked in surprise. What was this? A Legate's wife and her daughter, here in his fort. For a moment he struggled to think of something to say. Then he nodded towards the woman.

"You and your companions are safe here with us lady."

"Good," Claudia snapped haughtily, "for we will expect you to provide us with a strong escort on our journey south. I want to leave as soon as possible."

***

The long line of neat freshly dug graves lined the southern bank of the Eden. It was afternoon and the sun was fierce and high in the sky and brightly coloured flowers were poking up amongst the reeds, lining the river's edge. Marcus stood watching the Batavian priest as the man slowly and solemnly made his way down the line. The flow of the water over the rocks in the river and the gentle breeze in the trees was the only noise and he could smell the wild garlic, that grew along the river bank. Marcus held his helmet tucked under his arm and he looked tired. At the water's edge the party of Batavian grave diggers, with their shovels slung over their shoulders, were watching the sombre funeral rites being administered to their comrades.

At last Marcus grunted and turned away and started to make his way back to the fort, a couple of hundred paces away. Fridwald and the trumpeter, lugging his conical trumpet, followed him in silence. Marcus stomped along, oblivious to the towering column of black smoke, that was billowing upwards at the southern edge of Luguvalium. The enemy dead were being burned on a great heap. He couldn't afford the possibility of disease breaking out amongst his troops. Marcus looked thoughtful as he strode through the gate and headed towards the Principia. The Batavians along the ramparts were fortifying their positions with sharpened wooden stakes and the carpenters were hard at work, hammering and sawing away. The men's good- natured curses and cries abounded around the camp, as if their very activity had for the moment pushed away the seriousness of their situation. At the southern gate a line of men equipped with buckets, was hauling river water into the camp. Amongst them were Lollius's Legionaries, easily distinguishable by their fine segmented armour and uniforms from the more plainly clad auxiliaries.

"Tell Lucius and Adalberht to come to my quarters at once," Marcus said, turning to the trumpeter. "And find that Centurion, Lollius as well. I need to speak to him, too."

The trumpeter peeled away without a word and Marcus strode past the guard and into the Principia building. Once inside he glanced awkwardly at the doorway leading to Cotta's old private bedroom but there was no noise from within. He'd given up the room to Claudia and her daughter and the two women must be asleep. Annoyed, he turned away and placed his helmet on the table. His wife had not been happy about the arrangement but what could he do. The lady was a legate's wife. One word from her and his army career would be over.

"We have a decision to make," Marcus said quietly in Latin, once his principal officers had assembled. Stiffly they stood around the wooden table in the centre of the square room with their helmets tucked under their arms. Marcus studied their faces carefully. Lucius looked calm, Adalberht seemed impatient and full of energy and Lollius, the Centurion from the Twentieth, looked sombre. The officers remained silent, waiting for him to continue. Near the door Fridwald had his arms folded across his chest and was looking bored.

"As I see it, we can do a number of things," Marcus said, tapping the table with his fingers. "We can either break out towards the east and try and join our comrades at Magnis, if they are still there. Or we can, as lady Claudia suggests, move south and hope that the Twentieth is pushing north. Or," Marcus paused, "we can remain here and hold the fort and wait for a relief column. I want to know your thoughts, that's why you are here."

The room fell silent as the assembled officers glanced at each other. Adalberht was the first to speak and he did so in his native Germanic language.

"Once the wounded can be transported we should march towards Magnis and join our comrades. If this rebellion is as widespread as we think we will be more effective as a combined unit," he growled.

"Latin, Adalberht, today we speak in Latin," Marcus said sharply. "Lollius here does not understand your language."

"Well maybe he should learn it then," Adalberht muttered in his native tongue.

"Our standing orders are to hold this fort until we are relieved," Lucius interrupted, speaking in Latin. "I say we stay where we are and hold our position. Luguvalium is an important strategic position. We are here to guard the crossing over the Eden and the supply roads leading north to the forts in Caledonia. Those are our orders. We cannot abandon our comrades."

Marcus nodded and glanced at Lollius. The Centurion was looking down at the table.

"I say we kill every damned last rebel we can find Sir," the Centurion said looking up. "Those bastards are not going to give up. They know that they must either win or die. There can be no middle ground, not now. They slaughtered my men. I have unfinished business with these rebels."

Marcus sighed as he glanced idly at the doorway leading to his private chamber. No one had spoken out in favour of Claudia's demand and for that he was glad. It was impossible for him to agree to her demand for he couldn't spare the men, but telling this to the legate's wife was not going to be a pleasant task. The woman was obviously well connected, and refusing her request was not going to do him any political favours. It would be even worse if she or her daughter were killed whilst under his protection. The Legate of the Ninth would never forgive him.

A sudden commotion outside the door had them all turning round. The watch commander appeared in the doorway, his face flush with excitement.

"The enemy have appeared on the other side of the river Sir, " the officer gasped, "They have brought something with them. You have to come and see this, Sir."

*** 

The Batavians were muttering amongst themselves and gesturing at something across the tributary, that flowed along the south-western ramparts, as Marcus clambered up onto the parapet. He pushed his way to the edge of the palisade to get a better view and as he reached the wooden rampart, he grunted in dismay at the sight across the swollen river. Rebel tribesmen had appeared in amongst the trees, their bodies painted blue and white. The Britons were shouting and beating their weapons against their small hide-bound shields and, at the water's edge, in full view of the fort, some fifty paces away across the river, were three wooden crosses, upon which hung the spread-eagled figures of three men. As Marcus stared at the scene, one of the rebels calmly strode up to the crosses and sliced open the stomach of the first and then the second man. Blood and intestines tumbled out and the screams of the dying men were horrific. The Briton paused beside the third man and turned to face the Batavians in the fort before raising his arms and sending a stream of foul mouthed curses across the river.

"Get a party of men across the river and cut the poor fellows down from those crosses," Marcus bellowed. His cry was taken up by the Batavian officers as they shouted orders at their men. Marcus turned back to stare at the grizzly scene across the river. The two men, whose guts had been ripped out had fallen silent, but the third man was still alive and screaming. The rebels however, seemed to be in no hurry as they lounged about taunting the Batavians from across the river. Then as the assault party poured forwards behind the shelter of their long flat shields, the Britons cried out to each other and vanished into the trees leaving the remaining captive, screaming and dangling on his cross.

Marcus was waiting beside the southern gate as the officer in charge of the assault party returned with his men and the freed prisoner in their midst. The officer looked grim as he came up to Marcus.

"Those two on the crosses were our men Sir," the officer said. "Some of the lads recognized them. They were with the patrol that went missing yesterday. I cut them down myself and we will bury them alongside their comrades."

"What about him?" Marcus said gesturing towards the prisoner stumbling along amongst his liberators.

The Decurion shrugged, "He's not one of ours, Sir. He's a Briton but he says he wants to speak to the officer in charge. They've beaten him up pretty badly Sir but he will live."

"What does he wish to discuss?" Marcus asked with a frown, as he gestured at the Batavians to bring the man to him.

The Briton was in a bad state. He was supported by two Batavians as he was half carried over to Marcus. The man was young, in his late teens, barefoot and his bare chest was covered in blue tattoos. Spittle and dirt clung to his spiky hair and he smelt as if someone had pissed on him. His left eye was swollen shut and marked by an angry, dark red bruise and across his back were lacerations caused by a whip. His hands and feet showed the red angry marks, where the ropes had fastened him to the cross.

"Why did they put you on that cross?" Marcus said addressing the man.

The Briton's head rolled back and he groaned, blinking rapidly with his one good eye. Then he steadied himself and peered at Marcus.

"Thank you Sir," the man groaned in his native language. "I thought they were going to kill me. I must speak with the officer in charge. I have urgent news."

"You can speak to me," Marcus replied, folding his arms across his chest.

For a moment the Briton eyed him carefully. Then his body sagged and he groaned again.

"I am loyal Sir," he whimpered. "My people, all of us; we are loyal to Rome. We have no quarrel with you. Blessed is the image of great Domitian. Blessed are the Eagles that protect the Legions. You must believe me Sir. This rebellion, it is not something we wanted." The man coughed and fixed his red feverish eye on Marcus. "But the rebels, they are besieging our settlement. They want our cattle and our grain, they want our women and they say they are going to kill our leader, Drustan because he refused to join them." The man coughed and for a moment he was silent as he turned to stare at the ground. "Drustan is a great man, Sir. He, knows things; he knows things about these rebels and their plans. He sent me here to warn you, but they caught me." The man collapsed onto his knees before Marcus and held up his hands in a pathetic plea. "Drustan sent me," he sobbed, "You must come to our village at once and break the siege. We won't be able to hold out for much longer. They are threatening to kill us all. You must help us Sir. We are the Emperor's loyal subjects."

Marcus stared down at the miserable man before him.

"Where is your village?" he said.

"To the south and west," the man whimpered, as he kept his eyes on the ground, "a day and a morning's walk. We live on top of the hill above the western shore of Bassenthwaite lake, a few miles east from the watch tower at Derventio."

"How many of you are there? How many rebels besiege the place?" Marcus snapped.

The Briton groaned and did not answer at first.

"There are fifty of us," he muttered. "Women, men and children. You must hurry. The rebels are our kin, Sir, but the druids have poisoned their minds with hatred. I think there are about a hundred of them."

From the corner of his eye Marcus caught Lucius beckoning to him. Leaving the Briton on the ground, he strode over to the first Centurion. Lucius turned and took a few steps away from the Briton. He looked grave.

"I know this Drustan and his people," Lucius said quietly, "He is a good man and loyal like the prisoner says. He is no enemy of Rome. On our patrols my men and I often visited his settlement and we always received a warm welcome. I believe him Sir."

Marcus turned to glance at the prisoner. "Is this Drustan as important as the man claims?" he muttered.

Lucius shrugged. "He is their leader; he commands the respect of his extended family and he is wealthy, but beyond that I don't know. Still, it is possible that he will have contacts amongst the rebels. It may be worth finding out what he knows and it will give us a chance to discover the fate of the eight men stationed at Derventio. There has still been no news from them."

"The Briton thinks there are around a hundred rebels," Marcus said carefully.

"The hill fort above Bassenthwaite is well protected," Lucius replied, "It's an old fortress with walls and ditches. The inner ring can be held by a few dozen determined men. Maybe the rebels wish to avoid bloodshed. Drustan and his people are their kin after all Sir."

Marcus sighed and bit his lip as he stared at the man, cowering on the ground. For a moment he was torn by indecision.

"We will stay and hold Luguvalium," he muttered at last. "That is our duty and those are our standing orders, but we are not going to abandon our allies."

"I don't like it," Adalberht said gruffly, speaking in his native language as he came up behind Marcus. "I don't like the look of that piece of shit," he growled, glancing at the Briton kneeling on the ground. "They executed my boys, Marcus. Why did the Britons let him live, when they could have so easily killed him?"

Marcus shook his head. "I don't know," he murmured, "but we are going to defend our allies." He turned to look at Lucius and Adalberht in turn. "I have made my decision. Who knows how long it will take the Legions to restore order. We are not going to just hide behind our walls and allow our allies to be destroyed." Marcus's face darkened. "I meant what I said to the men," he snapped, "Before this is over I want these rebels shitting themselves when they hear of our approach."

Adalberht spat onto the ground and muttered something under his breath. Lucius however nodded in agreement.

Marcus turned to Adalberht.

"I want you and all seven cavalry squadrons ready to move out at dawn, I want every rider and horse that we can muster," Marcus said quickly. He turned to Lucius. "You will remain here with the infantry and hold the fort. Keep the men alert Lucius. If all is well, we should be back at dusk. Place the Briton in the infirmary tonight and see to it that his wounds are looked at. He may be useful to us."

"Very good Sir," Lucius said snapping out a quick salute.

Marcus nodded, turned and strode away with Fridwald close behind him.

"What now Sir?" Fridwald said.

"Now," Marcus replied sourly, "We are going to tell the lady Claudia that she is not going anywhere."

# Chapter Eight - The Island of Vectis

Corbulo stood watching his daughter Dylis playing with the dog on the beach. It was noon and along the wide beach, with its soft golden sands, the waves came rolling and crashing onto the shore, sending their ice-cold sea water racing and hissing across the sand. The fresh western wind tugged at his cloak and with it came the tangy smell of the sea. Far out to sea the sea gulls rolled, dived and rose on the air currents. Eleven year old Dylis, his adopted daughter, was shrieking with laughter as she threw the stick as far as she could into the waves, only for her dog to bound out into the surf and retrieve it. Corbulo smiled at her antics. The wide beach was deserted apart from a solitary youth playing with a wooden plank in the surf.

Slowly Corbulo pulled the hood of his Palla over his short white hair. He looked rugged and older than his 51 years but his eyes were still alert. Absentmindedly he stroked the grey stubble that covered his chin and cheeks. Then he opened his mouth and rubbed his three remaining teeth. He was a survivor he thought. They all were. Efa, his beautiful Briton wife, young Dylis his daughter, Marcus his son by his first wife and Quintus, retired Centurion and old army comrade. They were all survivors in a world where women routinely died in childbirth, where babies and children died like flies from disease and malnutrition and where few Legionaries reached retirement age. Corbulo grunted. Twenty five years long he had served Rome, following the Eagle of the Twentieth. He'd marched the length of the Empire, fought and bled in more battles and skirmishes than he cared to remember, drunk himself silly and whored in every forsaken tavern and army post he'd been sent to but now, now when he had finally managed to retire, all that seemed to matter to him was the happiness and welfare of his family. He nodded to himself. Securing their future was what mattered now.

A sudden movement made him look up. High above him, soaring into the pale blue sky was an eagle. Gracefully the sharp-eyed bird circled over the beach and opened its mouth, but it's high pitched scream was lost amongst the noise of the crashing waves, Dylis's laughter and her dog's excited barking. The smile slowly faded from Corbulo's eyes as he watched the eagle drift away. Half turning so that Dylis would not see him, he lowered his hand and touched his crotch. The lump on his scrotum had grown larger since he had first noticed it in the military bathhouse at Deva Victrix and a few months ago he'd started coughing up blood. Corbulo sighed. The disease that inflicted him was surely and steadily draining the strength from him. He'd tried to keep it hidden at first but Efa his wife had not been so easily fooled. She had insisted he call the doctor but the Greek had only confirmed what Corbulo already knew. A year, maybe eighteen months the doctor had told him.

"I love the sea," Dylis cried out, as she came running towards him. Her dog came bounding after her, barking loudly before shaking itself and sending water droplets flying everywhere. Corbulo ruffled his adopted daughter's blond hair affectionately. Dylis was growing up fast. Since they had moved from Londinium to the farm at Brading, she had turned into a confident, inquisitive and occasionally cheeky girl, who had taken to her private Latin lessons with gusto. In her free time she was always running wild around the farm and the surrounding fields and woods, bringing home weird pets, making friends with the slaves, setting traps and learning to shoot a bow. She and her dog were inseparable. Corbulo glanced down at her as Dylis wiped her hands on her tunic. Efa his wife was always going on about how he should be stricter with his daughter but Corbulo had grown to tolerate Dylis's wildness, gently reining her in when she went too far. He still remembered the deeply traumatised girl he and Quintus had rescued along with Efa from a life of slavery on the Crannog in Caledonia. It was good to hear her laughing and see her confidence.

"We should get back to the farm," he said.

Dylis nodded and giving the sea a final glance she slipped her hand into his.

"I am not afraid of the outer ocean father," she said thoughtfully as the two of them started out towards the green field's further inland. "I don't believe all those stories about sea monsters. I think they were invented to scare little children."

Corbulo looked serious as he gripped his daughter's hand.

"I have seen an entire company of battle hardened Legionaries refuse to board a boat," he said sternly, "Are you saying that you are braver than the finest soldiers in the Empire?"

"Maybe," Dylis replied with a cheeky smile.

The two of them were content to be silent for a while as they crossed a field heading towards a narrow meandering river, further inland. In the spring sunshine the lush, gently rolling countryside looked magnificent. Corbulo could feel the warmth of the sun on his face. Amongst the green grassy edges of the meadows, slender colourful flowers were poking up and birds and small animals rustled in the trees and bushes provoking Dylis's dog to bound away to inspect them. Corbulo headed towards the stepping stones that spanned the river.

"When will we go and see Christiana and Petrus again? I miss Christiana." Dylis said, looking up at him with that enquiring look of hers.

Corbulo muttered something under his breath. It had been nearly two years since he'd last seen the nine Christian children he'd help rescue from the pogrom in Londinium. Christiana was Dylis's age and the two had become firm friends on the chaotic flight northwards. Petrus, insolent rebellious Petrus, would be a young man of fifteen by now. The children it seemed, had found a good home with Efa's people but the thought of seeing Aidan, his father-in-law, did not fill Corbulo with a great sense of joy.

"Maybe in the summer," he muttered, "when we go north to visit Marcus at Luguvalium."

"He's an important soldier now, isn't he?" Dylis said as they approached the stepping stones across the river.

"He is," Corbulo replied.

"Just like you once were, father," Dylis said, looking up at him.

Corbulo grunted and a little colour shot into his cheeks. "Did I ever tell you that you are my favourite daughter," he said abruptly, changing the subject.

Dylis rolled her eyes. "That joke is getting really old, can't you think of a new one," she replied with a loud sigh. "I am the only daughter you have."

Corbulo grinned as he stepped out onto the stone in the river and as he did so, Dylis let go of his hand and before he could stop her she was out on the river, leaping expertly from stone to stone. As she made it to the other bank, she turned and glanced back at him.

"Mother says that one day soon I am to marry," she called out with a sudden tension in her voice. "Mother says that you will choose a husband for me. Do you already know who he is?"

Corbulo paused on a stone in the middle of the river and turned to look down into the dark brown water. Her words had caught him by surprise.

"You are free born, Dylis," he said at last turning to look at her, "When the time comes you will be free to choose your own husband."

"I will be able to choose?" Dylis asked, as a fierce flush spread across her cheeks. She looked away and Corbulo could see that she was pleased. A moment later her dog came bounding and crashing into the water.

As Corbulo stepped onto the riverbank Dylis came towards him and wrapped her arms around his waist and for a long moment she clung to him in silence.

"You are my favourite father," she muttered.

***

Corbulo sighed as he caught sight of his villa through the trees. The simple stone building, with its smart new red roof tiles, looked out of place amongst the crude smelly animal pens and the two thatched Briton round-houses which housed the slaves and the free born farm workers. A clump of trees shielded the villa from the western winds and around the complex, the traces of the ditch and earthen embankment that had once protected the original Briton farm house, were still visible. In the field beyond the trees the slave women were milking the cows and in the adjacent field men were labouring away under Quintus's watchful eye. The women milking the cows were singing as they worked and as he and Dylis approached he caught the smell of freshly baking bread. Corbulo loved his farm. The villa at Brading of course was not his, nor did he own the slaves, the cattle or the farm's profits. Everything belonged to Agricola, ex Governor of Britannia, but as official caretaker of Agricola's business interests in the province of Britannia, he was allowed to live there as if he was the master himself. He had even drawn up plans for a massive expansion of the farm, if only Agricola would give him permission.

Leaving Dylis outside, Corbulo entered the modest looking stone house. Efa was sitting in the front room mending a pair of boots. She looked up as he came in. Her long black hair was neatly bound in the Roman fashion and she was wearing a simple white woollen tunica. Corbulo sniffed and ignoring Efa he glanced at the large iron cauldron filled with meat stew that hung over the fire. Without saying a word he stepped through the internal doorway into the back of the house. There were three small bedrooms and one larger room in this part of the farmstead. The smaller rooms were each just large enough to fit in a stone bed, upon which lay a straw filled mattress. Corbulo entered the larger room and strode towards a corner and knelt down on the stone floor. A few animal skins lay scattered across the paving stones. He kicked one aside and glanced round to check if he was alone. Then inserting his fingers into a crack in the floor he quickly lifted up one of the paving stones to reveal a dark hole. He thrust his hand into the hole and retrieved two leather bags. The bags made a soft clinking noise as he gently placed them on the stone floor.

"Counting your money again?" Efa said from the doorway.

Corbulo glanced round at his wife. Efa had her arms folded across her chest and there was an inquisitive look on her face. Corbulo turned his attention back to the bags.

"It's not my money," he muttered, "It belongs to Agricola as you well know."

"The smaller bag is ours," Efa said sharply, "and Agricola is a lucky patron to have a man like you looking after his affairs. Most men, whom I have known, would slip a few extra coins into their own pocket, but not you Corbulo. No, you are the most honest man I know."

"I am no damn thief," Corbulo growled, as he started to count the coins. "Agricola has been good to us. He deserves my respect and honesty."

Efa sighed and entered the room and gently laid a hand on Corbulo's shoulder as he crouched on the floor.

"If you want," she said, "we can leave earlier for the north this summer. That will give you more time with Marcus. It will be the last time you will see him. You should make the best of it."

Corbulo nodded and for a while he was silent as he concentrated on stacking the coins into small neat piles. Then he cleared his throat.

"I have drawn up my will," he said, without looking up, "a copy is inside our bag here and another copy is at the bank in Londinium. It has been witnessed by the garrison commander at Londinium. There are no surprises Efa. Everything that I own will be divided three ways, between you, Marcus and Dylis. You will be free to do what you like and if you wish to marry again you will have my blessing. I only ask that you and Marcus remain friends and look out for each other."

Efa tightened her grip on his shoulder.

"Of course we shall," she replied quietly. "We're family Corbulo and family stick together. You do not need to tell us this every day."

"Yes," Corbulo nodded solemnly, "family must stick together."

***

The slaves were strung out in a line across the field as Corbulo trudged up to Quintus. The big man, retired Centurion of the Twentieth, stood a little apart, keeping a watchful eye on the slaves. He was clad in a black tunic over which he was wearing a wolf-skin Palla, cloak. A sheathed gladius and a coiled whip hung from the belt around his waist. Quintus turned as Corbulo came up and nodded at his old army comrade with a slightly bored expression. A small bronze cross dangled from a chain around his neck.

"Have you not yet grown bored of being a Christian?" Corbulo said, as he handed Quintus the cup of sour wine he'd been carrying.

Quintus took the mug and downed the contents in one go before wiping his mouth on his sleeve.

"One day the whole Empire will be Christian," he replied confidently, "Even the Emperor in Rome will be one of us. One day, Corbulo, one day."

"It's my turn to supervise the slaves," Corbulo said, gesturing towards the farm. "Tell the boy to come and relieve me in an hour."

Quintus nodded, but instead of leaving he turned to look to the north with a sudden pensive expression.

"Have you heard the news?" Quintus said slowly. "I fear evil times ahead Corbulo. I met a couple of imperial postmen in the tavern yesterday. The Emperor Domitian has crushed Saturninus's rebellion on the Rhine and captured the Eagles of the 14th and 21st Legions." Quintus shook his head. "The shame those boys will now endure will be endless. Saturninus is dead and so is our own Governor Lucullus. Domitian forced him to commit suicide. The official excuse was that it had to do with the naming of a new spear," Quintus paused, "what a load of horse shit." He spat onto the ground. "Lucullus was deeply involved in this rebellion. So getting his letters back did not save our Governor after all. Domitian is triumphant. The rebels are utterly defeated."

Corbulo ran his hand across his cheek and frowned. News travelled slowly when one did not live in a town.

"Governor Lucullus is dead, I didn't know that," he muttered as he was reminded of the arrogant overweight man to whom he had handed back the stolen letters, the letters that had incriminated the rebels, on his return to Deva Victrix from the disastrous expedition to Hibernia.

"The only good that ever came out of our expedition to Hibernia was that you saved my fat arse," Quintus exclaimed.

"What about Agricola?" Corbulo said sharply, "Did you ask whether there was any news about him?"

Quintus shook his head.

61

"Oh for fuck's sake," Corbulo growled irritably, "He's only our patron, Quintus. You know he was involved in the plot against Domitian. If his head is now resting on a spike in the forum in Rome, then it won't be long before some arsehole of an official will arrive here on Vectis and take over our farm, kick us out or worse..."

"Sorry I should have asked," Quintus muttered.

Corbulo shook his head as he turned to stare at the slaves and for a while the two of them were silent.

"There is more news and it's bad," Quintus said with a shrug. "The messengers told me that in the north the Brigantes and Caledonians have risen in rebellion. It's widespread and several of our forts have been attacked. My drinking companions had heard the news from dispatch riders out of Deva."

Corbulo did not reply at first. Then he lowered his head towards the ground.

"Fuck," he muttered.

"Marcus will be alright, he's a fine a soldier and he has a thousand hairy-arsed Batavians to protect him," Quintus said, managing a grin.

Corbulo however, did not look amused.

"The southern tribes are losing their tribal identity," he said at last, shaking his head, "but in the north; in the north they still refuse to forget. We will have to change our travel plans. I can't take Efa and Dylis into a war zone. Maybe this summer I will travel north on my own."

"Don't be stupid," Quintus replied glancing at Corbulo, "The Britons will capture you and cut your heart out and then what use will you be to me and your family?" Quintus sighed. "Maybe the rebellion will be over by summer. The Legions will sort it out; they always do."

Corbulo was about to reply, when he heard a voice crying out his name. He and Quintus turned and saw a boy running towards them across the field. As the boy approached he called out again.

"Master, master, you have a visitor," the boy shouted.

"Who is he? Has he come alone?" Corbulo said sharply, as Quintus's hand dropped to the pommel of his sword.

Gasping for breath the boy came to a halt in front of Corbulo.

"Yes master, he's alone," the boy gasped, "and he says that you know him."

## Chapter Nine – No Escape from the Past

"He's waiting in the hall," the boy said, as he skipped along keeping pace with Corbulo as the older man strode towards the red-tiled farm house. Corbulo ignored the boy. In the field with the cows, the slave women had fallen silent as they watched him pass. Corbulo looked troubled. The northern revolt amongst the Brigantes and Caledonians had complicated matters, but Quintus was right; the Legions would crush the uprising. It was just a matter of time and Marcus was a capable soldier who knew how to look after himself. Corbulo clenched his fist in frustration. He couldn't give a damn about the failure of Saturninus's revolt, but if evidence had been uncovered that Agricola was involved in the plot against the Emperor then, he and his family, through his close association to the retired ex Governor of Britannia, would be in danger. The fact that he just didn't know what was happening was beyond frustrating. If Agricola was in trouble, there would be little warning before the Emperor's men came to seize his farm.

As he stomped into the farm yard he peered suspiciously at the front door of the house. A horse that he didn't recognize stood tethered to one of the wooden enclosure walls and was drinking from a bucket of water. The beast looked in good condition. Corbulo muttered something under his breath. He hardly ever received visitors, apart from the merchants with whom he did business and the occasional messenger. Who was this visitor who claimed to know him?

Corbulo stepped through the doorway into the hall and as he did so, a figure clad in a tired and frayed brown riding cloak, rose from where he'd been waiting. A fierce blush spread across Corbulo's cheeks as he instantly recognized the man. The visitor was old, in his early sixties but still in good shape and his chin was covered by a dirty white beard. He was leaning on a stout stick and a short hunting knife was stuffed into his belt.

"You have aged since I last saw you," the Briton said, speaking slowly in his native language. "Now, how long ago was that Corbulo?"

"Fergus!" Corbulo dipped his head respectfully as he felt his cheeks burn. "I believe it has been nine years." he muttered awkwardly.

For a moment the hall was silent as Fergus took his time studying him.

"Will you come in?" Corbulo said at last, gesturing at the open doorway into the house. "I will have the slaves bring us some wine and food."

"I will," Fergus replied as he stepped into the front room.

Efa rose quickly as Fergus followed by Corbulo entered and as they did, she shot her husband a quick questioning glance.

"Efa," Corbulo said, gesturing at the visitor, "this is Fergus. He is the father of my first wife Alene. He's Marcus' grandfather."

Startled, Efa stared at Corbulo. Then she turned to Fergus and muttered a polite greeting. Fergus returned the greeting and slowly lowered himself into a chair beside the cooking pot containing the meat stew.

An embarrassing silence followed. Then Fergus coughed.

"Nine years sounds about right," he muttered turning his pale eyes towards Corbulo. "The last time we met was before Alene killed herself; do you remember? After her death you did not come to pay your respects to me and my family. You simply vanished. It has taken me months to find you."

"I am sorry," Corbulo replied, lowering his gaze. "I should have come. But I am no longer that man whom you knew."

Fergus was examining him carefully. Then he glanced at Efa and gave her a gentle smile.

"Alene told me," Fergus said quietly, "that upon your retirement you were thinking about returning to Italy and taking her and Marcus with you. She didn't want to go. Her life was here."

Corbulo shifted his weight awkwardly. "It was a mistake," he muttered, "and it has taken me a long time, but I have made my peace with Marcus. Together we erected a memorial stone in her honour. It stands on the road just north of Luguvalium." Corbulo ran his fingers across his cheeks and turned to gaze at Fergus. "I know what you must think of me. I know what kind of man I once was but that man no longer exists. Marcus brought me back; he healed me."

Fergus's face was difficult to read and for a long moment the room remained silent. Then at last he nodded.

"Yes I know about the stone. Marcus is a good man," he said. "He has his mother's spirit in him. I only wish I could see him more often. He told me where I could find you."

"He has named his son after you," Efa said suddenly from the corner to which she had retreated.

Fergus gave her an appreciative glance. He looked pleased.

"I no longer have a quarrel with you, Corbulo," Fergus said, turning back to look at him. "I am old and do not wish to be burdened with anger and hatred. You did not treat my daughter with the respect she deserved and that is something you will have to explain to her when you meet her again, but I am glad I have found you and that we have talked."

Corbulo nodded his appreciation.

"I have also come to ask for your help," Fergus said quietly.

"Of course," Corbulo replied stiffly, "What can I do for you?"

Fergus sighed wearily. "It's a question about land," he replied. "My people and I have not moved from the earth that I inherited from my father and the home where you first met Alene. My land is sacred ground. It was given to us by the great King Cunobelinus himself. However the Roman settlement, your colony at Camulodunum is growing and is attracting many wealthy and ambitious Roman settlers. They like to build stone houses and erect statues to their gods and set pictures in stone floors. One of these Romans by the name of Timion, a salt merchant, has grown interested in my land and is trying to force me to leave." A troubled look had appeared in Fergus' eyes. "He has asked me to sell my land but I refused and now he is intimidating me into leaving. His thugs have threatened me and my people. I am an old man Corbulo, I cannot fight against a man like Timion."

"What can I do to help?" Corbulo murmured.

Fergus glanced at the iron cauldron over the fire. "Marcus tells me that you enjoy the protection of Agricola. He is no doubt a powerful patron," he said. "I may not be much of a match against this Timion but you, on the other hand..." Fergus paused. "You are a powerful man Corbulo; you have influence and I need your help. I have come here to ask you to come back with me to Camulodunum and persuade Timion to leave me alone? I have no one else to turn to."

For a moment Corbulo looked surprised. Quickly he glanced at Efa and then lowered his gaze towards the floor. The room fell silent.

"Of course," he muttered at last, "it is the least that I can do, but if I go with you my woman and daughter will come with me. These are unsettled times and I do not dare leave them behind on their own."

Fergus nodded.

"You are all welcome in my home," he said gratefully, "but you will not like everything that you will find there."

## Chapter Ten – The Bankers of Londinium

"Pull!"

The helmsman's deep voice was followed by the placid swish of the oars in the water as the oarsmen propelled the sea-going galley up the river. It was mid-morning and grey rain clouds were building in the west. High above the vessel the shrieks of the sea gulls had not ceased since they'd left Vectis, three days ago. Corbulo stood beside the main mast clasping the smooth wood with one hand. The Thames was in flood and the wide river had extended to over a thousand yards from bank to bank, covering the many sand banks and mud flats he knew were out there and making inroads into the low-lying, swampy southern shore.

"Pull," the helmsman cried out again and, like some strange insect with many legs, the banks of oars dipped into the brown, placid water in steady, perfect harmony.

Corbulo turned to glance at Efa and Dylis, who were sitting at the rear of the galley. Efa had her head in her hands. She had hated every second of the sea journey and had been sick every day, vomiting the contents of her meals over the side at regular intervals but Dylis... Dylis had loved the journey and for a moment Corbulo looked intrigued. He had never seen her as excited as she had been these past three days. The ocean certainly held no terrors for his daughter. His gaze shifted to Fergus, who was asleep on the deck behind the two women. What had Fergus meant when he'd said, that he wouldn't like everything he found at Camulodunum? He'd never really got to know the old man. Alene, his first wife had not often spoken about her family and for most of his career he'd been posted away from Camulodunum. But Corbulo was glad he'd come. Fergus was the final person to whom he owed an apology for the way he had once been.

"Pull!"

Carefully Corbulo made his way forwards to the figurehead of Neptune that proudly adorned the prow of the ship. On both sides of him the rowers, their faces covered in sweat, were rhythmically moving forwards and backwards on their benches and piled into the hold and the middle of the ship were a cargo of amphorae, around which clustered the three slaves he'd brought with him from the farm and a few passengers, hitching a ride to the capital of Britannia. At the prow Corbulo clasped hold of the wooden side of the galley and grunted with sudden nostalgia, as in the distance he caught sight of the magnificent wooden bridge that spanned the Thames. The bridge was still just as he remembered it when he'd been a stone merchant hauling stone up the river from the quarries to the south-east.

"Why are we going to Londinium," Dylis asked, as she pushed her way to his side. "Fergus says that he lives in Camulodunum."

Corbulo laid his hand on his daughter's shoulder.

"Don't you like being back here?" he asked.

Dylis shrugged as she gazed at the northern shore of the Thames and the approaching harbour of Londinium, with its massive box-like quays, cranes and docks. "I don't mind," she replied indifferently, "but I like Vectis more. The air is cleaner." Then she looked up at him with that inquiring look of hers. "But you didn't answer my question?"

"I have some business to take care of in Londinium," Corbulo sighed. "It's on the way to Camulodunum, so it makes sense to pay the place a visit, I suppose."

"Is that with the bank?"

"Yes, it's with the bank," Corbulo nodded. "I work for Agricola, our patron and it's his bank. I need to just check that everything is being managed correctly. We won't be staying here longer than a day."

"I wish Quintus had come with us," Dylis said, as she looked up at the screeching sea gulls; "he always has the funniest stories to tell. That would cheer Mum up. She is not feeling so well."

"Really," Corbulo exclaimed in mock alarm, "I thought she loved the sea?"

For a moment father and daughter shared a bemused smile.

"Someone needs to look after the farm whilst we are away," Corbulo said at last, "and anyway his stories are not that funny. Quintus is a Christian and those people are far too serious for their own good."

\*\*\*

The harbour front of Londinium was crowded and the noise was tremendous. Eagerly Corbulo clambered up onto the embankment and turned to stare at the activity along the river. Londinium, capital of the province of Britannia, was booming and as he looked around Corbulo felt a familiar excitement at the prospect of seeing the city, where he had once made his home. Ships of all sizes lay moored alongside the massive wooden quays that had been driven into the northern river bank like some gigantic wooden palisade, and on the shore cranes were lifting the precious cargoes from their holds and depositing them onto the cobble-stone embankment where slaves, carts and mules were whisking the goods into the large warehouses that lined the Thames. The shouts and cries of the sailors, overseers and merchants, speaking to each other in a multitude of different languages, mingled with the hammering and sawing of the boat builders, barking dogs and the creaking groan of the carts. Hanging over the whole scene was the sour stink of raw sewage.

Further along the water front in the area reserved for exporters, Britannia's tin, iron, gold, silver, grain and oyster exports were being loaded onto large sea-going galleys. As he stared at the scene, Corbulo suddenly noticed something he had not seen before in the city. A line of bedraggled looking men, women and children were shuffling towards one of the continent-bound galleys. The slaves were chained together in leg irons and were being driven on by a man holding a whip.

"Want to fuck, Sir?" a prostitute called out as she ambled up to him. The girl looked no older than eighteen.

"No," Corbulo snapped, as ignoring the woman, he turned and helped Efa up onto the embankment. His wife looked pale and miserable and unsteady on her feet. Once his little party of seven were all ashore and standing around him, Corbulo fished a small leather pouch from his pocket and handed it to the eldest of the three slaves who had accompanied him from Vectis.

"Here is some coin," he said, "Arrange for us to have two rooms tonight at a tavern called Cum Mula Peperit. You will find it close to the Forum. Also we will need a horse and a wagon. I want everything to be ready, so that we can leave tomorrow at dawn. Once you are done, come and find me in the Forum, understood?"

The slave nodded and without saying a word, he hurried away into the crowds. Corbulo didn't watch him go. Instead he turned and walked over towards the quayside and stared out across the river. Then he reached into his pocket and flipped a single copper coin into the river.

"What was that for?" Dylis asked as she came up beside him.

"That's for Priscus," Corbulo grunted, "May his soul rest in peace."

Dylis was silent as she stared at the brown river. Priscus had been Corbulo's young business partner in Londinium until Bestia had murdered him and thrown his body into the Thames.

"He is not gone unless we forget him," Dylis said suddenly, looking up at her father and for a instant Corbulo was struck by the wisdom in her eyes.

Slowly he nodded in agreement.

"Come on," he said at last, giving Dylis a wink, "let's get this business over with."

***

It was a short walk from the harbour to the Forum. People thronged the street and the advertising cries of the merchants and shop owners were everywhere. Along both sides of Watling Street the wooden-framed strip houses, with their narrow frontages, were packed tightly up against each other. Smoke was rising from holes in the thatched roofs and at intervals the terraces were separated by a narrow rubbish- littered alley, from which a drain protruded to merge with the drainage ditches on both sides of the main street. With the rest of his party following close behind, Corbulo strode up the street. As he glanced around, he grunted in approval as he noticed that some of the wood, daub and wattle strip homes had been replaced by stone houses with proper roof tiles. Stone was surely and steadily changing the look of the city.

As they approached the Forum, the heart of the city, where the banking and legal practices were concentrated, Corbulo gasped and came to an astonished halt in the middle of the street. The two-storied stone Forum building was still there, but the tightly packed strip housing that had once surrounded it, had been demolished. In the large, cleared space, labourers were at work laying the foundations of a huge, square looking building that dwarfed the existing Forum. A section of a stone- colonnaded, covered walk way was rising up from the ground and the construction was surrounded by wooden scaffolding. The cries and shouts of the workmen mingled with the sound of hammering and sawing. Corbulo stepped aside as the driver of an ox-drawn wagon laden with stone cried out a warning as he rattled past him up the street. Corbulo shook his head, as he stared at the building site. So they had finally started work. The new Forum at Cornhill was going to be one of the largest buildings he had ever seen, only eclipsed by the Colliseum in Rome.

His eyes narrowed as he suddenly caught sight of the gang of youths hanging around outside a fast food shack. The young, shaven-headed men could be no older than eighteen. Knives hung from their belts and they were laughing, staring at the shoppers and towns folk with confident aggressive looks. Corbulo muttered something under his breath. Some things had not changed. The gangs that roamed the streets of the capital were as visible and dangerous as ever.

"Stay close," he said turning to look at Efa and Dylis, "and watch your belongings, the Forum is full of pickpockets and thieves."

***

In the court yard inside the Forum, the farmer' market stalls lined the edge of the open space and from behind their stalls, the merchants and farmers were doing a brisk trade. Alone, Corbulo made his way through the crowd towards the Forum's eastern wing, where the bankers had their offices. Squeezing in between two stalls, he stepped into the shade of the stone-paved and covered walk way, that separated the Atrium from the shops and offices. A line of wooden posts, driven into the ground, stretched away along the side of the Forum, holding up the sloping roof. He strode along until he came to a door, above which hung a sign.

"Argentarii Agricola. Authorised moneylender and foreign exchange dealer. First class service for veterans."

Corbulo grunted. The last part of the sign had been his idea. Agricola had been a late entrant into the cut-throat competitive banking market and to survive, it had been necessary to carve out a niche, and with Agricola's military reputation, angling the business towards veterans had proved to be a good and profitable move. Without knocking on the door, Corbulo barged into the office.

A man of around thirty with curly black hair was sitting behind a messy looking desk, across which lay scattered papyrus scrolls and small leather bags. He was grunting and his eyes were closed. A young woman was on her knees in front of him, her head bobbing up and down over his crotch. She was making a slurping noise. As Corbulo stepped into the room, the man cried out in shock and nearly tipped over backwards.

"Good to see that you are keeping yourself busy Romulus," Corbulo growled as he folded his arms across his chest. The woman rose to her feet as Romulus hastily tried to pull up his under garments.

"Corbulo!" the man exclaimed, "This is a surprise. I didn't know you were coming to pay a visit. You should have warned me in advance, I could have arranged a proper welcome for you."

Corbulo glanced at the woman who smiled back him.

"Get out of here," Corbulo snapped.

"He hasn't paid me yet," the Temple whore retorted.

Corbulo said nothing as he stepped up to the desk and emptied one of the leather bags into his hand. Selecting a few coins he thrust them into the prostitute's hand and pushed her towards the door.

"Get out!" He ordered.

Once the whore had gone, Corbulo turned to look at Romulus. The banker was blushing with embarrassment as he tried to straighten his clothing. It had been Agricola's decision to hire Romulus to look after the bank and it had been a bad decision, Corbulo thought. Romulus was one of the dozens of Romanised local Celtic aristocrats, who had flocked to the new and burgeoning Roman cities that had popped up across the south. These southern nobles had taken Roman names and had bought into the new way of life that Rome had imported into their island. Once their eyes had been opened to the luxury and wealth and the temptations of the new possibilities, there had been no holding back.

"I want to inspect the books, so get them out and clean up this desk," Corbulo snapped in an annoyed voice. "Those money bags should be in the strong box. Damn it Romulus, we can't have money lying around like that. Where is your security man?"

"He should have been outside by the door," Romulus muttered, as his eyes darted nervously across the desk.

"And I want to count all the money in the strong box," Corbulo said.

Startled, Romulus looked up at him and his face suddenly grew pale.

"Surely there is no need for that," he protested. "Come Corbulo, you must have had a long and tiring journey. Surely these matters can wait?"

Corbulo ignored Romulus' protestations and began picking up the scrolls from the desk. Without another word he pulled up a chair and began to sift through the documents.

"It will be months before Agricola's secretary arrives to collect the profits," Romulus whined, as he watched his boss.

"Get to work," Corbulo growled, not taking his eyes off the papers.

Romulus sighed irritably and slowly started to collect the bags of coins and, as he turned to place them in the iron box, Corbulo glanced thoughtfully at his employee. Romulus looked tense and uncomfortable.

***

It was a few hours later when it became clear to Corbulo why his employee was so tense and uncomfortable. The accounts and the money inside the strong box did not add up. Romulus had to be stealing from his employer. As the realisation dawned, Corbulo slowly lowered the scroll he had been reading and looked down at the stone floor of the office. Romulus sat behind his desk watching him. The Briton was silent and there was a resentful look on his face.

Corbulo raised his head and looked Romulus straight in the eye.

"In the Legions," he growled, "when a man was caught stealing, we would take turns in whipping him."

The resentment on Romulus' face did not change. "Agricola already has so much wealth," he sneered suddenly, "he is not going to miss a few coins."

"So you admit that you are stealing from your employer," Corbulo snapped.

Irritably Romulus shook his head and rolled his eyes. "Wake up Corbulo," Romulus retorted bitterly, "all the bankers around here are involved. They all take a bit for themselves and why not? You, Corbulo, have a family. I know you have. You could do very well for yourself if you turned a blind eye now and then. You could secure their future without any trouble."

Corbulo stared at Romulus in silence.

Romulus's face suddenly seemed to brighten and he leaned forwards hopefully.

"Think about it Corbulo; the money we could make here would set us and our families up for life. Think about the possibilities."

Corbulo slowly rose to his feet as he stared at Romulus, sitting behind his desk.

"If I see you around here again," Corbulo bellowed, "I will have your balls cut off. You are nothing more than a common thief. Now get out of my sight. You are lucky that I am not going to report this to Agricola."

Romulus was silent as he blinked in rapid succession.

"Suit yourself grandpa," he sneered, rising to his feet, "But you and I are not so different. One day it will be you who will be sucking my cock."

Corbulo was across the room in a flash. He grabbed hold of Romulus's neck and flung him in the direction of the door.

"Get out," Corbulo roared, "Before I change my mind and cut your balls off right here."

Romulus staggered into the door but his reflexes were quick and sharp. A small knife suddenly appeared in his hand. He held it up threateningly, his chest heaving and his face contorted in rage.

"Watch yourself Corbulo," Romulus hissed, "you won't get rid of me so easily. I have friends and these are dangerous times."

And with that he disappeared out through the door. Corbulo watched him go. Then he shook his head and turned to look around the office. Getting rid of Romulus was the right decision but it had created another problem. With Romulus's departure he had no one to manage the bank for him. Corbulo sighed. Who else did he know in Londinium whom he could trust?

He groaned as an idea came to him.

***

The sign outside the office in the forum a few doors down from his own office read.

"Argentarii Britannia, Owner Gaius Valerius Falco, authorised money lender and foreign exchange dealer, good rates for all."

Someone had tried to scratch out the word 'good' and insert the word 'awful' in front of the 'rates for all' part and someone else had tried unsuccessfully to erase the graffiti. Without knocking, Corbulo entered the office. Two armed men were lounging about in a corner. Swiftly they rose to their feet as they saw him. Corbulo ignored the guards and grunted as he caught sight of Falco. The banker was examining the breasts of the same temple whore he had ejected from his own office just a few hours earlier. As he caught sight of Corbulo, a surprised smile appeared on Falco's face.

"Lovely tits love," Falco grinned turning to the whore, "but I am not buying today. Go on, get out of here now, I have business to attend to."

The prostitute raised her eyebrows at Corbulo as she glided past him on her way out.

"Well well, this is a surprise," Falco bellowed, "The great and famous Corbulo here in my very own office. I would say 'good to see you Sir,' but as you are my competitor, I will settle by shaking your hand."

Corbulo extended his arm and Falco clasped it with a wary grin. Falco was a small man with thick bushy eyebrows and a fat belly. He looked in his mid-forties. When Corbulo had first come to live in Londinium he had sold the amber stone he'd found in Caledonia to Falco and the man had become Corbulo's banker when he'd started his stone haulage business. Corbulo quickly glanced around the office. Falco's main business was lending money to the lower end of the market, to the desperate and poor and the occasional legitimate business. The banker had helped him during the flight from Londinium with the nine Christian children, but if there was anything that Corbulo knew about Falco, it was that the man's loyalty was dependent on the size of the profit he would make.

"What can I do for you Corbulo?" Falco said, with a fake smile. "If you have come to give me a hard time about that wagon I sold you, we already spoke about this, remember."

"It's not about the wagon," Corbulo replied, "I have a proposal Falco. I want us to merge our banks."

For a moment Falco looked genuinely surprised and lost for words.

"What's brought this on?" he muttered at last.

"I need someone to manage Agricola's bank and accounts here in Londinium. I want you to take on that job."

"But what about Romulus, isn't that his job?"

"I sacked him, just now," Corbulo replied, "He was stealing from me."

Falco raised his eyebrows and emitted a chuckle. "Well I could have told you that when he was first hired," he exclaimed. "The man had thief tattooed across his forehead."

"Will you take the job?" Corbulo pressed.

Falco sat down in his chair and leaned back, examining Corbulo thoughtfully.

"So you trust me," he said, "You are not afraid that I will do the same and steal from you? I want to hear you say it Corbulo."

"You are an unscrupulous bastard," Corbulo said, staring at Falco, "You would sell your own mother if the profit was worth it but I think you have got just about enough honour to not steal from your own employer. So yes. I will trust you Falco."

Falco was staring at Corbulo with a pleased look. For a long moment he was silent as he considered the offer. Then his eyes narrowed suspiciously.

"Do you know who killed Classicus, the Procurator Augusti?" Falco asked. "There is a rumour that he was murdered in Hibernia but his body was never found. You were in Hibernia at the same time, weren't you?"

"Do you want the merger or not?" Corbulo growled.

Falco shrugged and looked down at his desk. "Personally I am glad that arse is dead, along with Governor Lucullus. The two of them were not good for business." Falco looked up and there was a sudden cunning gleam in his eyes.

"I want ten percent of the profits," he snapped.

"Six," Corbulo replied.

"Nine," Falco retorted.

"Seven and that's my final offer," Corbulo growled. "You are not the only banker to whom I can go."

"Done!" Falco grinned, extending his hand.

Corbulo clasped it as the two men shook on the deal.

"Agricola's profits are about to soar," Falco exclaimed rubbing his hands together in sudden glee. He pointed a finger at Corbulo. "You did well to come to me Corbulo. I will not forget that my friend."

## Chapter Eleven – The Royal Burial Ground

Corbulo gasped for breath as the coughing fit finally started to subside. He stood bent over, with one hand leaning against a willow tree. It was late on the second day of their departure from Londinium. Through the trees a short distance away, the horses and the open-topped wagon, carrying his family and slaves, stood motionless on the gravel road as they waited for him to return.

"Is he alright?" he heard Dylis say.

Corbulo tried to steady his breathing as he looked down at his hands. They were covered in speckles of blood. He closed his eyes, straightened up and wiped his hands against the tree trunk. His left arm was shaking.

As he emerged onto the road, he felt the eyes of everyone in the cart upon him. Ignoring his daughter's worried look, he got back up onto the wagon and took the reins from the slave.

"Fergus," he called out without looking at the man, "how much further?"

"Not far," the Briton replied quietly, "not far now, Corbulo."

\*\*\*

An hour or so later Fergus suddenly pointed to the right. Corbulo brought the wagon to a sharp halt and peered down the rough country track that led away from the Roman road. The track across the open fields was nothing like he remembered, but then again, it had been many years since he'd visited Fergus's home. Further up the Roman road he could see a mile-stone and in the distance a horseman was coming towards them from the direction of Camulodunum. Nervously Corbulo fidgeted with the horse's reins. Then with a grunt he forced the horses and wagon off the road and onto the country track. The wagon groaned and swayed as they started off across the fields. Birds were singing cheerfully in a copse of trees and beyond the meadows he caught sight of a long earthen dyke, that marked the outer defences of the old royal fortress of Camulodunum. The sight brought on a sudden gush of memories. It was here, in Fergus's old round house, that Marcus had been born and it was here too at Camulodunum's river harbour, as a raw recruit, that he'd first come ashore in Britannia and had been assigned to the Twentieth Legion. At that time the town had been the largest Roman settlement in Britannia and capital of the fledgling province. The Roman colony had been constructed within the boundaries of the old Briton settlement that had once been the seat of King Cunobelinus, King of the Britons. It was still surrounded by numerous earthen dykes, whose main purpose were as anti-cavalry and chariot defences. Corbulo shook his head dismissively. Not that they had provided any effective defence against the barbarian Queen, when she and her horde of barbarians had over run and slaughtered the entire Roman town, thirty or so years ago.

Fergus's home was a cluster of round houses, which stood in a tight circle surrounded by a ditch and a low and grassy inner embankment. Smoke was drifting upwards from a hole in the low-slung thatched roofs and a few people were tending to some farm animals in the adjacent field. Close by, a cow was mooing and out of sight Corbulo could hear a barking dog. The labourers in the field looked up as the wagon and horses trundled towards them. Then, as they recognised Fergus, an excited cry rose up and more people emerged from the wattle and daub homes. As they caught sight of Fergus they rushed over to greet him.

Corbulo forced the horses to a halt as the Britons surrounded the wagon, calling out to Fergus as the old man was helped down onto the ground. Corbulo swallowed awkwardly and remained sitting on the wagon. Amongst the Britons the only people that he recognised were Alene's brother and sister. They had not recognised him yet. He glanced for support at Efa but his wife had her back to him.

"What is he doing here?" a loud and hostile male voice exclaimed. Corbulo turned to see Alene's brother, a mature man of around forty with a black beard and spiky hair pointing a finger at him.

The excited chatter around the wagon came to an abrupt halt. For a moment no one spoke. Then Fergus came up to the Alene's brother and calmly laid a hand on his son's shoulder.

"He is here to help us with our problem," Fergus said, "So you will treat him with the proper respect that we provide to a guest."

"He should not be here," Alene's brother growled. "Not after the way he treated my sister. She is dead because of him. Damn you Corbulo. Damn the sight of you. How dare you come back here."

Stiffly Corbulo rose from his seat and jumped down onto the ground and turned to face Alene's brother.

"I have come here to help you," he muttered, "To make amends. That is all that I want to do, brother."

"Fuck you," Alene's brother hissed as he threatened to lunge at Corbulo, only to be held back by Fergus's restraining hand. "You have a cheek to show your face here again, you Roman bastard."

"That's enough," Fergus said sharply. "I will hear no more such talk." Fergus turned to look at the people around him. "Come, tonight we shall feast and I shall tell you about my journey and tomorrow we shall discuss how to handle Timion and his thugs. Corbulo and his wife and daughter are our guests and I will not have them mistreated in my home. Is that clear?"

The people, clustered around the wagon, remained silent as they stared at Efa and Dylis. Efa blushed at the sudden attention but Dylis managed a little shy smile.

"Go with Fergus," Corbulo said quietly turning to his wife, "I am going to tend to the horses. I will join you in a little while."

Efa nodded without saying a word and Corbulo watched her go, as the people led by Fergus, streamed back into the small settlement, leaving him alone with the horses and the wagon. As Dylis crossed the ditch, she turned to quickly glance back at him before disappearing behind the low earthen embankment.

*** 

Corbulo stood on top of the dyke peering out across the fields towards the east. It was dusk and in the round houses behind him he could hear the sound of laughter and singing. He would have to go inside soon and join them he thought, although he didn't want to. To the east, a little distance away, he could see the outline of the small wooden Roman fort that guarded the market and the Roman temple in the Briton settlement of Gosbecks. He sighed and lowered his head. Helping Fergus was the right thing to do but he hated being here. He hated looking at, and speaking to Fergus and his family. The farmstead and it's people constantly reminded him of Alene. She was everywhere, unseen, untouchable and unheard. He took a deep breath. But it was right that he was confronting the guilt that had first propelled him to leave Rome in search of Marcus, all those years ago. He needed to make his peace with the past and if this was the final part of that journey, then that was a good thing. Fergus was indeed a wise man. He nodded to himself. Soon when he went to be judged by the immortal gods, he would meet her again and he would be ready to explain himself but not yet, he thought, not yet.

He turned as he heard a noise behind him. In the fading light Dylis appeared clambering up the dyke towards him. Silently she came and stood beside him.

"Will you come to join us in the house?" she asked, looking up at him. "Fergus has slaughtered one of his sheep in our honour."

"Soon," he muttered.

"What are you looking at?" Dylis frowned as she turned to look eastwards.

Corbulo raised his finger and pointed at the cluster of farmsteads of the Briton settlement of Gosbecks, a little distance away to the east.

"Over there," he said quietly, "in that small settlement is where Emperor Claudius took the surrender of eleven Briton kings over forty-five years ago. When I first joined the Legion I knew soldiers who had taken part in the surrender ceremony. It is the place where the great King Cunobelinus had his home. He lies buried there beneath the Roman temple."

"Is that why Fergus doesn't want to give up his land, father?"

Corbulo glanced down at Dylis. Then he shrugged.

"Who knows," he muttered, "he will have his reasons."

Dylis was silent for a long moment. Then she looked up at him with a frown.

"Well I think he is right to fight for his land," she said, "and I hope he wins. And I am glad that you are helping him."

Corbulo stared at his daughter, struck by the determination in her voice. Then he felt her slip her hand into his hand.

"Come on, let's go and join them," she said pulling him after her down the earth embankment.

*** 

Inside the round house all the Britons had gathered in a large circle around a fire. A pair of beautifully forged, iron fire dogs stood gleaming in the fire and slung in between them, was the carcass of a sheep. The delicious smell of roasting meat mingled with the strong smell of wood smoke. The flames roared, exploded and crackled as the juices from the animal trickled down into the fire and Corbulo felt himself sweating from the heat, as the firelight cast eerie shadows across the walls and roof of the house. The round house was surprisingly large and the feasting people were in a boisterous mood, talking, laughing and crying out to each other. Cups of mead were being passed around and as he took his place, he caught sight of Efa. His wife looked relaxed and seemed to be enjoying herself. A girl whom he didn't recognise, came up to him with a jug and without a word she poured Roman wine into his cup. He looked up in surprise but the girl had already moved on.

Across the fire he caught Fergus watching him. The old man gave him a sly little nod and raised his cup. Corbulo did the same, before draining the contents of his beaker in one go.

"Corbulo," a voice suddenly boomed, as Alene's brother fixed his eyes on him, "why don't you tell the younger folk here how you fought against Boudicca in her last battle. Tell us how you defeated the Queen."

"That's enough," Fergus interrupted, but Alene's brother silenced his father with a sharp wave of his hand. Bitterness was written clearly across his face. The people around the crackling fire slowly fell silent.

Corbulo turned slowly to look at his former brother-in-law.

"What would you like to know?" Corbulo replied sourly, "That I lost many good friends that day. That Rome was victorious? But I will tell you this, if I had to do it all again, I would and I wouldn't hesitate to slice the barbarian queen's head off, if I got the chance. The bitch deserved nothing less."

"Arsehole," someone muttered.

Alene's brother's eyes blazed with cold fury but he managed to control himself.

"Yes, I am sure that you served Rome well," he hissed, "But it's a shame you cannot say the same about your family. Do you know what we did when Governor Paulinus and his men marched into our land seeking revenge? Do you know what we had to do to survive?"

Corbulo lowered his eyes to the fire. He didn't know. He had never asked Alene about it and she had never dared tell him, or maybe she had and he had not bothered to listen.

"For half a year we hid in the marshes," Alene's brother snarled. "We hid out like wild animals in order to evade the Roman patrols. Paulinus acted like a demon. He sent his men from village to village burning, killing, raping and destroying. Nothing was sacred to that man, nothing."

Corbulo stared stubbornly at the fire and said nothing.

"So where were you Corbulo?" Alene's brother snapped, "where were you when our farms went up in flames and our wealth was stolen from us? Why did you do nothing to help us? Why do you only come now to help us?"

"Perhaps he was one of the soldier's doing the looting," a voice cried out.

"That's enough," Fergus said in a calm voice whose authority carried around the room, "All of you," he said turning to look around the gathering, "you should know that Alene, my daughter never spoke a harsh word about this man, so neither shall we. Corbulo has come here to help us, he is our guest and he is our friend."

"If you needed help you should have gone to Marcus," Alene's brother retorted with a shake of his head, "Marcus is of our blood. He was born right here in this house. He would have been a far better choice than this prick here."

At the mention of his son, Corbulo stirred and cleared his throat and his eyes found Fergus across the fire.

"Yes, Alene killed herself because of me," he said. "Her blood is on my hands but Marcus and I have been reconciled. We have made a fresh start and I am here to do the same with you. So in compensation for your family's loss, I am willing to pay you. Name a price in gold and I will provide it?"

The house fell silent until the only noise was the roar of the fire. Across from Corbulo, Fergus smiled and lowered his eyes to the floor.

"No," the old man said shaking his head. "We do not want your gold Corbulo. You will repay us in another way."

***

Beneath the iron fire dogs the blackened, smouldering embers of last night's fire still glowed amongst a circle of stones and mixed in between them were animal bones. Corbulo sat cross legged on the floor, sipping warm milk from a wooden cup as he listened to Fergus. The stale smell of unwashed bodies and smoke filled the round house and in a corner two sleek hounds lay curled up together. One of the dogs raised his head, as a black mouse shot across the floor and vanished into a crack in the wall. It was dawn and apart from Fergus and Corbulo the only other person in the house was Alene's brother. The man was staring at Corbulo with sullen and silent resentment.

Fergus was speaking in a slow measured voice. He looked tired. "The land around here is rich and fertile," he said. "Before the rebellion it supported a large population. People were prosperous but afterwards, after Governor Paulinus had his revenge, for a long time there was nothing left but burnt out villages, ruined fields and corpses hanging from trees. It has taken us a very long to recover." Fergus sighed. "The Roman settlers have taken advantage of this. Timion wants to use our land to build a new villa," he said. "At first he offered to buy us out but when I refused, he sent some of his hard men to frighten us and get us to agree to leave. They beat up one of my grandsons and threatened to rape the women, but my son here drove them off. But they will be back. Timion is determined to get his way. He is a stubborn and powerful man. The women can no longer go into the Roman town to shop without protection."

"You said Timion controls the salt trade in these parts?" Corbulo muttered.

Fergus nodded.

"He does and it's made him wealthy. His salt pans are everywhere along the coast and in the salt marshes. From his warehouse along the river at Camulodunum, his merchants trade the salt across the whole province. He has friends everywhere. He is a dangerous man Corbulo, so we must be cautious."

"Where does he live?" Corbulo said.

"He has a town house in Camulodunum," Fergus replied, "He spends most of his time there but I think he owns other houses too. It's difficult to say."

Corbulo nodded.

"So what are you going to do?" Alene's brother sneered. "How are you going to help us?"

Corbulo looked up at Alene's brother and raised his eyebrows.

"I am going to scare the shit out of him," he replied.

***

Corbulo was sharpening his gladius on a mill stone when Fergus came up to him. It was mid-morning and the sky was dark and overcast. Gently the old man took Corbulo by the arm.

"Before we leave for Camulodunum," Fergus said, "there is something that I need to show you. Come with me."

Obediently Corbulo slid his sword back into its sheath and turned to follow Fergus as the old man made his way across the ditch and into the fields that surrounded the small settlement. Fergus seemed in no rush as he started out towards the long earthen dyke.

"It is time that you understood why I will not surrender this land," Fergus said quietly, as the two of them strode across the field. "In the time of my father this land was given to us by King Cunobelinus. It is sacred land of great significance to all Britons, who have not forgotten their ancestors. I am its caretaker and my son will be the caretaker after I am gone. We have a sworn duty to protect this land. We are not leaving. It is not going to happen."

"Why?" Corbulo muttered as he turned to look around him, "what is so special about this place?"

Across the open grassy field the wind had picked up. Fergus was silent as he made his way towards five, grass covered mounds. Corbulo frowned. He had not noticed the mounds on his previous visits and Fergus had certainly never spoken about them before. The low mounds were covered in grass and laid out in two rows, one of three and one of two. Fergus halted beside the first one and looked down at the earth.

"It is because of these," he said with a strange emotion in his voice, "these mounds Corbulo, are royal graves. My father was given the task of looking after these graves and when he died, that responsibility passed to me. This one here contains the cremated remains of Cunobelinus's physician, a druid. The others are members of the king's family and here," Fergus said with a sigh as he came to a halt beside one of the mounds, "is where Queen Boudicca is buried."

Corbulo's eyes widened in shock and for a long moment he stood motionless, staring at the grassy mound at his feet.

"I told you that you wouldn't like everything that you would find here," Fergus said slowly as he turned to look at Corbulo. For a moment the old man did not speak. "After she died," he said at last, "some of her loyal followers brought her body here. The Iceni were afraid that Governor Paulinius and his men would desecrate her grave if they found it, so they decided to give her a secret burial. I have looked after her grave ever since."

Corbulo did not reply. His eyes were fixed on the grass mound.

"So now I hope that you understand why I need your help?" Fergus said quietly.

Corbulo said nothing and for a moment the only noise to be heard was the wind, as it swept across the field.

"We leave for Camulodunum once you are ready," Fergus said abruptly, as he turned away, leaving Corbulo alone beside the graves. Corbulo did not watch him go. He seemed distracted. Then carefully and slowly he undid his tunic, fumbled with his undergarments and sent a stream of piss arching onto the grave.

## Chapter Twelve - Colonia Victricensis

The five of them strode along the Roman road towards Camulodunum. It was nearly noon and it was raining. Corbulo looked grim as the rain plastered his face. At his side Fergus was silent and behind them Efa and Dylis were hurrying along, huddled under an improvised woollen blanket. Bringing up the rear and carrying a leather satchel was one of Corbulo's slaves, clad in a simple white tunic.

"Why did you never tell me that the bitch was buried on your land?" Corbulo snapped suddenly, turning on Fergus.

"What would you have done if you had known?" Fergus retorted.

Corbulo shook his head and kept on walking. In the distance he could see the walls of the Roman colony.

"You cannot speak to anyone about this Corbulo," Fergus said, as he wiped the rain from his face. "I will die before I see those graves desecrated or robbed."

"I know," Corbulo growled, "Do you think I don't know that?"

As they drew closer to Camulodunum, Corbulo peered at the city walls. The formidable looking stone ramparts were brand new and interspersed with watch towers and a wide V shaped ditch ran along the outside of the wall. Someone had gone to a lot of trouble and expense to provide the colony with first-class fixed defences. He sighed as he wiped the rain from his face. The city he had first known had been completely destroyed by Boudicca but out of the ashes a new city, Colonia Victricensis had risen, brash, industrious and commercial. As a fully-fledged Roman colony its inhabitants were all Roman citizens, enjoying the privileges that came with being part of the top class of the Empire's strict, hierarchical, social class system. The status of Roman colony had however not prevented the provincial government from moving to Londinium in order to be closer to the supply roads, that converged on the only crossing point across the Thames.

He turned to look behind him at Efa and Dylis. The women were doing their best to keep the rain at bay. The weather had put them off and they hadn't really wanted to come along to the city, but Corbulo had insisted. He'd told them they would enjoy the shops and the market. He'd kept the real reason, that he did not want to leave them behind in the company of Alene's brother, to himself.

As they approached the Balkerne gate, the main gate into the city, Roman tomb stones started to appear along the side of the road and in the distance beyond the grey city walls, he could just make out the glorious tiled roof of the great temple of Claudius, centre of the imperial cult. The original temple had been the last desperate refuge of the town's folk, trying to escape Boudicca's wrath, but the gods had not prevented the barbarian queen from storming the building and slaughtering everyone inside.

The huge triumphal arch and double-gated entrance into the city were open and the guards were busy collecting the city taxes from the merchants, who were entering the colony. As they approached the gates Corbulo glanced down into the V shaped ditch. The decapitated heads of convicted criminals lay half buried in the mud and raw sewage was pouring into the ditch from the drainage pipes, that were set into the stone walls. The small party entered the Roman town and Fergus led them eastwards down the main street towards the newly restored temple of Claudius. The colony's streets had been laid out in a precise grid and every hundred paces the city blocks, Insulae, were connected to side streets leading north and south. Corbulo glanced up at the terraced strip houses with their narrow frontages. Some had been built of stone and were two or even three stories high, but most were simple single storied buildings, constructed of wood, daub, wattle and with thatched roofs. Here and there however, a plot of land lay unused and covered with debris and blackened-ash and earth, a reminder that the colony had not yet fully recovered from the devastation wrought by the barbarian queen. The chatter of the pedestrians mingled with the advertising cries of the shopkeepers and in the street, the wagon drivers shouted warnings as they negotiated their horse and oxen-drawn carts through the crowds.

As they approached the fourth intersection, Fergus paused at the corner and gestured up the side street leading towards the northern wall and the harbour along the river Colne.

"Timion lives at the end of the street on the left," he muttered.

Corbulo turned to Efa and slipped a small bag of coins into her hand. "Go and buy something for Dylis and yourself," he muttered. "I will meet you back at the entrance to the temple."

Then he turned to the slave, carrying the leather satchel, "Keep an eye open," he ordered, "the market will be full of thieves."

The man nodded and Corbulo watched him follow the two women as, arm in arm, they set off up the street.

"Alright, let's go," he grunted, turning to Fergus.

\*\*\*

As the two of them strode down the paved street, Corbulo heard a loud voice. Up ahead a small group of people had gathered around an officious looking man, who was standing on a barrel and holding up a parchment. The man seemed to be reading aloud.

"By order of Governor Aulus Vicirius Proculus," the man cried, "Any person found aiding or supporting Brigantian or Caledonian rebels will be executed and his corpse left unburied outside the town walls. No sedition will be tolerated. No appeals will be heard. No clemency will be extended."

The crowd of onlookers remained silent as the town crier got down from the barrel and started up the street. As he drew level, Corbulo reached out and grasped the man's arm.

"What news from the north?" Corbulo asked.

The man examined Corbulo hastily. Then he shook his head.

"The situation is serious, that's all I know," he muttered darkly, before continuing on his way.

Timion's house was on the corner of an intersection, close to the northern wall and a block away from the brand new theatre. The stone entrance had a small vestibule, within which stood a miniature statue of the emperor Domitian. Corbulo looked up at the two-story building. Whoever had built the house had done a fine job, for the stone masonry looked solid and grand. Corbulo stepped into the vestibule, grasped the brass door knocker and rapped it a couple of times against the oak door. After a few moments the door was opened by a slave.

"We are here to see your master, Timion," Corbulo growled.

The slave glanced quickly from Corbulo to Fergus. Then he gestured for them to come in and Corbulo stepped into a small square hallway. A colourful and expensive looking mosaic, forming the letters SPQR, had been inlaid into the stone floor and beyond it, an open doorway led into the atrium and the heart of the house. The smell of incense was everywhere and from somewhere inside the house, Corbulo could hear the noise of splashing water and a girl's laugh.

"Wait here," the slave said, as he disappeared into the atrium.

Corbulo and Fergus were silent, as they stood waiting in the hall. At last they heard the sound of approaching footsteps.

"I am Timion," a confident sounding man in his early thirties said in Latin as he appeared in the doorway to the atrium with the slave at his side. Timion was athletic, handsome, and his hair had been dyed blond. He was clad in a white toga and a multitude of brightly coloured rings adorned his fingers. He gave Corbulo a cautious examining look but, as he noticed Fergus a little contemptuous smile appeared on his lips.

"Ah it's you Fergus," Timion said, switching effortlessly into the native Celtic language, "I hope you are here to tell me that you have changed your mind and have come to sell up at last?"

"No," Corbulo said in Latin, shaking his head, "That is not why we are here."

"Who the fuck are you?" Timion said aggressively, as he turned to glare at Corbulo.

Corbulo calmly looked the younger man in the eye.

"My name is Corbulo," he growled, "and I am here, as one Roman citizen to another, to give you a message. Fergus, his people and his land are under my protection and patronage and they shall not be harmed." Corbulo took a step towards Timion. "So if I hear that you are continuing to threaten and intimidate him and his people, you will be dealing with me. You got that arsehole?"

Timion grunted in surprise and for a moment he stared at Corbulo in silence. Then he shook his head in feigned confusion.

"And who do you work for?" Timion sneered, "You look like a common soldier to me. Why should I be kissing your feet?"

"My employer is the house of Agricola," Corbulo said, "I look after Gnaeus Julius Agricola's business interests here in Britannia. That's who you are dealing with."

At the mention of Agricola's name, Timion raised his eyebrows.

"Agricola," he muttered with a hint of puzzlement, "So the great and famous Agricola has taken an interest in a piece of farmland in the middle of nowhere?"

"He has," Corbulo replied, "So you will order your thugs to leave these people alone or else I assure you, matters will work out unfavourably for you."

"Is that a threat?" Timion's eyes narrowed, "Are you threatening me in my own home?"

"Damn right I am," Corbulo snarled. "They tell me that many of Agricola's veterans have retired around this town. They will not be pleased if they hear that you are pissing on their old boss." Corbulo raised a finger in warning. "One word from me and I will destroy your salt trading business and run you out of town."

For a moment Timion's face was unreadable. Then with an effort he composed himself.

"You have delivered your message," he snapped. "Now get out of my house."

\*\*\*

The door slammed shut behind them and as it did, Corbulo started off up the street. The rain had grown heavier and was pelting down, creating small rivers in the gutters.

"Thank you, Corbulo," Fergus said, as he caught up with him. The old man looked pleased and also a little impressed.

"I will stay with you for a week to see how he reacts," Corbulo replied, as he glanced up at the grey skies. "If Timion returns after I am gone, send me a message and I will come and help you. I am also going to leave you some money. If you have to, use it to bribe the land commissioners until we can organise a proper response. Your days of taking shit from that prick are over."

"I hope so," Fergus muttered, "I truly hope so." He paused as the rain clattered onto the paving stones. "We are all grateful Corbulo. It's not only about Timion. We are just grateful that you have come."

Corbulo nodded but said nothing, as he stomped on along the street.

Efa, Dylis and the slave were waiting for them beside the entrance to the majestic, colonnaded temple of Claudius. The three of them were sheltering from the rain under the tiled roof of the building. Dylis was holding a new pair of leather shoes in her hands. She waved, as she caught sight of him. Efa gave her husband a quick searching glance as he greeted her.

"Everything alright?" she said.

Corbulo nodded and glanced up at the grey skies. "This rain doesn't look it's going to stop any time soon. We should be heading back," he said.

The party said little, as they slipped out of the city through the Balkerne gate and started out on the two and half mile trek back to Fergus's home. The rain did not cease and the gutters, that ran alongside the Roman road, were full to overflowing. As they left the last of the Roman tombstones behind, Corbulo saw a solitary wagon pulled along by a horse approaching from the opposite direction. The driver sat hunched under the hood of his Palla as he gripped the reins.

Suddenly something whizzed past Corbulo's head and behind him he heard a thump and a small cry. Startled he turned round. His slave was lying on the road with blood oozing from his head. The man was not moving. Then Efa screamed. A dozen paces away, a man stepped out of the cover of the trees. He was whirling a sling above his head, as he advanced purposefully towards Corbulo. Then with a flick of his wrist and arm, he flung a stone straight at Fergus. The projectile struck the old man square in his chest, sending him staggering backwards onto his arse with a sharp cry of pain. Corbulo's eyes bulged. They were under attack. From behind the slinger, six horsemen came charging out of the forest. The men were armed with spears and their faces were covered by Roman ceremonial, parade-ground cavalry masks. Efa screamed again as Corbulo pulled his gladius free from his belt.

"Efa, get Dylis into the cover of the trees, now," Corbulo bellowed, but there was no time. The horsemen had already surrounded them. The riders lowered their spears threateningly, as two of them slid from their mounts and rushed to grab Efa and Dylis. The women screamed as the men caught them and forced them down onto their knees. Along the road the solitary driver was desperately trying to turn his wagon around as fast as he could. Corbulo lunged at the nearest rider but it was useless as man and beast retreated only a short distance. On the ground Fergus groaned, as he pressed his hand against his chest.

"Drop your sword and get down on your knees, or else we will kill the women," one of the masked riders cried out, raising his spear.

Desperately Corbulo went into a crouch as his attackers circled around him.

"It's over Corbulo, drop your sword and get down on your knees," a voice cried.

Corbulo cried out in frustration. Efa and Dylis were on their knees and their attackers were pressing knives into their throats. One of the riders had grasped hold of Efa's hair and had pulled her head backwards exposing her tender white throat. Then Corbulo caught sight of Dylis. His daughter was crying, her face contorted in pure terror.

"Alright," he cried, "alright." Slowly he dropped his sword on the road and raised his hands as he got down on his knees. "Don't harm my wife and daughter. Take me. I am the one you want. Let them go. They have nothing to do with this, please."

One of the riders dismounted from his horse and, as he came towards Corbulo he peeled away his face mask. It was Timion. The handsome man was silent as he strode up to Corbulo and without warning smashed his fist into Corbulo's face, sending him sprawling onto the ground with a painful cry.

"No one threatens me in my own home," Timion hissed with cold fury and with an enraged cry he gave Corbulo a vicious kick. "Do you think that you could scare me with all that talk about Agricola and his veterans? Do you think that I was afraid of you! I knew what you were, the moment you stepped into my hall, a nobody, a dead man. So who cares if you know Agricola," Timion hissed as he gave Corbulo another kick in the ribs, "He is far-away in Gaul and I doubt very much that he would really give a shit about a piece of land, in the middle of nowhere."

Timion stood over Corbulo, glaring down at him. "In any case it doesn't matter," he said, "For you will never speak with Agricola again, not where you are going."

Corbulo groaned as he turned his head in the direction of Efa and Dylis. One of their attackers was binding his wife's hands behind her back and a hood had been thrust over her head. Her screaming had stopped. For a split second he caught Dylis's eye. The girl was crying as she desperately sought to reach him. Helplessly he stretched out a hand towards her.

"Spare the women," he groaned, "They are innocent, they are not involved, please, I beg you."

Timion gave him another kick and Corbulo cried out in pain.

"Say goodbye to your wife and daughter," Timion sneered. "For this is the last time that you will ever see them."

101

## Chapter Thirteen - Cohors II Batavorum Milliaria Equitata

The two hundred Batavian cavalrymen clattered swiftly down the road in a long column. The men were silent and their feathered-helmets and chain mail armour glinted in the dawn-light, as they rode along clutching their spears. The soldiers had slung their small, round cavalry shields over their backs and a few of the riders had adorned the manes of their horses with the gleaming white skulls of dead rebels. Marcus, clad in Cotta's splendid armour and helmet, rode at the front of the column, leading his men in a south westerly direction. At his side Adalberht was silent. The old warrior was staring moodily up the road and riding just behind him was Fridwald, flanked by the Cohort standard bearer, holding up the proud boar-headed unit banner. The young body-guard was scratching at the iron torque around his neck. Marcus looked satisfied, as he glanced back down the column. He'd managed to assemble all seven remaining cavalry squadrons for the rescue mission. Every cavalryman in the Cohort had wanted to go out. Even the wounded had forced themselves from their camp beds, so that they could be with their comrades on the expedition to relief Drustan and his Briton loyalists.

To the south, the hills and mountains stretched away to the horizon. The lower slopes of the uplands were densely forested with green pines, but their summits were brown, bleak and rocky and in places covered with patches of snow. High in the pale-blue sky a hunting bird cried out, as it circled searching for prey, and to the west the lush rolling green fields and meadows were deserted. Marcus peered down the road. They had not encountered a living soul since leaving Luguvalium. It was as if the local population had vanished into thin air, but the rebels were out there. Twice already the column had encountered abandoned road blocks of felled trees and upturned carts and at the second road block, the corpse of a man had been nailed to a tree. Marcus turned to glance at the young tattooed Briton who was riding a few ranks behind him. The young man's eyes were fixed on the road. He had not said a word since they had left the fort.

"Marcus," Adalberht growled in warning.

Up ahead three Batavian scouts were galloping back towards the main column. Marcus peered at the riders as they approached.

"Well," he barked as the foremost Batavian rode up to him.

"The bridge is intact Sir," the soldier cried, "and the watch tower still stands but there is no sign of our men."

"What about the rebels?" Marcus snapped, but the horseman shook his head.

"Nothing Sir, there is no sign of them."

Marcus glanced at Adalberht who shrugged. Without a word Marcus raised his arm above his head and clenching his hand into a fist, he pumped his arm up and down as he urged his horse to quicken its pace. Behind him the Batavian cavalry too began to pick up the pace. As they surged down the road, Marcus suddenly caught sight of the Derwent, through a break in the trees. The river looked swollen. A few hundred paces away across the field was the wooden bridge, that carried the road across the river. Beyond, standing within the protection of a square palisade and V shaped ditch, was a solitary Roman watchtower. Marcus peered at the tower as he and his men approached. The purpose of the eight man garrison had been to guard the cross roads with the Roman road coming from the south. He stared at the wooden observation platform that surrounded the top floor of the tower and, for a moment, it reminded him of the watch tower that he and his father had sought refuge in during their flight from Caledonia. The building looked exactly the same.

Marcus, surrounded by his principal officers and the Cohort standard bearer clutching the boar-headed banner, sat waiting on his horse beside the road when Hedwig appeared on the balcony at the top of the tower.

"There are four dead inside," the Decurion shouted as he caught sight of Marcus. "No sign of the others Sir."

Marcus frowned and was just about to call out, when a cry rose up from some of the Batavian riders near the river. Marcus turned to look in the direction of the tumult. The riders were shouting to each other.

"What's going on over there?" Marcus cried, as he urged his horse in the direction of the noise. The river bank was muddy and lined with tall and thick river reeds. As Marcus reached the water's edge, a party of mounted Batavians came riding towards him escorting four dirty, exhausted looking men. Marcus stared at the men, as they staggered towards him before sinking wearily down onto their knees in the mud. They looked like they'd been through hell.

"Thank the gods, thank you, Sir," one of the miserable looking soldiers cried, "You came at last Sir."

Marcus took a deep breath as he stared at the men.

"What happened here?" he cried.

"They came at night," the soldier stammered, "they killed four of my men before we knew what was happening. My boys here and I, we managed to escape Sir. We have been hiding in the reeds for two days now. We haven't eaten in two days Sir."

"Give them some food," Marcus snapped turning to one of his Decurion's beside him, "and find them someone with whom they can ride. We will take them with us."

"Bless you, Sir," the Batavian called out, "but there is something else you should know Sir. The men who attacked us - they were not local men. They were from the north, they were Caledonians Sir."

Marcus's head whipped round and he stared at the soldier.

"Caledonians, here, this far south," he exclaimed, "Are you sure?"

The soldier nodded eagerly. "I was at Mons Graupius with you Sir. I know what these Caledonian tribesmen look and sound like. They were Caledonians. I am sure of it."

***

"What do you think?" Marcus said, glancing at Adalberht. The two of them sat on their horses within the cover of the trees, as they peered at the lone Briton fort, perched on the crest of the steep rocky hill. It was mid-morning and it was drizzling.

"Not much of a siege," Adalberht grunted, speaking in his native language, "The Briton boy told us there would be a hundred men besieging the fort. I only count twenty eight, where are the rest of them?"

Marcus muttered to himself, as he peered at the rebel pickets across the open field. Adalberht was right. The rebels were clustered in small groups, huddled around open fires, as they formed a loose line surrounding the western approaches to the hill fort. He shifted his gaze to the hill fort. Nothing about the tight cluster of thatched, round-houses inside the fort looked unusual, but he could see no defenders up on its earthen embankments.

"The lake protects the fort from the north and the southern approaches are too steep for our horses," Marcus muttered, "that leaves the west and the east. Boy," he said turning sharply to the young Briton behind him, "you said there were a hundred men; where are the rest?"

"The entrance into the fort is from the east," the Briton muttered with a strange excited tension in his voice as he avoided Marcus's gaze, "they are probably on the other side of the hill. Let's attack them Roman."

Marcus frowned and for a long moment he examined the Briton. The youth seemed keen to fight but he was unarmed. Slowly he turned his attention back to the hill fort.

"Adalberht," he said, "At the head of the lake over there is a ford across the river. Send a squadron to secure it. That will be our line of retreat if things go badly." Marcus paused as he turned to look to the west. "Take two squadrons and move around their flank. Once you hear my trumpet signal, attack them from east. Until then, do not show yourself. Understood?"

Adalberht nodded. "They won't know what's hit them," the veteran warrior growled as he turned and rode away.

Marcus glanced at the massed ranks of his cavalry. The Batavians were silent as they clustered around their officers amongst the cover of the trees, their eyes fixed on the enemy in the fields, a couple of hundred paces away beyond the tree line. The only noise was the occasional nervous whinny of a horse.

"Stay close to me," Marcus snapped, turning his attention back to the Briton youth. The young man again avoided Marcus's gaze, but he gripped the reins of his horse in eager anticipation.

"Drustan will be grateful, he will be eternally grateful," the youth muttered. "Let's attack now Roman."

Marcus ignored the youth. Instead he gestured at Hedwig. There was a serious expression on the Decurion's face as he caught Marcus's eye.

"Form the men up for the attack," Marcus snapped. "Once you hear the signal sweep up the hill. No prisoners Hedwig. We cannot take them with us."

"Thunder and lashing rain, so Woden commeth..." Hedwig muttered in his Germanic language, as a dark-spark of adrenaline fuelled excitement, appeared in his eyes. "No prisoners, Marcus."

***

"Now!" Marcus cried, turning to his trumpeter.

A moment later, the long, mournful trumpet blast echoed away across the fields and the forest around Marcus erupted into movement and noise. With a cry, Marcus urged his horse forwards and burst from the forest. Along the tree line the Batavian cavalrymen had broken cover and were surging forwards up the grassy slope, their wild yells and cries mingling with the thud of hundreds of hooves. The earth seemed to shake, as the line of horsemen bore down on the Briton pickets. Dimly Marcus was aware of Fridwald, galloping along at his side. The young man was practically standing up in his saddle. Up ahead, the Britons had risen to their feet and were staring at the approaching cavalrymen in stunned horror. Then with a cry, the rebels scattered and fled, racing up the hill towards the fort.

The Batavian cavalry surged forwards and the foremost riders were in amongst the enemy before the Britons could reach the outer ditch. Shrieks and screams rose up as the fleeing enemy were mown down, struck and cut down by the Batavian spears and long cavalry swords. They didn't stand a chance. As Marcus reached the outer defensive ditch, the fight was already over. The corpses of the Britons lay spread out across the grassy slope, as the Batavian troopers rode up and down, crying out to each other as they dispatched the wounded and dying. Marcus reined in his horse, gasped and turned to stare at the hill fort. There was still no sign of anyone inside the fort. Irritably Marcus twisted in his saddle.

"Where are Drustan and your people?" he roared as he caught sight of the young Briton.

The youth was staring at the blood-soaked grass slope. Silently he shrugged as he dismounted from his horse and started out towards the cluster of round houses inside the fort.

"I said stay close to me," Marcus roared but the Briton took no notice.

Annoyed, Marcus growled out loud and urged his horse into the ditch and up the other side. As he made it to the first earthen embankment, he heard a man crying out his name. He turned and saw Adalberht and his riders galloping full pelt towards him. Confused Marcus wheeled his horse round as Adalberht cried out again. The old warrior looked in a hurry and as he approached Marcus felt a sudden unease. Something was wrong. Something felt wrong.

"It's a trap Marcus," Adalberht bellowed, "We have been set up. We have to leave now, right now!"

"What?" Marcus blinked in confusion, "What are you talking about old man?"

Adalberht came to a halt beside him. He was panting with exertion and his face was flushed. "It's a trap," he cried. "They are moving around to cut us off. I saw them. On the eastern side of the hill. We must get out of here!" Adalberht fell silent as he struggled to regain his breath.

"There are hundreds of them," he gasped, his eyes flashing wildly, "and they are mounted. They have been waiting for us to enter the hill fort. They knew we were coming."

"Fuck," Marcus exclaimed as he felt a hot flush spreading across his cheeks. For a moment he stared at Adalberht in horror. Then before he could say another word a Celtic Carnyx sent a long defiant blast reverberating away across the lake. The trumpet blast was followed by cries of alarm amongst the Batavian cavalry, as a line of rebel tribesmen suddenly appeared along the southern     slope.

"They set us up," Adalberht hissed bitterly as Marcus's head whipped round to stare at the young Briton. The youth was clambering up the earth embankment and as he caught sight of Marcus, he sprang forwards with renewed urgency and speed.

"Seize that man, seize him!" Marcus bellowed furiously. Frantically the youth scrambled up the embankment but just as he was about to reach the top a Batavian flung himself against the earth wall and caught the man's foot. It was Fridwald. With a cry, Marcus's bodyguard pulled the Briton back down the steep, earth embankment. The Briton cried out as he tried to cling to the grass, but it was no use. Fridwald caught his arm and pinned it against his back, as the two of them wrestled in the mud at the base of the embankment. A moment later another Batavian came to his aid.

"Bind his hands and put him on a horse," Marcus yelled as he stared at the Briton, "I want him alive. He is not to be harmed."

Marcus's head whipped round to stare at the advancing line of rebel tribesmen. The infantry were coming on at a steady confident pace. His eyes blinked rapidly as he turned to look towards the west. Sure enough in the fields, half a mile, away a large contingent of Briton cavalry were thundering northwards.

"Order the retreat," he yelled at his trumpeter. "We need to reach the river ford before they can hem us in against the lake."

He had hardly spoken the words before a trumpet blasted away. Marcus wheeled his horse around and gave the Briton hill fort a final derisory glance.

"So much for fucking Drustan and his loyal subjects," he snapped. Then he was away crying out to his men to follow him.

The retreat was chaotic. Marcus urged his horse on as he tried to keep the lake to his right. Trees flashed passed as he wove his way through the forest, ducking under branches, as around him the disordered Batavian riders did the same. At last he emerged into an open meadow.

"Move, to the river, to the river," he roared, wheeling his horse round as his men thundered passed him. Wildly, Marcus stared around him but there was no sign of Adalberht or Fridwald or the Briton. It was everyone for himself now. As the Batavian horsemen surged past him, the standard bearer holding aloft the boar-headed banner came galloping towards him.

"Follow me," Marcus cried at the soldier as he turned and joined the retreating riders.

To his left Marcus was suddenly conscious of a movement. Then he heard the deep and low note of a Carnyx and as he did, the Batavians to his left started veering towards him. Marcus snatched a glance to his left and groaned. The Briton cavalry, riding their small shaggy and fast horses were closing in from the west. There were hundreds of them and their wild excited whoops and cries were drawing closer. He wrenched his gaze away. How far to the river? If they could cross the river and make it to the opposite bank they would have a chance.

"Ride, ride," he screamed at the men around him.

The ground shook as the horsemen thundered across it. Where along the river was the ford? With rising panic Marcus realised he couldn't remember. Desperately he peered at the fields ahead. Where was the fucking crossing point? Where the fuck was it? Just as his panic was about to turn to despair, he suddenly heard the noise of a Batavian horn. It was not standard army equipment but had to be part of one of the soldier's personal belongings. His eyes bulged. Then once more he heard the horn, its distinctive noise was unmistakeable. It had to belong to one of the men from the squadron he'd sent to guard the ford and their line of retreat. They were signalling to him.

"Follow that horn, follow the horn," he roared at the riders around him.

A minute later, Marcus suddenly caught sight of the river and as he did, the Batavian horn rang out once more and this time it was closer. Marcus cried out as he saw the Batavian riders on the opposite bank. Without pausing, he and his horse crashed into the river. The horse staggered and raised its head in protest but the river was not deep and with Marcus crying out and urging the beast on, the animal began to swim, snorting and tossing its head. All around him the Batavian cavalrymen were crashing into the water, sending waves rippling away into the far bank. There was no time to look behind him. Marcus bit his lip as his horse struggled through the water. Then with a snort the beast rose from the river and struggled up onto the opposite bank. Marcus turned to look behind him and gasped. The river was filled with swimming Batavian horsemen and a hundred paces away across the river the meadows were filled with rebel cavalry. There were hundreds of them. The Britons were charging towards the river as they cut down the Batavian stragglers.

Wildly Marcus looked around him. Close by Fridwald and his horse, carrying two men struggled up onto the bank, sending droplets of water flying in all directions. His bodyguard looked exhausted as he gripped the young tattooed Briton around the neck with one arm.

"Form a line, form a line," Marcus roared as more and more of his men and beasts struggled ashore.

But as the Britons neared the river their pace suddenly slowed until their foremost men came to a halt at the water's edge. For a moment the rebels seemed uncertain about what to do. Then they raised their weapons and jeered at their enemy across the river. Marcus wiped the spittle from his mouth. His chest was heaving. The enemy were not going to try and force a crossing.

"Let's get back to Luguvalium," he cried at the men around him.

## Chapter Fourteen - The Face of the Enemy

"Who are you? Marcus cried.

Inside the room the oil lamps had been lit and bathed the principia of Luguvalium in a dim flickering reddish glow. The Briton did not reply, as he knelt on the ground. His hands had been tied behind his back and the youth was staring moodily at the floor. He had not said a word since they'd returned to the fort. Behind him, Fridwald stood looking down at the prisoner. The bodyguard had his arms folded across his chest. Wearily and irritably Marcus turned and glanced at Adalberht and Lucius. The two officers were staring at the Briton with a mixture of shock and outrage.

"They set us up, Lucius," Marcus growled. "That piece of shit over there was leading us straight into a trap. If we had entered Drustan's village the enemy would have surrounded us and annihilated every one of my men." Marcus closed his eyes and rubbed his face. It had been a long day and he needed to rest, but it could wait. "We are facing a cunning enemy," he muttered, "We must not underestimate them again."

"Well boy, are you going to tell us who you are?" Adalberht roared as spit flew from his mouth.

"Fuck you Roman," the youth hissed.

Marcus caught Adalberht just in time, as the veteran was about to lunge at the prisoner. He shook his head sharply and pushed the old man backwards.

"You are a brave man," Marcus said turning to face the prisoner and the tone of his voice was suddenly softer and quieter, "You showed courage coming into our midst like you did and your acting was first class. You did well."

112

The youth did not reply as he stared moodily at the floor. Slowly Marcus came up to him and crouched before him. "But at the end of the day you failed," he said, as he grasped the youth's chin and forced the boy to look at him. "We are still here and we are going to crush this rebellion. Twenty eight of your comrades are dead tonight and you have nothing to show for it."

"You will never defeat us," the youth hissed, as a proud look appeared on his face. "This is our land. Rome is not welcome here."

Marcus nodded. "Tell me who your leader is," he said quietly, "tell me the name of the man who has planned this rebellion and I will let you go free."

The youth looked at Marcus in surprise. Then surprise gave way to suspicion.

"You would do that? I don't believe you."

Before Marcus could reply however there was a commotion at the door to his HQ. He looked up as one of the guards hastened into the room. The soldier saluted quickly.

"Sir, it's that merchant, Urbanus, he says he wants to speak to you."

"Tell him to wait," Marcus growled irritably, "I am busy."

The soldier nodded, turned and disappeared out of the doorway and into the night.

Marcus turned to look at his prisoner.

"I will organise a prisoner exchange. Just tell me the name of the man who is leading this rebellion and I will let you go," he said.

The youth peered at him suspiciously and for a long moment he did not reply.

"The tribes have chosen Faelan to be High King, "the Briton muttered at last, "Faelan unites the Brigantes. He is our leader."

"Faelan," Marcus frowned in surprise. "I have heard this name before. Where have I heard this name before?"

"In Hibernia," Adalberht growled, "there was a druid who went by the name of Faelan. He claimed to be the bastard son of the barbarian queen herself. Your father had dealings with him. The prick only had one eye."

"He is the son of Queen Boudicca," the prisoner snapped defiantly.

Marcus was silent as he rose to his feet. "Faelan," he muttered, "I remember him now. He was at the siege of Tara. He advised the Hibernian High King. So he has returned to Britannia to cause trouble."

"He has returned to claim his birth-right," the young Briton hissed.

Coldly Marcus turned to look at the prisoner.

"Adalberht," he said sharply, "Take the prisoner away and make him talk. Torture him if necessary. By dawn I want to know everything he knows."

"Gladly," Adalberht muttered as he strode across the room, caught hold of the Briton and yanked him up onto his feet. The prisoner's eyes bulged in shock.

"But you promised, you promised a prisoner exchange, I would go free," the man cried out.

Marcus stared at the youth with a hard cold look.

"I lied," he replied.

***

114

Alone, Marcus paced up and down beside the table in the Principia. The night was far advanced but despite his crushing tiredness he could not rest. Outside in the camp all was quiet, except for the high pitched screams coming from one of the barracks blocks where Adalberht was interrogating the prisoner. Marcus ran his hand across his face. He had very nearly gotten all his men killed today. How could he have been so stupid? The ambush had unsettled him. How could he have been so gullible? The prisoner had made a fool out of him. As he paced up and down his face darkened as outside the screams intensified. Torturing the prisoner was not a pleasant task and he took no satisfaction from it, but it was necessary. The boy had refused to talk and he needed to know everything he could about the rebels. They had already proved themselves determined and cunning opponents.

Marcus was sitting slumped in his chair half asleep when Lucius shook him awake. The officer looked grim.

"He talked," Lucius said smoothly, "and he had a lot to say."

Marcus raised himself up in the chair. Outside the screaming had stopped. "Go on," he muttered.

Lucius took a deep breath. He looked bone tired. "Most of what the prisoner told us confirmed what we already suspected. Faelan is the mastermind behind the uprising. The Brigantes have allies to the north amongst the Caledonian tribes. The Caledonians and even some of the Hibernian tribes are sending war bands south. There is active support and contact and it goes in both directions. The prisoner said that many of the Brigantes have sent their families north, to the safety of the unoccupied lands. It's easy for small war-bands to slip past our northern outposts or land on the coast. Rome does not have enough soldiers to stop the infiltration and seal the northern border. The rebels," Lucius sighed, "also seem to have a lot of gold and silver. The boy said he had seen chests filled with the stuff but he doesn't know where it's coming from."

Marcus nodded.

"I have heard similar complaints from other officer's," he murmured, "Maybe one day someone should build a wall across the land from coast to coast and cut the Brigantes off from their Caledonian friends. This infiltration has to be stopped. It is feeding this uprising. It's giving the rebels hope."

Lucius looked serious.

"A wall. It's not a bad idea," he admitted. Then he fixed his eyes on Marcus and Lucius' normally calm face grew tinged with sudden excitement. "But the prisoner also told us something that we didn't know. Something that I think you will find very interesting," he murmured.

Marcus raised his eyebrows and leaned forwards across the table but just as Lucius was about to speak they were interrupted by Fridwald. The Batavian bodyguard cleared his throat.

"Sir, Urbanus, the merchant is still outside. He says he really needs to speak to you at once."

"Tell Urbanus that he can fucking well wait," Marcus snapped in an annoyed voice.

"Yes Sir," Fridwald said as he saluted and left the room.

Marcus turned to stare at Lucius.

"Well? What did the prisoner tell you?"

Lucius was stroking his chin thoughtfully. Then he looked up at Marcus.

"The youth revealed to us where we can find Faelan. The rebel leader has gone to the old stone circle at Castlerigg to celebrate Beltane, the festival to mark the start of summer. The stones are two days march from here. The prisoner said that Faelan

116

usually travels alone with a small band of men." Lucius eyes sparkled with sudden glee. "I know that stone circle. It is sacred ground for the druids and Beltane is in three days. We know he will be there. If we were to move fast, we could seize Faelan before he moves on. We could capture the rebel leader, Marcus. Such a feat would surely get our names noticed in Deva and Londinium and possibly even in Rome."

"How do we know the prisoner was telling the truth?" Marcus snapped "He fooled you into thinking that village was being besieged. What if this is another trap?"

Lucius shrugged.

"It's possible," he muttered, "but unlikely. Adalberht and his men were quite thorough. The man experienced a lot of pain before he talked and it's unlikely that the rebels would have planned two ambushes. I think it's worth it. Beltane is a sacred day for the druids. Their minds will not be on fighting. We cannot just sit here behind our walls Marcus. If there is a chance we can capture Faelan then we should take it. This opportunity may not arise again."

Marcus grunted and once more ran his hand across his face.

"The men and horses are still exhausted from yesterday's encounter," he growled, "They need to rest and cavalry alone will not be enough if Faelan is holed up in a fortified settlement near the stones, which is likely."

"I know, I know," Lucius replied. "But we could put together a mixed battle group comprising our horsemen and say, three infantry companies. That should be a sufficiently strong force."

Marcus took a deep breath as he considered the plan. Then he turned to look at Lucius. "Alright," he nodded, "make the preparations. We will leave at nightfall but you, my friend will remain here and guard the fort and my family."

Lucius looked disappointed but he was too good a soldier to complain. Instead he nodded and got to his feet.

"What shall we do with the prisoner?" he said slowly.

"Put him up on a cross outside the fort," Marcus said harshly, "I want everyone to see what happens to men who murder my soldiers."

## Chapter Fifteen - An Unnecessary Death

Marcus was asleep when he was woken by a hand shaking his shoulder. It was Fridwald. The bodyguard was clad in armour and he was wearing his helmet. He looked agitated.

"Sir, it's the woman, Lady Claudia, " he exclaimed. "The watch at the gate told me to wake you."

"What about her?" Marcus growled.

"She and her daughter have taken two horses and have just ridden out of the southern gate. They told the watch commander that they were heading south to Deva, Sir."

"What?" Marcus exclaimed, suddenly fully awake, "They left together, just the two of them, on their own?"

Fridwald nodded.

"This is madness. Why did the watch officer not stop them from leaving?" Marcus bellowed, as he jumped to his feet and grabbed his helmet from the table. "They won't stand a chance out there on their own. Two high born Roman ladies on their own. The rebels will have them swinging from a tree within the hour."

"I don't know why he didn't stop them," Fridwald muttered as Marcus rushed out of the door, shouting at his bodyguard to follow him.

Marcus ran across the muddy parade ground and as he did so, he pushed his helmet onto his head and tightened his sword belt around his waist. Around him the Batavians paused to stare at their commander as he rushed passed them towards the southern gate.

"Mount up, hurry, hurry," Marcus roared at the eight fully armed and armoured troopers of the cavalry detachment, who were on

119

permanent stand by. The Batavians had been huddled around a camp fire playing a dice game but as Marcus stormed towards them they dropped what they were doing and ran towards their horses.

"Not you," Marcus cried as he caught up with one of the men before the soldier could throw himself into his saddle, "I need your horse."

With a smooth movement Marcus hoisted himself up onto the beast and grasped the reins before wheeling round towards the gate.

"Open the gate," he yelled. "Follow me, stay close."

With a creaking groan the gates swung open and Marcus charged out of the fort. He was followed a few moments later by the squad of Batavian riders as they struggled to catch up with their boss. The horses' hooves thundered as they galloped off down the road, sending clumps of mud flying in all directions. As the guards were about to close the gate, Fridwald, mounted on a horse, shot out of the gateway with his cloak flying behind him and his horse's hooves thudding into the ground as he veered sharply to the right and raced after the riders, desperately seeking to catch them up. Marcus thundered down the road crying out to his horse. The round houses and huts of the civilian settlement quickly disappeared behind him as he galloped south down the Roman road. The two women could not have got far. The officer of the watch had said that they had only just left the fort. Anxiously he peered down the road but there was no sign of them. Behind him he heard the beat of hooves and his men's cries. A minute passed and he could feel his horse starting to tire. He snatched a glance behind him. The Batavians were strung out along the road, as they tried to keep up with him. On both sides of the road the open fields looked deserted but ahead the path led straight into a small but thick wood. There was no sign of the enemy.

Suddenly Marcus heard a scream. It was followed rapidly by another, a high pitched female scream. Instinctively he pulled his sword from its scabbard. Up ahead in amongst the trees a rider-less horse came galloping towards him. Then he caught sight of the two women. Claudia was lying on the ground, screaming as she was being dragged into the forest by her leg. On the road her daughter was wrestling with a man, who had pinned her arms behind her back. The girl was biting the man's hand. Around them six rebels stood laughing and jeering. Then as they caught sight of Marcus charging towards them, the laughter faded and they cried out in alarm. As he swept into them Marcus raised his sword and slashed at the closest man sending him spinning to the ground. Then he was wheeling round and moving in to attack again. The rebels were shouting and one of them raised his spear and flung it straight at Marcus. The projectile struck his horse in the flank and the beast screamed and reared up flinging Marcus into the road before crashing sideways into the gravel. Marcus hit the ground hard and yelped in pain. For a moment he was utterly disorientated. As he tried to focus a man suddenly loomed over him and raised an axe intending to smash the blade into Marcus' neck but, just as the blade started its downward swing a horseman flashed passed and a sword sliced half the man's head from his body. With a gurgle and a great spurt of blood the corpse collapsed beside Marcus, splattering him with blood and the axe clattered onto the road.

Marcus groped for the war axe and staggered unsteadily to his feet, pressing his other hand up against his ribs. Around him everyone was screaming and yelling. The Batavian riders had caught up and were locked in a fierce and desperate struggle with the remaining rebels. Marcus blinked as he saw one of his men lying motionless on the ground, with a growing pool of dark red blood seeping out from under him. Then with a cry he took a step forwards and sent the war axe slamming into the exposed back of one the rebels. The man groaned and stiffened as a Batavian finished him off by ramming his sword into the man's face. Marcus staggered backwards as the corpse flopped onto the road. The fight was over. The bodies of the seven rebels lay spread out where they had fallen. Marcus stared at the bloody carnage unable to speak, and up on their horses, the Batavians were panting and gasping with exertion as they too gazed at the blood and gore strewn across the road. As he heard movement behind him, Marcus whirled round raising his axe. Close by a rider was sitting upon a horse. It was young Fridwald and his chest was heaving. He looked enraged as he pointed a bloodied sword straight at Marcus.

"Are you insane! What do you think you were doing Sir," he roared with real anger in his voice, "You would have been killed if I hadn't reached you in time. Have you completely lost your senses? I am your bodyguard Sir. It is my job to make sure that you stay alive." Fridwald's eyes blazed furiously as he gasped for breath. "And I like my job. What would the men say if I had allowed you to be killed, Sir? This is my fucking job." Fridwald's hand shook as he pointed the sword at Marcus. "That was the most stupidest thing I have ever seen you do Sir."

In stunned surprise Marcus stared at his bodyguard. Then he opened his mouth to say something but no words came out. Abruptly he turned away and staggered towards the two women. Claudia was on her knees in the road clasping her daughter who clung to her with wide open terrified looking eyes.

Without a word Marcus grasped Claudia by the arm and lifted her up onto her feet.

"That was foolish," he hissed, "What did you think you were doing? Did you expect to reach Deva without running into trouble?"

Claudia managed to compose herself. She turned and glared at Marcus. Her daughter however refused to let go of her, as she clung on to her mother's waist, her whole body shaking with terror.

"I told you once Prefect," she said sharply, "I asked that you provide me with an escort south to Deva, but you refused. I want to go to Deva and if you are not going to give me any of your men then I and my daughter will go alone. You are not going to stop us."

With the flat of his hand Marcus slapped her hard in the face and Claudia gasped and recoiled in shock and pain.

"Damn you and your arrogance," Marcus shouted, "You are coming back with me right now. I am going to show you something."

*** 

The horses clattered towards the southern gate of Luguvalium at a steady trot but instead of entering the fort, Marcus led them through the abandoned civilian settlement; past the crucified prisoner and towards the Eden. The small party were silent as Marcus, with Claudia sitting in front of him on the horse, approached the river bank. The Legate's wife had retreated into a sullen and furious silence and an angry red mark was etched across her cheek. At the water's edge, Marcus dismounted and grasping hold of the horses reins, he walked the beast and Claudia up to the first of the long line of freshly dug graves. For a long moment he was silent as he stared at the freshly turned soil.

"One hundred and nine of my men lie buried here," he said sharply. "I do not care that these rebels think this is their land. I do not care about the glory of Rome or how large the empire has become. But I do care about my men and the honour of the 2nd Batavian Cohort," he said, looking up at the Legate's wife, "They are my men. I am their commanding officer and I am responsible for them and today, this morning, another one of my soldier's is dead because of you, because of your arrogance and stupidity."

Marcus stared straight up at Claudia but the Legate's wife refused to meet his gaze as an embarrassed blush appeared on her cheeks.

"So go on ride away with your daughter," Marcus snapped, "I will not stop you again. My men are not going to die unnecessarily."

Claudia was silent as Marcus turned his back on her to stare at the graves.

"You are right," Claudia said stiffly, "and I am sorry. I was not thinking straight. We will do as you command, of course."

"Take the Lady and her daughter back to their quarters," Marcus said, turning to one of the Batavians, "I will be along in a moment."

"Sir," the soldier nodded and grasping the reins to Claudia's horse, he and the others turned and trotted back towards the fort.

As the men moved out of earshot, Marcus frowned and turned slowly to look at Fridwald. The young body-guard sat on his horse staring defiantly at his boss. For a long moment Marcus studied him. Then he shook his head.

"Thank you," he muttered, "I think the time has come for you to take that iron torque from your neck. You are a warrior Fridwald; you killed a man and you saved my fucking life today, I won't forget it."

Fridwald nodded as a proud look appeared in his eyes. Slowly he reached up to his neck and pulled the iron ring off before flinging it away into the river.

"And if you brag to anyone in the fort about your insolence, I will have you whipped in front of the whole Cohort," Marcus said grimly as he started out towards the fort.

\*\*\*

As the two of them passed the crucified prisoner hanging from his cross at the edge of the civilian settlement, Marcus looked up at him. The young man was dead and a black bird was perched on top of his head.

"Shall I order the men to cut him down Sir," Fridwald asked, as he to gazed up at the corpse.

But Marcus shook his head.

"No, let him rot," he said harshly, "This is revenge Fridwald. These rebels butchered and crucified two of our men right before our eyes. He will hang there until the birds have had their fill."

Fridwald was silent as the two of them approached the southern gate-house. As the gates swung open, Marcus suddenly felt exhausted. He needed to get some rest before they left at dusk but there was still so much to do. As he and Fridwald entered the camp, two figures came hastening towards him. With a weary sigh Marcus recognised the merchant Urbanus and one of his sons.

"So what do you want?" Marcus asked, as Urbanus fell in beside him as he strode towards the Principia.

Urbanus ran his fingers through his hair. He looked worried.

"It's too late now," he whined, "I tried to warn you but now it is too late. You crucified him. You just had to crucify him."

Marcus came to a halt and with a frown he turned to look at the merchant.

"What the fuck are you talking about?"

Urbanus jabbed a finger in the direction of the crucified prisoner.

"I tried to warn you but you refused to see me," he whined. "I came to tell you that I know who the prisoner was. My son here recognised him. Do you know whom you just crucified, Sir?"

"Who?" Marcus frowned.

"Only the eldest son of Faelan, High King of the Brigantes," Urbanus cried out. "That youth was going to be next king upon his father's death."

## Chapter Sixteen - The Stones of Castlerigg

"My trade takes me everywhere," Urbanus was saying, as he stood in the Principia surrounded by Marcus, Adalberht and Lucius. The three officers were studying him closely. "A few weeks ago we made a trip to the Brigantes at their meeting place at Stanwick. It's a huge fort on the eastern side of the central mountain range," Urbanus added, looking around at his audience.

"We know where Stanwick is," Marcus interrupted. "Please tell us what you know about the High King."

Urbanus nodded. The merchant seemed to be enjoying the attention. "Well," he said licking his lips, "It was at Stanwick that we first saw Faelan and his sons. I did not know he had been chosen to lead this uprising, I swear it. The man is a druid and the Britons do not usually choose such men to be their military leaders. Faelan's youngest son is called Arvirargus. He is a year younger than the brother you crucified but they are already talking about him as a great leader. Men twice his age are happy to follow him. They say that he has all of his father's qualities and none of his faults."

"The youth out there on the cross," Marcus muttered, "the older brother. Why did we not know that he was Faelan's son. Did he not talk? We fucking tortured him, didn't we!"

Adalberht shrugged, "Well we never asked him who he was," he replied. "So he never told us."

Marcus closed his eyes and wearily rubbed his face with his hand.

"What else?" Lucius said quietly.

"Faelan is a wealthy man," Urbanus continued, "he seemed to have plenty of gold, so much of it, that I wondered where he was getting it from." The merchant paused and glanced around at the officers.

Marcus opened his eyes.

"My father told me a strange tale about his time in Hibernia," he said, stroking his chin thoughtfully, "He said that the Hibernians on the forbidden islands were unloading cargoes of gold and silver from boats that had come from the west. He said he'd seen one of these ships for himself."

"There is no land to the west of Hibernia," Urbanus said confidently. "It must have come from Hispania or from Caledonia."

Marcus nodded and rapped his fingers on the wooden table.

"A more important question," Lucius said calmly, "Is what Faelan intends to do with all that gold and silver?"

"That's obvious," Marcus said quickly, "He must be using it to pay Caledonian and Hibernian mercenaries to join the uprising."

"There is another possibility Marcus," Lucius said suddenly, as he glanced at his commander. "Faelan may be using the gold to bribe our men. He may be using it to buy their loyalty and encourage them to desert. There are many Germanic and Gallic auxiliary Cohorts stationed throughout the north. Some of these may be susceptible to the right amount of gold."

"Fuck me," Marcus muttered as he took a deep breath.

"If that is true," Adalberht growled in his native language, "Then I take it as a compliment that the rebels have not tried to bribe us. They must have decided that trying it on with the 2nd Batavians was pointless. For once those bastards got it right."

"Maybe they did try us," Lucius said slowly, "Maybe that was why Cotta did not listen to your warnings Marcus. Maybe he was planning to have us all killed in exchange for rebel gold and silver?"

Marcus caught Lucius' eye and shook his head.

"Those are spurious claims and I will not have them repeated," he snapped, growing annoyed, "As far as we are concerned, Cotta died a heroic death trying to drive the rebels from his camp."

"If you say so," Lucius muttered lowering his eyes.

***

It was dark when Marcus, clad in his splendid armour and plumed helmet and holding a burning, torch strode down the ranks of the Batavian soldiers. The two infantry companies that formed the vanguard, had been brought up to full strength with replacements from other companies and the men stood in two long single files, waiting patiently and silently for the order to march out of the fort. The men's helmets, torso armour and large, body-shields glinted in the faint light and each man was clasping a long Hastae thrusting spear. As he strode down the ranks, Marcus sensed an excited expectant atmosphere amongst his men, as if they were relishing the chance to close with the enemy. They had been stuck inside their fort for far too long, he thought.

As he reached the front of the column where a small cluster of horsemen were waiting for him, he handed the torch to one of the slaves and hoisted himself up into the saddle of his horse. Then he turned to give the fort a final glance.

"The men want to fight," Adalberht said from the darkness, "They are gagging to kick the shit out of someone."

"Good," Marcus replied, "Then let's not disappoint them." He turned his beast around as his horse whinnied nervously, "Open the gates," he called out softly to the men beside the southern gatehouse.

Marcus was the first out of the fort. He was followed closely by Fridwald, his trumpeter and the standard bearer proudly holding aloft the boar-headed Cohort standard. As they turned south and vanished into the swirling darkness the Batavian infantry companies and cavalry squadrons followed, until all four hundred men had disappeared into the night.

***

It was dawn before Marcus allowed his men to rest. Wearily Marcus dismounted from his horse and led the beast through the trees towards the spot, where Adalberht and his cavalry squadrons were in the process of making their camp. In amongst the forest the Batavian infantry were settling down onto the ground individually and in small groups, as their officers moved in amongst them, issuing orders and detailing men for guard duty in low urgent voices.

"No fires; eat the bread and cheese you brought with you," Marcus called out quietly to the men, as he led his horse through the trees; "and no noise, no noise. The enemy are close."

As he caught sight of Centurion Lollius and his forty Legionaries, Marcus veered towards him. Lollius was sharpening the blade of a gladius as Marcus approached. He looked up and nodded in greeting.

"That was good of you to take me and my men with you," Lollius said with appreciation in his voice.

Marcus placed a hand on the man's shoulder. There was a strange sadness in Lollius's voice that he found slightly unsettling.

"Get some rest," he muttered, "We will remain here for a few hours only. Following the road south was the easy part. The hard part comes next. From here we must leave the road and turn westwards and enter the mountains. There are no roads and the country is broken and difficult and fuck knows what enemy war bands we may run into, as well. I want to reach the stone circle by dusk."

Lollius looked down at his sword grimly.

"My men and I have sworn to avenge our fallen comrades," he said. "We are not going to show any mercy. You can count on us, Sir."

Marcus nodded and without a further word he turned and led his horse towards where the cavalry squadrons were making their bivouac. Adalberht was sitting on the ground, leaning with his back against a tree. He had his eyes closed but opened them as Marcus called out to him.

"We will stay here for a few hours," Marcus said quietly, as he crouched down beside the old warrior on the forest floor. "See to it that your men and horses get as much rest as possible. I want to reach the stone circle by dusk. Beltane is tomorrow. If Faelan is where we believe him to be, we will strike at dawn. I want him alive, Adalberht, understood. Only kill him if he is likely to escape. Make sure your men are aware."

"Let's hope he runs away," Adalberht muttered as he closed his eyes again. "Then I will kill him. The arsehole deserves death after all the problems he's caused."

Marcus turned to look towards the west. "We have been lucky so far," he said, "hopefully our night time departure did not alert the enemy to our intentions, but later today we are going to be out in the open, with little cover and no darkness to conceal us. If we run into any rebel war bands, I am going to need you and your cavalry to ensure that they meet a swift end. If Faelan gets word of our approach, he will disappear and all of this will be for nothing."

"I know. I know what is required," Adalberht grumbled irritably. "Or have you forgotten that I was a warrior before you were even born."

\*\*\*

Marcus crouched beside the small river and scooped some water into his hands before raising them to his mouth. It was dawn and the sky above him was cloudless and blue. Dew clung to the grass at his feet and for a moment he closed his eyes, allowing the young rays of the sun to warm his face. Along the northern bank of the river the four hundred men of his battle group were clustered together in their company and squadron formations. The men were silent, as they sat waiting and crouching in between the great tumbled boulders and rocks of the narrow river valley. Marcus took another drink from the river and then straightened up. The bleak, rocky and treeless mountains rose all around him, green and brown, empty, windswept and magnificent. Immediately to the south, across the bubbling and gushing river, was a steep rocky ridge and beyond that, a mile away or so out of sight, was the stone circle of Castlerigg. As he stared at the bleak, treeless ridge a wolf suddenly appeared on the skyline and turned it's inquisitive head to stare at the men in the valley below. At the sight of the wild animal, a stir passed through the troops along the river bank and a few of the soldiers stood up and pointed at the animal. Eagerly Marcus peered at the wolf, willing it to come down to the river but after a moment the beast turned away and vanished from view.

"They're back Sir," Fridwald cried out with sudden excitement, as he pointed to the west. Marcus turned to look in the direction his bodyguard was pointing. Sure enough two Batavians were scrambling down the ridge towards his position. As they ran towards him, every soldier in the battle group turned to stare at them.

"Well?" Marcus growled as the two, panting men stumbled towards him.

"He's there Sir," the scouts cried out, unable to hide their excitement, "A tall man, white beard and a black eye patch over his eye, just like you said. There is a crowd of people, men, women, children, dogs too."

"What about fighting men?" Marcus snapped, as from the corner of his eye he caught sight of Adalberht, Lollius and Hedwig scrambling toward him.

The scouts bent forwards and paused to catch their breath.

"Yes a small party of mounted men, maybe twenty in all. But that's it, Sir. We saw no others. They are gathering around the stones."

Marcus stared at the scouts in silence. Then as Adalberht, Lollius and Hedwig reached him he turned sharply.

"Adalberht," he said in an urgent voice, "take half our cavalry and circle around towards the lake and close in from the south. Don't let them see you. If Faelan tries to escape you will cut him off and capture him." Marcus turned to Hedwig. The Decurion was staring at him with a face filled with eager anticipation. "Hedwig, you and I will take the rest of cavalry, ride west along the river and attack from the north. You will block any northern escape." Marcus turned to stare at Lollius. The Centurion looked grim and composed. "You will form the centre of our attack," Marcus said quickly. "Upon my signal take the infantry and lead them over that ridge towards the stone circle. Wait for my signal. Then drive everyone before you; don't let them break through your line. I want the enemy driven back towards the lake. We will trap them against the water." Marcus turned to stare at his officers. "Is that clear; understood?" he snapped.

The officers nodded in silence and Marcus grinned as the adrenaline-fuelled excitement    started to grow.

"Thunder and lashing rain, so Woden commeth," he muttered, as one by one his officers quietly repeated the Batavian battle cry.

Without another word, Marcus strode towards his horse and flung himself up onto the beast's back. Fridwald and the trumpeter, clutching his shiny conical instrument, and the standard bearer holding the boar-headed standard, rode towards him as he placed his plumed helmet on his head. Marcus turned and pumped his fist up and down and then he was away, splashing through the water of the shallow river. He was followed moments later by his staff and dozens of Batavian horsemen, clutching their long lances.

The ground was rocky, uneven and difficult as Marcus and his troops picked their way along the gurgling and tumbling river. Soon they had lost sight of the rest of the battle group. All around them the beautiful barren treeless mountains rose up, crisscrossed with deep gulley's, small streams and gigantic, moss-covered boulders. Sheep were everywhere, munching on the sparse vegetation and nervously skittering away as the horsemen approached. Marcus looked up at the pale, clear blue sky as a V shaped formation of birds flapped away towards the west. To his left, the ridge of the river valley kept him from seeing the stone circle in the meadows beyond, but they had to be close. He was just about to say something to Hedwig when a low, mournful horn blasted away, it's noise echoing away into the mountains. Marcus instantly raised his fist and came to a halt. That had not been a Batavian horn. He twisted round but the trumpeter was shaking his head. Then he heard it again, a low mournful blast. The noise had come from the direction of the stones.

"Fuck," Marcus cursed, as he urged his horse up towards the ridge. As he reached the crest he cursed again. Across the green, open meadows less than half a mile away, stood the magnificent stone circle of Castlerigg and gathered around it were a crowd of people. A dog had started to bark and a group of mounted men were galloping towards the standing stones.

"Damn him," Marcus cried out as he caught sight of the long line of Batavian and Legionary infantry that was advancing upon the standing stones, "He has started out too early. Lollius did not wait for my signal. We have been spotted."

Before anyone could reply, the Briton horn rang out once more. The noise was coming from the small group of rebel horsemen.

"Sound the signal and follow me," Marcus roared, as he unsheathed his sword and urged his horse on. The beast leapt forwards and with a great roar the Batavian cavalrymen surged over the crest and out into the open meadow. Marcus kept his eyes on the crowd around the standing stones as he galloped towards them. Where was Faelan, where was the king? A Roman trumpet blasted away behind him and as they caught sight of the approaching Batavian horsemen, screams and yells rose up from the crowd of people. Then the crowd scattered as the people started to run. Amongst them Marcus suddenly recognised druids, clad in their long white robes. Wildly Marcus stared at the fleeing figures. Where was Faelan? Then suddenly he caught sight of a chariot. Three figures were racing towards it.

"There he is, get him, get him," Marcus roared, as he raised his sword and veered towards the chariot and its two attendant horses. The three running figures had reached the vehicle and were desperately whipping the horses as they started out westwards towards the lake. Marcus shouted at his horse as he set off in pursuit. Behind him the hooves of the Batavian horsemen thudded into the ground as the riders yelled and cried out.

"Marcus," Hedwig screamed suddenly in warning, "Look, to the left."

But Marcus had already seen the approaching threat. The small band of rebel horsemen who had first sounded the alarm, were streaking across the meadows on a intercept course with the Batavian riders. Marcus grunted with reluctant admiration as instantly he understood what they intended to do. The Britons were trying to protect their king. They were going to buy Faelan time to get away.

"They are riding to their deaths," Hedwig screamed as the two cavalry formations thundered towards each other.

There was no time to reply. With a savage roar the outnumbered group of Britons crashed into the Batavian riders. A screaming rebel horsemen flashed past Marcus as he slashed at the man with his sword. In the confused melee, desperate yells, shouts and screams rose up as the two groups of horsemen slashed, hacked and stabbed at each other. Marcus parried a blow with his shield from a bearded warrior as he furiously tried to break free from the melee of grunting and groaning men and snorting horses. At his side a Batavian thrust his lance savagely into the exposed back of a rebel rider, sending the warrior tumbling to the ground. Wildly, Marcus hacked at a Briton who was trying to attack him, but the man fended off the blow and before Marcus could close again, Fridwald had gotten in the way.

Marcus stared wildly around him. The fight was always going to have just one outcome. The Britons were heavily outnumbered and already more than half their number were lying dead in the grass. Then he caught sight of the distant chariot. It was racing straight towards the lake. It was getting away.

"Follow me!" he roared as he broke free from the melee. "The king must not get away. A hundred Denarii for the man who brings him to me!"

Then he was away, galloping off in pursuit of the chariot and its three occupants. As he thundered across the grassy meadow, he was joined by Fridwald and a few of his men. Marcus snatched a glance behind him. His riders were strung out in a disordered line as they finished off the last of the Briton horsemen. Up ahead he suddenly noticed the lone running figure of a druid clad in his long white robe. As Marcus closed in, the man came to a halt and calmly turned to face the horsemen. Defiantly the druid crossed his arms across his chest and spat onto the ground as Marcus and the Batavians flashed past. Then as the small group of Batavian raced away, the druid slowly sank to his knees and toppled sideways into the grass with a spear impaled in his chest.

He was gaining on the chariot. Marcus stared at the vehicle and its occupants. They were no more than a couple of hundred paces away now. Fiercely he cried out to his horse, urging the beast onwards. Up ahead the long and large, placid-looking blue lake came into view surrounded by magnificent, treeless mountains. They were going to trap the chariot against the water. Faelan was trapped. The High King of the Brigantes was going to fall into his hands. The chariot however, did not change course as it raced straight towards the water's edge. Marcus frowned. Did his quarry not realise what was about to happen? Then, as they reached the edge of the lake, the three occupants leapt from the chariot and sprinted across the rocky beach and as they did, Marcus recognised a tall bearded man with a black eye patch and a golden torc around his neck. It was Faelan and for a moment Marcus was transported back to the ramparts of Drumanagh in Hibernia, where he had first watched his father stride out into no-man's land to negotiate with the one-eyed druid.

"Seize him," Marcus roared pointing his sword straight at Faelan and as he cried out the High King looked up and glanced straight towards Marcus. The Batavians were less than fifty paces away when Marcus groaned in sudden dismay. On the lake shore the three Britons were pushing a simple log boat into the water. As he galloped towards them the three men scrambled hastily into the log and started to paddle furiously out into the lake. Marcus roared in frustration as he reached the water's edge, slid from his horse and splashed into the water. But the log boat was steadily pulling away and with the water coming up to his waist Marcus came to a halt. The High King was going to escape after all. Frustrated, Marcus raised his sword and pointed it straight at Faelan. In the log boat Faelan sat calmly staring back at Marcus. Then he raised his hand in a crude gesture.

"Fuck you Roman," the High King roared in Latin.

## Chapter Seventeen - Vengeance

Marcus took his time as he made his way down the lines of his wounded men, pausing here and there to speak to a soldier. It was evening and five days had passed since Faelan had managed to elude him. The wounded lay on camp beds and on make-shift, straw mattresses that had been laid out on the floor. The long barracks block inside the fort was quiet except for the occasional groan and cry. The doctor and his three medical orderlies followed a step behind Marcus. They looked utterly exhausted. Marcus passed on down the line. The wounded were watching him intently and expectantly as if he somehow had the power to heal them and make their pain go away, but all he could do was offer words of encouragement and shake the hands of those who had the strength. Two more wounded men had died since he'd set out to try and capture the High King. He was nearing the end of the line when the door to the barracks block opened and the officer of the watch hastened towards him. The officer looked concerned.

"Do what you can," Marcus nodded at the doctor, as he caught the look on the watch commander's face. Then he was heading out of the door.

"Well, what is it?" Marcus snapped as the watch commander fell in beside him.

"The sentries report movement outside the walls Sir," the officer replied.

Marcus was silent as he headed straight for the nearest ladder leading up onto the ramparts. Faelan's escape had weighed heavily on him and he'd given Lollius a public dressing down for his failure to follow orders, but apart from that there had been not much more he could do. The Cohort had taken substantial casualties and he needed those forty Legionaries. The Centurion had taken the rebuke with a simple, silent shrug. Lollius seemed overwhelmed by a desire for revenge, so much so, that it seemed to have started to cloud his judgement.

As he scrambled up onto the parapet, one of the Batavian sentries cried out in alarm. Marcus moved across to the edge of the wooden palisade and peered into the darkness beyond the fort. He could see nothing. There was no moon and the night was pitch black. Then he heard a quiet metallic jingle and the snorting of a horse. Quickly he turned and started out along the parapet. But as he approached the southern gateway he came to an abrupt halt. With a crackling whoosh the roof of one of the abandoned, civilian round-houses burst into flames, instantly lighting up the night. Marcus stared at the scene, rooted to the ground as beyond the fort, one by one the roof's of the round-houses started to burst into flames. Along the parapet the Batavian sentries stared at the burning, crackling buildings as their watch commander shouted a hurried order. A moment later the rapid clanging of the alarm bell rose up from one of the watch towers. Down inside the fort, the Batavian soldiers came streaming out of their barracks blocks as their officers shouted and yelled out orders. Marcus did not move, as all around him the Batavian infantry, fully armed and armoured rushed towards their allotted posts.

"Are the cranes ready?" Marcus snapped turning to Fridwald, who stood behind him.

"The carpenters finished them an hour ago," Fridwald replied quickly.

Beyond the walls of the fort, the civilian settlement of Luguvalium was on fire. The flames were soon out of control, roaring, crackling and leaping upwards as one by one the thatched roofs collapsed inwards with a great crashing noise. Marcus could feel the heat from the flames on his face. A line of Batavian infantry, clutching their long, Hastae spears, came jogging passed him before turning and taking their positions along the wooden battlements. Then a new sound rose up overwhelming everything else and Marcus felt an involuntary shiver pass down his spine, as all of a sudden the night was filled with thousands of roaring voices and the thunderous clash of weapons against shields. The roar fell and rose like waves crashing onto a beach. Marcus turned to look behind him. The noise seemed to have enveloped the fort. It was coming from all around them. Dimly he could hear the Batavian officers screaming orders at their men.

"Oh fuck." Marcus muttered to himself.

\*\*\*

Marcus was sitting, slumped on the parapet with his back leaning up against the wall, when a hand shook him awake. It was Fridwald. Marcus blinked and for a moment he looked confused. Then quickly he got to his feet. It was dawn and all along the parapet the Batavian's lined the walls.

"Looks like they want to talk, Sir," Fridwald said grimly pointing.

Marcus turned to stare at the blackened, smoking and smouldering ruins of the round-houses and huts. Beyond the cluster of civilian dwellings he caught sight of the numerous small camp fires of the enemy. The rebel tribesmen squatted or stood around in small groups, as they formed a continuous line around the fort. Marcus grunted, as for a split moment he felt the hair on his neck stand up. There had to be thousands of rebels out there. Their massed ranks vanished into the trees beyond the settlement and extended as far as the banks of the Eden. As he stared at the Britons, a small party of mounted warriors clasping a white flag, trotted towards the entrance to the southern gate. They halted a few paces from the barred gates and their leader, a huge hulk of a man clad in a wolf-skin cloak, looked up at the defenders who were peering down at him.

"I have a message from High King Faelan to all of you Roman dogs," the Briton roared in Latin, "We have no quarrel with slaves. King Faelan is prepared to offer you all, each man of you, a year's salary in gold and safe passage south, if you abandon your fort and hand over the man who commands you. Those are his terms. One year's salary in gold for the man who butchered and crucified the King's son. You have one hour to decide."

And without waiting for an answer the messenger turned and trotted away back to his own lines.

Marcus took a deep breath as he stared at the retreating Britons. Along the ramparts the Batavians remained silent as they gripped their spears and peered down at the enemy from behind their shields.

"Don't worry Marcus, the lads are not about to sell you out," Adalberht said with a faint smile as he strode towards his commanding officer, "Not for just a year's measly salary at any rate."

Marcus did not reply, as he struggled to stop himself from blushing. Then he turned to look at the men lining the walls and the two, tall wooden cranes with their large leather sacks that loomed awkwardly over the walls. For a long moment he was silent.

"Order the scorpion crew to shoot the next bastard who comes into range," he muttered, "and have the archers in the towers stand by and wait for my order. We are going to give these arseholes something to remember us by, if they dare attack us."

"Already done," Adalberht growled. "And by the gods, I do hope they try. I am ready to kick the shit out of someone. It's been too long since we've had a proper fight."

Marcus nodded grimly. "You are a good man Adalberht, so don't go getting yourself killed. I have a feeling this uprising is not going to end soon."

"Don't worry about me," Adalberht growled as he stomped away, "I am not the one who has made a personal enemy out of the rebel king."

***

With a twang the scorpion shot it's long, iron-tipped bolt straight at the rebel tribesmen, swiping a man boldly from his horse and hurling him straight into the ranks of his comrades behind him. The death however was hardly noticed by the thousands of rebel infantry. The Britons with their full body tattoos, blue-painted faces, spiky-hair and outlandish tunics, stood massed and armed, baying, screaming and yelling insults at the silent defenders inside the fort. The noise and sight of the wild barbarians was terrific.

"Looks like they are preparing to attack Sir," one of the Batavian officers yelled, as along the ramparts the Batavians started to lower and point their spears at the enemy.

Marcus did not reply as he strode down the line staring at the enemy. He'd gotten every available soldier up onto the parapet and only the wounded, who were unable to move, the women and children and the slaves remained down below inside the barracks blocks but despite this, the line of defenders still looked pitifully thin. Quickly he glanced at the two, newly-constructed cranes that stood close to the ramparts. The wooden cranes had been fastened and secured onto two wagons to make them mobile and now the strange machines, each with a large, bulging, leather sack attached to their tops, loomed awkwardly over the walls. A squad of eight men stood to attention beside the two machines and along the north eastern wall, were two more cranes.

Marcus turned his attention back to the men up on the wall.

"When they come," he roared, as he passed down the line, "we will hold them and we will throw them back. We have nowhere to run to boys. These walls are it. We either beat them here or

143

we die. We are not going to run and we are not going to let those bastards enter our fort. We are going to kill them."

The Batavians, standing shoulder to shoulder, remained silent as they stared at the baying, screaming mass, of hostile tribesmen. Then a solitary soldier suddenly raised himself and defiantly turned to face the enemy.

"Come and get us you arseholes," he yelled at the tribesmen.

The soldier's defiant outburst was followed a moment later by the low mournful blast of a Carnyx, that reverberated across the fields and from the mass of tribesmen a line of bowmen calmly stepped forwards and raised and aimed their bows at the fort.

"Shields up, shields up," the shouts of the Batavian officers could be heard along the parapet, as a moment later a hail of arrows hammered into the wooden palisade and shot over the wall to strike the empty parade ground. The volley was followed by another. Half crouching behind the shield wall, Marcus ran along the parapet towards his command post at the southern gate as another long blast from a Carnyx reverberated across the fort.

"Here they come," a Batavian voice screamed.

Marcus made it to the edge of the wall, where the standard bearer and his trumpeter were waiting for him. With a heaving chest, he turned to stare at the enemy. Instead of the massed, all-out charge that he'd been expecting, the Britons were advancing on the ramparts in tightly packed scrums, like slow moving tortoises, bristling with weapons and holding their small shields above their heads for protection. Marcus gasped in surprise. The Britons were advancing in Testudo formation; they were copying Roman, army tactics. As he stared at the unfolding scene, the scorpion bolt- thrower sent a bolt straight into one of the advancing formations. The projectile went straight through a shield impaling a man to the ground, but the rebel ranks quickly closed again. Suddenly Marcus felt something whizz passed his head. It was followed moments later by a thud as a stone smacked into a Batavian shield.

"Slingers Sir," the standard bearer, clutching the boar-headed standard said calmly.

Marcus bit his lip as he caught sight of the enemy youths, whirling their slings above their heads. There was nothing he could do to slow the enemy advance. He neither had the artillery nor the archers. Another volley of arrows came flying towards him and instinctively Marcus and his staff flung themselves against the protection of the wooden palisade, as the missiles zipped over their heads. As he raised his head a great roar rose up from the enemy ranks and the tight scrums suddenly dissolved, as the Britons stormed forwards and into the V shaped ditch. Some of the men were carrying ladders. As the foremost men started to scramble up the steep side of the turf rampart towards the wooden palisade, the massed tribesmen behind them surged forwards in a mad rush towards the fort. Marcus took a deep breath. The land seemed to vanish, covered by hundreds and hundreds of screaming, running men.

Along the pathway leading to the southern entrance, a party of rebels came charging towards the gate. In their midst they were carrying a sturdy tree trunk with a sharpened and fire hardened point. With a wild yell, the Britons slammed the battering ram into the gate. The wood creaked, swayed and groaned but held as the party fell back a few steps, before charging forwards again.

"Clear those men from the gate," Marcus yelled furiously.

Up on the ramparts the Batavian defenders raised their spears and flung them at the charging Britons and at such short range, they struck home, impaling the attackers and sending them tumbling and shrieking to the ground. The wooden battering-ram dropped unceremoniously into the mud. There was no time to finish off the wounded. Along the length of the ramparts the rebel assault ladders were crashing up against the wooden palisade, and the Britons were clambering upwards, clutching their swords, knives, battle axes and small, hide-bound wooden shields. From the walls the Batavian auxiliaries thrust their spears at the enemy, sending their leading men shrieking and tumbling back into the ditch, but their place on the ladders was quickly taken up by others. More and more ladders appeared amongst the rebel ranks and came thumping up against the wooden wall. In the ditch below, the corpses of the dead and wounded were being trampled into the mud by the press of the attackers as they tried to get up to the walls. Marcus stared at the scene, the adrenaline pumping in his veins. The Batavian officers were screaming orders at their men, as the Batavians were becoming locked into a vicious and desperate stabbing and thrusting contest.

Close by, a Batavian cried out as he was struck by an arrow. The man staggered backwards and tumbled off the parapet and into the fort. A moment later the painted face of a Briton appeared above the wall and with a shout the man leapt over the parapet and landed on the wooden deck. Marcus drew his sword and ducking under the man's clumsy, swinging axe, he darted forwards and thrust his sword into the man's exposed chest. The Briton groaned and gurgled up some blood as Marcus grasped him by his hair and sent him flying into the camp. Then Marcus cried out in pain and staggered backwards as something struck his helmet. Another Briton appeared on the top of the ladder. Marcus raised his hand to his head as a trickle of blood ran down his cheek. The Briton, a huge man clasping a spear, landed on the parapet and with a wild slashing blow he sent a Batavian cannonading into his comrades. Marcus staggered backwards in alarm, as another Briton appeared at the top of the ladder and with a wild triumphant cry jumped down to join his comrade. With a roar the Briton with the spear jabbed it at Marcus and struck his armour with a glancing blow. There was no time to feel any pain. With a scream Marcus launched himself at his attacker and punched his sword straight into the man's face. The blade sliced into the man's head with a sickening crunch. The momentum of his attack sent him and the

Briton crashing into the side of the wall. Blood and gore spattered onto Marcus's face, as he struggled to pull his sword free. At his side with a dull thud, a Batavian shield suddenly parried the sword thrust of the other Briton. Marcus yelped in fright. It was Fridwald. The young bodyguard's face was grim as he drove the attacker back against the wall with his shield. As the rebel tried desperately to push Fridwald back, a Batavian decapitated him with an abandoned axe.

Marcus wrenched his sword free from the corpse and staggered backwards. His face and torso armour were covered in blood. Along the parapet the Britons were clambering over the ramparts in increasing numbers. The Batavians were locked into snarling, desperate hand-to-hand combat and down in the ditch more and more rebels were pushing and shoving their way towards the assault ladders. Marcus heard his own laboured breath and suddenly he felt the pain in his ribs. Inside the fort he could see the corpses of his men lying in the mud.

"Give the signal," he snarled turning to the trumpeter behind him, "light the bastards up."

The Roman trumpet blasted two sharp notes but along the walls the shrieking melee did not pause as the defenders desperately tried to stem the rebel assault. Then the two cranes inside the fort started to move lumbering along the wall, until they were poised over two of the rebel ladders. Marcus stared impatiently at the machines as suddenly the bulging leather bags turned upside down emptying a shower of black liquid down onto the attackers climbing up their ladders. The black liquid splattered and completely drenched the men moving up the ladder.

"Now," Marcus roared as he turned to stare at the men high up in their watch tower. A moment later a trumpet rang out in three quick blasts, and from the tower two flaming arrows streaked through the air and smacked into their target. Instantly the whole ladder and the unfortunate attackers on it burst into flames with a great whooshing roar. The men's high-pitched screams were horrifying, as they clawed at their burning tunics and tumbled back towards the ground. From the watch tower a fresh set of fire arrows hammered into a second ladder, setting it alight. The attackers leapt from the ladder and crashed into their comrades below as inside the fort, the men manning the cranes rushed to lower the cranes and refuel the leather bags.

"Drive those men from our wall," Marcus roared as he leapt forwards. "Clear those ladders," he yelled as he felt a savage, blood-lust taking over. "They are not going to enter our fort." As Marcus struggled along the wall, a burning assault ladder groaned and collapsed, sending its occupants tumbling to the ground. Stepping over a corpse Marcus rammed his sword into the back of a rebel, who was grappling with one of the defenders, grasped his hair and sent him spinning off the parapet and into the fort.

"Drive them back," Marcus roared savagely.

Close by, a Batavian clambered up onto the top of one of the ladders and started hacking at the enemy who were climbing up. Then with a splintering crack the ladder gave way and attackers and defender vanished over the side of the palisade with a startled shriek. Marcus roared as he picked up an abandoned spear and thrust it into the head of a rebel, who had appeared above the wall. The man collapsed backwards without a sound taking the spear with him.

"Drive them back!"

"Sir, look over there, the gate!" Fridwald yelled suddenly. Marcus blinked as he swung round to stare at the southern gate. The gates were open and as he stared at them uncomprehendingly, a mounted squadron of Batavian riders charged out and into the screaming mass of rebel tribesmen. Marcus gasped in shock. The Batavians were being led by Adalberht. The force and momentum of the charge sent the old veteran deep into the enemy ranks. Then the Batavians around the entrance rushed to close the gates and Marcus lost sight of his men.

Beyond the ramparts a Carnyx bellowed defiantly as another ladder burst into flames. Marcus struggled to the edge of the palisade. Out amongst the burned and blackened ruins of the civilian settlement, he suddenly caught sight of a chariot flying a black pennant. The chariot was surrounded by a tight-knit group of horsemen and standing up in the chariot was Faelan. The tall, one-eyed figure with the golden torc around his neck was unmistakeable. The High King was staring at the fighting. Marcus groaned as he caught sight of Adalberht and his remaining men, as the Britons surged around him like an angry sea playing with a piece of flotsam.

"What is he doing?" Marcus cried out in horror.

No one around him answered as the desperate, vicious struggle for control of the wall went on without a pause. Then Marcus gasped as he realised Adalberht's purpose. The man was trying to fight his way towards Faelan. Adalberht was trying to single handily kill the enemy king.

"Fool," Marcus whispered hoarsely, "Oh you heroic fool."

There was no way Adalberht was going to make it through the enemy mass that was pressing towards the walls. As Marcus stared at the fighting, Adalberht was pulled from his horse and swiftly disappeared into a frenzied mass of hacking and stabbing rebels. Marcus snarled and wrenched himself away from the edge of the wall as the blood-lust, that had been growing inside him, came to a boil.

"Kill them, kill them all," he roared as he seemed to go berserk. Near by, a rebel jumped down onto the parapet but before the man could straighten up, Marcus shoved a Batavian out of the way and grasped the Briton by his throat before slamming him up against the palisade. With a savage snarl he smashed his forehead into the attacker, stunning the rebel before thrusting his sword straight through the man's mouth.

"Thunder and lashing rain, so Woden cometh," Marcus screamed, raising his blood- stained face and arms to the sky before thrusting his way along the parapet, with a crazed, ferocious look.

\*\*\*

The fort was quiet. It was late in the afternoon and the exhausted Batavian survivors crouched and stood along the battered ramparts, staring warily at the enemy who had retreated to their campfires. Corpses were everywhere, filling the ditch and littering the ground around the base of the ramparts, their contorted figures twisted into crazy shapes or burnt and blackened. The charred, blackened remains of sixteen assault ladders lay crumpled and wrecked at the base of the walls and amongst the debris lay countless swords, spears, broken shields, discarded helmets. limbs and severed heads. Here and there a wounded man was crying out for help and in the sky the first of the scavengers were starting to circle.

Marcus was supervising the repairs to a section of the palisade, where the Britons had tried to pull down the wall with ropes and iron hooks, when he heard the standard bearer call out his name. Leaving the repair work, he clambered up the ladder and onto the parapet. He'd had no time to wash the blood from his face and torso armour and the pain in his ribs was constant and irritating. Fridwald followed a few steps behind. The bodyguard had sustained a blow to left arm and a white bandage was wrapped around the wound. Moodily Marcus came to a halt beside the standard-bearer clutching the Cohort Standard. The officer was staring at the rebel lines a couple of hundred paces away.

"Think they have had enough Sir?" the standard bearer said calmly.

"Maybe," Marcus muttered sourly, as he turned to look at the enemy. "It will take them some time to build new ladders."

"Then we shall burn those too Sir."

Marcus did not reply as he craned his neck and peered at the spot where he'd seen Adalberht fall.

"I am going to try and arrange a truce," Marcus said quietly, "Just a little bit of time to bring Adalberht's corpse back into the camp. It's not right that his body should be left to the beasts. He deserves a proper funeral."

The standard bearer nodded. "You are right Sir, but I don't think they are in the mood to allow that. They have lost a lot of men today."

"So have we," Marcus growled, as he turned and started back along the parapet.

However just as Marcus was about to descend the ladder leading down into the fort, a Carnyx shattered the peace. The long, powerful and mournful blast reverberated across the land. Along the walls of the fort, the weary Batavians stirred and rose to their feet. Marcus turned and peered in the direction from which the noise had come and there riding towards the southern gate, was a single chariot with two occupants. The chariot was flying a white flag. As the vehicle approached the gate, one of the occupants leapt off it and turned to face the Batavians up on their walls. It was the same herald clad in his wolf-skin cloak, who had offered them the bribe that morning.

"Roman slave dogs," the man roared in Latin, "You continue to hide behind your walls like cowards. King Faelan thinks you are scared. The King thinks your commander, the man called Marcus is shitting himself with fear. He thinks your commander is a worthless dog, who prefers others to do his fighting and dying for him. So King Faelan challenges him to a duel to the death. Man to man outside these gates, like a true warrior." The herald paused as he stared at the defenders up on their ramparts. "Well, what say you? Does your General have the balls to come out and face our    champion?"

The Batavian defenders remained silent as they stared down at the rebel. Marcus shifted uncomfortably as he shook his head. Standing orders throughout the army were that soldiers were strictly forbidden from accepting offers of single combat.

"No man is to accept an offer to single combat," he shouted turning to his men.

Hardly had he spoken the words when Marcus heard a sudden commotion along the wall. He turned in the direction of the noise. Along the section of the wall that was defended by the Legionaries, the soldiers were raising their swords and shields in the air and shouting at something beyond the fortifications.

"What is going on over there?" Marcus roared as he strode towards the Legionaries. Then as he reached the edge of the wall he came to an abrupt halt. Outside the fort a man was picking his way purposefully across the battlefield towards the rebel herald. It was Lollius, the Centurion.

Marcus raised his hand to his chin and shook his head in silent dismay as the Legionaries around him cheered their commander on. Lollius had cracked. There was something sad and tragic about the way the Centurion made his way towards the herald, as if the memory of his butchered men had become too much to bear. Marcus opened his mouth but then closed it again. There was no point. Lollius was not going to come back. Not after half the fort had seen him accept the rebel challenge.

As he halted before the Briton Lollius spat at the man's feet and as they saw the gesture a great encouraging roar rose from the Legionaries up upon the wall. The herald looked disappointed. Then he shrugged and turned towards his own lines and raised both his arms in the air.

From the enemy ranks a solitary horseman detached himself and came trotting towards the southern gate. As the horseman approached Marcus saw that the rider was young, no more than eighteen and he was clad in common leather torso armour and armed with a simple, hide-bound shield and an axe. The young man's long flowing black hair fluttered in the breeze as he examined Lollius in silence. Then as he reached the chariot, the youth turned to look up at the defenders peering down at him from their ramparts.

"Who is he?" Fridwald muttered.

Marcus did not answer as the tension up on the wall started to grow. The handsome youth slid smoothly from his horse and handed the reins to the driver of the chariot. Then silently and calmly whirling his axe in his hand, he strode towards where Lollius was waiting for him.

"See dogs," the herald roared, turning to face the defenders, "Your commander has proved his cowardice. Why does he not come himself? Why does he allow others to do his fighting for him? He dares not even face a youth of barely eighteen. King Faelan spits on you Marcus; you are no warrior, you are not even a man and we shall treat you lower than a dog when we get you and make no mistake we will get you."

The herald's eyes gleamed contemptuously as he stared up at the defenders.

"Rome does not offer us a fair fight," the big herald shouted, "but we shall show you what it means to be a great warrior. We shall give you a fair fight; we shall show you why our people are better than you."

And with that the big man turned and cried out to the two fighters.

"To the death, only one man leaves alive. Now fight."

Down beside the gate Lollius drew his sword as he slowly started to circle his opponent. The youth however hardly moved as he studied Lollius's movements. Then with a cry Lollius lunged, aiming his sword at the youth's midriff, but the Briton parried the thrust with contemptuous ease. On the ramparts the Legionaries were shouting and yelling encouragements at their commander. Then, as Lollius lunged again, the Briton cried out and with a speed that caught everyone by surprise he parried the thrust, spun away sideways and in one smooth movement buried his axe into Lollius's neck. The blow caught the Centurion by surprise and he staggered backwards, with the axe still embedded in his neck and blood spurting out. Instantly the Briton was upon him and with a loud cry the youth kicked Lollius to the ground. As the horrified Legionaries fell silent, the youth yanked his axe free and severed the Centurion's head. Along the wall the shocked Legionaries looked on helplessly as the Briton turned and held up the bloodied head of his opponent.

"I am Arvirargus," the Briton yelled, turning to face the defenders up on the wall, "and you will remember my name for I am the bringer of death and your champion here is the first to die, to satisfy the soul of my older brother."

## Chapter Eighteen - The Death of Heroes

The Batavian priest stood in the fort's muddy parade ground close to the north- eastern wall. He was speaking in his native Germanic language and as he did he raised his arms up towards the grey heavens. It was morning and it was raining heavily and the lashing wind plastered the priest's face with water, as if the gods themselves were in mourning. Marcus, Lucius, the principal officers of the Cohort and a small group of Batavians stood in a circle around the funeral pyre upon which lay Adalberht's body. The corpse had been covered with a simple woollen army blanket upon which someone had placed a sword, a shield and a piece of green amber. The men around the pyre were silent and had removed their helmets as the rain and wind swept across the fort in great, grey gusts. Finally the priest finished his incantation and nodded at Marcus.

Marcus sighed as the men around him waited for him to speak.

"He was our eldest," he cried out, "and he was our bravest but he is home now, with his gods and I have no doubt he sits at the table of the greatest in the feast halls of Woden. We shall miss him and we shall honour him. He served his people and Rome well. So farewell old comrade, may you rest easy and happy."

And with that Marcus nodded at the Batavian who was holding the flaming torch. The soldier lowered the torch to the pyre and instantly the pitch caught alight and despite the rain the fire began to greedily claim and consume the wooden pyre and the body that lay upon it.

"Thunder and lashing rain, so Woden commeth," one of the Batavians cried out, raising his sword into the air as around him the others did the same. As the noise died away, Marcus turned and strode towards one of the ladders leading up onto the parapet. Around him the parade ground was covered with an assortment of pots, individual mugs, jugs, barrels and blankets, all of which were trying to catch the rain water. Marcus wiped the rain from his face. To his surprise the Britons had agreed to his request and had allowed a party of unarmed Batavians to search for, and retrieve Adalberht's body from the battlefield. The rain and wind continued to soak him as he caught sight of the huddled shapes of the defenders along the ramparts. The men were exhausted. For two days now they had not left their positions along the walls. The Britons had not renewed their assault on the fort and had instead settled down to besiege them. As he clambered up the ladder a few slaves came shuffling past the ranks of the defenders handing out pieces of stale bread and cups of sour wine.

Marcus wiped the rain from his face as he stepped onto the wooden deck. Down below in the fort the dead Batavians had been laid out in rows. There had been no time or opportunity to bury them. Marcus turned to stare at the enemy. The Britons had not moved. He could see them huddled around their camp fires. Their numbers seemed undiminished despite the fearful carnage that surrounded the fort. Faelan had it seemed, decided to starve the defenders into submission. Marcus sighed as he knew he had a decision to make. That morning the quarter master had told him that there were two week's worth of food supplies left in the camp, but that the garrison would run out of water long before that. The only commodity that seemed to be in plentiful supply was the pitch, with which he'd set the enemy ladders on fire and repulsed the rebel assault. Marcus scratched at the stubble on his cheeks. He'd tried to send out a party to the river but the rebel cavalry had driven the Batavians back before they could reach the water's edge.

He glanced at his men. The stoic defenders had pulled the hoods of their winter cloaks over their heads as they crouched along the walls trying to shield themselves from the lashing rain. The men were silent as they munched on their bread and sipped their cups of sour wine. Marcus sighed again and turned to stare at the enemy lines. In full view of everyone, Lollius's headless corpse hung from a cross that the Britons had erected along the road leading north towards the Eden. It was the same cross upon which he had crucified Faelan's eldest son. Marcus stared at the corpse unable to look away. The prominent sight of their Centurion upon the wooden cross had had a dreadful effect on the morale of the forty Legionaries, but every attempt to try and cut him down had met with the same aggressive response that the water foraging party had received.

"What are we going to do Sir?" one of the Batavians said looking up at Marcus.

"We're going to defeat them," Marcus replied, "That's what we are going to do."

The Batavians were silent as Marcus slowly started out along the wall offering his men words of encouragement.

\*\*\*

A long mournful blast from a Carnyx made Marcus turn away from where the slaves were picking up the hundreds of jugs, cups and pots and carefully pouring the precious rain-water into barrels. It was afternoon and the rain had ceased, but the dark, gloomy grey clouds still covered the sky. The low, powerful trumpet blast reverberated once more and as it did, Marcus ran across the mud towards the walls. As he clambered up onto the parapet, the sentries high up in the watch towers started shouting and pointing. Marcus turned to stare at the rebel positions.

"Looks like they are leaving," Lucius cried excitedly as he came running along the parapet towards Marcus.

Marcus grunted in surprise. Could it be true? Beyond the slaughter and destruction of the battlefield the Britons were indeed beginning to move out. As he stared at them small parties of warriors started to fade away in every direction. The rebels did not seem to be in a hurry.

"It could be a trap to lure us into lowering our defences," Lucius said calmly as he stared at the retreating enemy. "We should be careful Marcus. This doesn't make sense. The enemy have us by the throat. Why would they decide to leave now?"

Marcus nodded. "Look," he said pointing eagerly, "they are moving off in small war bands. They are scattering. Faelan is breaking up his army. If the High King is splitting up his forces then he must be returning to his earlier strategy of avoiding a pitched battle. The Britons look like they are going back to their hit and run tactics."

For a long moment the two officers stared at the rebel retreat in silence.

"Send out two mounted pickets," Marcus snapped, as he turned to Lucius. "I want one watching the northern road, the other the southern road. They are to report any rebel movements immediately."

Lucius saluted and turned away without saying a word.

"And assemble a party of men to get water from the river," Marcus shouted as Lucius clambered down into the fort.

"And Lucius," Marcus cried out as Lucius reached the ground, "Get someone to cut Lollius down from that cross. I want his body brought into the camp."

***

The rider was shouting as he galloped towards the fort. It was afternoon and a full day and night had passed since the Britons had abandoned their siege and vanished. As the Batavian thundered through the open gates, Marcus with Lucius at his side strode towards the horseman.

"Well, what's going on?" Marcus snapped as the man veered towards him. The rider looked excited as he brought his horse to a halt.

"Sir," he cried out, "Soldiers    approaching from the south."

Marcus frowned at the rider. "What are you talking about man," he snapped.

"Legionaries Sir, thousands of them and cavalry too. They are marching down the road. I saw a standard but it was too far away to make out who they are."

Marcus turned and glanced at Lucius. The Senior Centurion's eyes sparkled with sudden fervour and excitement.

"It must be the Twentieth marching north from Deva Victrix," Lucius exclaimed, "They are coming to our relief. Thank the gods."

"How far away are they?" Marcus asked turning back to the rider.

"Couple of miles Sir, they will be here within the hour."

Marcus nodded as he turned to look down at the mud. "Trumpeter, let them know that we are still here," he snapped.

Marcus was up on the walls when the first Roman Legionary cavalry squadrons appeared on the road to the south. The heavily armoured and armed riders, led by a man wearing a magnificent Greek-style Attic helmet, came on at a trot as they headed straight towards Luguvalium. At the sight of the Roman relief column, the Batavians along the walls raised their weapons and shields in the air and roared and roared, crying out in their guttural native language.

"Open the gate," Marcus cried as a smile appeared on his lips too.

The Legionary cavalry, clad in their chain-mail armour and infantry-style helmets, came to a halt a short distance from the fort. The riders were clutching their short lances and oval shields and from their belts hung their long Spatha cavalry swords. Marcus peered down at the man who was leading them. The officer was wearing an Attic helmet and was clad in a white tunic with a broad purple vertical stripe, over which he was wearing finely-decorated bronze, muscled cuirass, body-armour. A large rectangular cloak was draped over his shoulders and fastened with a pin. Marcus grunted in surprise as he recognised the officer's rank from his clothing. The officer was a Tribunus Laticlavius, a Tribune of Senatorial rank, the second in command of a Legion. At the man's side a standard bearer, his head covered and draped in a wolf's head and fur, was holding up the vex illation standard of the Twentieth Legion.

The Roman Tribune took his time as he paused to stare around him at the decaying corpses, destroyed and blackened houses and discarded and broken debris, that littered the ground. Then he looked up at the Batavians manning the walls. Behind him along the road, the first of the heavily-armed Legionary infantry companies came marching into view and mixed in with them were ox and horse-drawn carts and wagons, laden with supplies, sacks, barrels and amphorae.

Without a word the Tribune raised his arm and trotted through the open gate and into the fort. Marcus with Lucius at his side, hastened to meet the newcomers as the Roman cavalry followed their leader into the camp.

"It's good to see you Sir," Marcus cried out in Latin as he approached the officer wearing the Attic helmet and saluted. "We have been besieged for two days but the enemy left yesterday. They must have learned of your approach."

"Where is Cotta?" the officer snapped in a stern and unfriendly voice, "I want to speak to the Prefect right away."

Marcus glanced quickly at Lucius. Then he cleared his throat.

"Cotta is dead Sir," Marcus replied stiffly, "He was killed during the first attack on our fort. I am in command. My name is Marcus, I was the Beneficiarius."

"We were nearly overrun Sir,"    Lucius added.

"Marcus, the Beneficiarius?" the Tribune muttered with a sudden frown.

The Tribune turned to fix his eyes upon Marcus and Marcus saw that he was about the same age as himself. For a long moment the officer said nothing. Then he clicked his fingers and behind him one of the riders slid from his horse and hastened to kneel head down beside the Tribune's horse. Slowly the officer dismounted using the man's back to step onto the ground. He turned and removed his helmet and glared at Marcus with a stern, hard and disapproving look.

"That is unfortunate," the Tribune snapped, "Cotta was a good man. Well Beneficarius, give me your report."

Marcus quickly rattled through what had happened. As he was about to finish the Tribune held up his hand for silence.

"That's enough," the officer barked, "this fort and its defence are no longer your concern. My name is Titus Cornelius Gallus, I am the Senatorial Tribune and second in command of the Twentieth Legion. The Legate of the Twentieth has sent me north to form a battle group and crush the rebellion in this district. You and your men will from now on be under my command."

"Yes Sir," Marcus nodded.

"How do you plan on defeating the rebels Sir?" Lucius said stiffly, "The Britons are avoiding a pitched fight. They are operating in small scattered war bands, attacking us where we are weak and making the roads too dangerous to travel on except for large companies of armed men."

Titus sniffed as he looked Lucius up and down.

"I have brought two and half thousand Legionaries with me," he said sharply, "and I have the authority to command all the auxiliary Cohorts and garrisons in this district. Defeating the enemy is simple. We are going to kill every rebel war band we meet. We are going to burn and destroy their villages. We are going to ruin their fields and crops, so when winter comes the enemy will starve." Titus's lips curled contemptuously. "We are going to turn this district into a wasteland, so that before I am done these Britons will know what it means to rebel against Rome."

Marcus glanced quickly at Lucius as the first of the Legionary infantry companies marched through the gate. The rhythmic tramp of the Legionary boots reverberated through the camp.

"Very good Sir," he replied tonelessly.

Titus turned to examine the fort. "Beneficarius," he said coldly, "You should know that I will not tolerate any disobedience under my command and that any offense or breach of discipline by you or your men will be dealt with using the severest punishment. Do I make myself clear?"

Marcus frowned in confusion.

"I am not sure I understand Sir?" he muttered.

"There is a charge against you or have you forgotten," Titus snapped as he turned to look at Marcus. "Cotta, your commanding officer sent the Legate of the Twentieth a message. He said that you had refused to obey a direct order and that he wanted to have you punished."

"Oh that," Marcus replied as he blushed.

"You are lucky," Titus hissed as he took a step towards Marcus, "That this is not the time or place to haul you in front of a military tribunal but rest assured than when this rebellion has been crushed, that Tribunal will take place. We cannot have officers disobeying orders. You know this."

"Yes Sir," Marcus muttered as he lowered his eyes.

"I will be appointing one of my officers to take command of the Second Batavians," Titus exclaimed, "It's not only your disciplinary record that bothers me. An auxiliary Cohort cannot have a non-citizen as its commanding officer, it's absurd. You will retain your former rank until your tribunal. Is that clear?"

Marcus was about to reply when he was interrupted by a woman's voice.

"Is that you Titus?" Claudia exclaimed as she came towards them, closely followed by her daughter.

The Tribune turned abruptly as he heard his name being mentioned. For a moment he looked confused. Then a broad smile appeared on his lips.

"Lady Claudia," he exclaimed, "This is a surprise, a most welcome surprise."

Marcus shook his head wearily in dismay as Lady Claudia briefly embraced the Tribune.

"But I am confused," Titus said grinning, "What are you doing here? Your husband is on the other side of the mountains."

"Yes he is," Claudia replied, glancing idly at Marcus, "The uprising caught us by surprise. It's a long story but the most important part is that I and my daughter are still alive."

"Indeed," Titus said with a curt nod. "Indeed, it is good news."

Claudia sighed and gave the Tribune a sweet smile. "I am alive because of the actions of that man over there," she said pointing at Marcus, "If it were not for him I and my daughter would be dead or worse, prisoners of these rebels. Gods forbid what they would have done too us."

"I see," Titus said awkwardly as he turned to glare at Marcus.

163

"He may have disobeyed his commanding officer," Claudia purred, "but I have been speaking to these Batavians and to a man they say that it is he who saved this fort and every living soul inside it. He has the respect and loyalty of his soldiers, Titus. If you demote him now, they will not like it." Lady Claudia reached out and gently touched Titus's arm. "And neither will I," she added raising her chin. "I owe him a debt, Titus."

Titus took a deep breath as he studied Marcus. Then he turned to look at Claudia and her daughter.

"I see," he muttered awkwardly, "Alright, if it pleases you lady Claudia, I shall allow him temporary command of his Cohort until this rebellion is settled."

"Thank you," Claudia purred as she gave Marcus a quick glance, before taking Titus's arm and leading him away towards the Principia building. "Come you must have had a long journey and I and my daughter are keen to head south at the earliest possible moment," she exclaimed.

"What an arrogant bastard," Lucius murmured as he caught Marcus's eye.

\*\*\*

It was evening when the slave found Marcus sitting around the camp fire with some of his exhausted men.

"The Lady Claudia requests that you come to her chamber at once," the slave said lowering his eyes to the ground.

Marcus looked up at the slave and then turned to stare into the flames before slowly getting to his feet with a deep sigh.

"What does she want," he muttered.

"She did not say," the slave replied.

The guards standing outside the door to the Principia were no longer Batavian but Roman Legionaries. They said nothing as Marcus, accompanied by the slave entered the building.

"I shall leave you here," the slave said with a little respectful bow. Marcus folded his arms across his chest as he was left alone inside the room.

"So what do you want," he snapped as he heard movement in the adjoining room.

For a moment there was no reply.

Then the door to the Prefect's private room's opened and Lady Claudia appeared in the doorway. She was clad in one of Cotta's old white toga's. As she made eye- contact with Marcus she slowly allowed the garment to slip to the ground revealing her stark naked body.

"The Tribune is going to provide me and my daughter with a mounted escort," she said staring at him intently, "We leave for Deva tomorrow at dawn, but before I go I want to repay you for what you did for me and my daughter. Once we are done here we shall be even and I shall owe you nothing. Do you like what you see Marcus?"

Unable to take his eyes off her Marcus stared at her fit, attractive body. The woman was beautiful but something held him back.

"I have a wife," he muttered. "I am loyal to her."

Claudia came towards him and ran her fingers slowly across his chest and as she circled around him she allowed him to get a whiff of her perfume.

"I shall not take no for an answer," she said sharply. "You are in no position to reject me. You will please me Marcus. I assure you that will not be disappointed."

Marcus looked up at the ceiling and groaned. All his life he had tried not to be like his father, Corbulo, and yet here he was, he had disobeyed his commanding officer, he had used violence and torture on prisoners and now he was about to be unfaithful to his wife. This was his father, he thought, this was what Corbulo had been like. This was exactly the man he did not want to be. As Lady Claudia's hot mouth closed around his penis he groaned again and closed his eyes. There was no point in fighting against Fortune. However hard he tried, he could not escape, slowly but surely he was turning out to be just like his father had once been.

## Chapter Nineteen - The Caledonian Bog Iron Ore Mine

The thick, green, pine tree forest that covered the slopes of the hill resounded to the noise of the wood-cutters, as they chopped away at the tree trunks with their axes. It was morning and Corbulo stooped and groaned as he heaved the tree trunk up onto the back of the wagon. His chin and cheeks were covered by a dirty beard and his hands were blackened with grime and he had a bruise around one eye. As he caught his breath, he glanced down at the heavy, iron slavers chain that was clasped around his ankle and which shackled him to his fellow prisoner.

"Eh", Corbulo muttered, glancing at the prisoner, but the man, a Briton ignored him.

"You there, get back to work," one of the guards yelled at Corbulo as he spurred his horse towards the wagon.

Silently Corbulo stooped and reached for the next tree trunk from the growing pile in the forest clearing. It had been ten days since he'd arrived at the Caledonian, bog iron-ore mine beside the lake and more than a month, since the attack in Camulodunum. He closed his eyes as he lifted another log onto the wagon. The memories haunted his sleep and weighed him down during the day. The last image of Efa and Dylis he had, was of Timion's men dragging the two women into the trees beside the road. That same night, he'd been bundled onto a galley at anchor along the Colne river and taken north. It had taken him two days to discover that Timion had sold him to a Caledonian slave merchant from the Orcades. The merchant had taken him to the far north, to his treeless and rocky island home, where he'd been sold to another Caledonian, who had brought him to this forsaken iron mine. Corbulo opened his eyes and grimly heaved another tree trunk onto the wagon. He had no idea of what had happened to his wife and daughter.

A Caledonian horn suddenly blasted away and the noise reverberated through the dense forest. Corbulo looked up. From amongst the trees, the first of the wood- cutters came shuffling into the forest clearing. The men, chained together in pairs dropped their axes into a pile and started to form a silent line, as the Caledonian guards went down the line counting the slaves. More armed guards appeared from amongst the trees. Some of them were holding dogs on leashes and the animals growled and barked at the slaves. Corbulo tried to ignore the dogs. Only yesterday he had seen the beasts maul and bite a man to death. In the forest clearing a prisoner was busy stirring a large, iron cauldron that hung suspended over a small fire. The food smelled of fish. Corbulo and his partner flung the final log into the wagon and turned to join the line of prisoners queuing for their meal. As he reached the cauldron, Corbulo held out his small wooden bowl and the prisoner dumped a helping of fish stew into it. There was no time to warm his hands beside the fire, for the prisoner to whom he was shackled was already yanking impatiently at the chain that bound them together.

Wearily Corbulo sat down in the grass and with his fingers he started to spoon the food into his mouth. All around him the prisoners were doing the same. No one spoke and the only noise was the growling of the dogs and the scrape of fingers on the wooden bowls. Corbulo looked around him. There had to be over a hundred men, most of them Britons, slaves taken in raids or local feuds, but amongst them too, were a few Romans.

"You two," one of the guard's shouted, pointing at Corbulo, "Take the wagon down to the shore and unload the wood. Then come back here for the next load."

Corbulo did not reply, as he quickly finished his food. He had lost another tooth on the sea voyage north and he was now down to just two teeth. As he licked the remainder of his food from his bowl his partner yanked bad-temperedly at the chain.

"Get up Roman," the slave hissed in a thick accent.

Silently Corbulo rose to his feet as his partner shuffled off towards the ox drawn wagon, upon which they had been piling the logs. Two Caledonians armed with spears were waiting for them.

"Move, move it," one of the guards growled as he gave Corbulo a push.

Corbulo clasped hold of the back of the wagon as the Briton did the same. He could smell the man's stinking clothes and his own were no different, but the smell had long ago stopped bothering him. There was just one thing on his mind. He had to get out of this desolate place. He had to find Efa and Dylis. They were alive and they needed his help.

A moment later the wagon started out down the forest path.

***

The long and narrow lake appeared through a gap in the trees, as the wagon trundled and swayed down the forest path. Beyond the lake the bleak rocky and barren mountains, some of them still covered in snow, vanished into the distance and to the west the grey, dull-looking lake widened until he could barely see the opposite shore. The heavy iron chain trailed behind him and now and then it yanked him backwards, as it got caught or snagged on a stone or rock. As it did, the guard striding on behind them would slap his spear into Corbulo's back, forcing him onwards down the path.

At last they emerged from the forest and onto the flattish, treeless land that led towards the water's edge. The land around the shore was an industrious hive of activity, people and noise. Dozens of small hearths, a yard high and enclosed with clay and brick, stood in rows and from the tops of the hearths, plumes of smoke were rising up into the sky. Slaves crouched beside the furnaces, operating the bellows that were blowing air into the bottom of the hearths. The wagon trundled slowly into the miners' camp and joined a line of men, who were carrying leather sacks, filled with wet, mud brown, iron ore on their shoulders. Corbulo glanced in the direction of the bog from whence the iron-ore was being taken. The men were taking the ore directly to their hearths, where it was being mixed with charcoal and heated to separate the iron from the slag. The ore miners were not prisoners but free men who operated their own, private hearths and made their profit from selling the resulting iron to the nearby blacksmiths, who crafted weapons and other iron objects.

As they approached the section of the camp where the wood was being turned into charcoal, Corbulo caught sight of the slaves chopping the tree trunks into small logs and passing them on to others, who were using the logs to build large conical piles. The wagon came to a creaking halt beside one of the conical, clay-covered mounds and silently Corbulo and his partner started unloading the fresh tree trunks onto a pile of old trunks. As he dropped a tree trunk onto the pile, Corbulo glanced sideways at one of the wood choppers. The Roman briefly raised his eyes and gave Corbulo a brief, grim nod. Corbulo straightened up and together with his partner he heaved the next tree trunk from the cart and onto the pile. The two guards were chatting together and not paying the prisoners any attention. Corbulo turned and glanced in the direction of the blacksmith huts from whence he could hear a dull metallic hammering.

"Where are we?" he whispered loudly and quickly in Latin.

The Roman prisoner did not look up as he split another log.

"This is the western coast," the man murmured in Latin, "who are you?"

"Twentieth Legion, my name is Corbulo."

"Lepidus, Ninth Legion. They caught me six months ago whilst I was out on patrol," the man murmured quietly.

"Tonight when they give us our meal, I will come and find you," Corbulo whispered. He was rudely interrupted by the Briton's

170

bad tempered cursing. Hastily Corbulo turned and lifted the next log from the wagon.

"No talking over there," one of the guards cried out.

***

The stars twinkled in the night sky as Corbulo shuffled into the line to receive his evening meal. The miners' camp was settling down to its evening routine and, interspersed between the hearths and conical mounds, dozens of small, camp fires crackled and spat sending showers of red sparks, shooting into the dark, cold night. The miners clustered around the fires eating their food and from somewhere in the darkness he could hear men singing. Corbulo looked down at the stew, that was dumped unceremoniously into his wooden bowl. It was the same fish stew he'd had earlier that day, and the day before and the day before that one. Irritably the Briton yanked on the iron chain and Corbulo was unceremoniously propelled forwards.

"No," Corbulo snarled as he drew his leg back, bringing the Briton to an abrupt halt. "Tonight we sit where I tell you."

Corbulo caught the Briton's eye and for a moment the two men stared at each other in silent fury and rage, each trying to force the other to look away. But there was something in Corbulo's eye that brooked no disagreement. Without a word, Corbulo turned and started towards one of the camp fires. Behind him the Briton hissed but followed, the heavy, metal chain clanking as it hit the ground.

The miners seemed to have little appetite to talk as they sat around their fires. The older ones looked exhausted, pale and in bad health. Their chains snaked from one ankle to another and here and there, an armed guard stood keeping watch. Corbulo lumbered past several fires until he spotted the Roman, who had called himself Lepidus. Dragging the chain behind him, he limped towards the man and sat down beside him and after a moment's hesitation, the Briton too, crashed to the ground, muttering curses under his breath. Corbulo stared at the fire and then glanced sideways at the Roman. The Legionary had drawn his legs up to his chin and was staring moodily into the flames.

"How do I get out of here?" Corbulo muttered in Latin.

Lepidus did not look up, nor did he move as he continued to stare at the flames.

"There is no escape from this place," he murmured at last in Latin. "This is it, my friend. This is the rest of your life; get used to it."

Corbulo blew the air from his mouth as he slowly shook his head.

"I need to get out of here," he whispered, "how do I do that?"

Lepidus sighed and stirred, glancing quickly at Corbulo. Then it was his turn to shake his head.

"You will never make it," he murmured. "This place may not have any walls but the guards have weapons; they have horses and they have dogs. They will hunt you down and kill you if you try and get away. You are not the first to try and escape but every man who runs, ends up being caught. No one gets away. Have you not seen what those dogs are capable of?" Lepidus's eyes widened in horror. "Did you not see them eat that man? Is that how you want to end up?"

"I need to get out of here," Corbulo hissed, "Tell me what you know, please."

Lepidus turned his eyes back to the fire and for a long moment he was silent. Then he looked up at the stars.

"Beyond the hills where you cut the wood," he muttered, "there is a lake. Its long, maybe seven or eight miles. Follow it and it will take you to the coast. From there you will need to cross the sea to the mainland. I think our northern most forts are maybe two or three days walk from there, but I can't be sure."

Corbulo looked down at the grass.

"How do you know this?" he murmured as in the firelight he caught sight of a guard, walking slowly towards them.

"That is the route by which I reached this place," Lepidus muttered, "They bound a cloth around my eyes to prevent me from seeing, but they didn't do a very good job." Lepidus glanced at Corbulo and a little smile appeared on his lips. "I kept my eyes open."

Corbulo grinned.

Thank you," he murmured. He paused as the firewood crackled and sent sparks shooting off into the darkness. "Come with me," Corbulo murmured at last.

But Lepidus shook his head in weary resignation.

"What are you two talking about?" the Briton sitting behind them, suddenly hissed.

Corbulo turned and glanced idly at the man. "None of your fucking business," he replied in the man's native language.

"Sure it is Roman," the Briton snapped with a contemptuous snort. "We share a chain; everything about you is my business. What are you talking about?"

Corbulo turned his attention back to the fire and for a moment he did not reply.

"We were talking about our women and children," he muttered.

The Briton grunted and tossed a pebble into the fire. "Forget about them," he said gruffly. "We are going to be here for a long time and the only relief you are going to get is with your hand Roman, so don't you dare look to me to help you."

Corbulo shook his head in disgust. Then as the silence lengthened he turned to the Briton.

"Do you have a woman? Is she not waiting for you to come back?"

The Briton muttered something to himself, as he tossed another pebble into the fire.

"I do," he replied, "but I shall not see her again." The prisoner turned to look at Corbulo, "and neither will you see yours. Sure your woman will wait, maybe a month, maybe two but in her heart she will know that you are not coming back. She will move on; she will find someone else; she will forget you."

Corbulo stared at the Briton.

"Efa and Dylis will not forget," he said slowly. "They need me; they are relying on me."

The Briton shook his head contemptuously.

"You are a fucking idiot if you think like that," he snorted. "You, Roman," he added pointing a finger at Corbulo, "will never see your woman or daughter again."

With a loud cry Corbulo smashed his fist into the man's face, sending him sprawling into the ground. Then Corbulo was on top of him pummelling the prisoner with blows.

"I will meet them again," Corbulo roared in Latin. "They are alive. They are still alive, damn you. By all the eternal gods, above and below, I will see them again in this world."

## Chapter Twenty - The Running Man

The wagon laden with fresh tree trunks trundled down the forest path in the direction of the miners' camp. It was the last load of the day and Corbulo shuffled on behind the cart, feeling the tiny, invisible wood splinters stinging his hands. Behind him the guard was humming a tune to himself. Corbulo glanced at his sullen and silent companion shuffling along at his side. The prisoner's face was covered in dark, angry bruises and he had not uttered a single word all day.

Corbulo looked away. He would have beaten the man to pulp if the others had not pulled him off. He lowered his eyes to the ground. There was just one thing that was keeping him going. One thing that was preventing him from giving up and throwing himself onto a guard's spear was that Efa and Dylis needed him. They were alive and they were counting on him. He was sure of it. He had to get back to them. As he stared at the ground, his lips parted in a murmured prayer.

"Immortal Jupiter, keep them alive, keep them safe, and I shall give you everything I have, everything without exception."

"Shut up Roman," the Briton hissed beside him. "Shut your fucking moaning."

***

Corbulo sat staring at the camp fire. It was night and around him most of the miners had crawled into their tiny and rudimentary straw and turf shacks to sleep. The fire was dying and the flames crackled and spat. Close by he could hear the Briton snoring in the shack that they shared. The living space was just big and high enough to allow the two of them to crawl inside and lie down. It stank of unwashed clothes, urine and sweat. Corbulo sighed as he turned to glance in the direction of the sea. A gentle, western breeze was blowing and he could smell the saltiness on the air. A miner had fallen asleep beside the fire and from the darkness he could hear one of the guards

175

coughing. The man had been coughing all evening. Corbulo sighed again and turned his attention back to the fire. Efa and Dylis would be alright he told himself. They would still be alive. They would be alright. He had to hold onto that, but the truth was that he no idea what had happened to them or where they could be. He closed his eyes as the thought brought on a wave of depression. No he could not give in to that. Grimly he opened his eyes. He did not fear death nor did he fear a life of slavery. But before he went to meet his ancestors, he needed to settle one last matter. He needed to make sure that Efa and Dylis were safe and provided for and as he pictured their faces, he felt himself seized by a fierce and stubborn determination. He was going to do this. He was going to find them. No man or beast was going to stop him.

"You Gods, if you are listening," he murmured to himself, "I could do with a little help here." Corbulo looked up at the dark, night sky. "You fuckers owe me," he hissed, "After everything I have given you, you damn well owe me."

Then he shook his head, sighed and turned to stare at the flames. He might not have been a model father or husband, but he had always paid close and expensive attention to the gods, the immortals who controlled a man's fate. As he stared wearily at the flames, he suddenly frowned. Abruptly he leaned forwards and took a closer look at the fire. Then slowly his eyes widened in excitement. Among the blackened stones and remnants of wood, an iron poker was sticking out of the fire. The metal rod was glowing red with heat. Corbulo stared at it in stunned silence. One of the guards must have forgotten to retrieve it when they had started the fire. Startled, he looked around him but he could see no one.

Quickly he inched towards the fire taking care not to make a sound. As he reached the limit of what the chain around his ankle would allow, he leaned forwards, stuck his hand into the flames and pulled the poker from the blackened earth. The hot iron burned his hand and a little yelp of pain escaped from his mouth. He moved backwards rapidly and dropped the poker onto the grass, with a painful grimace and for a long moment he stared at the glowing, metal rod. Then he shook his head as his heart began to thump away with growing excitement. Taking a deep breath he inched backwards until his fingers found the loose soil around the edge of his shack. Quickly he dug a hole in the soft soil and laid the poker at the bottom, before covering it up with earth.

"Fuck me," Corbulo whispered with large, startled eyes as he looked up at the dark heavens with renewed respect. "Thank you."

***

The familiar thud of the axe men at work in the forest, reverberated through the trees. Corbulo grimaced and groaned as he lifted another log up onto the wagon. It was afternoon. The skin of his hand where the poker had burned him was raw and blistered. The Briton working beside him glanced at him and as he noticed Corbulo's discomfort, a dark look of satisfaction appeared on his face. Corbulo ignored him as he stooped to lift up the next log. In the forest a tree tumbled and crashed to the ground. The noise was followed by that of another falling tree. Corbulo was just about to lift up the next log when the forest suddenly erupted in shouts and yells. He straightened up and turned to stare at the trees, as his companion and the two guards beside the wagon did the same. Amongst the trees the guards were shouting to each other. A moment later four guards led by a pack of barking and snarling hunting dogs came running passed them. Corbulo looked around in confusion.

"What's going on?" he muttered turning to the Briton.

His companion was staring at the trees where the guards and their dogs had disappeared. In the forest more shouts and yells rose up.

"Someone has made a run for it," the Briton replied with a shake of his head.

"Get back to work over there," one of the guards yelled as he caught Corbulo staring at the trees.

Reluctantly Corbulo stooped and heaved another log up into the wagon. The shouts and yells from the forest were more distant now as was the barking of the dogs. Then as he heaved another log up onto the cart, a high pitched scream erupted from amongst the trees.

"The dogs caught him, poor stupid bastard," the Briton muttered with a shrug as he heaved a log up onto the wagon.

From the forest the high pitched screams lasted for a few more seconds. Then abruptly the noise ceased.

"See what happens to men who try and escape," one of the guards yelled triumphantly at Corbulo and his companion, "You end up becoming a meal for the dogs. No one escapes from this place."

\*\*\*

Corbulo was tense and silent as he sat outside his tiny turf shack waiting for the others to fall asleep. It was drizzling and in the miners camp the usual fires had been lit. The night sky however was dark and there was no sign of the stars or the moon. As he watched the last of the miners crawl into their shacks, Corbulo's fingers started to claw and dig into the soft earth. The iron poker was still where he had buried it. Carefully he examined it with his fingers. The metal had cooled. He paused to glance around him, but the night was quiet and peaceful. Slowly he brought his leg up and thrust the poker into the tight space between his skin and the metal clasp of the slavers chain. He grunted as he felt the iron digging painfully into his flesh. Then slowly he began to work the poker up and down, trying to loosen and bend the clasp.

It was an hour later when with a little metallic crack, the clasp around his ankle snapped and he was free. Corbulo steadied his breathing and reached down and touched his ankle. It was covered in blood and it hurt like hell. Quickly he looked around him, but he could see no one in the faint light. He rose to his feet. The release from the heavy iron chain felt wonderful. He turned and paused for a moment, trying to get his bearings. Crouching, he crossed the empty space around the fire and knelt down beside the turf shack in which Lepidus was sleeping. From inside he could hear a man's steady breathing. Silently Corbulo placed the poker beside the sleeping Roman, before vanishing into the darkness.

The camp was quiet except for the occasional snoring and cough. Corbulo strode calmly past the array of hearths and turf shacks. There was no one about at this time of the night. The drizzle seemed to have driven the guards to seek shelter, for he could not see or hear them either. Then as he reached the edge of the miners' encampment he broke into a run. The sense of being free was intoxicating and he wanted to shout and scream. In the darkness he nearly collided with a tree. He slowed his pace as he vanished into the forest. The trees loomed up out of the darkness and he had difficulty keeping to a path. How long did he have before the guards discovered he had escaped? There was no way of knowing, but come dawn the pursuit would start for sure. All he could do was run and trust in his plan. As he stumbled on through the trees, the pain in his ankle grew worse and soon he was limping. On a ridge he paused to catch his breath and get his bearings. The drizzle soaked his face as he tried to recognise a feature in the darkness but it was difficult. He groaned in frustration as he wiped the rain from his face. Cross the hills and you will find a long and narrow lake, Lepidus had said. But where was it? Where was the fucking lake. He could see nothing in the darkness.

Grimly he plunged on into the forest thrusting his way past trees and up a steep slope. The tangled undergrowth grasped and scratched at his legs and tree stumps tried to trip him up and at one point he heard an owl hooting in the night. As he moved deeper into the forest, he struggled to fight off a growing panic. What if he was going round in endless circles? What if he was going in the wrong direction? He paused again and leaned against a tree as he tried to calm himself. If the ground was rising it meant that he was heading in the right direction. It had to. Forcing himself on, he started out again clambering up a steep rocky slope and as he reached the crest, he suddenly realised that the trees had gone. He must have reached the top of the hill. Wildly he looked around. Yes he was on the summit. Clenching his hand into a relieved fist he started off over the ridge and down the other side of the mountain. The terrain grew increasingly tricky and his pace slowed even more, as he was forced to negotiate great jagged stone boulders and deep narrow ravines. The pain in his ankle had become a dull ache. Then at last he was back below the tree line. The dark fir trees were dripping wet as he pushed past them. Suddenly he paused and turned to look back the way he had come. Had that been a horn? He strained to listen but all he could hear in the darkness was the steady patter of the rain. Then once more he was off limping down the slope as fast as he could.

"Where the fuck is it?" Corbulo muttered as he crashed through the trees. The minutes passed and still the dense forest went on. Corbulo was panting when he suddenly stumbled straight into the mountain stream. Startled, he cried out as his foot went into the ice cold water and he nearly lost his balance. Wildly he flung his arm out to steady himself against a rock. The stream however was not very large and it was shallow. Corbulo's eyes widened as he heard the water rushing and splashing over the rocks as it made its way down the mountain side. Of course! Without hesitation he started down the slope keeping close to the stream. The descent was strewn with boulders and rocks but as he finally emerged onto flatter land, he cried out in delight. In the distance, gleaming in the faint light, was a lake.

## Chapter Twenty One - The Hunters and the Hunted

The rain had ceased and the night sky was losing its darkness as Corbulo hobbled to the water's edge. In the early dawn he could see the lake. The placid and still water faded away southwards twisting away until it was out of sight. Corbulo paused at the water's edge as he struggled to catch his breath. How long had Lepidus said the lake was? Seven or eight miles. It didn't look very wide. He tried to steady his breathing, but it was no use. With a groan he was sick, spewing the contents of his last meal onto the moss covered rocks. For a moment he crouched, breathing heavily with his eyes closed. He was no longer the fit and healthy Legionary he had once been. He needed to pace himself and conserve his energy for when it would be most needed.

Stumbling over a rock he set off along the edge of the lake. The ground around the water's edge was flatter and easier to traverse and the growing light was making it easier to see the path ahead. On the opposite shore the dense, fir-tree forest came right up to the water's edge, extending half way up the steep mountain slopes. The mountains enclosed the lake in a tight grip; their rocky crests, treeless, barren and beautiful. As he hobbled on through the trees, Corbulo suddenly remembered the time in Caledonia when he and Marcus had fled for their lives from that fanatical woman. Oh, what he would give to have Marcus at his side right now.

It was dawn and across the mountains to the east the sun had emerged, bright and powerful as it started out on its eternal journey across the sky. Corbulo turned and glanced behind him along the shore of the lake. Had that been a horn? The guards must by now have discovered his escape. They and their dogs would be coming after him. There was no doubt about that. Breathing heavily, he came to a halt and turned to stare at the placid waters of the lake. How far had he come along the lakeside? Maybe two or three miles. On the shore a piece of wooden flotsam lay wedged in between two rocks. Corbulo stared at it. Then he turned again to look back the way he'd come. This was a good a place as any. With a groan he veered from his path and without hesitating he plunged straight into the lake. He gasped at the coldness of the water. Grimly he turned and yanked the piece of wooden flotsam from the rocks. As the wood floated free, Corbulo wrapped his left arm around the log and started pushing out into the lake. As his feet lost contact with the ground he cried out as panic began to seize him.

"No," he spluttered. "No."

Stubbornly he clung to the log and with his right arm he desperately clawed at the water. No, he was not going to drown in this place. The lake around him was still and there was no current. Grimly Corbulo pushed out further into the water as he headed for the opposite shore, half a mile away. He was no good in the water and he hated swimming, but it had to be done. He could out run men; he could fool them and hide from them but there was no escape and no hiding from tracker dogs, once they had his scent. The hounds would not give up; they would find him whatever he did and they would lead his pursuers straight to him. It was just a matter of time. No, the only thing he could do was try and delay the dogs for as long as possible and hope that in that time he found a means to get away from his pursuers.

As he struggled across the lake clinging to the piece of flotsam, he felt the welcome warmth of the sun on his head. He was nearing the opposite shore when he heard the horn echoing away across the lake. Startled, he twisted round to look at the shore he'd left behind. He was too far away to see any movement amongst the trees. For a moment all was silent. Then across the placid waters he heard the unmistakeable barking and baying of dogs. Corbulo's eyes widened. He had expected this, but the noise still sent a shiver of terror down his spine. Desperately he clawed at the water with renewed energy. The dogs would have found the spot where he'd entered the lake. It would confuse them momentarily, but once the dogs failed to reacquire his scent their handlers would soon realise that he'd crossed the lake. Grimly Corbulo let go of the wooden flotsam and staggered onto a small stony beach. His pursuers would now have to go back around the lake, a distance of five or six miles. He'd bought himself one or two hours but no more. Gasping and with water streaming from his soaked clothes, he stumbled into the forest. On the opposite shore he could still hear the barking.

"Move old man, move," he cursed as he hobbled through the trees, keeping the lake within sight. It was a race now. What had Lepidus told him? Follow the lake and it will take you south towards the coast. He had to reach the sea before his pursuers and their dogs. And then what? Corbulo shook his head. He was not going to think about that yet. He had to stay positive.

The pain in his ankle where the poker had cut into his flesh was a dull throb as Corbulo stumbled through the trees. He shivered in his wet clothes but a remorseless, primeval, instinct drove him onwards. He was not going to die here in this forsaken and beautiful place. It was not yet his time. Efa and Dylis needed him. They were waiting for him to rescue them. As he pictured their faces, a tear appeared in Corbulo's eye. He had been responsible for getting them into this mess. It was he who had insisted on taking them to Camulodunum. It was all his fault. Why was he always getting his family into trouble? What kind of man did that? Grimly he stumbled on through the forest.

"No, this is not how it is going to end," he cried at the trees.

Veering sharply from his path he plunged back into the lake. The water no longer felt cold as he waded out and started along the shore. A dozen paces further he turned and struggled back towards the shore. The move may help to confuse the dogs and buy him some more time. Stoically he hobbled on through the trees. Thoughts of hunger, coldness and tiredness seemed to fade as a primeval fear drove him onwards through the forest.

Corbulo groaned in surprise when he suddenly caught sight of the end of the lake. The ground beyond it was heavily forested and rose steeply towards a ridge. How far still to go? He hadn't a clue. Stubbornly he pushed on and, as he started up the steep slope, his pace slowed. He'd reached the barren, treeless crest when, from the forest beside the lake, he heard barking. Corbulo didn't pause or look behind him. The ridge was jagged and covered in great boulders and rocks.

"Come on," he muttered to himself.

As he hobbled past an exposed rock face, Corbulo caught sight of the forested valley beyond the ridge. A small white stream was running through it into the lake and in the distance two or three miles away he suddenly caught a glimpse of the sea. At the sight of the ocean he clenched his hand into a fist and cried out. Without pausing, he started down the side of the mountain towards the valley floor. As he stumbled down the mountain, he tore a piece off his tunic and flung it into the entrance to a dark cave. With a bit of luck it might fool the dogs into thinking he had taken shelter in the cave but the decoy would not delay them for long. He was panting when he finally reached the stream and splashed through the water. Behind him he could hear the barking of the dogs clearly now. His pursuers were closing the distance. They were maybe half an hour behind him.

Quickly Corbulo looked up at the sun. It was past noon and he was downwind from the dogs, which helped. Gods don't let the wind change direction, he thought as he crashed on through the trees. The valley was forested and here and there a giant boulder barred his way. Corbulo struggled on. He was starting to tire; he could sense his legs slowing. How far had he come since he'd escaped from the miners' camp? He had no idea, but the chase could not go on forever. Sooner or later the dogs were going to catch up with him and when they did, they were going to tear him to pieces. Desperately he looked around for something with which to defend himself, but there was nothing he could use. He was utterly defenceless.

Up ahead the trees started to thin out. Then at last the forest gave way to flat open meadows that funnelled gently down towards a stony beach. As he emerged from the trees Corbulo stared around him. The fjord that led out into the open sea was surrounded by steep, majestic and treeless mountains, some of which still had snow on their crests. Smoke was curling up from a solitary, round house that stood close to the shore of the sea loch. Corbulo peered at it. He could see no one about, but the inhabitants would not be far away; the smoke gave them away. Quickly he stooped and picked up a stone. It was all he had to defend himself. Then he was off limping across the open space towards the shore.

A cow stood alone in the meadows chewing on the sparse grass. It looked up as Corbulo rushed past. Corbulo ignored the beast. His eyes were on the round house and its thatched conical roof. Further up the valley the barking and baying of the dogs was drawing closer. As he reached a low earthen embankment, Corbulo paused and crouched, struggling to control his heaving chest. From the round house a woman emerged and started walking towards the cow. She was carrying an iron bowl. Corbulo watched her go. Then his eyes flicked back to the house. A man and a boy had appeared in the doorway. They seemed to be arguing and the man was pointing at something in the sea.

From the valley behind him a horn suddenly blasted away and the occupants of the house turned sharply to look in the direction from which it had come. Corbulo groaned with rising panic. The horn was close. He was out of time. His heart was thumping in his chest. What now? What could he do? He was trapped between the sea and his pursuers. Wildly he looked around him but there was nowhere to go. There was nowhere to hide. There was not even anywhere where he could make a final stand. His panic and desperation grew. It would be better to drown than to be torn to pieces by the dogs. Then from the forest, a few hundred paces away, a pack of dogs burst into view. The hounds came streaking straight towards him, barking and baying as they sensed that their prey was close. Behind them came the running figures of their handlers. The men were shouting to each other in excited voices. Corbulo yelped in pure terror. They were onto him.

Stiffly he rose to his feet and dashed over the embankment straight towards the stony beach and as he did so he went tumbling head over heels over a log that had lain unnoticed on the opposite side of the embankment. Corbulo cried out in shock. Then as he righted himself his eyes widened. The log was not some washed up piece of flotsam. It was a log boat complete with paddle. It had to belong to the family in the round house. Without hesitation he stooped and began to tug the log towards the water. There was no time to wallow in his good fortune or think about anything. The dogs were nearly upon him. With a surge of renewed energy, Corbulo roared as he staggered into the gentle surf. The dogs barking was terrifyingly close as he struggled out into the sea. Corbulo kept roaring as the energy flooded into his veins. He was not going to die here. It was not going to happen. With a supreme effort he gave the log boat a massive thrust through the water, as his head briefly submerged into the sea. He surfaced still roaring and flung himself onto the log as his momentum pushed him out to sea. Behind him he could hear men's cries and shouts. They were followed by a wild crashing splash as the dogs charged straight after him into the sea. Corbulo was half inside the hollowed out log as he turned. One of the dogs was swimming madly towards him with open jaws that revealed a line of razor sharp teeth. As it reached him Corbulo screamed and smashed the stone he was holding into the beasts snout.

"Fuck off," he roared as the dog disappeared under water.

## Chapter Twenty two - Alone

Corbulo drove the paddle into the water with steady strokes as the log boat swiftly cut through the gentle sway. The log was surprisingly agile and easy to steer. It was late in the afternoon and an hour had passed since he'd made his escape from the stony beach. Around him the sea was calm. The sea loch was behind him and he now found himself out in the middle of a wide estuary, several miles wide. In the distance he could see the grey outlines of hills that marked the far shore. He paused to catch his breath as a seagull was suddenly hanging above him. The creature's sharp eyes were examining him. Then lazily the bird drifted away screeching as it left. Corbulo glanced over his shoulder. There had been no sign of a pursuit since he'd managed to escape from the beach, but that didn't necessarily mean they were not coming for him. As he stared at the entrance to the sea loch he took a deep breath and allowed himself a loud relieved sigh. Oh how he hated dogs; how he hated swimming and how he hated running and yet here he was, being forced to confront them all. The gods were taking the piss. They were having a laugh at his expense.

Grimly Corbulo paddled further out into the sea. Well, let them have their laughs. Let them mock him and play with him. He couldn't give a shit. There was just one thing that mattered. Efa and Dylis.

"Yeah, fuck you," Corbulo cried raising his hand at the sky in a crude gesture.

The gods could not know or understand what he felt for his family for they were immortal and did not suffer loss, nor did they experience regret. To really live, to really experience life in all its glorious forms, a man had to be doomed to die.

As he paddled on he glanced down at the harpoon he'd found at the bottom of the hollowed out tree trunk. The spear point was tipped in iron. The people who'd owned the boat must have used it for fishing. He grunted as he turned his attention back to the land on the horizon. At least he now had a weapon with which to defend himself. Things were looking up.

*\*\*\**

It was early evening and darkness was setting in when the log boat finally slid onto a gravelly beach. Stiffly and awkwardly Corbulo clambered over the side of the tree trunk and with a splash he landed on his back in the shallow water. For a moment he just lay there staring up at the sky as he floated in the gentle surf. Then wearily he rolled over and staggered to his feet and turned to look at the boat that had saved his life. With a sigh he stooped and shoved the log out into the sea current. At least now no one would know where he had come ashore. Clutching the harpoon he turned away and started out along the rocky shore. What had Lepidus said? A three- day walk to the nearest Roman fort. He had no idea where the Roman forts were, but a good bet was that they were to the south.

Soon he had disappeared into a vast, thick forest that seemed to stretch for miles in every direction. The ground was uneven and the lichen-covered trees were old and interspersed with moss-covered rocks and sharp, muddy gullies. As the light faded he stubbornly plodded, on glancing up at the stars to find his direction and as he did so, he shook his head in bewilderment. He had never thought he would ever have to use the orientation skills that a twelve year old Petrus had once taught him on a long night outside Viroconium some three years ago. But tonight the skill was proving very useful. As he stumbled along through the trees, he thought again of Efa and Dylis. How was he going to find them? He had no idea where they were or what had happened to them? What had Timion done to them? He shook his head. It didn't matter, he was going to find them.

As the darkness became complete the stars faded from view and it started to rain. Quickly the drizzle turned into a torrent. To the west, the night sky lit up with jagged lightning forks, followed moments later by a deep rolling crack of thunder. Corbulo

188

hastened into the shallow shelter of a rock face and slid down to the ground with his back leaning against the rock. As he sat staring at the jagged forks of lightning in the night sky, he suddenly realised how incredibly exhausted and weak he was. The flight had taken everything out of him. His breathing came in ragged gasps and suddenly he sneezed. As he opened his eyes again he looked around. He had nothing to eat or drink. He took a deep breath and closed his eyes. It didn't matter. Tonight he would do without food and water. Tomorrow would bring new opportunities. Whatever he did, he had to keep his spirits up. If he allowed the enormity of the task ahead to depress him then he would be finished.

***

The solitary round house stood in a clearing surrounded by the thick, wild forest. Smoke was drifting upwards from the smoke-hole in the thatched roof. Corbulo crouched in the undergrowth, clutching his harpoon and peered at the three cows that stood tethered to a wooden post in the small meadow, behind the house. It was morning and he was starving. The cows had their heads to the ground and were munching on the lush grass. Corbulo's eyes turned hungrily towards the bucket of milk that had been left beside the animals. Was it a trap to get him to show himself? Carefully he examined the simple hut but there was no sign of its occupants. The forest around him was quiet. Uneasily he shifted his weight. On another occasion he would not have taken the risk, but today he had little choice. He had to eat. Hunger had become the new enemy and if he didn't eat soon his body was going to give up.

With a grunt he abruptly rose to his feet and bolted out of the undergrowth towards the cows. The animals did not look up as he snatched the bucket of milk and made off towards the trees. As he stumbled towards the forest, he braced himself for the inevitable shout and cry of alarm but as the seconds passed no cry came. Grimacing from the dull pain in his ankle, he staggered into the cover of the trees and came to a halt beside an old oak tree. There was no sign of a pursuit. Elated he lifted

189

the bucket of milk to his lips and poured the frothy milk straight down his throat. The milk was still warm and it had delicious clumps of cream in it and, as he gulped everything down, the liquid splashed across his face and beard, dribbled and ran down onto his clothes. Corbulo groaned as he felt his stomach filling up. At last he closed his mouth and eyes and emptied the remainder of the bucket over his head, revelling in the feel of the warm milk on his skin. Then he sneezed, wiped his nose and mouth on his sleeve, rose to his feet and giving the round house a final grateful glance he set off purposefully into the forest. The milk would sustain him for a while but if he were to retain his strength, what he really needed was meat.

The forest seemed to go on forever. Wearily Corbulo picked his way through the trees, now and then glancing up at the sun to check his position. The gods were making amends with him today, for last night's storm had been followed by clear blue skies. They must be impressed that he'd survived for so long, he thought sourly. At dawn he'd tried to hunt for food with his harpoon, but he'd lacked the strength and the forest animals were far too quick and alert for him. No, he would just have to keep going until he ran into a Roman fort or patrol or watch tower. They were out there and they couldn't be far away. Lucullus, who had succeeded Agricola as Governor of Britannia, might have ordered the retreat from Inchtuthil and the Roman outposts along the highland line, but Rome still retained a grip on the fertile lowlands, north of Luguvalium and the Stanegate road. The coast to coast system of forts, garrisons, watch towers, fort-lets, all connected by military roads had been built to control the local tribes and encourage them to turn away from their simple barbarian lifestyles, for this was Roman land now. Corbulo spat onto the ground and shook his head. But the Caledonians had rejected the civilised lifestyle offered to them by Rome. They had not taken up the seductive luxuries, the new technology, the new ideas that the Empire had brought into their midst. They had refused to follow the southern tribes of the island province, who had embraced Roman civilisation. No, up here in Caledonia and further south in Brigantia the local tribes had chosen to retain their old, wild and free way of life. It was a major problem. It was the reason why fifty five thousand Legionaries and auxiliaries were needed to hold down the north.

***

It was late in the afternoon when Corbulo heard the men's voices. Instantly he scampered from the forest path and into a tangle of thick bushes. The thorns dug painfully into his skin but he hardly felt the pain. Keeping himself as silent as possible he peered in the direction from which he'd heard the voices. A few moments later a man appeared on the path. He was tall and clad in furs and armed with an axe. A shield was slung over his shoulder. He was followed by another and then another man. Corbulo tried to control his breathing and his nose began to twitch. No, not now, he groaned inwardly as he desperately struggled to stop himself from sneezing. With a supreme effort he managed to control himself, as the band of men came striding passed him in a single file along the forest path. The Caledonians looked relaxed and were talking to each other and they were armed to the teeth. Corbulo watched them vanish around a bend in the path. Then he lowered his head and groaned. This was all that he needed. A Caledonian war band heading south on the same path he was following. He glanced up at the sky. The gods were back to their old tricks.

Corbulo crouched behind the tree on the natural earthen embankment as he watched the woman washing the clothes down below in the shallow stream. It was early evening and hunger had driven him towards her. The woman was singing quietly to herself as she soaked the pile of clothes in the water. She seemed oblivious to his presence in amongst the trees. Corbulo stroked his beard as he peered at her. The woman did not seem to have any food on her. Disappointed he was just about to rise and move off when from the corner of his eye he caught a sudden movement on the far side of the stream. From the trees a man appeared and came splashing through the brook towards the woman. Corbulo tensed as he caught sight of the brace of dead rabbits dangling from the man's belt. Meat. He licked his lips as he stared at the rabbits. He could already taste them. Down in the stream the woman looked up and noticed the newcomer and abruptly her singing stopped. As the man came towards her she rose unsteadily to her feet and Corbulo suddenly noticed the dark bruise across her cheek.

The man looked angry as he strode up to her and with a snarl that took Corbulo by complete surprise he slapped the girl hard across her face. The blow knocked her to the ground and she cried out in pain. Corbulo's eyes widened. The man was shouting something he couldn't understand. Then he hit her again. The woman screamed. She was crying now as she raised her hands to ward off the next blow. Warily Corbulo looked around him. The woman's screams were bound to attract other people. He should leave. This was none of his business but something kept him from rising to his feet. As he stared at the man beating up the woman, Corbulo felt a sudden shame. He had once been like that. He had once treated his woman in this way. Corbulo sighed. But he was no longer that man. He had tried to make amends. He had done what he could for his family. He had tried to make something of himself with the few years left to him. As the woman screamed again he looked up at the sky. He should go. This was none of his business. He was putting himself in danger.

"Fuck," he cursed as he rose and went sliding down the embankment.

When the man saw him coming it was already too late. With a fierce cry Corbulo smashed the stone against the man's face sending him flying backwards onto the ground. In an instant Corbulo was upon him and hitting him with the stone until he was no longer moving. As he threw away the blood stained rock Corbulo turned and raised his harpoon at the woman. The girl was lying in the mud beside the stream and staring at him in astonishment. Corbulo raised his finger to his mouth.

"Not a sound," he said in the Briton language.

The woman opened her mouth but made no noise. Her face was swelling up with a fresh set of bruises and her cheeks were stained with tears.

"I am not going to hurt you," Corbulo said quickly holding up his hand, "I just want those rabbits and I will be on my way."

The woman was staring at him in stunned, trembling and terrified silence. Quickly Corbulo reached down to the unconscious man and ripped the brace of dead rabbits from his belt. Then he slipped the man's hunting knife into his own belt. As he glanced up at the woman, he saw her watching his every move. Corbulo straightened up and lowered his harpoon.

"Do you want me to kill him for you?" he muttered.

The woman shook her head and stared at him with large tear filled eyes.

"Alright," Corbulo muttered, looking away awkwardly, "but I am not like that man, you understand. I am not like him anymore. I am somebody. I have made something of myself. I have. The gods know it."

And with that he was up the side of the embankment and heading into the trees. Just as he reached the cover of the forest a piercing female scream echoed through the wood. Corbulo felt the hair on his neck stand up. From down beside the stream the woman screamed again. Corbulo's eyes widened. She was calling for help. The bitch had given him away.

Corbulo started to run as he heard men's voices through the trees. The woman screamed again. As he stumbled on through the forest the men's voices started to come closer and closer. They were shouting to each other. A sudden rustle and movement amongst the bushes to his right startled Corbulo and he veered sharply to the left.

"He went that way," a voice cried out terrifyingly close by.

"I see him, I see him," another voice yelled.

Behind him Corbulo heard the noise of someone crashing through the undergrowth. Wildly he changed course and plunged on through the forest. How many men were after him? It was impossible to tell but there were at least three. He could hear them shouting to each other. Too many to fight at once. His chest was heaving and a stitch was starting to develop in his side. With growing panic he raced on through the trees as the noise of his pursuers drew steadily closer.

Corbulo burst from the trees and into a sloping clearing, covered with moss and colourful flowers that ended in a jagged and solid rock face. From the corner of his eye he noticed a dark hole in the rocks. A cave, it was a cave mouth. Instinctively he changed direction and with the last of his energy he made straight for the cave. As he fled into the dark cool cave, four men came storming out of the forest and into the clearing. There was no time to see whether they had spotted him. Panting with exertion Corbulo halted and spread his arms out wide as he started to fumble his way deeper and deeper into the cavern. The air inside was cool but the cave stank and the walls were damp and moist. Up ahead he could see nothing but pitch blackness. Painfully his knee struck a rock and Corbulo bit back a strangled cry.

"Did you see him?" a voice outside the cave cried.

"No," someone shouted.

"He's gone into the cave," another voice shouted.

"I'm not so sure," the first voice cried.

"Go on, get in there, the bastard can't be far," one of the men shouted.

Corbulo steadied himself as he felt the cave start to narrow. In the pitch blackness he inched forwards until his hand touched solid rock. He'd reached the end of the system. Breathing heavily he crouched and started to feel his way around but everywhere he placed his hands he felt solid rock. Grimly he raised his spear and turned to face the cave entrance. He was trapped. They had cornered him. At the cave entrance he suddenly sensed movement. Then he heard a man's heavy laboured breathing. It was coming straight towards him.

"Are you in here you bastard?" a voice muttered close by in the darkness.

Corbulo held his breath as he tensed ready to lunge forwards. The man was close. A few more steps and he would be upon him.

In the darkness the man seemed to pause and for a long moment the cave was completely silent. Then he heard the man backing away towards the entrance.

"He's not in here, nothing but bat shit, I am coming out," the man shouted to his comrades.

Corbulo slowly exhaled as the noise of the men outside the cave faded. For a long time however he did not move as he stood peering into the darkness. Then as he felt his legs start to cramp up he finally lowered himself to the ground. Relieved he closed his eyes and groaned. The relief was short lived as his shoulder touched something that moved in the darkness. Startled Corbulo turned and peered at the object that lay propped up beside him but in the darkness it was impossible to see what it was. Carefully he lowered his spear to the ground and stretched out his second hand and in the darkness his fingers found the object and started to feel their way over it. Abruptly Corbulo froze in shock as he realised what he was leaning against. It was a human skull and skeleton.

***

195

The little fire flickered and crackled as Corbulo sat beside it slicing the rabbit meat into pieces that were small enough for him to swallow whole. The dancing, fire-light cast strange shadows and shapes onto the rock of the cave and the smoke made him cough. Outside the cave, the dark, night sky was lit up by a multitude of stars. Hungrily Corbulo opened his mouth and dropped a piece of meat into it. The two teeth he had left were not much use to him when it came to chewing. As he swallowed the meat, he cast a glance at the skeleton that lay propped up against the far wall. The man must have been here for a very long time, for his bones were bleached white and his clothes had almost completely rotted away. As he finished the first rabbit and started on the second, he felt some of his strength start to return. Tomorrow he would raid a farm and steal a chicken and maybe some eggs. Gods what would he give for the taste of an egg he thought, as he dropped another piece of meat into his mouth.

As he finished the last of the rabbit he glanced warily at the skeleton. The empty and sightless eye sockets of the skeleton stared straight back at him. With a sigh he took the animal's small dark livers, which he'd reserved for last and held them up over the small cooking fire.

"Immortal gods, hear me," he muttered, closing his eyes, "and accept this offering. I cannot give you much and yet I have a great favour to ask of you. Show me how I can find my wife and daughter. Guide me to them, immortals. Show me what I must do for I seek your blessing and help; I beg you, please."

And with that Corbulo opened his eyes and dropped the livers into the fire.

\*\*\*

It was growing dark on the following day, when Corbulo heard the howl of a wolf. He paused in mid-stride and turned to look in the direction from which the noise had come. Throughout the day, as he had trudged southwards, he had not seen another living soul. The dense forest had started to give way to open fields and sometimes in the distance, across the gently rolling hills, he had spotted small isolated settlements. They had however been too large and populous for him to approach without fear of being spotted. He frowned as he heard an answering howl. What was this? A pack of wolves. Up ahead through the trees, he could just about see a large open meadow and a small wood beyond it. He glanced up at the sky. Maybe it was time he found a place to rest up and spend the night. The howl came again and this time it seemed closer. Uneasily Corbulo started walking again.

Soon the growing darkness and a night mist started to limit his view. He plodded on across the open field, glancing wearily at the swirling eerie mist that began to envelope him in a thin, moist cloak. Suddenly he blinked. Something had moved in the mist. Something that was fast. He was sure of it. Warily he lowered his spear in the direction in which he'd seen the movement, but the night remained quiet. Then from close by he heard a growl, a low ominous hungry sounding growl.

"Oh fuck," Corbulo gasped as something flashed passed him and disappeared into the swirling mist and gloom.

He was being hunted. He was being hunted by a pack of wolves. Corbulo started to run as he struggled to contain his rising panic. Around him the night mist suddenly seemed filled with moving shapes, the thud of running paws and hungry growls and yelps. As he raced across the field a shape loomed up out of the mist and launched itself at him. With a cry of terror Corbulo whirled round and brought his spear up just in time. The wolf, a great, grey beast, swerved aside and vanished into the darkness. There was no time to see where the wolf had gone for the first attack was swiftly followed by another as a black wolf came hurtling out of the mist straight at him.

"Get out of here," Corbulo roared as he frantically jabbed his spear at the beast. The black wolf too, swerved away from the weapon and as it did Corbulo cried out in fright as from all around him, amongst the darkness and mist, he heard the wolves excited yelping, whooping and growling as they milled around him. There had to be a whole pack of them and they seemed to be starving.

Terrified he turned and started to run. He was horribly vulnerable out here in the open. How could he have been so careless? The wolves were starving or else they would have never have left the cover of the remote forest. Desperately he stared around him for a means of escape, but in the mist and growing darkness he could see very little. Corbulo whirled round as he sensed movement close by. A shape streaked passed in the thick mist. Stumbling backwards he crashed straight into a pine tree and the collision knocked the spear from his hand. Instantly a growling shape came lunging out of the darkness. Corbulo yelled in fright as he twisted away and struggled to his feet. He could not see his harpoon in the gloom. Instinctively he grasped hold of a tree branch and frantically pulled himself up as he started to climb the tree. It was not a moment too soon, as another wolf came leaping towards him from out of the mist. Panic stricken, Corbulo kicked at the beast striking him on his snout. The wolf vanished into the darkness without making a noise. With desperate energy Corbulo forced himself up the tree, ignoring the needles and sharp branches that tried to push him back down to the ground and which dug painfully into his skin and flesh. As he paused to look down he saw that the wolves had converged on the tree and were milling about around the base, growling and snapping at him with their large jaws as they looked up with hungry, excited eyes.

"Go on, find someone else to eat," Corbulo roared as he shifted his weight to a more comfortable position on the tree branch. "You are not going to have me, so why don't you fuck off."

***

Corbulo was woken by the snorting of a horse. Rapidly he blinked as his eyes grew accustomed to the morning light. He was still perched high up on the branch in the tree, his legs

198

dangling into space. As he looked down his eyes widened in alarm. The wolves had gone and instead several men on horseback were gathered around the tree and were staring up at him. The men were clad in iron helmets and chain mail armour and they were holding spears and oval shields. The riders were laughing.

"Looks like someone or something chased him up there," one of the soldier's was saying in Latin.

"Reminds me of the time the Prefect's cat got stuck up that tree. What trouble that was. Who do you think he is?" another of the horsemen quipped.

The riders of the mounted patrol sniggered as they stared up at him.

Corbulo leaned forwards and peered down at the cavalrymen from his perch high up in the branches of the tree.

"Yeah take the piss, have a laugh, but know this," he roared in Latin, "You are talking to a veteran of the Twentieth, who stood in the line facing the barbarian queen, you ignorant cock suckers."

## Chapter Twenty Three - Payback

Corbulo sat on the pavement with his back leaning against a wall as he held up his hand like a beggar. On the paving stones at his feet stood a small wooden bowl containing a few copper coins. He was clad in a ragged cloak with a hood, which he'd drawn over his head so that his face was not visible. It was morning and the city street was busy and crowded with pedestrians going about their business. Corbulo could smell the stink of stale urine and rotting garbage coming from the alley beside him. As an ox drawn wagon trundled passed him, he called out for charity but the traders sitting on the wagon did not even seem to notice him. Corbulo however did not mind. From under his hood his eyes remained firmly fixed on the door of the house across the street. During the two days he'd sat in this spot, pretending to be a beggar, he'd been spat on, solicited by some shady characters and told to get a job. He'd endured it all in stoical silence, for none of it mattered.

Nineteen days had passed since the auxiliary, cavalry patrol had rescued him from the tree and his encounter with the pack of wolves. The soldiers had taken him to their fort at Loudoun and from there he'd hitched a ride southwards with various Roman supply and relief columns, until he reached Eburacum from whence he'd taken the road to Camulodunum. The journey had been hard for he'd lacked money and food, but an unceasing restlessness and growing determination had driven him onwards. He could not afford to waste time. Efa and Dylis needed him. They were alive and he was going to find them and the gods were going to help him. To survive he'd begged for money from passing merchants and he'd stolen food from farms and villages and he'd kept heading south towards Camulodunum, as fast as his feet could carry him.

From under his hood Corbulo stared grimly at the door across the street. For two days now he'd been watching that door, observing the people who came and went. The temptation to get up and kick that door down was strong but so far he'd resisted the desire. Timion, the salt merchant was the only man who knew what had happened to Efa and Dylis. Timion was the key. He could not afford to squander his only lead. If he lost Timion, he would also lose the only chance he had of finding his wife and daughter. No, he needed to be cautious and patient.

A girl clutching a man's hand stooped and dropped a copper coin into his wooden bowl and Corbulo gave her a little nod of gratitude. From across the street the door suddenly opened and two women emerged. They were clad in expensive looking clothes and they seemed happy and excited as, arm in arm they strode off down the street in the direction of the temple of Claudius. Corbulo watched them go until they had vanished into the throng of pedestrians. Then slowly he shifted his gaze back to the door. Today was a public holiday and if he was right, the two women were off to see the Matralia celebrations, the festival of women. It was just a guess, but it meant that there were just two occupants inside the house right now. Grimly Corbulo raised his hand to his chin and carefully stroked his beard. Timion and his slave were alone at last. Four people had been too many, but two he could handle. He'd seen them all enter the house late last night and he was sure they had not come out since then. Nor had he seen any of Timion's men. Could there be another door he didn't know about? Could there be another occupant he was unaware of? It was unlikely but he couldn't be sure. Would Efa and Dylis be inside that building? Corbulo closed his eyes as he made his decision. It was time to find out.

Stiffly he rose to his feet and picked up the copper coins from the wooden bowl. Then slowly he crossed the busy street and as he did so, his hand slipped into the folds of his worn and dirty brown cloak. No one paid him any attention as he stepped into the small stone vestibule of the two story house, with its small stone statue of Emperor Domitian. Quickly he knocked on the wooden door. It had been only two months or so since he had stood here in this very spot, waiting to give Timion a message, but it felt more like a lifetime. As he waited Corbulo glanced tensely over his shoulder at the people in the street.

With a creaking noise the door was opened by the slave. The man gasped in shock as the sharp point of a gladius was suddenly hovering at his throat. Swiftly Corbulo drove the slave back into the hall way and closed the door behind him using his foot.

"Not a word," Corbulo muttered as he drew back his hood. "Where is your master? Where is Timion?"

The slave was staring in horror at the sword point hovering over his throat. He swallowed nervously.

"My master is upstairs in his study," the slave stammered. Then as he looked up at Corbulo his eyes widened with sudden recognition. "I know you," the slave spluttered, "You came here..."

Without a word Corbulo drove his sword straight into the man's throat. The slave gurgled and made a feeble attempt to claw at his throat as he collapsed sending a torrent of blood shooting and pouring onto his tunic and the fine mosaic stones. Corbulo placed a foot on the man's chest as he wrenched his sword free. For a long moment, he stood looking down at the slave as the man tried to speak, croaking and drowning in his own blood. Then at last the slave's head lolled to one side and he lay still in a growing pool of blood.

"Who is it Julius?" a man's voice called out from somewhere deeper inside the house. Corbulo said nothing as he stepped over the body and started out across the atrium. A small water cistern stood at the centre of the large room and in it colourful fish were swimming about. Corbulo paused and looked around him. A number of small bedrooms led off from the atrium but he could see no one inside them. The house looked empty apart from the voice upstairs.

"Julius, who was that at the door?" a man's irritated voice cried out.

Corbulo looked up. The voice had come from the upper floor. In the corner of the atrium beside the door leading to a small kitchen, a stone flight of stairs led up to the second floor of the house. Swiftly he crossed the atrium and started to climb the stairs. He had reached the top when a figure appeared on the landing. Timion was naked from the waist upwards and he was unarmed. Corbulo lunged forwards and as Timion saw him coming his eyes bulged in shock and confusion.

"No. It can't be," the salt merchant cried out as he staggered backwards into a large room, "You came back, you were not supposed to come back."

Holding his sword up before him Corbulo grimly drove Timion backwards against the wall and as he did so Corbulo's face darkened.

"Your man downstairs is dead," he snapped, "and if you try to shout for help I will kill you too."

Timion raised his hands.

"I won't be a problem," he stammered. "If its money that you want, take it. No hard feelings Corbulo, I was just doing what you would have done. It's just business, right? You understand. Just business."

Corbulo snatched a quick glance around the room, but apart from an unmade bed and a wooden desk and chair they were alone.

"Where are they?" he hissed fixing his eyes on the salt merchant. "What did you do with my wife and daughter?"

Timion swallowed nervously and glanced down at the sword point hovering at his throat.

"There is no need for this," he said weakly, "I have money, lots of money, I can compensate you for your loss."

"Where are they?" Corbulo roared.

"Alright, alright," Timion stammered as a little colour crept into his cheeks. "I don't know where they are. That's the truth. I swear it. I sold them both in the slave market to a man whom claimed to be from Londinium. They were alive when the deal was done. I swear it."

Corbulo was breathing heavily as he stared at Timion, but the salt merchant seemed to be telling the truth.

"Who bought them?" Corbulo growled. "Tell me the name of the man who bought them. I want a name," snapped Corbulo as he pressed the steel tip of his sword into Timion's throat.

"He never gave me his name," Timion whined, "I swear it. I don't know his name. All he said was that he'd come from Londinium and that he was here on behalf of a banker called Falco."

Corbulo relaxed the pressure on Timion's throat.

"Falco," he muttered trying to hide his surprise.

"Yes, yes," Timion nodded eagerly, "That's the name he gave me."

For a long moment the room remained silent as Corbulo considered what had been said.

"You are a piece of shit aren't you? I want you to say it," Corbulo snapped as he turned his eyes towards Timion.

"I am a piece of shit," Timion said swallowing awkwardly.

"What happened to Fergus? He was with me when you attacked us. Is he still alive?" Corbulo said in a challenging voice.

Timion nodded as he looked down at the blade pressing into his throat.

"He lives," Timion muttered sourly.

"Did you make him sell his land to you?"

Timion looked up at Corbulo and a little of his old defiance seemed to return.

"Fergus signed the contract on his own free will. The land is legally mine now and there is nothing that you can do about it," Timion replied lifting his chin.

"Yeah, fuck you," Corbulo snapped angrily, "I know Fergus. He would never have willingly sold his land. You are a lying bastard."

"Think what you like," Timion sneered, "But I have his mark on the contract and that is all that matters in the eyes of the law."

For a moment Corbulo was silent. Then he nodded. "Maybe you are right," he said, "So now you are going to write a letter declaring this land sale contract null and void. You are going to do this right now if you want to save your own and the lives of those two pretty ladies who left this house this morning."

Timion was staring at Corbulo with barely concealed rage.

"I will do no such thing," he hissed.

"Yes you will," Corbulo retorted, "For I will kill you all and forge your signature if you don't. Either way you are going to write and sign that fucking letter."

And with that Corbulo grasped Timion's shoulder and shoved him towards the desk upon which lay an assortment of scrolls and wooden writing tablets.

"Write the fucking letter," Corbulo roared.

Sullenly Timion sat down on the chair and reached for an iron tipped stylus and a wooden   writing tablet.

"You are an arsehole," Timion hissed, "But if I do this you must promise to let me and my family go free. Those are my conditions."

"Agreed," Corbulo snapped.

As Timeon started to write he shook his head. "This is the most outrageous thing I have ever been forced to do," he sneered.

Corbulo said nothing as he pressed his sword point into the man's neck.

"Do you know what the difference is between you and me," Timion said as he scratched the neatly written words onto the thin wood, "I would never have exposed my family to danger like you did. What kind of man brings his wife and daughter along to such a business meeting as you had in mind?"

As Timion finished scratching his signature into the wooden tablet, Corbulo snatched the letter from his hands and read it carefully and quickly.

"So I have kept my end of the bargain. Now get the fuck out of my house," Timion snarled as he turned to look at Corbulo.

Corbulo slid the wooden tablet into his cloak pocket. Then as he turned to look at Timion his hand started to tremble with sudden emotion, as the iron discipline with which he'd kept his emotions in check started to break down.

"What," he said quietly, "so that you can go back to harassing Fergus? You are a fool to have believed me."

Corbulo stared at Timion as a growing and uncontrollable fury took hold. " I am a dying man," he cried in an unsteady voice, "I was looking forward to spending a last summer with my family and my son, but instead of that I find myself searching for my wife and daughter amongst the arseholes and scum of the Empire. I did not want to do this. But you have robbed me of my precious time with my family. You fucking bastard. Did you really expect that I was going to let you live after what you did to us?"

And with that he thrust his sword deep into Timion's throat.

## Chapter Twenty Four - It is time that our demons left us

The round house fell silent as Corbulo finished telling them the tale of his escape from Caledonia. It was night and Fergus's whole extended family had crowded into the thatched house, taking up all the available space. In the centre of the hut beside the beautiful iron fire-dogs, the fire crackled and spat, sending sparks flickering and dying into the darkness. The air was smoky and humid as two children moved carefully through the crowd, refilling the many eager cups of mead. Then at last Fergus stirred. The old man looked tired and for a long moment he said nothing. In his hands he was holding Timion's letter that Corbulo had given him.

"Our enemy is dead," Fergus said choosing his words slowly and carefully, "and for that we should all be grateful. The gods have listened to our prayers. They gave us Corbulo. Now our land shall remain ours because of our loyalty to our ancestors and our determination and through this piece of wood here in my hands."

Fergus held up his hand for silence as he turned to look at Corbulo sitting across from him.

"But others will come, they will try and evict us from our land. We must not let this happen, for here, in our small settlement, we shall remember our ancient freedoms and the kings of old, even when a new world is being constructed around us. Our future does not lie in rebellion against Rome. No, those days have passed. But we shall honour our ancestors by not forgetting them. We shall keep their memories alive. If we can do this, Rome will never conquer us."

The crowd of men and women around the fire remained silent.

"Will you stay with us Corbulo?" Fergus called out. "We could do with a man like you around here. You have always been a member of our family."

Corbulo looked down at the sandy floor of the hut.

"Thank you," he muttered, "but I must find my wife and daughter."

Fergus looked away.

"Mine was a selfish request," the old man said as a sad smile appeared on his lips. For a moment Fergus seemed to be mulling something over in his mind.

"I have often wondered what my daughter saw in you Corbulo," Fergus said at last. "And now I think I know what it is. I hope Alene, my daughter is watching you sitting here amongst us as a true friend. I will ask her spirit to find its peace, like I have. It is time that our demons left us."

A tear trickled slowly down Corbulo's cheek as he drew a sharp breath. For a moment he could not speak.

"Many years ago when I left Rome and set out to find Marcus I asked my son to forgive me. Now I ask for it from you all," he gasped as another tear rolled down his cheek.

"It is done," Fergus replied gravely, "It is never too late for a man to find his soul and ask for forgiveness. I shall pray to the gods that you find your wife and daughter, Corbulo and when the time comes for you to pass into the next world you will meet my daughter again and you will explain yourself to her."

Corbulo nodded solemnly.

"I will," he replied.

## Chapter Twenty Five - The Slave Trade

It was evening when Corbulo trudged past the scaffolding and building work on the new Forum and entered Londinium's old Forum. The centre of the bustling capital of Britannia was deserted except for a few farmers and traders packing up their stalls and merchandise after a long day. The fading scent of perfume mingled with that of garlic, incense, bacon and wood smoke. Corbulo looked worn out as he ignored the lingering glance of an old temple whore and strode straight towards the office where Falco had his banking head quarters. Corbulo's grim looking face was covered in dust and streaked with sweat. At least Efa and Dylis were together he thought and for that he was grateful. If they'd been split up it would have made matters far worse. The gods had rewarded his sacrifice in the cave. But how was it possible that his own bank had been involved in buying Efa and Dylis? What could Falco possibly have wanted with his wife and daughter? Did the banker not know who they were? The questions had gnawed at him on the depressing journey from Camulodunum. They had haunted his dreams, until he had been unable to sleep but now at last he was going to find out.

The banking offices along the edge of the Forum looked closed and locked up. As he approached Falco's office, Corbulo suddenly launched himself at the door. With a crack of splintering wood his momentum sent him crashing through the doorway and into the office beyond. Falco was sitting at his desk. The banker yelped in shock and fright as the violent intrusion sent him tumbling backwards from his chair. In his panic he sent a scroll he'd been reading, flying into the air. Corbulo staggered to his feet oblivious to the searing pain in his shoulder. One of Falco's guards was staring at him in complete, stunned surprise. The other guard however was quicker and was already reaching for his knife.

"Falco, you little shit," Corbulo bellowed, "What have you done with my wife and daughter?"

The security guard came at him with a hoarse cry but Corbulo caught the man's knife arm in his left hand and smashed his right elbow into the guard's face. The man screamed in pain as the blow broke his nose and sent him staggering backwards against the wall with blood pouring down his face.

"Get up you miserable arse," Corbulo roared. "Get up and answer the fucking question."

From behind the desk Falco's head suddenly popped up as he stared at Corbulo with shocked eyes.

"Is that you Corbulo?" he stammered.

The second security guard seemed to have recovered from his surprise and was coming at Corbulo with a knife in his hand.

"It's alright," Falco yelled loudly, "It's the boss. Stand down, both of you."

The security guard hesitated as he stared warily at Corbulo before glancing questioningly at Falco who was still cowering behind his desk.

"Put the knife away," Falco scolded as he quickly rose to his feet and dusted down his clothes, "It's the boss, you fool, can't you see."

Slowly the guard lowered his hand and took a step backwards, his face sullen and angry. Against the wall, his comrade was groaning as in vain he clutched his bleeding nose.

"Corbulo," Falco exclaimed as he recovered from his shock and mustered a fake smile, whilst raising both arms in greeting, "What an unexpected pleasure, I was not expecting to see you here but it doesn't matter. What can I do for you?"

Corbulo slowly shifted his gaze away from the guards and to the banker standing behind his desk.

"Do you take me for a fool," he hissed, "I will ask you one more time. What did you do with my wife and daughter?"

Falco frowned and shook his head in confusion.

"I am not sure I understand you," he stammered, "I haven't seen your family. Why would I? Are they not with you?"

Corbulo looked Falco straight in the eye and for a long moment he searched the banker's face for clues to whether he was lying. Then with an irritable growl Corbulo wiped the sweat from his forehead. Falco was undoubtedly an immoral person who would shaft his clients to fill his own pocket if he could get away with it and who didn't give a shit about his clients fortunes, but on this occasion he seemed to be genuinely telling the truth.

"I lost them," Corbulo said tersely, "They were taken from me and sold as slaves. The man who sold them said that it was one of your agents who bought them. He gave me your name."

"Oh fuck," Falco muttered running his hand over his head and for a moment he looked genuinely concerned.

"Where and when did this happen?" Falco asked as he sat down at his desk and began to sort through the mess of scrolls and leather money bags.

"In Camulodunum, about two months ago," Corbulo replied.

Falco frowned and closed his eyes as he tried to remember something. The banking office fell silent as Falco scratched feverishly at his forehead. Then he snapped his fingers and opened his eyes with a triumphant look.

"Yes I remember now," he exclaimed, "Yes. We received the order just after you left us. The client wished to invest in slaves. They were very specific. Female, preferably young, healthy, obedient and most importantly they had to be able to speak and write fluent Latin as well as the local language."

212

"So it was not you who bought them?" Corbulo snapped.

Falco shook his head. "Argentarii Agricola and Britannia did buy them. After I received the clients instructions I ordered my agents to start looking for suitable investments. My man must have picked up your wife and daughter in the slave market at Camulodunum. He had orders to bring them back to Londinium and hand them directly to the client. I never saw them Corbulo, I swear it. I never saw the slaves."

"Who was the client?" Corbulo growled.

Falco blew the air from his mouth and shrugged. "They never gave me a name and I did not meet them," he sighed. "He or she was not one of our regular accounts but they must be very wealthy for they paid over the market rate and upfront. The profit margin was very good. One of the best deals we've had all year."

Falco looked up at Corbulo and a little colour shot into his cheeks. "Sorry," he muttered.

"What else?" Corbulo said impatiently. "What would such a client want with my wife and daughter?"

"Well," Falco sighed," it's unlikely that they are destined for manual labour, prostitution is a possibility but I think their real value lies with their language skills. Female slaves who can speak good Latin and also the local language are fairly rare. Whoever this client is, they were very specific about what they wanted. If I had to guess then I would say that your wife and daughter are destined to be teachers or translators in the household of some large country villa. It's not a bad position. There are far worse fates that befall slaves."

Corbulo turned to look down at the floor as he considered Falco's words. If Falco was right then his insistence that Efa and Dylis both learn to speak and write proper Latin was what had kept them together.

"Who actually placed the order?" he growled.

Awkwardly Falco raised his hand to scratch his forehead. "You are not going to like this Corbulo," he said clearing his throat, "But the man who came here and placed the order and paid us was that arsehole, Romulus, the banker you fired on your last visit. He told me he was working for a new client but he refused to give me their name. That's all I know, I swear it on Juno's naked tit."

"Romulus," Corbulo hissed as his face darkened. For a long moment he was silent. Then he looked up at Falco. "Where I can find him?"

"I am not sure," Falco replied blushing, "but you could try the Banging Bed. It's a brothel along the Walbrook. I know Romulus frequents the place."

Corbulo nodded and turned towards the door.

"One more thing boss," Falco called out, "I don't know if its relevant but two men came calling here last week. They were looking for you."

"What kind of men?" Corbulo said as he paused in the doorway.

"Not sure," Falco frowned, "Not really the type who would come to a bank looking for a loan. They didn't tell me their names but they said they would be back. They were very eager to speak with you."

# Chapter Twenty Six – The Game of Cat and Mouse

It was growing dark as Corbulo strode out of the Forum. The last of the market traders had packed up their belongings and had gone home, leaving the empty courtyard strewn with the usual rubbish of discarded vegetables, squashed tomatoes, broken shoes, lost hairpins and a solitary pile of dirty clothes. At the entrance gate the Legionary on fire watch examined Corbulo with an idle and bored expression. Corbulo did not seem to notice the soldier. He looked worried as he turned westwards, his boots crunching over the gravel. The lead that he had on the whereabouts of Efa and Dylis was as fragile and slender as ever but now that Romulus was involved it had got a whole lot worse. He knew Romulus. The man was a shallow, self obsessed prick, who had a grudge against him. Had Romulus met Efa and Dylis? Corbulo stroked his beard nervously. He couldn't remember. But if he had then there was the possibility that Romulus would have recognized them and abused them all in order to take revenge for being sacked. Corbulo closed his eyes and groaned in dismay. Outside the Forum the levelled and cleared ground was strewn with piles of building materials, stone, sand and wood and the wooden scaffolding that abutted the unfinished walls of the new Forum was deserted. A solitary security guard, armed with a spear was wandering around the site whistling a tune.

As he headed westwards along the street, Corbulo glanced up in the direction of the tavern where he'd used to drink for over twenty years when he'd still been in the army. The Cum Mula Peperit sign above the tavern had been taken down and the place was boarded up. Corbulo shook his head in disbelief. What had happened to the woman who'd run the place? Had she died or moved away? With a dispirited look he lowered his head and kept on walking. The world he'd known was slowly disappearing bit by bit.

The Wallbrook was peaceful and silent as Corbulo finally reached it. The stream was narrow at this point, no more than a few yards wide and a simple wooden bridge made of a few wooden planks, spanned the water. Corbulo paused and turned to glance at the narrow and densely packed, strip houses that lined both sides of the street. The road was quiet and there were few people about and smoke was rising from several smoke-holes in the thatched roofs of the nearby homes. To the west the sun was slowly vanishing below the horizon. He sniffed and glanced at the stream. The Wallbrook divided Londinium into two and, as it flowed southwards into the Thames its width increased making it navigable by boat. Corbulo grunted. It was used both as a sewer and as a source of fresh water and, judging from the smell, he was in the section of the river that was used as the sewer. He glanced again at the dying sun. He would have to hurry if he wanted to catch Romulus before nightfall.

The Banging Bed backed up against the revetted bank of the Wallbrook and a gaily coloured sign above the door was the only clue to the nature of the establishment. From the cover of an alley, Corbulo studied the simple, two-storey strip house across the street. Would Romulus be coming here tonight? It seemed unlikely but he had no other leads and so he would wait. That was all he could do. He peered at the brothel. The place had to be new for he had never heard of it before and in his time, he'd known all the brothels in Londinium. There was no security outside but no doubt the brothel owner would have some men inside who were capable of sorting out trouble. The owner would be a fool if he hadn't. Thoughtfully Corbulo stroked his beard. He needed to be cautious. If Romulus spotted him would he fight or would he flee? There was no real way of knowing, but he would have to be prepared for both eventualities.

As he leaned back against the alley wall, Corbulo could smell the raw sewage from the Wallbrook filling his nostrils. Idly he watched as along the revetted embankment a woman upended a leather bag of rubbish into the river, sending a shower of broken shoes, dinner plates, shards of pottery and old wooden writing tablets into the dirty brown water. Further along the gloomy, litter-strewn alley a drunk was sitting on the ground

216

singing to himself and slurring his words as he did. Corbulo folded his arms across his chest and settled down to wait, resisting the temptation to cross the street. Asking the brothel owner if they had seen Romulus could alert Romulus to his presence and he didn't have enough money or the desire to pay for a whore. No, he would wait. He would wait until the prick finally showed up.

It was just before dawn when in the alley Corbulo was woken by a high pitched female scream. Instantly he staggered to his feet and his hand went for his sword hanging from his belt. The alley however was deserted and he could see no one apart from the drunk who had not moved. Quickly he turned to stare at the door to the brothel across the street. A few pedestrians were going about their business but no one seemed concerned about the scream. Corbulo rubbed his hand over his face as he felt his stomach growl with hunger. Then he froze. The door to the brothel had opened and a man stumbled out into the street. He was closely followed by a huge bear of a man with an angry-looking face, who gave him a shove.

"What the fuck do you think you are doing?" the larger man cried. "House rules say no hitting the girls. Can't you read? Get out of here, you swine."

Corbulo felt his body tense. Standing no more than six paces away from him was Romulus. The ex-banker was pressing his hand painfully against his jaw as if someone had hit him.

"I paid, right," he retorted, "So I get what I want, that's fair. Anyway you are not the only place in town so go fuck yourself."

"Don't let me see you back here again," the bouncer cried as he strode back into the brothel and slammed the door shut behind him.

Corbulo was half way across the street when Romulus turned and saw him coming. The ex-banker's eyes lit up in shock as with a fierce cry Corbulo, with his head down, came barrelling into him like a wild boar, sending both of them tumbling and rolling onto the street.

"You," Romulus cried out in a confused shocked voice, "You bastard."

Corbulo grunted painfully as he hit the gravel and the wind was knocked out of him. Wildly he tried to grasp Romulus's belt but the younger man was fitter and more agile and with desperate energy he kicked himself free from Corbulo's grip and rolled away. As Corbulo staggered to his feet Romulus was already sprinting away down the street. Gasping for breath Corbulo set off in pursuit. The street was almost deserted and the few passers-by stopped to stare at the scene, but Romulus was fast and Corbulo had difficulty keeping him in sight. Desperately he ran on feeling a stitch developing in his side. If he lost Romulus he would lose the only chance he had to finding Efa and Dylis. It must not happen. Ahead, Romulus suddenly darted into an alley. Grimly Corbulo followed him in. The alley was strewn with rubbish and it stank of stale urine and rotting food. He was just in time to see Romulus disappear around a corner into another alley. Panting, Corbulo shot around the corner and tripped over a pile of garbage sending him tumbling to the ground. As he righted himself and looked up the alley Romulus had vanished.

Corbulo closed his eyes and lowered his head as a wave of crushing despair and hopelessness engulfed him. He had failed. Romulus had gotten away. Now the task of finding Efa and Dylis had grown even harder. He groaned and rose wearily to his feet. He was bleeding from a cut to his arm and the stitch in his side was not subsiding. Dispirited he turned and made his way back to the main street. There was nothing for it but to go back to Falco and ask him for some money so that he could eat and get a wash in the bathhouse. After that he would start the search for Romulus afresh.

As he strode back along the main street towards the Forum the sun rose and from somewhere in the city a bell rang out. Corbulo had just passed the entrance to an alley in between two

218

rows of thatched strip houses when from the corner of his eye he suddenly noticed movement.

"Die," Romulus screamed as he came running out of the alley and launched himself at Corbulo. Corbulo cried out in shock as he saw the knife in Romulus's hand. Instinctively he raised his arm and caught the man's knife hand before he could plunge the weapon into his body. Romulus's momentum sent them both tumbling to the ground in a ball of kicking legs and twisting arms as passers-by scattered in panic. Corbulo hit the ground hard as he lashed out at his attacker. Romulus was yelling, his mouth spraying Corbulo with spit as he tried to force the knife into his throat. Grimly Corbulo held on, groaning and straining as the two of them grappled and rolled across the street. Around them the passers-by were shouting. But Romulus was younger and stronger and as the vicious murderous struggle continued Corbulo felt himself starting to lose the fight. Gritting his teeth he tried to force the knife away from his throat but Romulus was not having any of it. His attacker's eyes were bloodshot and his face contorted with hatred, as with vicious determination he forced the knife down towards Corbulo's exposed flesh.

Suddenly from out of nowhere a fist came smashing into Romulus's jaw and the powerful blow sent the banker flying backwards and his knife clattering away into the street. Corbulo gasped, his chest heaving with exertion, as the pressure on his body instantly vanished. A man calmly strode past him and without saying a word kicked Romulus in the head with such force that the blow knocked him out. Corbulo struggled to his feet and stared at the unconscious body lying in the road. Then furiously he lashed out at the limp body striking it with his boot. As he heard movement behind him he turned and came face to face with a second, younger looking man. Corbulo's eyes bulged in surprise as he instantly recognized him. The man had a hunting bow and quiver full of arrows slung over his shoulder.

"We have been looking for you, Corbulo," the older man who had knocked Romulus unconscious said speaking in the Briton language with a thick accent,   "You are not easy to find."

Corbulo stared at the two men in stunned silence and for the first time in his life he seemed happy to see Efa's father and brother. The two Britons however looked unimpressed.

"Aidan, Logan," Corbulo exclaimed unable to contain his surprise, "By the Gods. What are you doing here?"

"We heard you had lost Efa and Dylis; we heard they went missing," Corbulo's father in law snapped-unhappily, "so we have come to help you get them back."

## Chapter Twenty Seven – The Little Shit

"So this is the little shit who knows where my daughter and granddaughter are?" Aidan growled as the three of them stood over the unconscious body in the alley into which they had dragged Romulus.

"Yes, that's him," Corbulo nodded as he looked down at Romulus.

The shock and surprise of seeing Efa's father and brother had finally started to subside but the close brush with death had rattled Corbulo. His left hand would not stop trembling and he'd already been sick twice, puking up blood-laced vomit. As they had stood waiting for Romulus to come round, Aidan had told him about the message he'd received from Fergus telling him of his daughter's and granddaughter's fate. On hearing the news they had immediately set out for Camulodunum only to arrive to find that Fergus had no idea of what had happened to Efa or Dylis. So they had come to Londinium in the hope that Falco, the banker would know the whereabouts of Corbulo and his family and it had been just pure luck that they had come across Corbulo during his street fight with Romulus.

"How could you lose them?" Aidan rounded on Corbulo angrily. "How could you put them in such danger? This is your fault. This whole mess is your doing."

Corbulo stood his ground. He and his father in law had never gotten on, for Aidan had never approved of his daughter's marriage to Corbulo. But recently their frosty relations had been showing signs of improvement.

"Well I am not the only one who lost them," Corbulo retorted, "I seem to remember that Caledonian raiders snatched them both from under your very nose."

"That was different," Aidan snapped, "I was not there to protect them."

"Yes well, it was me who brought them back from Caledonia," Corbulo sniffed. "That was after you lost them the first time," he added.

For a moment both Aidan and Corbulo refused to look at each other as they tried to maintain their dignity and pride.

"This is taking too long. I will wake him up," Logan said as he stooped and slapped Romulus hard across the cheek with the back of his hand.

On the ground Romulus groaned and slowly his eyes flickered open. Aidan leaned forwards and hauled the ex-banker roughly up onto his feet.

"So now we are going to talk," Aidan snarled as he brought his face close to that of Romulus, "Tell me what you did with my daughter and granddaughter and I may let you keep your cock and balls."

Romulus looked pale as his eyes darted nervously from Aidan to Logan and then to Corbulo.

"I don't know what you are talking about?" he groaned.

"Efa and Dylis, the two female slaves whom Falco the banker bought for your client and whom were handed over to you. Do you remember now or shall I thump you again to remind you?"

Romulus blinked rapidly and looked down at the ground.

"I handed them over to my client like I was instructed to do. It was a just a job," he stammered, "I didn't know who they were. I didn't know they were yours Corbulo. I swear it. I was just following my instructions. It was just business."

"Just like now when you tried to kill me," Corbulo cried angrily. "Was that just business too? Who was the client? Who bought Efa and Dylis? Where are they?"

Romulus blushed and tried to avoid Corbulo's fierce gaze.

"Tell me the name of your client," Corbulo hissed seizing Romulus by the throat, "Tell us now who he is and where we can find him or by the gods, I will squeeze the very life out of you?"

"Not a man," Romulus gasped as he struggled to breath, "My client is a woman," he wheezed. "Her name is Emogene, a Caledonian woman from the free north beyond our borders. She doesn't live here. She keeps moving around. She and her husband are just down here in the south on business. Her husband works in the slave trade but it was she who placed the order."

Corbulo let go of Romulus's neck and frowned. Emogene, he had heard this name before. Where had he heard this name before? Then slowly he opened his mouth in silent consternation. Emogene, of course, the young woman who had spent some time locked up with Marcus in the dungeon, in the village in northern Caledonia where the sea washed the amber ashore. It had been Emogene who had chased him and Marcus halfway across the Caledonian mountains. Corbulo took a step backwards in shock and groaned. How was this possible? What evil fortune had conjured up this set of events and coincidences? Corbulo looked up at the sky. The gods were laughing at him. His sacrifice had not been enough. Once more they were playing tricks, demanding more from him.

"Are you sure that was the name she gave you?" he muttered, turning to look at Romulus.

The ex-banker nodded.

"I know this woman," Corbulo said gravely as he looked up at Aidan and Logan. "She, Marcus and I share some history together. It's a long story."

"So where can we find her?"    Aidan growled.

"Like I said," Romulus replied coughing, "She and her husband move around a lot but I think they have a place at Aquae Sulis. She mentioned the town a few times. I think that is where her husband is running his business from, but they could have already returned to the north."

"You wouldn't be lying to us now would you?" Logan said sharply.

Romulus hastily shook his head. "It's the truth, I swear it," he stammered.

"What did Emogene want with my wife and daughter?" Corbulo asked.

Romulus shrugged, "She didn't tell me," he muttered, "I don't think she was looking for specific individuals. My instructions were to find at least four, female slaves who were able to speak both Latin and our own language. She didn't seem to care where they came from. So I delivered four such slaves to her. I really don't know what she wanted them for. I swear it."

"You are doing a lot of swearing today," Logan growled with a mistrustful look. "So what are we going to do with him?" he said glancing at Corbulo and his father.

"We can't just let him go," Aidan snapped, "The moment he's out of sight he will go straight back to his client and warn her about us. Let's put the little shit out of his misery, right here and right now in this alley."

"I would not go back to her," Romulus said in an alarmed tone and his eyes darted from one of his captors to the next. "I really wouldn't."

Aidan pulled a knife from his belt and placed it against Romulus's neck.

"No," Corbulo said suddenly holding up his hand, "I agree with you Aidan, we cannot let him go, the risk is too high but he was after all just following instructions. He didn't know the identity of the slaves and it wasn't his idea. He may be a little shit but he doesn't deserve to die for that. No, I have a better idea."

"What's that then?" Logan asked.

Corbulo turned to look in the direction of the Thames. "I still have some contacts in the shipping business," he replied slowly. "The long-distance, ocean-going-boats are always short of crew members. We'll hand him over to a captain I know. My friend will see to it that this shit here gets to go on a very long voyage to Alexandria in Egypt. He will be gone for months if indeed he ever comes back." Corbulo turned to stare at Romulus. "Maybe a bit of hard, honest labour will turn him into a proper man."

"Where is Alexandria?" Logan muttered with a puzzled look.

"It doesn't matter, it's a fucking long way away from here," Corbulo growled.

## Chapter Twenty Eight - The Waters of Aquae Sulis

The three horsemen reigned in their horses as the small town of Aquae Sulis hove into view amongst the pleasant rolling hills. There was no city wall and the fields and woods that surrounded the small, wealthy Roman settlement were green and lush whilst the Avon river looked cool and welcoming as it lazily wound its way westwards. Amongst the numerous, outlying farms and villa's, flocks of sheep and herds of cattle were grazing peacefully. From his vantage point Corbulo stared down at the town. Once long ago he had considered retiring to this settlement, for it was one of the most sought after retirement places in the whole province. He bit his lip. If he had only come here then maybe Alene, his first wife would still be alive. Wearily he wiped the sweat from his forehead. Aquae Sulis was known for its large, natural, hot-springs that bubbled up from deep within the earth. He'd been here when they had still been building the temple to Minerva over the source of the hot springs. Now he could clearly see the magnificent stone and red-roofed temple as it rose above the cluster of simple, thatched roofs of houses that surrounded it. The Britons had built a shrine to their god Sulis on this spot and when the Roman settlers had first arrived they had identified Sulis as the goddess Minerva. Corbulo gave Aidan a little contemptuous smile. If the Britons wanted to call Minerva by a different name that was fine with him. Worship of the goddess was binding the Britons and Romans into an ever closer religious union for the similarities between Sulis and Minerva were so close that the one was undistinguishable from the other.

"We will need to split up," Corbulo said, glancing up at the sun to gauge the time. "Logan," he said turning to Efa's brother, "You will go to the market. See what information you can find on Emogene and her husband, but don't be too open about it. Stick to the story that we agreed upon. We don't want them hearing that someone is making inquiries about them. That would not be good. Got it?"

Logan nodded with a serious    look on his face.

"Aidan, you will go to the taverns and whore houses," Corbulo said stiffly, "and do the same. Someone, somewhere must know something about these people."

"And you?" Aidan growled in his thick Briton accent, "Where are you going? What are you going to do?"

"I am going to the baths and the temple," Corbulo replied.

"Maybe I should go to the baths and you should go to the taverns and whorehouses," Aidan snapped turning to Corbulo with a challenging look. "You seem to know everything there is to know about whores."

"Look," Corbulo growled in an annoyed voice, "The baths are the place where it's most likely that you will come across proper Roman citizens like myself. You do not speak Latin and you stink. You probably have never been in a bath complex in your life. You will stand out like a fox in a hen house. No, it's obvious that I am far better suited to go to the baths than you are."

"Oh will you two stop bickering," Logan cried out with sudden irritation. "You are driving me mad. I have had to listen to this for the whole fucking journey from Londinium. Just stop it. We are here to find Efa and Dylis, remember? What would they say if they could hear you two now?"

Darkly Aidan muttered something to himself as Corbulo shook his head and looked away in disgust.

"We will do as Corbulo suggests." Logan snapped, as he urged his horse down the grassy slope towards the distant town. "Stick to our story," he cried, "and we will all meet back at the temple entrance at sunset."

\*\*\*

The stone statue of Tiberius Claudius Togidubnus, the town's founder, stood proudly at the entrance to Aquae Sulis along the road from Londinium. Idly Corbulo glanced at it as he led his horse on foot and into town. Togidubnus had been an important provincial figure, a client king of the Atrebates and an ally of Rome. It was he who had ordered the construction of the temple, around which the town had grown up, as a monument to the Roman conquest of Britannia. Amongst the Legionaries his name however, had become a bit of a joke as Togidubnus had tried to embellish the importance he himself had played in this conquest.

Up ahead through a gap in the tightly-packed strip houses and workshops that jostled for space along the lucrative main street, Corbulo caught sight of the wooden bridge across the Avon and beyond it, on the opposite bank, he knew was the small Roman fort that protected the town. Emogene and her husband had chosen a good location for a slave-trading business, he thought. The baths and the temple may be the star attractions of the town but the other reason for the town's wealth were the four important roads, that converged on the settlement, bringing trade, people and supplies to feed the local markets and turning Aquae Sulis into a major, strategic road junction and river crossing.

As Corbulo made his way down the main street of Aquae Sulis he could see that the town was filled with pilgrims who had come to worship at the great temple. The pilgrims, clad in dust and mud splattered travelling cloaks, stood around in large groups chatting to each other in loud voices and buying souvenirs and trinkets from the dozens of street stalls that lined the road. The smell of incense was heavy in the air and from the doorway of a strip house, two women were eying the newcomers with bemused looks. Further up the street, the sound of hammering was coming from a blacksmith's forge and smoke was rising from a potter's kiln. Corbulo pulled the hood of his Palla over his head as he approached the entrance to the temple and baths complex. Emogene may or may not be able to recognise him, but he could not afford the risk of a chance encounter.

The majestic stone bath and temple complex was surrounded by a warren of wooden workshops and maintenance huts. Muddy, unpaved alleys and lanes criss-crossed the dull, featureless industrial terrain and here and there gravelly, open spaces seemed to be waiting to be exploited and built upon. Workmen were repairing the paved street leading up to the temple entrance and from behind one of the maintenance sheds, he could see stone masons chiselling away. Corbulo strode across to the stables and gave the reins of his horse to a slave, who in return, handed him a small stone with a number written on it. Then he turned and joined the queue to enter the temple and bath complex.

As he waited in the queue Corbulo glanced up at the temple and the massive stone statue of Sulis Minerva that dominated the gateway. The stone walls of the complex were high and a squad of armed men stood guarding the entrance, watching the visitors with stern suspicious faces. When it was his turn, he handed a slave a couple of copper coins and received a small pewter vessel in return. Then he was through the gate and into the temple courtyard. The red tiled roof and colonnaded temple rose above him, more than three storeys high. In the courtyard a crowd of pilgrims had gathered around a central altar, upon which a man was sacrificing a rabbit to the goddess. Corbulo glanced at the pilgrims and the visitors shuffling into the building. There were no women to be seen anywhere and he sighed. How could he have forgotten? He should have checked. He had entered the temple during the time reserved for male visitors. The women would have their own assigned time to visit the baths.

Unperturbed he climbed the stone steps and entered the temple. Inside the heat from the hot springs instantly struck him as he walked up to the side of the rectangular pool of dark green water. Above him the vaulted roof blocked out the sun light. The green steamy waters were still and he could not see the bottom of the bath. Around him the visitors and pilgrims were silent as they knelt down beside the revered waters, bent over in prayer and contemplation. As Corbulo looked on, a man tossed a coin into the silent, steamy waters and beside him another man muttered a softly spoken, curse and threw a small pewter sheet into the green waters. Corbulo watched the curse tablet slowly vanish from view. The man was calling on the goddess to curse his enemies. He turned to look around at the pilgrims. Where to start? Nearly all the visitors looked like they were from out of town, travellers, soldiers and government officials, locals and Romans. Slowly he turned away from the steamy waters and headed down the corridor that led to the baths. This was where all the pilgrims went after they had paid their respects to the goddess.

In the changing rooms Corbulo stripped naked and handed his clothes, belt, shoes and sword to a slave boy whilst retaining the small leather bag of coins. The temple may be a highly respected place but inside the baths, stealing and prostitution was rife and he could not afford to have his remaining money stolen. Clutching the small leather bag in his fist, he entered the warm room. A group of middle-aged men were sitting together in one of the rectangular baths. They were laughing and seemed to be a high spirits. Corbulo slipped into the water beside them and nodded a polite greeting.

"Say gentlemen," he exclaimed in Latin with a friendly smile, "I wonder if you can help me. I am looking to buy some slaves for my employer. They say Aquae Sulis has a fine market. Any tips on which trader I should try?"

The conversation amongst his bath companions came to an abrupt stop as they turned to look at him.

"Slaves, you say? No Sir, you have come to the wrong town," one of the bathers chuckled. "There are no slave merchants in Aquae Sulis." His companions grinned good-naturedly and ignoring Corbulo they turned back to their conversation. Corbulo sighed and looked away. Somehow he could not quite believe that.

He had just left the hot room and was entering the cold plunge pool when a voice spoke behind him. Turning round he saw a Briton with a white towel around his waist. The man looked around thirty and his chin was covered in a black beard and his pale blue eyes contained an intelligent gleam. He was studying Corbulo warily. Corbulo frowned as he stared at the man's chest and shoulders which were covered in a multitude of coloured tattoos.

"Are you the one inquiring about buying slaves?" the Briton asked speaking in his native language with a thick accent.

"I am," Corbulo replied.

"Aquae Sulis is not known for its slave markets," the Briton retorted. "Everyone knows this. If you want to buy slaves you would be better off in Londinium or Camulodunum." The man frowned as he grew suspicious. "Who are you?"

"My name is Clodius," Corbulo said smoothly, "And I am here at my employers behest. My employer's name is Quintus of Hibernia. He owns land on the isle of Vectis. Maybe you have heard of him? Fat bastard and reputed to be a follower of Christus? He sent me here to purchase slaves. That's why I am here."

"What kind of slaves?" the Briton said sharply.

"Oh," Corbulo replied, feigning a casual attitude. "Let's see. He wants four men for farm labour and two women for household duties. Yes that's the lot." Corbulo grinned disarmingly as he looked at the stranger. "So are you a slave merchant, perhaps?"

The Briton did not reply, as he carefully examined Corbulo.

"Maybe," the tattooed man muttered, "But I am just passing through town. My business is in Isca. I am heading there tomorrow and I have nothing to sell. If you want my advice then head for Londinium. The northern rebellion will be bringing a glut of new slaves to the market."

And with a curt little farewell nod the Briton abruptly turned away and headed back into the hot room.

Corbulo watched him go. The man's tattoos extended to his back and Corbulo emitted a little contemptuous grunt. The tattoos were the only honest thing about the man for everything else he'd said had been lies. As the stranger disappeared Corbulo turned and poked his toe into the cold plunge pool.

"Who was that?" he asked turning to the two bathers who already occupied the pool.

"He's from the free north," one of the men replied, "He's a Caledonian. Can't you tell from the tattoos?" The bather turned to mutter something to his companion who smiled. "Be careful with these northerners, Roman," the man in the pool continued as he looked up at Corbulo. "They are easy to anger and insult. That one has an especially short temper."

"Don't I know it," Corbulo murmured sourly.

*\*\**

Corbulo was hanging around the Garum fish-sauce stand outside the entrance to the temple, when the Caledonian with the tattoos reappeared, clad this time in a black woollen tunic. As Corbulo pretended to study the fish sauce, he saw three burly- looking men with knives hanging from their belts, join the Caledonian. The four men swiftly set off up the street and as they did so, Corbulo left the food stand and began to follow them at a discreet distance. Soon the Caledonian and his companions had left the town and Corbulo found himself creeping through the trees, trying to keep them in view. The tomb stones of the dead lined the road and in the fields, the slaves and farm workers were gathering their equipment together after a hard day's work.

The four men seemed in a hurry and Corbulo had difficulty keeping up. As the trees ended and the road cut across an empty meadow, he paused and crouched in the long grass and peered at the four figures. Could the Caledonian be Emogene's husband? It was possible. He certainly seemed to be involved in the slave trade. It deserved further investigation. As the men vanished from view, Corbulo rose cautiously to his feet and started out across the field. There had been no time to alert Aidan and Logan. He was on his own.

Up ahead, the road descended into a steep wooded valley and in the late afternoon sun Corbulo caught sight of the Avon. The river looked peaceful as the water glinted and sparkled, reflecting the sunlight. A column of smoke was rising from somewhere in the forest. Corbulo crouched in the field and stroked his shaved chin thoughtfully as he caught sight of the Caledonian and his three companions. As he watched them striding down the hill, the men suddenly veered from the road and disappeared into the forest. They seemed to be heading in the direction of the column of smoke.

The pine trees stood close together and under their canopies it was darker than out in the fields. Corbulo slunk through the undergrowth. The smell of wood smoke was strong now. His right hand rested on the pommel of his sword. Had the Caledonian realised that he was being followed? Was he even now waiting to ambush him here amongst the trees? Corbulo paused to listen, but he could hear nothing except the cheerful singing of the birds and the rustle of a small animal amongst the bushes. Slowly he started forwards again. As he edged through the trees, ahead of him the forest seemed to thin out and through the tangled green branches he caught sight of a large thatched house, with several out buildings. He crouched beside a tree and peered at the building. Several horses stood tethered outside a barn and he could hear men's voices shouting to each other in a foreign language he couldn't understand. Smoke was rising from a hole in the roof of the main house and he could smell the scent of roasting meat.

Corbulo took a deep breath and tried to steady his nerves as he felt his heart thumping away. What was this place? The buildings were too crude and local to be the retirement villa of a wealthy Roman and if it was a farm it did not look like any he had seen before. Where were the farm animals, the ploughs, the huts of chickens, the pig enclosures and the actual grazing or planting fields? As he stared at the building, Corbulo frowned. There was something odd about this place. It was as if the house had no right to be here in this setting.

He stiffened as he suddenly heard the bark of a dog. From around one of the thatched out-houses, a large group of fifteen or so men appeared. They were talking in boisterous voices and in a language Corbulo could not understand. As he stared at them, he noticed that they were armed to the teeth. The men had been hunting and were dragging the carcass of a mature deer along with them. Corbulo's eyes widened in alarm as he caught sight of the three dogs padding along beside the men. Fucking dogs. If they caught his scent he would have to leg it.

But the dogs seemed content to follow their masters and as the group approached the house, a man suddenly appeared in the doorway to the main building and shouted at them to be silent. Corbulo slowly exhaled. The man in the doorway was the tattooed Caledonian he'd met in the baths. The hunters fell silent as they trooped inside in a single file and, as the last one vanished into the house the door slammed shut behind them. Corbulo, hardly daring to move, turned to study the buildings. Time passed and he began to feel his legs cramping up. He was about to rise and get a closer look at the house, when a second group of twenty or so men emerged from the forest and headed straight towards the house. Corbulo groaned in fright as he forced himself to remain still. The men were young and all of them without exception looked fit and confident. Like the first group, they too were armed to the teeth with spears, swords, slings and bows. What was this? A puzzled and confused look appeared on Corbulo's face as he stared at the newcomers. What were some forty, heavily-armed men doing here in this strange place? The men certainly were not farmers, nor were they slaves. Corbulo's eyes narrowed suspiciously as he suddenly realised who they were. The men were not hunters. They looked like warriors, trained fighting men. But what were they doing here in a settlement popular with retired Roman veterans?

Inside the main house, Corbulo suddenly heard a scream and the sound of a struggle. A moment later a small figure bolted out of the doorway. The figure was making a dash for the trees but she was swiftly followed by two men. They were laughing as they caught hold of the yelling, struggling girl and started to drag her back towards the house.

In his hiding place in the forest Corbulo gasped as he felt the hairs on his neck rise up. It was Dylis. The girl being dragged back into the house was Dylis.

***

Aidan and Logan were waiting for him beside the entrance to the temple complex. They looked annoyed and impatient and Logan seemed to have something urgent to say, but before he could do so Corbulo held up his hand.

"I found them," he exclaimed with feverish, excited eyes, "They are being held in a house in the forest, not far from here. I saw Dylis with my own eyes. That's the good news. The bad news is that there are over forty, armed men in there with them. We will have to think of a plan to free them. It's going to be difficult."

"You found them?" Aidan said, unable to hide his excitement. "Was Dylis alright? What about Efa? Did you see my daughter?"

"I only saw Dylis briefly. She looked alright. She tried to run away but they caught her," Corbulo said with a grim, satisfied nod, "If she has the strength and courage to be able to do that, then she must be doing alright. My girl is a fighter."

"Good, good, this is good," Aidan nodded looking down at the ground.

"But we have another problem," Logan blurted out, unable to contain himself any longer. "Whilst I was down in the market guess who I happened to see?"

Corbulo shrugged and shook his head.

"Romulus," Logan snapped.

"Romulus?" Corbulo exclaimed in surprise.

"He must have escaped from the boat to which we brought him," Logan said angrily, "Anyway you know what this means?"

Corbulo groaned and shook his head in bewilderment as he turned to stare in the direction of the house in the forest.

"Fuck," he hissed, "If he warns Emogene, she and her husband will know that we are here and what we are planning to do. Where is the prick now?"

"I don't know," Logan shook his head in defeat, "I lost him in the crowd. He could be anywhere."

"Well the next time I catch up with that little shit I am going to kill him like I should have done in the first place," Aidan growled, glancing at Corbulo. "What another fine mess you have made Corbulo, what another fucking, fine mess."

# Chapter Twenty Nine - The Battle Group Commander

Marcus looked grim as he rode away from the burning village. It was just after noon and behind him, the column of four hundred and fifty mounted, Batavian riders picked their way across the deserted and wasted fields. In the village behind them every house and building was on fire and towering, billowing columns of thick, black smoke rose up into the sky. Marcus did not look back at the inferno he and his men had created. The settlement had been completely deserted save for a single old man who had refused to leave. The Batavians had dragged him out of his house as they had set fire to the place, but the old man had broken free and had leapt into the flames and his dying shrieks had been heard by the entire battle group. Bewildered Marcus shook his head, as his eyes remained grimly fixed on the horizon. Such was the nature of the war he was fighting in these cursed mountains.

The Senatorial Tribune, Titus had taken over effective command of all Roman forces in the Luguvalium district and had immediately announced his strategy. If the Britons would not yield and surrender, then every one of their villages was to be destroyed, everyone of their war bands annihilated, everyone of their women and children sold into slavery. Rome would impose its will by a policy of complete and utter subjugation. There would be no negotiation, no concessions, no new freedoms. Everything was to be destroyed and turned to scorched earth, so that come winter the Britons would find they had no shelter and no food. The consequences of that would be mass starvation. It was tried and tested policy Titus had informed Marcus and it was going to work.

Marcus turned to look out across the ruined fields and for a moment, he allowed his real emotions to show. The 2nd Batavian Cohort would have to re-deployed to another province after this rebellion had been crushed. The locals would never forget or forgive him and his men for the destruction they had wrought in the past month. Marcus sighed wearily, as he led his men northwards away from the blazing houses. And then there was the matter of his court martial. Titus, the Legate had made it abundantly clear that the matter had not been forgotten, but simply postponed. It was highly probable that once the province had settled down he would be hauled in front of a disciplinary tribunal. Cotta may be dead but the prejudice against non-citizen officers, that existed in the higher echelons of the army, would be against him. Marcus's face darkened. Oh he knew how the system worked. Prefect of an auxiliary Cohort was a good job and there would be no shortage of candidates with political connections who would be enviously competing for the position. Yes he knew how the system of patronage worked, jobs for friends; I scratch your back, you scratch mine. He was an outsider in this system, a non-citizen, without wealth or connections save a single promise made by Agricola long ago. No, even if he was spared the death sentence, he would never command the 2nd Batavians again. This was as high as he would go.

"Where are we going Sir?" Fridwald asked, glancing across at him. The young bodyguard was sporting an unshaven chin and he looked dog tired.

"Home," Marcus growled, "Back to Luguvalium. The Tribune wants a report."

At the mention of Luguvalium Marcus looked away as exhaustion, depression and unhappiness conspired and threatened to overwhelm him. How would he ever be able to look his wife in the eye without knowing that he was a cheat, an adulterer? He had broken his promise to her. He had been unfaithful just like his father had been on countless occasions. He'd broken his oath. The shame made him blush.

Grimly he forced his horse on across the fields. Around him the colourful summer flowers poked up out of the green grass and to the east the wild, beautiful and heavily wooded mountains disappeared northwards across the horizon. Marcus bit his lip.

They had given him a thankless job to do with, as a reward, a court martial at the end of it, but he would not run from what was coming. He would trust in himself and in his men and in the blessings of the gods, for if he lost his belief in himself he would be truly finished. He still commanded a highly capable and powerful strike force of first class warriors. Raising his fist in the air he pumped it up down in rapid succession as he started to pick up the pace. Behind him the Batavian riders did the same. No, he thought, he was a soldier like his father had been and if this was to be his last command; he was going to make it into one hell of a memorable one.

***

The Roman task-force command HQ, in the Principia of Luguvalium had transformed itself since Marcus had last been there. The simple, wooden table around which he, Adalberht and Lucius had once planned the defence of the fort, over a cup of sour wine, was covered in large detailed maps; dozens of military counters and wooden writing tablets. At the door to the building, the Legionary guards stood stiffly to attention as staff officers and messengers came and went in a continuous stream. In a corner, a junior Tribune, a boy of no more than eighteen, was dictating orders to a clerk who was scratching them into a wooden tablet. Wearily Marcus looked around at the soft, animal furs that covered his old bed and the dishes of fine food that had been placed on a side table. The whole command post seemed to be humming with a sense of purpose and well organised efficiency.

"Prefect," a voice said sharply speaking in Latin.

Marcus took a step towards the large, wooden table and rapped out a quick salute. Titus, the task force commander, bare-headed save for a white Focale scarf tied around his neck and clad in his splendid armour, was stooped over a map surrounded by his staff officers. The officers seemed completely absorbed in their discussion as they poured over the map. Titus had placed both his hands on the table. He blinked and straightened up as he caught sight of Marcus and for a moment Marcus thought he saw a hint of disappointment on the senior officer's face.

"Welcome back Marcus, what news do you have for us?" Titus said sharply as his eyes wandered back to the map he'd been studying.

Marcus cleared his throat as he hastily tucked his helmet under his arm. Behind Titus, the standard bearer of the Legionary vexillation stood clutching the Eagle of the task force. The man's head and neck were covered in a wolf-skin head and he seemed to be staring rigidly into space.

Speaking quietly, Marcus delivered his report and as he did so, he felt the stern and contemptuous eyes of the staff officers upon him. They did not want him here. They all knew, they all knew that he was only still in command of his Cohort because of the favour of a woman. They would not ridicule him in front of Titus, but alone in the officer's quarters, it would be a different matter. Marcus ignored the looks and when at last he fell silent, Titus snapped his fingers at one of his officer's.

"See to it that the Batavians receive rations for a further two weeks and make sure their horses are tended to right away. Give them any supplies they need. I want them ready to move by tomorrow."

Marcus frowned. "My men need a rest Sir," he protested quietly, "We've been out there for nearly a month, we have taken casualties Sir. The men deserve a few days at least Sir, please."

But Titus shook his head.

"No Marcus," he growled, "I want this rebellion crushed as soon as possible. It is not my fault that the enemy refuses to fight a pitched battle or stand their ground. We need to push the enemy hard and we are. We are winning Marcus," Titus said with a hint of triumph in his voice, "I have four battle groups like yours out there and they are doing a fine job. The Britons are getting desperate. They know that winter is not far away. We are going to crush them."

"Yes Sir," Marcus said looking down at his muddy boots.

"The rebels are like sand, constantly slipping through my fingers but they are getting desperate," Titus repeated with a bemused smile, "They cannot keep on evading us. In the next month or so I expect we shall start to see individual war-bands coming in to surrender. King Faelan's strategy has failed and his coalition will collapse as his chiefs see their homes go up in smoke and their fields ruined. Faelan thought he could keep this province in perpetual unrest, but the one thing he didn't count on was me. Rome will not tolerate rebellious scum. That is the message we are going to ram down their throats."

Marcus nodded dutifully.

"Faelan is no fool Sir," Marcus replied quietly, "He will be adapting his tactics. We should remain cautious. These Britons are tough. They fight well. The rebels have allies to the north and they have money and they have been preparing for this fight for a long time."

Titus raised his hand in the air for silence.

"Enough," he said sternly, "between the Twentieth here in the west and the Ninth on the eastern side of the mountains, we will destroy them. But I have new instructions for you Marcus. Tomorrow you will take your battle group southwards along the road to Deva. We are expecting a supply column from the Legionary base. You will make contact and escort them back here. Once you have done that your orders are to head east into the mountains and search for enemy war bands and destroy them. I want you to wreak havoc on these rebels, slaughter them where you find them. I am not interested in prisoners, unless they have something important to say. Understood?"

"Yes Sir," Marcus replied staring wearily at the table.

Titus fell silent as he studied Marcus carefully. "There is one final matter," he said at last, "One of my officer's will be accompanying you this time. I will have them report to your tent at dawn."

Slowly Titus came around the table towards Marcus. His handsome aristocratic face displayed a little confident smile.

"Search and destroy Marcus," he nodded, "And I want your men to cut an ear off for each rebel they kill. The task force has a competition going for which battle group can amass the most ears."

"Ears?" Marcus said raising his eyebrows, "Of course Sir."

***

As he strode away from the Principia, Marcus raised his hand and touched his ear. The taskforce had a competition going? What madness. He shook his head in disbelief and glanced around at the fort that had once been his. Everything seemed to have changed since the arrival of Titus and the vexillation from the Twentieth. The parade ground was covered in row upon row of white tents and he had to be careful not to trip over the taught, mooring ropes. Up on the ramparts Legionary sentries patrolled along the parapet and beyond the walls he could hear the rhythmic thud of pickaxes, as the newcomers repaired and extended the defences. A queue of Legionaries were waiting alongside a mobile soup kitchen and in a corner of the fort he noticed the wooden, prisoner-enclosure. A few, dejected looking Britons were sitting on the ground chained together by the ankle.

Darkly Marcus muttered something to himself. Maybe he was lucky he thought. When the vexillation from the Twentieth had first arrived, a month ago now, they had given him fresh horses and weapons and ordered him to go out and hunt down the rebel, war bands in the wild, rugged mountains. At least out there he was his own man and far away from all his troubles. With the new resources, he'd been able to form a highly mobile and powerful battle group of four hundred and fifty mounted men. He'd done this by taking men from the Batavian infantry companies, but that had been no problem for every Batavian knew how to ride a horse.

As he made his way towards the corner of the fort occupied by the 2nd Batavian Cohort, Fridwald caught up with him. The bodyguard gave Marcus a quick questioning glance as he fell in beside him.

"We're off again," Marcus grunted as he caught Fridwald's glance, "The men are not going to like it."

"When Sir?" Fridwald asked.

"Tomorrow," Marcus growled," so if you want to shag that slave girl I have seen you hanging around with, you had better do it tonight."

"That sounds like a fine idea Sir," Fridwald replied with a straight face.

The two of them fell silent as they strode through the camp.

"Well one thing is certain Sir," Fridwald said cheerfully as he glanced at Marcus, "Remember that speech you gave to the men. It's coming true. Ah shit, here come those damned Batavians again. The rebels are saying it. I am sure of it. We are becoming famous Sir."

A little smile appeared on Marcus's lips but he said nothing as he strode past a group of Batavians who, were crouching around a fire over which they were warming up some old porridge. Fridwald was trying to cheer him up. The men beside the fire nodded a respectful greeting as they recognised him. Marcus sighed as he returned the gesture. Not only had everything in his fort changed, many familiar faces had gone too. Adalberht was dead as was Lollius. Lady Claudia and her daughter, together with Urbanus the merchant and his sons, had all headed south at the first available opportunity. Only his closest officers and men remained and as Marcus caught sight of Lucius and Hedwig he felt a sudden warm affection. At least here amongst his officers and men he was amongst comrades, true friends.

"Get out of here and go and make that girl happy," Marcus said laying a hand on Fridwald's shoulder and giving him a little push.

"Yes Sir," Fridwald nodded giving his commander a concerned look.

Hedwig was the first to catch sight of him. The officer looked pensive as he came towards Marcus.

"So what did Titus say?" the Batavian officer asked eying Marcus.

"He said that we are winning," Marcus replied gruffly.

"He said that," Hedwig muttered, turning to glance in the direction of the Principia.

"Yes and we're moving out again tomorrow," Marcus growled, "So see to it that the men are told. I want every soldier to get a good night's rest. Titus has promised us all the supplies that we need and we're going to have two Roman guests with us this time."

"Yes of course Sir," Hedwig said immediately.

Marcus nodded and glanced at the Batavian. He'd made the right decision with Hedwig. After Adalberht's death he'd promoted him to take overall command of the Cohort's cavalry squadrons and although Hedwig was a rather serious and unimaginative officer, he obeyed his orders instantly and to the letter and he was a good soldier who was widely respected by his men.

"What's wrong with Lucius?" Marcus said with a sudden frown. "He looks like someone has taken a shit and spread it all over his bed."

Hedwig turned and followed Marcus's gaze. Lucius, the Senior Centurion of the 2nd Batavian Cohort was sitting around a camp fire with a few of his fellow officers. He looked pale and moody.

"Shit," Hedwig muttered turning back to look at Marcus as he rubbed his hand across his forehead, "He hasn't had a chance to tell you yet has he." Hedwig sighed. "You know how he is always asking people whether they have heard anything about his brother, Bestia? Well whilst you were away at HQ, he found out that his brother is dead. One of the newcomers, a Roman, heard that Lucius was making inquiries and came and told him what had happened. Turns out that someone murdered Bestia. They stuck a knife into him. Can you believe that? I mean, Bestia knew how to handle himself, right."

Marcus stiffened and a little colour shot into his cheeks as he stared at Lucius sitting beside the camp fire.

"Where did it happen?" he muttered.

"In a tavern in Viroconium apparently, seems Bestia got into some kind of fight."

"Do they know who did it?" Marcus asked.

Hedwig shook his head. "All they have is a name, Corbulo. The man who brought Lucius the news was with Bestia when it happened. They were on some job in Viroconium, a couple of years ago. Lucius has already vowed to take revenge. He has sworn it before the gods. I know Bestia was a bullying prick but he was still his brother. I wouldn't want to be the murderer when

Lucius eventually catches up with him. He's really pissed. I mean really angry."

"Is that right," Marcus muttered looking away.

A sudden delighted squeal made him turn round and there, running towards him, was his three year old son. The boy was clutching his toy sword and behind him striding to catch up, came Marcus's wife.

Marcus took a deep breath and forced a grin onto his face.

# Chapter Thirty - Into the Mountains

Marcus raised his fist in the air and the horsemen behind him came to a clattering halt along the side of the Roman road. It was noon and up ahead, obscured by the trees, smoke was billowing up into the sky. Marcus peered at the smoke in the distance and then turned to Lucius who was riding beside him.

"What do you think?" he asked.

Lucius looked sullen and ill at ease as he leaned forwards on his horse and stared at the smoke. The Senior Centurion's armour was immaculate and in his right hand he held a spear, whilst his cavalry shield was slung over his back.

"It won't have been caused by one of our battle groups," he replied, "We're the only ones operating in this area. Must be enemy action, but if it's an ambush why alert us by creating smoke."

"Let's go and find out. Prefect, what are we waiting for?" Gaius the eighteen year-old Roman Tribune exclaimed impatiently, as he glared questioningly at Marcus. The boy and his private bodyguard, an experienced ex-soldier, had been attached to the battle group on Titus's orders and the boy had already managed to infuriate Marcus with his recklessness and arrogance. But there was nothing Marcus could do about it. Gaius was not his to command. The young Tribune hailed from an old and wealthy Roman family and had already been marked out for a career in politics. Titus had been keen to give the boy the battlefield experience he so desperately craved for without that, a political career in Rome was not likely to succeed. That was the only reason the boy was here. To gain some experience of war.

Ignoring the young Tribune, Marcus glanced out across the deserted, gently rolling fields that surrounded the road on both sides. There was no sign of anyone about. Warily he glanced at the dark green forest ahead. The wood however seemed large enough to hide an entire army.

"Get the men into an extended line, loose formation," he snapped, turning to his trumpeter who was sitting on his horse just behind him. "They are to wait here out in the open. First squadron will follow me into the forest. Give the order now."

Quickly Marcus turned to Gaius's companion, an older experienced ex-soldier with white hair, who was sitting on his horse beside the impetuous Roman youth.

"You two will remain here," he snapped.

As the trumpet rang out, Marcus urged his horse forwards up the road. He and his men were by now well versed in the war that was being fought against the rebels. If he wanted to live he needed to be cautious. Nothing was what it seemed and the enemy were cunning and resourceful. This was not a conflict of pitched battles and massed armies. It was a relentless, brutal and increasingly bitter duel between small bands of men, hunting each other across the mountains and forests of the north with each side striving to destroy and demoralise the other by ambush, dirty tricks, deceit and terror. The Britons had the advantage that they knew the land and they had the motivation, but the Romans were to a man, professional soldiers, well trained and well equipped.

Marcus raised his fist in the air as the fifteen squadrons of Batavian cavalry hastily deployed across the fields on both sides of the road. The horses' hooves sent clumps of earth flying up into the air and the jingle and rattle of their equipment mingled with the cries of the Decurions, as they struggled to get their men into position. Fridwald, the trumpeter, Lucius and the standard bearer, holding up the boar-headed, Cohort standard, stuck close to Marcus as he trotted up the road. They were followed by the thirty riders of the first squadron. All of them were staring at the billowing smoke beyond the forest.

Marcus did not hesitate as the road entered the forest. The green, dark and silent pine trees closed in on both sides. There was no way to see more than ten yards into the dense forest. As

248

he trotted up the road, the only noise Marcus could hear was the horses' hooves on the gravel road and the nervous whinny of the horses. The smell of smoke was growing stronger. Marcus glanced cautiously into the trees.

"Sir," Fridwald said suddenly. "Look."

Up ahead, tree trunks had been felled and laid across the road, forming a rough but effective barrier a yard high. Marcus slowed his horse to a walk as he stared at the trees lying across the road.

"Rebels, Sir," Fridwald muttered. "This is their work."

Marcus said nothing as he carefully guided his horse around the road block. The forest was already starting to thin out, but as he regained the road he raised his fist and the men around him came to an abrupt halt.

"Fuck," Lucius muttered as he opened his mouth in dismay and stared down the road. "Looks like we found the supply convoy Marcus."

Marcus did not reply as he stared at the carnage beyond the road block. As far as his eyes could see the road was littered with abandoned, broken and overturned wagons, dead horses, wagon wheels, slaughtered oxon, discarded clothes, smashed pottery, weapons, shields, helmets and the corpses of dozens upon dozens of men. The Romans lay where they had fallen, scattered across the gravel road and in amongst the trees. Further along the road beyond the forest, an overturned wagon lying in a drainage ditch was still on fire sending smoke billowing upwards. Marcus stared at the massacre taking in every detail. The carrion birds were already hopping from one corpse to the next and from amongst the trees he heard the Batavian riders on his flanks starting to call out to each other.

"Looks like they didn't stand a chance," Lucius muttered as he nudged his horse alongside Marcus, "Poor bastards. The rebels must have ambushed them and slaughtered them without mercy. What a way to go."

"That's not all," Marcus said quietly, "Look. The supplies the wagons were carrying are missing. The rebels must have taken them. That's what they were after." Grimly Marcus glanced at Lucius as he urged his horse on through the debris that littered the road. "I warned Titus about this," he snapped angrily, "I warned him the Britons would change their tactics. Maybe they are merging their war bands into larger groups. They must be targeting our supplies in the hope that it will see them through the winter. We should expect more of this shit. The high command are going to have to find a way to better protect our supply columns."

No one replied as the Batavian riders picked their way through the debris and blood soaked corpses that littered the road and nearby forest.

"Lucius," Marcus snapped at last, "Get your best trackers to find out which way the rebels went. They can't have gone far. These men here died this morning and the Britons will be laden with loot and booty. They will be moving slowly."

"I can do that Marcus," Lucius grunted as he stared down at the dead from his horse. "Should we not report this to HQ?"

"Fuck that," Marcus growled, "I have my orders. We're going to find whoever did this and pay them back. An eye for an eye!"

***

The green, rolling fields were covered in lush, long grass and to the west the sun was already sinking below the horizon. Marcus sat on his horse peering at the three scouts as they galloped towards him. Stretching away from him along the tree line and hidden in amongst the cover of the trees, the hundreds of Batavian horsemen sat quietly on their mounts waiting for the order to advance. All afternoon the battle group had followed the tracks left by the rebel war band. The rebels, laden down with loot, had been slow moving and had been easy to follow. Their trail had led eastwards towards the mountains.

"Sir," one of the scouts cried out as he reined in his horse before Marcus, "They are close, just beyond that hill. They are moving on foot, about a hundred men."

Marcus nodded and slowly turned round to look at the cluster of officers sitting on their horses. The men looked tense and pumped up.

"Hedwig," he said calmly, "Take squadrons ten through fifteen. Lucius, you will take the left flank squadrons. We charge upon my signal. The rest of you will follow me down the centre and remember boys, do not do anything stupid. I want you all alive after this."

"Thunder and lashing rain, so Woden commeth," Fridwald said unable to hide his fierce and tense excitement as he tightened his grip on his spear.

Marcus did not reply as he turned and caught the eye of Gaius's companion. The ex-soldier looked calm.

"Keep close to me," Marcus said. "And keep him out of trouble," he muttered gesturing at Gaius.

The white haired man replied with a confident little nod.

"I do not need a baby sitter," Gaius exclaimed as a furious blush spread across his cheeks. "I can handle myself."

Marcus ignored the youth's outburst and glanced along the tree-line. The Cohort Standard Bearer was right behind him, holding up the proud, boar-headed Standard and beside him the trumpeter was adjusting his conical instrument. Marcus waited until Hedwig and Lucius had vanished in amongst the trees. Then he raised his fist in the air and cried out to the men around him before slowly lowering his arm in the direction of the open fields. A moment later he was urging his horse out into the meadow. From amongst the cover of the trees the Batavian cavalry began to emerge in a long single and silent line. The riders' chain-mail armour glinted in the fading sunlight as the horsemen lowered their lances and presented their small, round cavalry shields. The metallic jingle of their equipment and the thud of the horses hooves were the only noise. Here and there a rider had adorned the mane of his horse with the gleaming and polished white skulls of the men he'd killed and some of the Germanic horsemen had painted their faces blue in the Briton fashion.

Marcus glanced to his left and right as he urged his horse into a trot. The Batavian cavalry squadrons were maintaining a solid line. His men knew what to do and as he watched them, he felt a sudden and fierce pride in his men. They may not belong to the elite formations of the Roman army but his band of semi-barbarian horsemen were the match of any enemy. Up ahead, the open meadows rose to a grassy ridgeline. Marcus raised his spear as he surged up the slope. As he reached the crest he caught sight of the fields beyond. The rebel war band were on foot and strung out in a disordered column, as they made their way across the grassy meadows towards the grey distant mountains.

"Give the order," Marcus yelled at his trumpeter.

A moment later the signaller blew on his instrument and the deep and low noise of the trumpet echoed away across the pleasant, green valley. At the sound of the signal the Batavian horsemen broke into a charge and came surging over the ridge. Their wild, blood-curling yells and screams mingled with the thud of their horses' hooves, as they thundered towards the enemy. Marcus cried out as the earth seemed to shake with the thud of hundreds of hooves. A familiar tension gripped his every muscle as he bore down on the rebels. Down in the valley the Britons had turned and were standing rooted to the ground, staring at the approaching tide of horsemen in utter shock. Then in the blink of an eye, all hell broke loose and the rebels dropped the sacks of grain and amphorae they had been carrying and scattered in wild flight. But there was no way they were going to outrun the horsemen.

The Batavian riders sliced through the running men, mowing them down with their spears and long cavalry swords. The Britons didn't stand a chance. Men tumbled to the ground and all around him Marcus heard terrified screams and confused yelling. A Batavian flashed past him with wild staring eyes and a blood spattered face. The man was roaring and he'd lost his helmet. As he stormed onwards Marcus raised his spear and flung it straight into the back of a tall Briton with red hair. The impact sent the fleeing man spinning and crashing into the grass. Wildly Marcus stared around him as his horse carried him deeper into the confused mass of horsemen and fleeing rebels. The grassy field was already littered with corpses. With a cry he reined in his horse and swung round to look at the carnage and as he did so, he was suddenly aware of Fridwald at his side. The young bodyguard was panting and clutching his sword. He was closely followed by the standard bearer holding up the Cohort banner.

Across the field the wild Batavian charge had petered out and the riders were milling about in small groups, as they closed and finished off the last of the rebels. Marcus stared at the scene in grim silence as he heard the desperate pleas for mercy. It had been an easy victory. The enemy had been outnumbered and careless and it had cost them their lives. As he looked down at the grass, he caught sight of a Briton crawling through the grass with his guts trailing behind him. The man was groaning. As he watched, a dismounted Batavian strode up to the wounded man, jerked the man's head up by his hair and sliced open his throat sending a torrent of blood gushing out onto the grass.

Marcus turned away and sighed in relief as he caught sight of Gaius, the young Roman Tribune and his companion. The two men had dismounted and were busy slicing off the ears from the enemy corpses that littered the field.

"Sir, over here," a voice cried out in the Batavian language. Marcus turned and saw that it was Hedwig. Urging his horse towards the officer he saw that Hedwig and his men had managed to capture two rebels. The Britons were kneeling on the ground with their hands pressed up behind their heads. They looked terrified. Their eyes darted from one Batavian to the next.

"Sir, they claim that King Faelan is close by. They say they were heading to his camp."

"The High King?" Marcus said as a gleam of interest appeared in his eyes. Carefully he turned to examine the prisoners.

"Where is Faelan, where is his camp?" he snapped speaking in his mother's language.

"A day's walk to the east. That way. He is camped beside the great waterfall, "one of the men gasped, pointing towards the mountains.

"How many men has he with him?"

"Four or five hundred," the Briton replied eagerly before stretching out his arms towards Marcus in a pathetic plea, "Please let us live," the man cried out. "My son and I did not want to fight. We have no quarrel with you."

Marcus ignored the man's outstretched arms and turned to glance eastwards towards the mountains. For a moment he said nothing.

"What shall we do with them?" Hedwig said gesturing at the two prisoners.

Marcus turned back to look at the two men kneeling in the grass. Then he looked up at Hedwig.

"We shall make camp on the top of that hill over there," he said pointing at the treeless summit of a hill a mile away. "Tie the prisoners up but don't harm them. Tomorrow they will earn their right to live and Hedwig, collect the looted supplies and burn them. We cannot take them with us and I don't want the enemy getting their hands on them."

"Yes, Sir," Hedwig replied with a stiff nod.

Without another word Marcus turned his horse away and rode off followed by Fridwald, the signaller and the standard bearer.

"What now, Sir?" Fridwald said glancing at his commander.

Marcus was eying the distant mountains. "That's where we are going," he said sharply. "That's where we will find the High King."

## Chapter Thirty One - Stalking the Enemy

It was night and as he sat, leaning back against a rock, Marcus could not sleep. Idly he drew the thin, army blanket closer around his body as he stared up at the bright multitude of stars in the night sky. The Batavian battle group had made their camp on the summit of a treeless hill and around him, the occasional cough and whinny and neighing of a horse disturbed the night. Marcus had forbidden the men from lighting camp-fires and the soldiers had been forced to eat their rations cold. As he sat, staring up at the stars from somewhere inside the camp, he heard a peal of laughter that swiftly died away. Marcus sighed. He had to keep going he thought. Oh how easy it would be to slip away from his command, ride back to Luguvalium, pick up his wife and son and vanish forever into the wild forests and mountains. Oh how easy it would be to run away from his pending court martial, his pending demotion and possible death. The Roman officers did not want him; they did not see him as their equal. He was not a citizen but, as he stared up at the stars he slowly shook his head. No, he wasn't going to do that. His father Corbulo had been an arse for most of his life and yet he'd managed to redeem himself. How had he managed that? How had that old tart managed to regain the respect of his family, friends and peers? Marcus frowned. Corbulo had never given up on him during his search in Caledonia and, as he tried to picture his father's face, a new strength seemed to flow into his veins. His father would be proud of him, no matter what happened to him.

"Can't sleep?" a voice muttered from the darkness.

Marcus turned as a dark shape appeared out of the gloom. He recognised the voice. It was Lucius. Marcus did not reply as the senior Centurion sat down on the hard rocky ground and for a long moment the two men did not speak.

"I heard about your brother, Bestia," Marcus muttered as he turned to look in Lucius's direction. In the darkness it was impossible to see the Centurion's face.

"He was an arsehole and I know you and he did not get on," Lucius replied with a strange tension in his voice, "but he was my brother and he did not deserve to be murdered. I have a duty to find his killer Marcus. When all this is over I will be applying for a leave of absence. Will you grant it?"

Marcus turned to look at the ground. Should he tell Lucius what had really happened? That Bestia had deserted because he wanted to go after the Caledonian amber; that his brother Bestia had tried to murder his father Corbulo on several occasions and that it was Corbulo who had ended his life?

"Bestia deserted," Marcus said sternly, "He abandoned his comrades. He abandoned you and his honour when he left the Cohort without permission. He does not deserve your respect even if he is of your blood. He should have hanged for what he did. There is no excuse."

In the darkness there was no immediate reply.

"The man who murdered my brother was called Corbulo. That started me thinking. Your father is called Corbulo, isn't he?" Lucius said suddenly.

In the darkness Marcus remained silent.

"Well?" Lucius's sharp accusing voice cut through the night like a knife.

"There are many men called, Corbulo," Marcus replied uncomfortably, "The name is popular. My father had nothing to do with your brother's death."

"That's not what my informant told me," Lucius snapped, "He told me that this Corbulo had a son serving with the 2nd Batavians."

"And who is this informant who seems to know everything?" Marcus growled irritably.

"That private bodyguard," Lucius replied bitterly, "The one who looks after Gaius, the Tribune. He was with my brother a couple of years ago. They were doing a job for the Governor and tracked Corbulo and a bunch of fugitive children to a tavern, the Pink Elephant, in Viroconium. It's there that my brother and two of his men were killed. The man was not there to see it happen but he found the bodies afterwards."

Marcus remained silent. Then at last he stirred.

"If I am still the Prefect, after this rebellion is finished," Marcus said in a strained voice, "I will grant you leave but you will never find your brother's killer. He is long gone."

"Maybe," Lucius replied darkly, "but I have a blood duty to avenge my brother. It is a sacred duty, the oldest duty a man has. It is not wise to stand between a man and his sacred duty."

"Your duty is to me and the Cohort," Marcus said sternly, "I need you to be sharp Lucius. This business about your brother is distracting you. Men will die if you are not focussed on your job. We are in the midst of a war. So this is the last time that we will discuss your brother. That's an order. Do I make myself clear?"

There was no immediate answer from the figure in the darkness and as the awkward stand-off and silence lengthened Marcus's hand idly dropped to the pommel of his sword.

"So what now," Lucius said as he seemed to change the subject, "What is the campaign plan? You have said nothing since we slaughtered that war band."

"The plan is simple," Marcus replied in a relieved voice, "We capture or kill the king."

"That didn't work out so well the last time we tried it," Lucius said, "Faelan came straight back at us like an angry bear. He's still out to avenge his son, Marcus. If he gets his hands on you, you will be wishing for a swift death."

"We were unlucky at the standing stones," Marcus replied, "But lightning does not strike the same spot twice; besides I have promised Juno that I will name my eldest daughter after her if she gives us the king." Marcus paused as a little smile appeared on his lips. "So what could possibly go wrong?"

In the darkness Lucius chuckled. He was joined by Marcus and for a few moments the night was rent with their soft, brittle laughter but the chuckles and darkness were hollow and without real feeling and could not obscure the fact, Marcus realised with growing sadness, that a long standing friendship was coming to an end.

***

Marcus said nothing as he stood on the summit of the rocky, treeless hill. Around him the Batavian camp was a hive of activity as the men busied and readied themselves to move out. It was dawn and the sun was a slowly rising, red ball above the mountains. At his side Hedwig, Lucius, Fridwald and the standard bearer were all staring in the same direction. A gentle wind was blowing in from the west, ruffling the mens' hair and beards and on the horizon dark, ominous-looking rain clouds were building up.

"How long have they been watching us?" Marcus growled, as he stared at the two Briton scouts up on the rocky ridge, a quarter of a mile away.

"Hard to say, Sir," Hedwig replied, "the sentries only spotted them at first light. Who do you think they are?"

"Who knows," Marcus growled as he studied the two horsemen, "But they are not afraid of showing themselves. That means they do not fear us. There must be another war band close by."

"Maybe it's the King," Lucius muttered.

Marcus nodded. "Well whoever they are, the Britons know that we are here. We will not be surprising anyone." He turned to Hedwig. "You will lead the advance guard, and the two prisoners whom we captured yesterday will show us the way to King Faelan's camp."

"Sir," Fridwald exclaimed, "look, they are leaving."

Marcus turned to stare at the two scouts as the Britons slowly and calmly urged their horses along the ridge line before turning away down the opposite slope and out of view.

"Get moving," Marcus snapped as he turned to his officers.

All that morning the battle group rode eastwards and as they did the Briton scouts kept pace with them, disappearing and reappearing but never getting too close to the Batavian column. As the low mountains drew closer the land started to change. The lush, green, rolling fields and meadows of the river valley began to give way to bleak, trackless uplands filled with jagged-rock-faces, gushing mountain-streams, strange outcrops and deep, boulder-strewn gorges. Here and there the slopes of the mountains were heavily wooded but the summits were treeless, windswept and covered in coarse, colourful heather. As the Batavian riders steadily climbed up through the tree-line the terrain grew more and more rugged and broken and their pace slowed. Marcus looked up, as he heard the high-pitched cry of a hawk circling above him. With nothing to stop it, apart from the tumbled boulders and deep gashes in the earth, the wind came sweeping in fast and furious and with it came the first drops of rain.

Marcus glared at the approaching rain clouds. Half a mile away standing out on the top of a peak, he could see an abandoned hill-fort. The neglected and forgotten ruins were from a different, older time. Marcus sighed as his horse followed the riders in front of him, up the rocky path. Around him the windswept, mountain peaks crowded around like spectators in the arena, watching the Batavian column as it slowly wound its way up the mountain slope. The magnificent, treeless mountains were hauntingly beautiful and the land felt old, terribly old. As the battle group plodded on, the rain came lashing and striking at the soldiers in fierce gusts and the men pulled their cloaks closer around their bodies and lowered their heads. But as soon as it had arrived the rain clouds passed away overhead and the rain ceased.

It was mid-afternoon when a Batavian rider from Hedwig's advance guard came trotting back along the desolate ridge towards the main column. Catching sight of Marcus and the standard bearer he rode up to his commander.

"We've made contact with the enemy Sir," the rider exclaimed, "Hedwig wants to know what he should do?"

Marcus acknowledged the soldier and without a word he spurred his horse forwards along the ridge, leaving the main Batavian column behind. He was swiftly followed by Fridwald, the standard bearer and his trumpeter. On both sides of the ridge the land dropped away towards a deep valley, through which a white mountain-stream was flowing. The bleak, boulder-strewn landscape was covered in purple and green heather and on a distant slope he could see a flock of sheep.

Hedwig's advance guard of ninety odd men had halted just below a peak. As Marcus approached, Hedwig spotted him and raised his arm.

"They are down in the valley beside the waterfall just like the prisoners said Sir," Hedwig said saluting smartly, "I counted fifty men, a mixed infantry and cavalry force, probably scouts. But it's the King, Sir, I recognise the banner on one of the chariots although I don't think he is with them."

Marcus nodded and swiftly dismounted from his horse. Half bent over he carefully clambered up to the ridge and crouched beside a large rock. A moment later he was joined by Hedwig. In the valley below him, a couple of hundred paces away, a group of armed men were lounging about around a waterfall. The roar from the water was clearly audible. Marcus stared at them. Beyond the water fall and the mountain stream the valley twisted away into a narrow gorge with steep, rocky and grey, slate- covered slopes. As he stared at the enemy the noise from a Carnyx suddenly echoed away across the treeless mountains. The men down in the valley beside the stream rose to their feet and a few raised their arms and pointed up at the peak behind which the Batavian riders had halted.

"Looks like they have spotted us, Sir," Hedwig said sucking in his breath.

"There was never any chance that we would surprise them," Marcus murmured shaking his head, as down below in the valley the Britons hastily splashed through the stream and started to move into the narrow gorge, "Not with those scouts dogging our every move. No, Faelan knows we are here."

"What are you waiting for?" a new voice beside them said impatiently. It was Gaius. The young Tribune edged forwards until he was crouching beside Marcus. His face was flush with excitement. "Come on, let's get down there and finish them off. We outnumber them. It will be an easy victory. What are we waiting for? They are going to get away if we don't do something."

Marcus stared at the youth for a long moment. Then slowly he turned back to the rebel war band in the valley below. The Britons did not seem to be in a hurry as they milled about in the entrance to the gorge.

"Hedwig," Marcus said sharply, "release the two prisoners and send them on their way. They have kept their word. I have no more use for them."

"Yes Sir," Hedwig replied stiffly as he turned and started to clamber back down towards his men.

"What are you waiting for?" Gaius said in an incredulous voice, "There can't be more than fifty of them down there. We can easily take them."

"No," Marcus snapped, "That is exactly what they want us to do. Those men down there look like bait and this looks like an ambush to me. Look carefully at that gorge, if we attack now they will surely lure us into it and straight into an ambush. See those steep rocky slopes; they are perfect cover for bowmen who will pick us off and once we are in that gorge; we will have very limited room for manoeuvre and gods knows what is waiting for us further in. Remember that the prisoners told us the King has five or six hundred men, so where are they?"

Gaius opened his mouth and then closed it again as his cheeks burned with sudden embarrassment.

"So what then?" the youth muttered sullenly.

"We wait and see," Marcus said, as he turned and started back towards his horse. "Patience is a virtue beloved of Fortuna, Gaius, remember that."

As he swung himself onto his horse, the rebel Carnyx bellowed out once more and its mournful tones faded away across the mountains.

"Hedwig," Marcus cried, "take your men down that slope and let the horses drink from the stream. Under no circumstances are you to engage the enemy, not even if they present you with a row of naked arses. Slacken your thirst and then get back up here."

"Yes Sir," Hedwig cried as he raised his arm and started to lead his men down the mountain slope.

"So are we to do nothing?" Gaius exclaimed. "How then will we ever beat them?"

"By letting them make the first mistake," Marcus replied grimly. "Don't be so eager boy, there is always tomorrow."

## Chapter Thirty Two - The Things to Come

It was night and in the dark skies the moonlight cast its pale light across the mountains. Marcus accompanied by Fridwald made their way silently across the barren hill-top as the two of them continued their inspection round of the sentry and guard posts. The soft crunch of their boots on the gravel was the only noise and a cool, fresh breeze was blowing in from the west. The Batavian battle group had pitched their camp in the midst of the ruined hill fort, he'd seen earlier that day, and inside the jumble of abandoned ruins, all seemed calm and peaceful. As they made their way from one post to the next Marcus was glad for the peace and quiet. He'd forbidden his men from lighting camp-fires and for a second day the soldiers had eaten a cold dinner, but despite that, morale was still high. The men seemed eager to close with the rebel High King for capturing or killing him would bring them a huge amount of prestige and reward.

As they left the last of the sentry posts, Marcus turned and glanced idly at Fridwald.

"The Decurion commanding the fourth squadron needs a second in command," he said quietly, "The post is yours if you want it."

There was no immediate answer from out of the darkness.

"Thank you," Fridwald replied as he cleared his throat, "but if it's all the same with you Sir, I would rather keep my position as your bodyguard. It is by far the best position within the whole Cohort."

Marcus nodded and a little smile appeared on his lips. There had been a reason why so many Roman Emperors had chosen to form their imperial bodyguard from Germanic troops. For the Batavians, loyalty to one's leader was a sacred oath, not to be broken under any circumstances. The man who did so would suffer everlasting shame and humiliation.

"There is something that you should know Sir," Fridwald said in a quiet voice. "Something I have been meaning to tell you for a long time. I had heard about you before I am joined the Cohort. We have a common friend, Sir."

In the darkness Marcus came to a halt and turned to stare at his bodyguard.

"What are you talking about?" he muttered.

"You used to call him Pig Face," Fridwald replied. "I am his younger brother Sir. He told me all about you when he returned to our home amongst the rivers."

"Pig Face," Marcus exclaimed as his eyes widened in surprise, "You are Pig Face's younger brother?"

"I am Sir," Fridwald replied with a hint of pride in his voice, "It was he who encouraged me to join up."

Marcus turned away and shook his head and for a long moment he said nothing. It had been six years since he had last seen or heard from Pig Face.

"How is the old, ugly, legless bastard?" he muttered at last.

"He is dead Sir," Fridwald replied swiftly, "One day, just before I joined the Cohort, he became ill and he just died." In the darkness Fridwald paused for a moment. "But he told me about you Sir," the young bodyguard continued. "He said that you saved his life during the battle of Mons Graupius in Caledonia. If you ever need friends, Sir or a new home, you will find it amongst my people."

Marcus closed his eyes and rubbed his forehead with his fingers.

"Thank you Fridwald," he muttered at last. "When this is all over we will have a proper chat about Pig Face. He was a good soldier and friend. I shall pray   to his spirit tonight."

At his command post Lucius and Hedwig were waiting for him. The two senior officers rose to their feet as they heard him approach. Inside the ruined house that acted as his HQ, Marcus wearily removed his helmet and took a drink from a leather drinking pouch before wiping his mouth with the back of his hand.

"Well what is it?" he said sharply. "I can see you have something on your minds."

Lucius cleared his throat and was the first to speak.

"We have been thinking Marcus," he said. "Maybe it would be better if tomorrow we retreated to lower ground. There is more food down in the river valleys for the horses and less chance of us being ambushed."

"Sir," Hedwig interrupted, "King Faelan can hide in these mountains forever. If he doesn't want to fight us it will be easy for him to avoid battle. We could be chasing him up and down these slopes and peaks for weeks. These mountains favour defence and the enemy know the land much better than we do. Would it not be wiser to retreat to lower ground and wait for the enemy to come to us?"

"No," Marcus said sharply, "We are going to capture or kill Faelan. I have made up my mind."

"Marcus," Lucius sighed in the darkness, "Every man in this Cohort knows that you are facing a court martial when this is all over. Capturing the enemy king is not going to change that. But remaining up here in these mountains is inviting disaster. Men are going to lose their lives."

"That's enough talk," Marcus growled irritably. "Men will die whatever I do. You have your orders. We are going to defeat this king or die trying. We're soldiers, damn it. What else are we supposed to do?"

\*\*\*

The column of Batavian horsemen was winding its way along the mountain ridge when Marcus spotted the scout galloping towards them. It was morning and dull, grey clouds covered the sky. Quickly he raised his arm in the air and the column came to a halt.

"Sir," the scout gasped as he brought his horse to a halt beside Marcus. "The enemy block the way ahead. They are no more than a mile away. They don't look like they are about to move Sir."

"Show me," Marcus snapped as he urged his horse forwards. Without a word the Batavian rider turned and started out across the bleak, treeless mountain-slope. As Marcus accompanied by his staff galloped after him, the sun broke through the clouds, bathing the rocks and coarse, colourful heather in warm sunshine. As he reached a rocky peak the scout reined in his horse.

Marcus cantered up the mountain slope towards him and came to a halt on the summit.

"They have not moved since we first saw them Sir," the scout muttered as he stared down into the valley below.

Marcus did not reply. Down in the treeless, boulder-strewn valley a mountain stream was meandering its way to lower ground and, drawn up along the length of the stream were hundreds upon hundreds of armed Britons. The rebels stood drawn up for battle with the infantry clutching long spears and the cavalry and chariots clustered together in dense groups on both flanks.

For a long moment Marcus peered at the enemy in silence. Then he turned sharply to the trumpeter beside him.

"Go and find Lucius and bring him here at once," he said calmly.

Marcus did not watch the scout ride away. Instead he turned to stare at the enemy lining the banks of the stream and as he did a lonely, Celtic horn blasted away, it's mournful, mellow sounds fading away across the mountains.

Lucius accompanied by a few of his men and with Gaius and his companion in tow said nothing as they trotted up to him.

"What do you make of it?" Marcus asked making eye contact with Lucius as he gestured at the rebels down in the valley.

Lucius took his time as he studied the enemy dispositions.

"They seem intent on denying our horses a drink," he muttered at last, "and they seem willing to fight us for it. They are offering battle Marcus."

"The High King is down there," Marcus replied. "See his pennant flying from that chariot beside that group of horsemen. That's Faelan alright. I can recognise that one-eyed bastard anywhere."

"I estimate they have around six hundred men Sir," Gaius cried in an excited voice.

Lucius nodded and exchanged a hurried glance with Marcus.

"We'll water the horses further upstream," Marcus said, staring at Lucius, "I am not going to go down there to fight them, even if that is what they want us to do. They outnumber us and they have the advantage of the terrain."

"Yes Sir," Lucius said avoiding Marcus's gaze.

"We are better than they are," Gaius cried, as his eager eyes darted across the enemy line along the mountain stream. "Man for a man we can beat them."

"The Prefect is right," Gaius's companion, the ex-soldier growled, "the enemy have the advantage of the terrain. No horse will charge onto a row of spears and the enemy will just retreat up the slope if we attack. That is what they want us to do. That's why they are standing there."

"Well, when will we ever get to fight in a proper battle," Gaius cried out in frustration. "I am wasting my time here."

\*\*\*

It was noon when Marcus heard a rider cry out his name. Eagerly he turned in the direction from which the cry had come. The mountain peaks and slopes were covered in wisps of mist that made it hard to see for more than a couple of hundred yards. From out of the mist, the patrol of thirty horsemen came cantering towards him with Hedwig leading them. Their dust and sweat-streaked faces looked excited as they rode towards the main Batavian force.

"There is an enemy patrol beyond that ridge Sir," Hedwig cried out, "I counted around fifty mounted men. They appear to be alone and they are heading straight for us Sir."

"They are alone?" Marcus exclaimed, "are you sure?"

"Yes Sir," Hedwig nodded stiffly. "I don't think they have seen us yet."

Marcus blew the air from his mouth and for a moment he seemed torn by indecision. Then he looked up at Hedwig and nodded.

"Take the advance group and rout them Hedwig," he snapped. "If they are stupid enough to blunder straight into us, then they don't deserve to live."

"Sir," Hedwig replied rapping out a quick salute as he raised his arm and started to wheel his horse around.

Marcus watched Hedwig and the ninety Batavian riders ride away across the barren mountain side. Then he raised his arm

270

and pumped his fist up and down and behind him the main Batavian column started to pick up the pace.

Ahead, the bleak mountain slope looked deserted and empty but as Hedwig's troopers went charging over the ridge line and out of sight, the silence was suddenly shattered by confused cries and shouts. Grimly Marcus bit his lip. It was impossible to see what was happening up ahead. Around him the thud of hundreds of hooves shook the earth as the Batavian riders began to form a wide line as they surged up towards the ridge-line. As he reached the crest of the hill, Marcus stared down the slope and into the swirling mist. Hedwig and his men seemed to be in full pursuit of the enemy patrol and, scattered across the hillside were the corpses of several rebels but the main enemy force seemed to be getting away.

"Sound recall," Marcus cried quickly, turning to his trumpeter as Hedwig and his men were about to completely vanish into the mist.

A moment later a trumpet blasted away sending its noise echoing away across the mountain slopes.

Marcus was breathing heavily at he stared at the scene. Hedwig and his men had heard the recall and had given up the pursuit and were slowly trotting back up the slope towards him.

"Bastards saw us coming Sir," Hedwig panted as he rode up to Marcus, "We managed to kill a few of them before they turned and fled."

"You will have another chance soon enough," Marcus growled as he peered at the mist into which the enemy patrol had disappeared.

At Marcus's side Fridwald stirred as a little smile appeared on his lips. "Ah shit here come those damned Batavians again," he muttered.

Hedwig heard the bodyguard's comment and for a brief moment his serious looking face cracked into a little sardonic grin.

"Take the horses down to the stream," Marcus said indicating the mountain stream in the valley. "We will halt here along the high ground. There is no point in looking for the enemy in this mist."

"The High King seems to want a fight," Hedwig replied thoughtfully as he turned to stare at the mountain stream in the valley, "If he didn't, he would have left this area long ago. We seem to be dancing around each other's shadows and that stream down there is the key."

"Why is that?" Gaius asked with a frown.

Marcus and his officers were silent as they peered around them into the advancing mist.

"It's the only place where we can we water our horses," Hedwig replied at last, as he raised his arm in the air and cried out to his men to follow him down the slope. Marcus watched the Batavian riders as they clattered down the mountain side. From somewhere in the distance a mellow Celtic horn rung out. It was answered by another horn and this one sounded closer.

"What are the enemy doing?" Gaius snapped in a bewildered voice as he stared at the swirling mist that was rolling over the top of the rocky ridge.

"They are signalling to each other," Marcus replied as he started to turn his horse in the direction of the main Batavian column.

"What are they saying? Why don't they attack us?" the youth growled.

"I don't know," Marcus muttered as he started back towards the head of the column. "But don't worry Tribune. You will get your fight. Hedwig is right. Faelan is sticking around. He too wants a battle."

***

The mist soon covered the entire mountain slope enveloping everything in a soft moist and impenetrable cloak. The Batavian riders sat and stood around in small groups, strung out along the rocky ridge line as they waited for the weather to clear. It had become impossible to see anything that was more than a dozen yards away. Marcus sat on his horse, surrounded by the standard bearer holding up the Cohort Standard and a close circle of officers. Hedwig was recounting an old Batavian story and the officers were listening in rapt attention and as always, when the Batavians turned to telling stories of their homeland and myths, Marcus felt left out for he was not of their blood. Nevertheless he smiled when Hedwig finished and was about to say something, when the noise from a Carnyx shattered the eerie calm. The noise had come from close by.

The group of officers abruptly turned to stare in the direction from which the noise had come.

"Shall I order the men into line Sir," the trumpeter gasped as he hastily raised his trumpet to his lips.

Marcus did not reply. In the mist he suddenly heard raised voices. Then, shouts. The shouting was coming from his men.

"Hedwig," go and see what is going on over there," Marcus snapped.

Hedwig did not reply as he quickly wheeled his horse round and headed off into the mist.

"Wait," Marcus muttered raising his hand in warning as he turned to his trumpeter, "Let's not give away our position. The enemy are not gods. They too can't see anything in this fog."

The officers around him were silent and tense as they waited. Marcus peered in the direction into which Hedwig had vanished. In the mist he heard more shouting. Then silence. After what seemed like an age, a figure on horseback emerged out of the fog. It was Hedwig. The officer was accompanied by a number of Batavian riders who were driving two men on foot before them. Marcus stared at the two men as they came towards him. One was holding up a mistletoe branch and clutching a Carnyx in his other hand. The other one, an older man with a grey beard was clad in a fine black sheepskin tunic over which he was wearing leather, torso armour. He was armed with a single, long-handled axe.

"That is far enough," Marcus cried, "What do you want?"

The Britons stopped in their tracks as they caught sight of him. For a long moment no one spoke. "Our King, Faelan has sent us," the younger man said at last speaking in the Briton language as he held up the branch of mistletoe. "We come under this sign of truce and expect you will honour the ancient terms."

"I know the sign," Marcus retorted irritably as he replied in the Briton language, "You have my word that you will not be harmed or detained."

"Not many Romans do," the older envoy said as he fixed his eyes on Marcus, "But then again you were not born to a Roman mother were you. Why does one whose mother was one of us fight against us? Why do you fight against your own people? What has Rome done to win your loyalty?"

Marcus's face darkened as he stared at the grey, bearded envoy.

"These men around me are my family now," he said sternly. "Rome is the light in a dark world. I have seen what civilisation is and it is better than what was before."

The envoy snorted contemptuously as he glanced around him at the hard faces of the Batavian officers sitting on their horses.

"They are no more Roman than you are," the Briton scowled. "and you are too young to know what it was like before, when we were truly free. You fucking southerners have been seduced by cheap Roman luxuries."

"What message do you bring with you?" Marcus said impatiently.

The grey-bearded envoy spat onto the rocks and looked up. "King Faelan has no wish to keep on killing you," he growled, "The King offers you terms. Come and join us. This is not your fight or that of your men." The envoy turned to look at each of the Batavians clustering around him. "He has promised each man who joins us twenty gold coins. He will expect an answer before sunset."

Marcus's face was unreadable as he stared silently at the Briton.

"Tell your King," he said at last, "That the 2nd Batavian Cohort is not interested in his gold. If you think these men can be bribed then you are wrong. Tell your master that we are coming for him and that if he values his life he still has the chance to surrender to us."

The grey bearded envoy took a step towards Marcus and shook his head.

"You are making a mistake," the Briton hissed. "The spirits are against you. You are going to lead your men into disaster. Our druids have foreseen the things to come. Farewell then, snake! Your bones will never find a final resting place."

## Chapter Thirty Three - The Mountain Ambush

Marcus sat on his horse surrounded by his officers. It was near noon and the sun was rising into a gloriously blue sky. The men were watching him with silent, tense faces as he spoke. A full day had passed since the envoys had approached the battle group and that morning the mist had finally lifted and the mountains had reappeared, wild, deserted, desolate and magnificent. Along the ridge and slopes, the Batavian cavalry squadrons stood clustered together as they waited for their officers to issue their orders. High above the soldiers, a hunting bird was hanging in the air, its wings spread wide, as its beady eyes searched the ground below and its high-pitched cry faded away across the treeless, mountain peaks.

"Our scouts report that this second rebel war-band consists only of infantry," Marcus said glancing around at his men. "We think they have around three or four hundred men. They are marching down from the north and if they keep going they will reach us within hours. It is important that they do not join forces with the King. So we are going to strike them before they can reach their allies." Marcus paused as he studied the faces of the men around him. "The enemy are following the river valley. Our scouts are watching them now. Hedwig you will take your three squadrons and flank them. Make sure the enemy do not see you. When you hear the signal fall on them from the north, Lucius," Marcus said turning to the old warrior. "You and your nine squadrons will block the valley from the south. The enemy is not to break through your line. Attack when you hear my signal. I will lead the remaining three squadrons into their flank. If all goes well they won't stand a chance. We will take no prisoners and there will be no looting. We will destroy them and we will get out." Marcus turned to look around at his officers. "Any questions?"

"What about the High King?" Lucius replied with a concerned look on his face. "Do we just expect him to do nothing whilst we destroy his allies?"

"It's a risk we will have to take," Marcus muttered, "We don't know where he is. Our scouts haven't seen any of his men since the mist lifted."

"Sir," Hedwig said with a serious looking face, "I agree with Lucius. We should have a plan just in case Faelan and his men do come to their allies rescue."

"If the High King appears," Marcus replied, "I will order a retreat. Our rallying point will be the abandoned hill-fort. It is the easiest defensible place. Make sure that your men are aware of this and listen out for my signal. If something happens to me Lucius will take command of the battle group. That will be all. Good luck and don't do anything stupid. I want you all to stay alive."

"Thunder and lashing rain, so Woden commeth," the standard bearer cried out. The grim cry was taken up by the officers as the gathering broke up.

"Marcus," Lucius said stiffly as the officers started off towards their individual squadrons, "I am sorry about the other night. The 2nd Batavian Cohort can always count on me. Fight well, friend."

Marcus reached out and gripped Lucius's shoulder affectionately but the first Centurion refused to meet his gaze and looked away instead.

"I never doubted you," Marcus replied. "You are a good man Lucius and I am a lucky to be able to command the finest auxiliary Cohort in the Empire."

\*\*\*

"There they are Sir," Fridwald muttered as he crouched beside Marcus in amongst the cover of the rocks. Marcus did not reply as he studied the valley floor below. Beside him Gaius's face was flush with excitement and his breathing was coming in rapid gasps. Down in the valley a hundred yards away, the mountain stream tumbled and wound its way across the uneven ground, a white, sliver of water in a barren, treeless world. A line of armed men, clad in sheep skin tunics and clutching spears and small round shields, were making their way up the valley straight past the position where Marcus and his ninety, mounted Batavians remained hidden from view. The Britons were strung out in a disorderly column and most were wearing little or no metal armour or helmets.

"They look like peasants straight off the land," Gaius sneered contemptuously, "They will die easily."

Marcus lifted his gaze away from the rebel war-band towards the north. Hedwig and his men should be in position by now. The Britons had followed the stream as he had hoped they would. Quickly he glanced up at the sky. The blue sky was cloudless and the hot, summer's day was undisturbed by any breeze.

"Give the order," Gaius muttered, turning to stare at Marcus, "We have the enemy where we want them. What are you waiting for?"

Marcus ignored the young Tribune and turned to stare at the war-band as it made its way slowly up the river valley. The enemy seemed oblivious to the impending danger. Gaius was right. The rebels were not professional soldiers. They had taken no precautions or sent out any scouts or patrols.

"Let's go," he muttered as he turned and carefully started to make his way back to the spot where the rest of his men were waiting.

As he swung himself onto his horse the Batavian riders around him began to form a wide line that extended along the ridge. The men were silent as they moved into their positions. Marcus glanced at Fridwald and gave him a little encouraging smile. Then he turned to the standard bearer who was sitting on his horse beside him.

"We will take the standard straight down the centre," Marcus muttered, "No prisoners will be taken. Stay close to me."

"Sir," the standard bearer replied with a curt nod of his head.

"Give the signal," Marcus said turning to the trumpeter behind him.

A moment later a long trumpet blast echoed away across the treeless hills and it was swiftly followed by two short blasts.

"2nd Batavian Cohort will advance," Marcus yelled as he raised his arm and urged his horse forwards and on down the slope.

Along the ridge the Batavian horsemen cried out as they charged forwards and on down the mountain slope. Marcus unsheathed his sword as his horse bore him down the open heather covered slope.

Down beside the stream, the Britons had come to a halt and had turned at the trumpet blast and for a stunned moment they stared at the Batavians in utter surprise. The moment however did not last long, as the valley floor erupted in shouts and yells. There was no time for the Britons to organise a defence. The Batavian horsemen slammed into the rebels in an ugly violent deluge. Marcus cried out as he bore down on a group of three rebels. As he crashed through them his sword caught a man square in the face, sending him spinning into the shallow stream. Marcus wheeled his horse around and caught Fridwald finishing off the man's companion. Wildly he stared around him. Where was the support? Where was Lucius? The peaceful, mountain stream had transformed into a chaotic, confused and swirling fight as the Batavian horsemen and the surrounded rebel infantry, hacked and slashed at each other. The men were shouting, screaming and yelling. A man shouting curses came splashing through the stream clutching a spear, intent on driving it into the flank of Marcus's horse but, at the last moment he tripped over a rock and went tumbling to the ground. Further up the valley a group of rebels pulled a Batavian from his horse and the unfortunate soldier vanished under a flurry of furious blows. Marcus kicked at a Briton who came at him with an axe and urging his horse up the slope he broke free from the melee. Where the fuck was Hedwig and Lucius? His men were outnumbered and the Britons would surely drive them off. Then, as he wheeled around he heard a noise and caught sight of Hedwig and his men charging up the valley towards him. The three Batavian squadrons had formed into a tight V shape formation with Hedwig at their very point.

Marcus cried out in fierce joy and raised his sword in the air. Two Britons with blue, woad-covered faces and armed with spears and small hide-bound shields, came storming towards him but before they could reach him, Fridwald and the standard bearer rode into the gap and blocked the men's path. One of the Britons rammed his spear into the standard bearer's horse's neck and with a panicked-cry, rider and beast collapsed sideways onto the hard, stony ground sending the boar-headed Standard flying and clattering onto the rocks. Without thinking Marcus urged his horse towards it and reached it just as a Briton stooped and grabbed hold of it. Marcus's slashing sword struck the man across his neck, slicing open his main artery and sending a fountain of blood gushing over the warrior's leather body-armour. The rebel staggered backwards and dropped the Standard as he clutched vainly at his neck. Then silently he toppled over backwards onto the ground. Marcus slid from his horse and grasped hold of the precious Standard. He was about to rise when something hit his horse and the beast reared up on its hind legs and bolted away. Marcus cursed but there was no time to go after the horse. A huge hulk of a warrior, clad in a black, sheepskin-tunic and wearing a horned helmet, came charging towards him clutching a long handled battle-axe. Marcus stumbled backwards in fright as the axe came sweeping down towards his chest. The warrior was snarling and spit clung to his black beard.

Desperately Marcus tried to block the next blow with his sword but the force and fury of the man's attack drove him backwards. Behind him he suddenly heard a horse's nervous whinny and snorting and a second later a rider, flashed past him and sunk his spear into the Briton's chest.

"The Standard, give it to me Sir," a Batavian rider cried out as he held out his hand. Shaken, Marcus handed it up to the rider who immediately rode away.

Where were Lucius and his men? Across the valley floor and the mountain stream the Batavians and rebels were locked in a loud vicious confused melee but the Britons were standing their ground and they still outnumbered the Batavians. As he stared at the fighting, a rider-less horse came cantering past. Then from further up the valley he heard a horn. It sounded close and it had come from the direction in which Lucius would come. Marcus's chest was heaving and he was panting with exertion. From a fold in the ground, horsemen suddenly appeared, charging towards the mass of fighting men. At the sight Marcus's face turned pale in dismay. The cavalry coming down the valley were not his men. They were Britons. Their small, shaggy horses and leather armour, painted faces and spiky hair were unmistakeable. Marcus groaned. What was this? What had happened to Lucius and his men? But there was no time to ponder what had gone wrong. The rebel cavalry were nearly upon him. There were hundreds of them.

Wildly Marcus turned to look around him. Corpses and dead horses littered the mountain slope and the stream. A wounded Batavian was trying to crawl away up the hill side.

"Sound the retreat," Marcus yelled, "Sound the retreat, fall back!"

There was no sign of Fridwald or his trumpeter but in amongst the desperate furious battle some of the Batavian troopers had already seen the approaching danger and were breaking away from the mass brawl.

"Fuck," Marcus swore with rising dismay. Where was Hedwig? But in the confusion he could    not see him.

281

"Sound the retreat, fall back," he roared with growing panic.

And a moment later from somewhere in amongst the mass of struggling, running and fighting men he heard a trumpet blast ordering the retreat. The blast however was cut off before it could be completed.

But it had been enough. Across the mountain stream and valley floor the surviving Batavians began to disengage and gallop away up the mountain slopes in a wild disorganised and humiliating flight. Marcus turned and started running down the stream. His boots splashed into the cold, mountain water as he heard the cries and shouts of the Britons behind him. What had happened to Lucius? Why had he not arrived as he'd been ordered to? A rider-less horse came cantering past and vainly Marcus tried to grab hold of it, but the beast was too terrified to stop. Behind him he heard the thud of horses' hooves and instinctively he turned and raised his sword. A large group of Britons on horseback came surging towards him. They were armed with spears. Marcus crouched in the stream and with his left hand he steadied himself on a rock. There was no point in running. The enemy cavalry were already upon him and surging around both sides of the stream. He was trapped. Desperately he turned to stare at the mountain slopes across which he could see his fleeing men. The surviving Batavians were vanishing over the crest.

Around him the Britons were crying out in triumph as they surrounded him. Then suddenly from out of nowhere, Marcus heard a deep and savage screaming roar and Fridwald, completely alone, came charging into the enemy ranks. The young bodyguard's sword nearly decapitated a Briton and sent the man tumbling into the mountain stream as he broke through the enemy ranks towards Marcus.

"Fridwald, ride, save yourself," Marcus roared.

But Fridwald seemed to take no notice. Furiously he lashed out at a Briton who tried to force his way past him. The blow forced the Briton back.

"Fridwald ride, that's an order," Marcus screamed as several Britons charged towards him.

"No," Fridwald shouted, "my place is at your side Sir."

Marcus ducked under a wild slashing sword swing and grasped hold of a rider's tunic and tried to pull the warrior from his horse but it was too no avail. Letting go he stumbled backwards and tripped over a rock and landed painfully in the middle of the stream. As he gasped at the coldness of the water, Fridwald roared and defiantly drove back a Briton on horseback but was as he did so he was struck in the back by two spears that knocked him from his horse. Marcus's bodyguard landed heavily on the ground and did not move.

Marcus gasped as he staggered unsteadily to his feet. The Britons surrounded him, closing in on all sides with their spears, their murderous intent plainly visible on their faces.

He closed his eyes and waited for death, but it did not come.

The Britons seemed to hesitate. Then their leader, a man with a blue-painted face and a long moustache raised his spear.

"The King wants this one alive. Take him," the man cried out.

## Chapter Thirty Four – The Watchers

With a start Corbulo opened his eyes and realized that he'd dozed off. Silently he cursed himself as he turned to stare at the secluded farm house in the forest clearing. It was night and the sky was covered with stars and in the pale moonlight the farm looked quiet and peaceful. In his hiding place in the forest Corbulo shifted his weight to a more comfortable position. Four days had passed since he'd found Efa and Dylis and for four days he, Aidan and Logan had taken turns to watch the farm hoping for an opportunity to free his wife and daughter but none had presented itself and Aidan was growing increasingly restless. Corbulo sighed as he stared at the dark building, fifty yards away. But they couldn't just force their way into a farm that was defended by forty, heavily-armed men. That would be the surest way to get everyone killed. No, the only thing they could do was to wait and see what happened. They had to be patient. There had been no more sightings of Efa and Dylis since his daughter had tried to escape, but Emogene, her husband and the forty warriors had not left the farm either. The warriors' daily routine had remained the same. Every day they had emerged at dawn to check the farm buildings, after which one party would disappear into the forest to hunt whilst the rest had remained indoors. What were they doing here? What were they waiting for? Corbulo opened his mouth and rubbed his finger thoughtfully over one of his two remaining teeth. Something strange was going on in that farm.

It had been a long time since his last encounter with Emogene, but two days ago he'd spotted her coming out of the main farm building. The young Caledonian woman, who years ago had chased him and Marcus half way across Caledonia, seemed to have become a mother for he'd seen her holding the hands of two small children. The eldest, a boy, looked no older than five. Corbulo stared vacantly at the farm as he remembered every last detail of that desperate flight on horseback and, as he did so, he frowned. What had Emogene said to him when she had trapped him and Marcus in that Roman watchtower beside the sea loch? She had told him that they would meet again and that when they did she was going to kill him. She wanted him and Marcus dead because he knew about the amber. He understood that. He knew the location of the amber cave and he was a threat. The amber seemed to mean a lot to that woman and she was probably frightened that if the knowledge and location leaked out, it would bring a steady stream of treasure-hungry Roman bandits, mercenaries, adventurers and thugs to her village. What she didn't realise was that he personally couldn't give a flying fuck about the amber or her village. He was never going back there again. All he'd wanted to do was to bring Marcus home. Slowly and bewildered he shook his head. The whole affair was a tragic misunderstanding. If only he could convince Emogene that he was no threat. Maybe then he could get Efa and Dylis back without conflict. But there was little chance of that. Too much had happened and too much suspicion and bitterness had built up between them for that to be bridged in a civilised manner. A wry, little smile appeared on Corbulo's lips. So the gods had decided to bring about a meeting between him and Emogene. He glanced up at the stars. Were the immortals even now gambling amongst themselves on who would emerge the victor?

"Yeah have a laugh, well fuck you," Corbulo muttered quietly, as he raised his hand towards the night sky in a crude gesture.

In the dark forest behind him a twig suddenly snapped. Corbulo spun round and drew his sword. Tensely he peered into the gloom. Someone was out there amongst the trees. Had that been movement in the darkness? He couldn't see anything as he crouched ready to lunge. In the forest another twig snapped and he heard a faint muffled curse.

"Corbulo," a voice hissed close by, "where the hell are you?"

Corbulo rolled his eyes irritably and lowered his sword. The voice belonged to Logan, his brother in law.

A moment later two figures appeared out of the gloom heading towards his hiding place.

"You are supposed to relieve me at dawn," Corbulo whispered, "and what is he doing here?" he said gesturing at Aidan who was accompanying his son. "I thought we agreed that someone would stay in Aquae Sulis at all times?"

"I am here to make sure you are doing a proper job," Aidan whispered in an annoyed voice. "You keep messing things up Corbulo."

"As if you were the perfect father," Corbulo retorted.

"Shut up, both of you," Logan hissed as he halted and crouched beside Corbulo and peered at the dark farm through the trees.

"Has there been any activity Corbulo, anything at all?" Logan inquired.

"Nothing," Corbulo growled, giving Aidan, his father in law, an annoyed look, "everyone seems fast asleep. They have a guard beside the main entrance and another around the back but I think they are both asleep. They are a bunch of amateurs. This would never have happened if I was still a watch commander. Falling asleep on duty is a serious matter."

Logan nodded and was silent for a while as he stared at the farm.

"We've been thinking," Logan whispered at last, "What if I went up to the farm tomorrow and told the owner that I was interested in buying his slaves. It may work and I would be able to get a closer look at Efa and Dylis."

"Is this your idea Aidan?" Corbulo whispered.

"Well we can't just sit here forever watching this damned place," Corbulo's father in law replied irritably. "They have my daughter and granddaughter. Gods know what they are doing to them inside that farm whilst we sit here and wait and do nothing."

"It's a stupid idea," Corbulo whispered, "For a start Emogene's husband told me they are not interested in selling slaves. Secondly if Efa and Dylis see you, they may reveal that they know you and thirdly, have you forgotten about Romulus? That little shit knows who we are and what we look like. How would you explain yourself if he is inside that farm with them? Only an idiot would make such a move."

"Alright, alright," Logan said quickly raising his hand and pre-empting Aidan's reply. "But my father is right. We cannot just sit here and do nothing."

Corbulo sighed and turned to stare at the farm.

"We must be patient," he whispered, "I know it's hard but if we make a wrong move then we will lose everything."

In the darkness Aidan muttered something under his breath. At his side Logan sighed and lowered his head in defeat.

"There is something unusual going on here," Corbulo whispered, "those men in that farm do not belong here. They are waiting for something."

"They are from Gaul," Aidan murmured. "All of them. I heard them talking a few days ago."

Slowly Corbulo turned to gaze at his father in law. In the gloom it was hard to make out Aidan's face.

"What? From Gaul!" Corbulo whispered, "And you decide to tell us this only now?"

From the darkness there was no reply. Corbulo rolled his eyes and turned back to look at the farm and for a while, the three of them, crouching in the darkness, remained silent.

"They are foreign mercenaries," Corbulo exclaimed suddenly. "That's what they are doing here. Emogene and her husband are recruiting a war band. I think they intend to join the fighting in the north."

At his side Logan exchanged a glance with his father.

"How do you know that she and her husband are in charge?" the younger man whispered.

"She's a druid and she has the money," Corbulo muttered, "I saw her once, a few years ago in Hibernia. She was with the druids on the Forbidden Islands. The druids were getting large amounts of gold and silver from somewhere, shipping it in. I saw the ships and treasure with my own eyes. Emogene and her husband will be in charge. I am sure of it. They must be using this farm as their base to organise their war band."

"But why hire mercenaries?" Logan whispered.

"I have been watching them," Corbulo said, turning to glance at Logan and Aidan. "They look like trained professional fighters. Maybe there are even some deserters from the Legions or auxiliary cohorts amongst them. Trained fighting men are expensive but they are also formidable opponents. The rebels in the north should be glad to have them fighting on their side."

"So," Aidan growled, "what does this druid bitch want with my daughter and granddaughter? Are they to be sex slaves for these mercenaries? If this is so then I am going to kill every last one of them."

Corbulo took a deep breath and shook his head. "I don't know," he murmured grimly. "But if they abuse Efa and Dylis I will join you in killing every last one of them. You have my word."

# Chapter Thirty Five – Moving in the Shadows

Something was not right as Logan came running through the trees towards their small forest camp. Corbulo and Aidan rose to their feet in alarm from where they had been preparing their porridge breakfast, over a small wood fire.

"What's happened?" Aidan cried, as he stared anxiously at his son.

Logan came to a halt beside the small camp which the three of them had constructed a mile away or so from the farm. He was panting.

"Another party of warriors have arrived," he gasped, "I counted around fifty men, all of them armed to the teeth. They came to the farm at dawn in small, separate groups of two or three. They nearly saw me."

"Any sign of Efa or Dylis?" Corbulo growled.

Logan shook his head.

Corbulo grunted and turned to look at Aidan.

"This must be why they were waiting," he said sharply, "So now Emogene has ninety armed men inside that farm. That's a proper war band. We should go and take a look right away."

"I agree," Aidan nodded.

Corbulo glanced at the three horses that stood tethered to a tree. Then he stooped and picked up the sharpened wooden spear he'd made for himself, and started to gather his belongings together as the others did the same.

The three of them crept through the woods towards the hiding place from which they had been observing the farm. Two days had passed since Corbulo had guessed the meaning of the strange gathering at the farm. As they drew closer, Corbulo could hear mens' shouts and the neighing of horses. Stealthily he slid into the observation post and peered at the farm through the bushes.

The doors to the two outlying barns had been flung wide open and three, four- wheeled, open topped, Roman wagons stood drawn up along the forest path. A team of two horses had been assigned to each wagon and stacked onto the wagons were piles of weapons, shields, sacks of wheat and numerous amphorae. Men were milling about loading supplies and beside the carts, fifty or sixty mercenaries wearing old and plain looking tunics, had formed up in a long, single file. The men were calling out to each other in good humoured banter.

"Looks like they are getting ready to move out," Aidan growled as he stared at the activity around the farm.

Corbulo did not reply as he stared at the scene.

"How are they going to avoid the Roman patrols?" Logan muttered, "Surely such a large band of men is going to attract Roman attention, especially if they are armed. They still have to travel hundreds of miles before they reach the north and there are patrols everywhere."

"Look," Corbulo said quietly, as he gestured towards the mercenaries. The men's laughter and spirited banter increased as their comrades began to weave a long, sturdy-looking rope around each man's neck. Corbulo watched as each man in the line became linked to the next man, until the whole group was bound together by a single rope. As the mercenaries finished tying up their comrades Corbulo turned to Aidan and Logan.

"There is your answer. They are going to pretend that the men are slaves or POW's," Corbulo muttered. "That's how they will disguise themselves. The ones not tied to the rope will act as guards. The mens' weapons will be in the wagons with their supplies and Emogene and her husband will act as slave owners." Corbulo paused. "This has been carefully thought out. It's a good, cover story. They know what they are doing."

"Rope instead of iron slavers-chains," Logan whispered, "Who is going to believe that?"

Corbulo shrugged. "Iron chains are expensive, not every slaver will have them."

"We need to find out where they are going?" Aidan said. "Then once they are out on the road, we should alert the nearest Roman patrol. I will give my left ball before I see my daughter and granddaughter get taken any further by these foreigners."

Corbulo gave Aidan a wry look.

"If there is a fight, Efa and Dylis could be killed. Are you willing to take that risk?"

"Then what should we do?" Aidan growled in exasperation, "You seem to know everything Corbulo except how to get Efa and Dylis back. Come on then, tell us your great, fucking plan."

"We follow them," Corbulo said resolutely, "we shadow them and we wait until an opportunity comes along, where we can free them."

"That's your plan?" Aidan grumbled.

"I agree with Corbulo," Logan interrupted with a weary sigh, "We can't do anything that may harm Efa or Dylis. An opportunity to set them free will come along. We just have to remain patient. Corbulo is right."

"He fucked it up the first time by letting them be taken," Aidan hissed furiously as he rounded on his son. "Then he screwed it up a second time by not slitting that shit, Romulus's throat and now you are allowing him to fuck it up for a third time."

"Quiet," Corbulo whispered as ignoring his father in law he peered at the farm. "Look, there they are."

Logan and Aidan abruptly turned to stare at the farm. Outside the doorway into the main house a woman had appeared, holding a small child in each hand. It was Emogene. Her long, dark hair fell to her shoulders and she was clad in a white tunic, over which she was wearing a short, travelling cloak with a hood. As she strode towards the nearest wagon, she was followed by her husband, the man Corbulo had met in the baths and bringing up the rear were Efa, Dylis and Romulus. Corbulo drew a sharp breath as he caught sight of his wife and daughter. They were too far away to see the expressions on their faces, but the two women seemed to be walking freely and were not tied up.

"They look unhurt," Logan gasped, "I can't see any chains on them."

Corbulo's eyes slid from Efa and Dylis to Romulus. His old employee was showing his new employers far more loyalty than he had ever shown to him. He would remind Romulus of that when he finally caught up with him. His face darkened as he watched Emogene pick up her children and place them inside the wagon, before climbing aboard. Where was she heading? Where was she taking his Efa and Dylis?

Just as Efa and Dylis reached the heavily laden cart, there was a sudden commotion. Dylis darted away from the group and shot off towards the forest. A loud cry rose up from the mercenaries milling about the small convoy and a few of the men moved to cut off the girl's escape. Dylis swerved and slipped passed the first man but just as she was about to reach the trees, two mercenaries caught her and roughly threw her to the ground. Dylis squealed and tried to break free but her yells were met by a barrage of laughter from the mercenaries as the two men dragged her back to the wagon. Behind him Corbulo suddenly sensed movement. He turned to see Logan struggling to keep his father from bursting out of the hiding place and towards the farm.

"Stay down you fool," Corbulo whispered angrily, "Or they will see us."

Aidan's face had turned a furious, blushing red but he was not staring at Corbulo. At the farm the two mercenaries had handed Dylis over to Romulus. Dylis was still yelling and struggling to break free as Romulus slapped her hard across the face. The blow silenced the girl and she ceased her struggle as Romulus hauled her to the wagon, dragging her along by her hair. A few of the mercenaries cried out in the Briton language calling on Dylis to try and escape again.

"That fucker is going to be the first to die," Corbulo said quietly as he stared at Romulus.

"He's mine," Aidan growled. "And I am going to make him bleed."

Corbulo turned his attention to Emogene. The young woman was seated beside her husband at the front of the cart. Her husband was holding the horse's reins and he seemed to be waiting on Dylis and Romulus. As Corbulo stared at Emogene she turned round and said something to Efa who had found a space behind her in amongst the supplies. Efa did not seem to reply but as Romulus forced a tearful Dylis up onto the wagon she turned and lent towards the two young children sitting across from her.

"So what do we do?" Logan murmured as he stared at the scene.

Down beside the farm Emogene's husband had stood up and was shouting at the mercenaries. Then abruptly he sat down and the small convoy started out along the forest path that led towards the Roman road.

"We follow," Corbulo said curtly, "All the way to Hades if necessary."

## Chapter Thirty Six – The Fosse Way

The Fosse Way stretched off into the distance, a perfect, straight, grey-stone line that looked out of place amongst the rolling hills, lush green and yellow meadows and dark tangled woods. It was mid-morning and a day had passed since Emogene and her mercenaries had left the farm. The road up ahead was deserted. Corbulo, Aidan and Logan trotted along at a carefully measured pace. The thud of their horses' hooves on the stone paving stones and gravel, mingled with the occasional snorting of their horses and the cheerful singing birds in the trees. A gentle, western breeze carried the smell of freshly-cut grass. Corbulo peered up the road to where it dipped out of sight over a hill. All morning he, his father and brother-in-law had been shadowing the column of mercenaries from a discreet distance. Emogene and her war-band had headed north as he had expected, but she had taken great care to avoid any towns and settlements, leading her men around them. Corbulo had been forced to slow his pace for the foreign war-band were nearly all on foot.

Where was Emogene heading? Where was she taking his wife and daughter? Corbulo glanced at his companions. Both Aidan and Logan had not said much all morning. They too must be wondering how this was going to end. Aidan caught his eye and his face soured. He was clutching a spear and an old sword was strapped to his belt. The man was never going to like him Corbulo thought, but it didn't matter. He was never going to enjoy his father-in-law's company either. Logan looked tense and worried as he searched the road ahead. His long bow and a quiver of arrows was strapped across his back and a Roman army Pugio, knife was stuck into his belt.

"Don't worry Logan. We will get them back," Corbulo said, trying to sound upbeat as he gave the younger man an encouraging nod.

"We are going to need luck to be on our side," Aidan growled darkly. "Our women have ninety, heavily-armed men to guard them and there are just three of us."

"Is he always so cheerful?" Corbulo snapped as he made eye contact with Logan.

"Shut up, both of you," Logan hissed in an irritable voice, "Your constant bickering is driving me insane. You are worse than a couple of feuding women."

Corbulo scowled and turned to look away. In Caledonia, Marcus had spent some time as a captive in the same dungeon as Emogene and although weak and delirious, he had remembered a few scraps of information about the woman who now owned Efa and Dylis. Corbulo sighed. The feud with Emogene had started out as a tragic misunderstanding that had been widened by bitterness, mutual suspicion and fear. What would it take for him to clear all this up? Could he just ride up to her and pay her to release Efa and Dylis? Would she let them go? It seemed unlikely and the risk that it would all go wrong was far too great. Corbulo growled and picked at his tooth. Mistrust was a powerful thing and killing seemed easier than talking. A sudden thought made him shiver with unease. What if Emogene had put one and one together and figured out who her female slaves really were? Romulus must have told her by now about himself and Aidan and Logan. She would know that someone, somewhere, was interested in taking her slaves from her. She would be on her guard. But would she remember his name and realise who he was? It had been several years since their last encounter in Hibernia and maybe, just maybe, she did not yet realise who was after her. Gods let it last, he thought for Efa and Dylis' fate depended on it.

"Romulus, you fucking weasel," Corbulo muttered as he shifted his weight uneasily. "I can't wait to get my hands on you."

"You said you know this Emogene," Aidan muttered glancing at Corbulo. "So what is it

296

between you and her? You shag her?"

Corbulo took a deep breath. "It's a long story," he replied sourly. "Just let's say I shouldn't have hit her, when I rescued Marcus from that Caledonian dungeon."

"We're not far from Corinium Dobunnorum," Logan interrupted as he suddenly brought his horse to a halt. "If the mercenaries keep to plan they should leave the road up ahead and cut across the fields and around the town." Logan turned to Corbulo. "There is a small Roman garrison in the town. We could alert their commander and get him to intercept the war-band."

"No," Corbulo replied with a firm shake of his head, "If there is a fight and Emogene knows she is going to die or be captured, she will slaughter her slaves before it happens. We must assume that she knows what we want. Romulus will have told her everything. We can't put Efa and Dylis at risk like that."

"We don't know what Romulus has told that bitch," Aidan said. "Maybe he has told her nothing. Maybe they don't know they are being followed."

"And why would he keep quiet?" Corbulo snapped.

Aidan shrugged. "Maybe to save his own skin and reputation. Those mercenaries may start to see him as a liability, if they know that their cover has been exposed and that they are being followed. It was Romulus after all who pointed us towards Aquae Sulis and gave us Emogene's name. He betrayed her."

"My father has a point," Logan said.

Corbulo grunted and muttered something under his breath. "Maybe," he said in a louder voice, "but the risks are still too great. We will keep on watching them for now."

The three of them were silent as they started out along the road again. In the distance Corbulo could see a small wood and along the sides of the road grave- stones had been erected in the Roman fashion. Logan was right. They were nearing the Roman settlement of Cirencester.

As Corbulo trotted on through the wood, a man stepped out into the road ahead of him. He was armed with a gladius and a white focale, a Roman army scarf was tied around his neck. The man raised his hand and from amongst the trees five more men appeared, forming a loose, semi-circle around the three riders. All of them were armed with spears, shields and swords and they looked hostile. Corbulo reined in his horse as beside him, Aidan and Logan did the same. The man with the scarf grinned but there was no warmth in his eyes.

"Say," he said addressing Corbulo in good Latin, "you three wouldn't happen to be following us now would you?"

Corbulo eyed the man warily. Then he turned to glance at the man's comrades.

"Sorry, following who?" he growled, turning back to the man who had addressed him.

The grin on the man's face widened as one of the mercenaries moved to block the road.

"I was told that three men on horseback were following my friends." The man with the white scarf shrugged and casually his hand dropped to rest on the pommel of his sword. "And here you are, three men on horseback trailing a couple of miles behind my friends. What a coincidence."

Corbulo leaned forwards on his horse and peered down at the man as a crazy little smile appeared on his lips.

"Where did you learn to speak such good Latin?" Corbulo asked in a bemused voice. "No don't tell me. Here's what I think. I think you are a deserter, possibly from the Legions. Forgot to hand over your scarf and sword when you left, did you? Stealing government property is punishable by a good whipping."

The man's grin faded and he was about to say something when Aidan's spear slammed straight into his chest with such force that it impaled him. The deserter with the scarf staggered backwards gurgling up blood and clutching at the stump of the wooden projectile before he went crashing sideways onto the road. Cursing, Corbulo tore his sword from its scabbard as everything around him descended into loud confused chaos. Two mercenaries came charging towards him. One drove his spear into Corbulo's horse's flank narrowly missing his leg. The beast screamed and collapsed, flinging Corbulo to the ground. He landed on his side with a thud that drove the air from his lungs and for a moment he just lay on the ground stunned. Then reality came rushing back. On the road he heard Aidan shouting and he caught a glimpse of Logan on horseback breaking through the cordon. Corbulo staggered to his feet as another mercenary came at him screaming a foreign battle cry, in a language Corbulo did not understand. With a roar born out of pure desperation, he grasped hold of the man's sword arm and drove his foot into the man's stomach, sending him stumbling backwards. There was no time to follow up his advantage. Another man was upon him thrusting a spear at his midriff, but just as he was about to strike, an arrow buried itself in the man's back and he flung up his arms and his spear clattered to the ground. Corbulo stared around him with wild eyes as he gasped for breath. Three of their attackers were down on the ground. The man he'd kicked came at him again. Corbulo twisted sideways as the man lunged. Then as his opponent lunged again, a little too eager this time, he caught the man's sword arm and with a grunt, drove his own sword into the attacker's unprotected side. There was no armour to stop his blade. The force of the blow sent him and his opponent crashing onto the ground and he landed heavily on top of the man. Corbulo let go of his sword and his fingers found the man's throat, but there was no further need. The man was dying.

Stiffly Corbulo staggered to his feet and swayed as he tried to maintain his balance. His right hand was sticky with someone else's blood and he'd lost his sword. Aidan was still sitting on his horse but his left leg was torn and bleeding heavily. He was shouting at Logan and grimacing in pain at the same time. Corbulo stared around him at the dead bodies lying scattered across the road. The two remaining attackers had turned and were fleeing down the road, running as fast as they could but as he stared at them, one of Logan's arrows slammed into one of the men sending him spinning into the drainage ditch.

"Get that last one, don't let him get away," Aidan roared as his son galloped off down the road in pursuit.

Corbulo bent over resting his trembling hands on his knees and was sick. His body shuddered as a spasm passed through him. Then he collapsed onto his backside, shaking uncontrollably. The front of his tunic was covered with the contents of his breakfast and yellow bile and mixed in amongst the sick were familiar droplets of blood.

"Are you hurt?" Aidan cried out as he turned to look at Corbulo.

Corbulo held up his hand but did not answer, as he tried to gather himself together. Slowly and unsteadily he rose to his feet.

"I am alright," he muttered, wiping his mouth with the back of his hand. "But it looks like they got your leg. Let me have a look at it."

Aidan turned to stare down the road in the direction in which Logan had vanished.

"It will heal," he grumbled, "bastard caught me with his sword. But it's worse for you. They killed your horse."

Corbulo turned to stare at the bloody carnage strewn across the road.

"That settles it," Corbulo said. "Those were Emogene's men. They belonged to her war-band. She must have left them here to ambush us. She knows we are on her trail. These men were sent here to kill us. She set a trap for us."

Aidan nodded grimly and for a moment he was silent. Then he gave Corbulo a little appreciative nod.

"Well they did a poor job," he growled, "No ranged weapons, no armour, no surprise attack. Did they think we were little, harmless boys? Now they are dead because of their overconfidence. What a bunch of arseholes!"

Corbulo did not reply as he caught sight of Logan galloping back towards them.

"You were right Corbulo," Aidan muttered and something in the tone of his voice made Corbulo look up, "Romulus talked," Aidan nodded. "Question is what will she do with Efa and Dylis? We were lucky today, bloody lucky. We will have to be more cautious from now on."

Corbulo stared at the approaching Logan as the young man slowed to a trot.

"Did you get that last one?" he cried out.

Logan nodded and ran his finger across his throat and Corbulo heaved a sigh of relief.

"But she doesn't yet realize who is following her," he muttered turning back to Aidan, as he stooped to pick up his sword and wipe it on the back of a corpse. "This is good."

Aidan grimaced with sudden pain and discomfort and pressed his hand against the wound in his leg.

"Why do you think that?" he grunted tensely.

"Because if she knew that it was me, she wouldn't have just sent six men," Corbulo replied, "She would have been here in person with her entire war band. That woman really doesn't like me. There is some bad history between us. She will eat my balls if she catches me."

## Chapter Thirty Seven – Carl Wark

Corbulo and Logan lay stretched flat out on their stomachs in the brown coarse heather beside a large, lichen-covered rock, as they peered at the rocky escarpment a couple of hundred yards away. It was early evening but the summer sun was still bright and strong. Around them the barren, treeless hills and bleak brown and reddish moor lands stretched away to the north. The two men did not move as they silently watched the steep, boulder-strewn slope that led up to the top of the hill, upon which sat the old abandoned Celtic hill-fort. It had been an hour since Emogene and her war-band had climbed the slope and had settled down to make their camp for the night. The mercenaries had posted guards at the main path into the fort and up on the crumbled, stone walls Corbulo could see another sentry.

It had been two days since the war band had left the Fosse Way and started to head north across open country. Corbulo glanced at the low, treeless, mountains around him. They were close to the old Brigantes tribal areas now and that meant they were entering the conflict zone. He sighed and turned his attention back to the abandoned hill-fort. There had simply been no opportunity to free Efa and Dylis since the war band had left Aquae Sulis. Corbulo bit his lip. But the longer he waited the harder it was going to be, for soon Emogene and her men would be in amongst the heart of the rebellion. He needed to act, but how? What could he and Aidan and Logan do against such a large number of armed men?

"I have heard of this place," Logan muttered quietly, without moving his head. "That hill-fort over there, forms part of a continuous line of fortifications and embankments. My father worked on these fortifications as a young man. The Brigantes built them all the way to the eastern sea. This was supposed to be the border between Roman land and that of the free Brigantes. They had a treaty."

Corbulo did not reply. It had been Governor Cerialis who had ordered the Roman invasion after the leader of the Brigantian confederation, the pro-Roman queen Cartimandua had been ousted from power by her estranged husband Venutius, who was hostile to Rome. Corbulo had been part of a battle group from the Twentieth that had crossed the border further west. As the Roman troops had poured across the border and into the highlands and mountains of the north, the Britons had put up a ferocious resistance that had never really ended.

"The north is not like the south," Corbulo murmured, "I don't think many Roman citizens are going to be building their villas up here. These mountains will never be fully pacified."

Just then a scream echoed away across the mountains. From the broken gateway into the hill-fort, a small figure shot out racing down the path straight towards where Corbulo and Logan were hiding. Corbulo's eyes widened. It was Dylis. His daughter was swiftly followed out of the gate by four men. The mercenaries being stronger and fitter easily outpaced the girl. They were laughing as they spread out to surround her. Desperately Dylis came to a halt as one of the mercenaries cut off her escape route. Wildly she looked around for a way out but there was none. The mercenaries however did not close in to grab her but kept their distance, laughing and taunting her. Corbulo's eyes narrowed as he felt a surge of raw, violent anger. The mercenaries were playing with his daughter. They were taunting and humiliating her.

"No," Logan hissed as he caught the look in Corbulo's eye. "Stay down. It could be another trap to flush us out. These men are cunning. There is nothing that you can do for her right now."

Grimly Corbulo stared at the scene as the men eventually tiring of their game closed in and caught Dylis and started to drag her back up the slope towards the hill-fort. Corbulo sighed and closed his eyes in silent helplessness.

"We should get back to my father," Logan whispered, "These mercenaries are not going anywhere tonight. We can come back at dawn."

Corbulo did not reply. Logan was right. There was nothing more they could do right now and Aidan's wound needed tending, for it had grown infected.

"Alright," he muttered as slowly he started to edge backwards into the cover of the large rock. Carefully Logan followed and the two of them were just about to slither away through the bed of a dried up stream when Corbulo froze and caught Logan's arm.

"Look," he hissed turning to stare at the hill-fort.

A party of ten armed men clutching wooden buckets, had emerged from the fort and had started out along the narrow path that led down towards a solitary, round-house a mile away. Corbulo peered at the men. It looked as if they were going to collect water. Then sharply he sucked in his breath as he caught sight of Romulus. The ex- banker was easily distinguishable by his clothes from the foreign mercenaries. Acting on instinct Corbulo turned to Logan.

"Go back to Aidan," he said quickly, "I am going to see what this lot is up to. I will join you later."

*** 

Corbulo crouched beside a large rock and peered at the solitary, round house. The building looked old and was in a state of disrepair. It's thatched roof had holes in it and a simple sheet of brown leather hung across the doorway. To one side stood a rough, stone enclosure made of slate and inside he could see a cow. A few chickens were prancing about and a dog was barking loudly from somewhere around the back. A few yards from the house, a small mountain stream gurgled and tumbled over the stones and rocky ledges, as it made its way down the gentle, treeless slope. The ten mercenaries were standing up stream from the home and were filling their buckets with water. The men were silent as they went about their tasks.

As Corbulo watched, a figure emerged from the house. It was a young woman and she was carrying a naked baby. She stopped just outside the doorway and stared at the men along the stream. Then she turned her head back to the entrance of her home, as if someone had said something to her. Corbulo frowned. The girl could not be much older than eighteen. Hesitantly and keeping a careful eye on the newcomers, the woman walked over to the stream, placed the child on a rock and began carefully washing the baby. Further up the stream Romulus had caught sight of the woman and, as Corbulo watched he peeled away from his comrades and strode towards her. Corbulo grunted in dismay as he guessed the man's intentions. The woman looked up as Romulus stopped before her and for a moment the two of them seemed to exchange words but Corbulo was too far away to hear what was being said.

Suddenly without warning Romulus grabbed the woman's arm and yanked her off her feet. The woman cried out in protest and tried to break free but Romulus had her in a strong grip and ruthlessly started to drag her towards the round house. Corbulo turned to stare at the doorway into the hut. Did the woman have no relatives willing to protect her? But no one emerged from the house as the woman screamed again and tried to bite Romulus's arm. Beside the stream the baby had started to cry. Corbulo growled with rising anger. Romulus was going to rape the woman. But just before the ex-banker could drag the struggling woman inside, a cry made him hesitate. He turned in the direction of the nine mercenaries beside the stream. Two of them were striding towards the house, gesturing at Romulus. They looked annoyed. Corbulo strained to hear what they were saying but he couldn't make it out. At the door to the hut Romulus raised his free hand in an irritated gesture and released his grip on the woman's arm before stomping away. The woman scrambled to her feet and rushed towards her baby, snatching it from the stone before fleeing downstream. Corbulo shook his head as he watched her go. Then slowly he turned to stare at Romulus and as he did so an idea came to him.

***

Carefully Corbulo smeared the vinegar salve into the ugly looking wound on Aidan's leg. The flesh around the wound had turned black and it had begun to stink. His father- in-law closed his eyes and groaned softly in pain. The deep, sword wound had got worse on the journey north and Aidan could no longer walk without being supported. He needed rest and time to recover, the woman who'd examined him had said or else he would lose the leg. But Aidan had refused outright to be left behind, threatening his son with violence if he tried to do so. But his leg was growing worse by the day and it was starting to hinder and slow them down. Corbulo had seen the black sickness before and he knew that it was incurable and, if left to fester it would kill Aidan. Logan too knew what needed to be done, but he lacked the courage to tell his father.

Wearily Corbulo glanced around at their small camp in a hollow in the hill side. The two remaining horses looked thin, miserable and malnourished. Corbulo knew how they felt for he too was exhausted and hungry. The camp was too close to the fort for them to dare to light a fire and for the past week they had not eaten a single hot meal. He turned his attention back to dressing the wound with a fresh white bandage.

"Logan is right," Corbulo muttered as he finished dressing the wound, "We should cut off your leg before it's too late. I too have seen these types of wounds and the infections that come with them. If we don't cut off that leg you are going to die."

"Every man has to die some day," Aidan growled with closed eyes. "But you are not cutting off my leg. When I die I want all of me to go. What kind of man goes into the next world with just one leg? Everyone would be laughing at me."

A little smile appeared on Corbulo's lips and he was about to say something else when, from out of the fading light Logan appeared. The younger man bounded into the camp and gave Corbulo a quick confirming nod.

"The woman has agreed to do it," he said with a glint of excitement in his eyes, "but I had to give her more money than we had initially offered. She will go when it's dark just like you said."

## Chapter Thirty Eight – Greed

It was a dark, moonless night and a warm breeze was blowing in from the south. Tensely Corbulo and Logan crouched in the heather. The jumble of stone walls and the entrance to the hill-fort was just ten yards away and they could hear the two guards quietly talking to each other. A couple of burning torches had been fixed to the sides of the ruined gateway, bathing the ancient entrance in a dim, flickering light. The mercenaries had parked one of their wagons across the entrance and through the gaps, Corbulo could see the reddish glow of a camp fire inside the fort. The mercenaries seemed to be sleeping. Corbulo turned and glanced at the girl who was crouching behind him. In the darkness it was impossible to see her face but he could hear her nervous breathing.

"Alright," he whispered, "You know the plan. Go up to the sentries and tell them that you want to see Romulus. Don't enter the fort. When he comes out tell him that you will agree to do what he wants as long as he pays you. Just get him outside the fort and we will do the rest."

From the darkness there was no reply. Then the girl rose silently to her feet and began to move towards the gateway and as she did, Corbulo got up and clenched his fist around a stone. At the entrance the guards had heard the girl's approach.

"Who is out there?" one of them cried in his foreign accent as he lifted a flaming torch from a wall socket and held it up above his head.

"I have come to see the man called Romulus," the girl replied in an unsteady voice. "We met down beside the stream."

"Are you alone?" the sentry called out.

"Yes," the girl replied, "Tell him I have a proposal for him, but for him alone."

The two sentries were silent. Then Corbulo heard a muffled laugh and some muttering.

It took a while before Romulus appeared. Warily he stopped just outside the gateway and peered into the darkness.

"Who are you? What do you want with me?" the ex-banker cried out.

The girl took a couple steps towards him and emerged into the faint circle of light thrown up by the guard's torch. Romulus grinned as he caught sight of her.

"Oh it's you," he said.

"I will do what you want," the girl said with a trembling voice, "but not here and you will agree to pay me."

"Who says that I am interested," Romulus leered, "You look like used goods. Maybe I have changed my mind. Why don't you come here so that I can get a better look at you?"

The girl hesitated and in the darkness Corbulo tensed.

"Why so hesitant?" Romulus snarled taking a step forwards. "What are you so afraid of? I won't bite."

The girl did not reply and remained standing, rooted to the ground. Suddenly suspicious, Romulus peered into the darkness.

"Why have you called me out here?" he asked frowning.

"Shit," Corbulo muttered as he lunged forwards. Romulus just had enough time to open his mouth in horror as Corbulo, head down, slammed into him sending them both tumbling down the slope in a frenzy of arms and legs. Corbulo grunted as he lost the stone he'd been carrying. Instead his grasping fingers found Romulus' throat and tightened their grip as in the darkness the banker squealed and frantically tried to push and kick him off.

From the gateway the guard holding the torch cried out a warning and his hand yanked his sword from his belt but, before he could act an arrow had buried itself into his chest sending the mercenary staggering backwards into the wagon. Logan loomed out of the darkness, stooped, struggled with Romulus' writhing body and then struck Romulus over the head with a stone, knocking him out with a single blow.

"Put him over my shoulder, I will carry him," Logan hissed hastily as he thrust his bow into Corbulo's hands.

In the hill-fort the sentry's cry had woken the camp and Corbulo could hear shouts and cries. Quickly he sheathed his sword and helped lift the limp body up onto his brother-in-law's broad shoulders. From the gateway the second guard was shouting in their direction but the man did not dare to leave the safety of the torch light.

"Move," Corbulo hissed as the two of them, carrying the unconscious Romulus, started to stumble away down the slope and into the night. It was hard going and their pace slowed as they navigated the rock-strewn slope in the pitch dark. Behind them the hill fort seemed to be in turmoil but there was no sign of any immediate pursuit. Logan was panting and sweating heavily from the exertion of carrying the heavy weight. Corbulo glanced back at the fort. The girl seemed to have vanished. It didn't matter. She had played her part. Suddenly he felt the bruises on his legs and shoulders, from where he'd hit himself when he'd crashed and tumbled down the slope. But his discomfort was overshadowed by a sense of deep satisfaction. His plan had worked. Now it was time to get some answers.

*** 

Romulus looked miserable as he sat silently staring at the ground. He was leaning up against a rock with his hands bound behind his back and his feet tied together. It was morning and the skies were covered in grey clouds and it was drizzling. Corbulo had deemed it wise to move their camp a further two

311

miles away, to a rocky treeless hill from whose summit they would have ample warning if the mercenaries came looking for their missing friend. But so far they had not seen a soul. Now the four of them were camped in between the great boulders on the summit, with the two horses tied up in a nearby gully. Corbulo stroked his chin thoughtfully as he stared at the prisoner. A large bruise and some dried blood caked the side of the ex-banker's face and the man had lost a tooth in the fight. Logan busied himself with preparing another cold breakfast and Aidan lay stretched out on his side on the rocky ground, one hand pressed to his infected leg as he glared at Romulus in grim anticipation.

"What do you want with me?" Romulus muttered in a dull, toneless voice.

Corbulo cleared his throat.

"You should have gone with that ship to Alexandria," he muttered. "You really should have. It would have been better for all of us."

Romulus shook his head in silent disagreement.

"When we are finished with you," Aidan growled in a voice that seemed to relish what was coming, "you will wish you had never been born."

"I was just doing my job," Romulus protested raising his head and staring at his captors. "You can't kill a man for that."

Corbulo raised his hand in warning for Aidan to be silent.

"Why don't you tell us about your employer? Where is Emogene heading?" Corbulo asked.

Romulus licked his lips nervously and looked away.

"They are going to the old Brigantian fort at Stanwick," he muttered, "There is some sort of gathering of the druids taking place. That's all I know."

Corbulo raised an eyebrow and exchanged a brief glance with Aidan. He had heard about the great fort at Stanwick. The Brigantes led by Venutius had started to construct it as a huge, fortified settlement and trading post some twenty years ago but the works had never been completed and the project had been abandoned shortly after the Roman conquest of Brigantia.

"So why are you going with them? Why did you show up in Aquae Sulis? Why did you warn your employer about us?" Corbulo growled as anger entered his voice. "You never showed me any loyalty when you worked for the bank, so why so much loyalty to your new employer?"

"She pays me well," Romulus replied avoiding Corbulo's angry blazing eyes. "She pays me very well, much better than you ever did."

Corbulo glared at Romulus for a long moment as his hand clenched into a fist.

"I think what he is trying to tell us," Aidan interrupted, "is that this little shit is greedy. He is just a greedy little bastard."

"There is nothing wrong with that," Romulus retorted.

"There is when it puts me and my family in danger," Corbulo cried out, as with an effort he controlled himself.

"Tell me about your employer; tell me everything you know," Corbulo said at last.

Romulus looked down at the ground. "I will make a deal with you," he said with sudden boldness. "If I tell you all I know you will promise not to kill me."

From the corner of his eye Corbulo caught Aidan turning to look at him.

"The time for making deals has passed," Corbulo said quietly. "Tell me what you know or else I will turn you over to my friends here. They are not civilized men like I am. They will make you endure pain like you have never experienced before. You are in no position to bargain with us."

Romulus's face grew pale and he gave Aidan a quick, nervous glance.

"Emogene is always angry," Romulus muttered looking away, "It's like something is eating her up inside. She is always snapping at people, always annoyed. Everyone has personally experienced her rage. The only time she seems content is when she is tending to her children. The rest of the men, the mercenaries, they fear her. She is a druid and they fear her magic. They have a nickname for her. They call her Possessed. Because some of the men think she mates with demons."

"Why is she so angry?" Corbulo asked frowning.

Romulus shrugged. "Who knows," he murmured, "Some of the men think it has to do with something that she was forced to do when she was young, some kind of trauma."

Corbulo grunted and scratched at the stubble on his chin.

"So what does she want with my wife and daughter?" Corbulo said. "Why did she buy them?"

Romulus leaned his head back against the rock, closed his eyes and sighed.

"I told you," he muttered, "The purchase order was for two female slaves who spoke Latin. Emogene wants her children to learn Latin. Your wife and daughter are teaching them the language and looking after them when Emogene is busy. They are house-hold slaves doing light duties and tasks, just like I told you. They are not being abused. My employer will not allow it."

Corbulo fixed his eyes on Romulus.

"Why does she want her children to learn Latin?"

Romulus swallowed awkwardly, "She told me that it was important that her sons grew up being able to understand the language of their enemy. She is a twisted fanatic, Corbulo. She hates Rome and everything to do with Rome. These mercenaries with her, they are all going to join the rebellion."

Corbulo said nothing. Then wearily he rubbed his hand across his face and muttered a little silent prayer of thanks to Fortuna. If he had not insisted on giving Efa and Dylis daily Latin lessons it was likely that his wife and daughter would have been split up and sold off separately.

Slowly Corbulo's eyes settled on Romulus.

"Did you tell your employer about me? Did you tell her that her slaves were my wife and daughter?" he said in a dangerous voice.

Romulus's face went white and for a moment he looked panic stricken.

"I may have," he muttered avoiding Corbulo's gaze. "But I swear, I never meant them any harm and I haven't touched them."

"That confession of yours cost me this wounded leg," Aidan roared with sudden fury.

"Does she know who I am?" Corbulo snapped.

Romulus shook his head in growing panic. "She thinks you are just trying to get your wife and daughter back. That's all. She doesn't know you." Then suddenly he stopped and his eyes bulged. "But you two do know each other," he exclaimed as realization dawned. "That's why you are so keen to know everything about her. You and her have met before haven't you? That's why you are asking all these questions."

Corbulo's eyes bored into Romulus and for a long moment the camp was silent. Then Corbulo looked away. The banker had guessed what this was about and in doing so he had signed his own death warrant. There was no way Corbulo could let him go now. If Romulus reported what he now knew to Emogene then Efa and Dylis would be in grave danger.

As if reading his thoughts Aidan turned and glanced at Corbulo. He looked grim.

"I will do it," he growled.

"No," Corbulo shook his head, "I will do it."

# Chapter Thirty Nine - The Eagle

Corbulo crouched beside the mountain stream and raised his cupped hands to his mouth and drank. The water was cold and it tasted good and as it filled his stomach he felt some strength return to his weary, battered body. It was a clear, hot afternoon and the fierce sun beat down on him. For five days now they had been following the mercenary war band north and the further they had gone, the more rugged and trackless the terrain had become. With a sigh Corbulo sat back down on the rock and glanced around him. The lush and beautiful, rolling uplands were heavily forested and to the west he could make out the bleak, treeless rocky peaks of the mountains that ran like a spine down the island of Britannia. Logan had said that they were close now to Stanwick; maybe another day's walk. What Emogene would do when they reached the abandoned Brigantian fortress was anyone's guess, but up here amongst the wild hills she was amongst friends and allies whilst he was not.

A sudden noise made him look up. In the clear blue skies a bird was circling overhead. Its magnificent brown-feathered wings spread out as it gracefully glided on the air currents; it's keen and sharp eyes taking in everything that moved below. Corbulo grunted. It was an eagle, the sacred god of the Legions. He had followed the Eagle of the Twentieth for half his life. As he stared up at the bird, the creature emitted another high pitched cry as it came swooping towards Corbulo only to climb away. A sudden melancholy seemed to take hold of Corbulo as he watched the eagle drift away towards the west. Was the eagle trying to tell him something? The bird suddenly reminded him of that day on the beach on Vectis with Dylis when she had delighted in playing with her dog and the sea. There had been an eagle in the sky that day too. That had been the last day on which he had been allowed to enjoy his comfortable life, looking after Agricola's farm. Corbulo lowered his eyes and stared moodily into the stream. Something was about to happen. He could sense it. Nothing good lasted forever, but shame and cowardice followed a man around like a shadow. The eagle was a sign. The gods were talking to him, they were telling him something.

"What," he growled irritably. "What do you want from me?"

*** 

Logan was tending to his father's leg when Corbulo returned carrying the two buckets of water. They had paused to rest in a small clearing in the forest and Logan had tethered the two horses to a nearby tree. Aidan had his eyes closed as he lay slumped up against a tree. Logan said nothing as he snatched the bucket of water from Corbulo's hand and knelt down to wash the infected wound. For a moment Corbulo stared at Aidan's blackened leg and the dirty blood stained bandage. They had run out of fresh bandages and disinfectant and the infection was growing worse. His father- in-law was deteriorating and for the past two days he had been unable to stay upright in the saddle and at night his groans and moaning had kept them all awake. Grimly Corbulo glanced at his brother-in-law. Logan was suffering from the stress and worry as he watched his father's weaken and it was distracting him from the task at hand.

"We need to cut his leg off," Corbulo said firmly as he strode towards the two, mangy-looking horses and placed the other bucket of water in front of them.

Logan did not reply as he crouched beside his father tending to the ugly, festering wound.

"You know I am right," Corbulo growled as he sat down on a rock to watch. "We have no more disinfectant, no garlic, no hyssop, no vinegar and no more clean bandages. I have seen wounds like this before. It's going to eat him. He may hate you when he wakes up to find he only has one leg but you will save his life. If we delay much longer it will be too late."

"I cannot do it without his permission," Logan muttered.

"Then let me do it. I know how it is done," Corbulo said rising to his feet but Logan shook his head.

"No," he said, "I have prayed to the gods. I have asked them to heal him. Give them a chance to perform their magic."

"He is slowing us down," Corbulo said harshly. "And he will be no use in a fight. Think about it Logan, when we free Efa and Dylis we are going to have to move fast. That vengeful bitch will be after us as soon as she realises what has happened. Trust me, I know her, she doesn't give up."

But Logan shook his head stubbornly and with an annoyed sigh, Corbulo sat back down again.

"How long until we reach the Brigantian fortress?" Corbulo asked looking away.

Logan paused as he studied his father's leg.

"We should reach it by noon tomorrow," he muttered. "But don't expect anything grand. The place was abandoned long ago. There is not much left."

***

Corbulo reined in his horse as he caught sight of the black smoke billowing into the sky above the green, tree tops of the forest. It was late in the afternoon and in the still blue sky the intense and oppressive heat beat down on him. Around him the forest was silent. Corbulo peered at the smoke. It seemed to be coming from a hamlet on top of a hill, a couple of miles away across the wooded valley. Wearily he wiped his brow with his hand and turned round to signal Logan, who was on foot leading his horse along the narrow, forest path. Aidan lay slumped over the horse with both arms dangling against the beast's flanks. His eyes were closed and his head lolled from side to side and he stank of shit. Logan had resorted to tying his father to the saddle, to stop him from slipping and falling to the ground.

All afternoon they had been following the trail left by Emogene and her men. It was not hard to follow for the mercenaries were slow moving with their three heavily laden wagons and they were being forced to use the flatter and lower ground along the valley floor. But the terrain was getting rougher and wilder and the fear that they would stumble into an ambush had made Corbulo take the higher path through the woods. That afternoon too they had seen their first refugees, miserable, frightened and desperate looking people heading south with all their worldly belongings on their backs.

Logan turned to stare at the smoke as he came to a halt behind Corbulo.

 "Must be from the fighting," Corbulo said as he reached for his water pouch. "Whoever did that may still be close."

"That's the second village today that's been on fire," Logan muttered sourly as he shielded his eyes and glared up at the sun. Then Logan's face darkened. "Looks like Rome is determined to burn everything to the ground. Is this what you call Pax Romana? No wonder the Brigantes are up in arms," he added in an accusing voice.

Corbulo ignored the jibe. The stress and worry of looking after his father was taking a heavy toll on Logan but there was no point in reprimanding him for his lack of alertness and his distracted nature. That would only make matters worse.

"I will ride on ahead and see if I can spot them. Stay here," Corbulo said as he urged his horse onwards up the path.

As he vanished from view amongst the trees, a trumpet echoed across the valley. Corbulo frowned as he urged his horse up a steep, loose, slate-covered slope. The trumpet had been Roman and he had recognized the signal to regroup. His horse snorted and stamped its feet as he made it up onto a small rocky plateau, from which he had a fine view of the countryside to the north. Eagerly he peered down the mountain side at the river that ran along the valley. A column of men and three wagons were winding their way across an open meadow about half a mile away. It was Emogene and her war band and she was still heading north. Corbulo licked his lips as he studied his quarry. The mercenaries seemed to have abandoned their pretence of being slaves, for the rope that had bound them had gone and instead the distant figures were moving forwards in small groups. Corbulo turned to stare at the wagons and strained to catch a glimpse of Efa and Dylis but he was too far away to make them out. He sighed and with his finger he prodded at one of his remaining two teeth. He was running out of time. Aidan was dying and Logan was growing weary and dispirited. How was he going to do this? How was he going to get his wife and daughter from out of the clutches of that mad druid?

A flash of reflected light suddenly caught his eye and he turned to stare in the direction from which it had come. Across the valley and along the opposite ridge a column of figures had appeared heading south. Corbulo sucked in his breath. The figures looked like Romans. No one else could possibly have so much metal, body armour. Sharply he turned to stare at the mercenary war-band but the two groups were moving away from each other and did not seem to have noticed each other's presence. Corbulo grunted as a sudden idea came to him. With a decisive grunt he made up his mind and urged his horse down the slope and into the forest.

The Roman infantry took no notice of him as Corbulo rode up the slope towards them. The sweating and tired looking Legionaries trudged along in a loosely spaced column, clutching their large oval shields and with their Pila, throwing spears, slung over their shoulders. There had to be over a thousand men and the tramp and thud of their army boots on the stony ground reverberated through the trees. Corbulo urged his horse along the flank of the column as he sought out the vanguard. As he drew closer to the front of the column, Corbulo caught sight of a Signifer clad in a wolf's head and fur skin carrying a unit standard. Beside him a Cornicen, was carrying his shiny G shaped trumpet, on his back. Ahead of them at the very front of the column, a small group of mounted officers clad in red-plumed helmets led the way. Corbulo cried out and raised his hand as he urged his horse towards the officers, but before he could reach them his path was blocked by a cavalry patrol. The thirty odd riders came cantering down the marching column and swiftly surrounded him. The riders were armed with thrusting spears. Corbulo reined in his horse and glanced at the men around him. Then his face broke into a wide grin and he raised his hands showing the men his empty palms. The horsemen looked like Thracians, dark looking auxiliaries from the east.

"Who are you? What are you doing here?" Their Decurion growled speaking in heavily accented Latin.

"The name is Corbulo, veteran of the Twentieth," Corbulo replied cheerfully in perfect crisp Latin, "and I am glad to see you boys. Now take me to the officer who commands this battle group. I have a proposition for him."

The Thracians did not look amused as they stared at Corbulo suspiciously.

"Get the fuck out of here little man," the Decurion snapped. "The officers are too busy to speak with the likes of you, little Briton."

The smile slowly faded from Corbulo's face.

"I am a veteran of Rome," he cried out indignantly jabbing his finger into his chest, "I was serving the Eagles before you were even born you piece of yellow Thracian shit." Angrily he glared at the horsemen. "I brought an entire battle group safely back from Hibernia. I stood in the line against the barbarian queen. I am one of the few left who can remember that day so, don't you tell me what I can and can't do, you brainless idiot. I demand to see your commanding officer right now."

The Thracians seemed taken aback by Corbulo's outburst but they refused to move and an awkward silence descended, broken only by the rhythmic tramp of the Legionaries' boots as they moved on past the standoff, glancing curiously up at Corbulo.

"What is going on here?" a Roman voice suddenly cried out in good Latin.

The scowl on Corbulo's face vanished instantly as he saw a young Tribune of no more than twenty, riding towards him. The man was wearing a red cloak and he had a plumed helmet on his head. He was accompanied by two cavalrymen who looked like bodyguards.

"Sir," Corbulo called out with a little respectful nod, "I don't mean to cause any trouble but I need to speak with you urgently."

The young Tribune frowned as he reined in his horse and gave Corbulo a quick and thorough examination.

"Well, what is it?" the aristocrat growled. "Hurry up man, I haven't got all day."

"I need to buy some equipment from you," Corbulo replied smoothly, "Let's see. I need some garlic, hyssop, clean bandages, a bone saw from your surgeon and oh a spare trumpet if you have one."

The Tribune looked puzzled. Then he leaned forwards in his saddle and peered at Corbulo.

"Who the fuck did you say you were again?" the young officer snapped.

***

Logan was waiting for him in the same spot where Corbulo had left him. The young man looked worried and annoyed as Corbulo dismounted but the disgruntled look faded as Corbulo dropped a sack at his feet.

"There was a Roman battle group up on the ridge," Corbulo said sharply. "I got us some disinfectant, new bandages and a bone saw. The army always has first class medical equipment." Corbulo folded his arms across his chest and there was something in his eye that brooked no protests. "I have a plan on how we can free Efa and Dylis," he said lowering his voice, "but it's going to require all three of us. I need him conscious. His leg is coming off tonight."

Logan looked away in weary resignation. Then he nodded his agreement.

"He is going to hate you for this," he said glancing at the slumped figure lying on the ground.

"He already hates me, it can't get any worse," Corbulo replied as he stooped and lifted Aidan up.

"So what are we going to do?" Logan asked taking a deep breath and stepping forwards to help Corbulo as Aidan groaned.

But Corbulo shook his head. "I will explain it all when we reach our destination."

"And what about that," Logan asked pointing at the straight, shiny bronze trumpet that was strapped across Corbulo's back, "is that part of your plan too?"

"Damn right it is," Corbulo grunted as he hoisted Aidan up onto the horse, "I didn't spend the last of our money because I wanted to play some fucking music to myself now did I."

## Chapter Forty – The Fortress of the Brigantes

Stanwick was a vast and empty fortress. Corbulo crouched in the tree line of a small wood, one hand touching the ground and peered at the earthen ramparts and ditches and the green, open fields beyond. It was dawn and two days had passed since his encounter with the Roman battle group. The fort's defences disappeared off out of sight and in places grass and brambles had started to reclaim the disturbed earth. Inside the abandoned fortress he could make out a low hill, upon which stood a cluster of thatched, round houses with conical roofs, surrounded by another earthen embankment, and rising high above the small settlement was a Celtic watch tower. Two figures clutching spears were standing guard. Corbulo ignored the sentries and turned to examine the makeshift Brigantian camp that had sprang up outside the village. Emogene and her mercenary war-band had not been the first to reach the fortress. Another war-band had already been occupying the inner enclosure and now over two hundred rebel warriors were encamped around Tofts hill. Emogene and her mercenary war-band had parked their three wagons in a field just outside the native settlement and her mercenaries lay sleeping and resting in small, spread-out groups in the grass. The men seemed relaxed and apart from the watchers in the tower they had posted no guards.

"Can you see them?" Logan muttered as he crouched at Corbulo's side.

Corbulo shook his head. There had been no sign of Efa or Dylis or Emogene.

"They must be inside one of those huts," Corbulo replied.

Suddenly Corbulo's face darkened as he caught sight of a small group of men walking through the camp. The men were clad in long, white cloaks and their hair was shaven in a traditional manner which he instantly recognised.

"Druids," he muttered giving    Logan a little nudge.

Logan nodded as he saw them. "So Romulus told the truth," he murmured, "Emogene has come here for a gathering of the druids. What do you think they are up to?"

"Nothing good," Corbulo growled as his right hand clenched into a fist. "It could be a ceremony or something or a council of war, who knows."

Logan was silent for a moment. Then he glanced sideways at Corbulo.

"So are you going to tell me about this plan of yours?"

Corbulo sighed irritably and rubbed his face with his hand. Then with an annoyed gesture he pointed at the settlement and the Brigantian camp. "The problem is that I don't know where Emogene is keeping Efa and Dylis," he growled. "I need to know exactly where they are being held, before we go in to get them. So we will just have to wait here and keep a look out for them. The damn plan can't work if we don't know where they are."

Logan was silent as he stared at the camp a couple of hundred yards away across the open meadow. Then abruptly he rose to his feet.

"Fuck that," the young man muttered as he strode out into the open and straight towards the warriors resting in the grass.

"Logan, what are you doing?" Corbulo hissed in alarm but it was too late to grab his brother-in-law and haul him back into cover. Corbulo groaned in dismay as he watched Logan cross the field and head straight towards the small settlement. Had he completely lost his mind? What did he think he was doing? The mercenaries caught sight of him and some rose to their feet. The men were all armed. Calmly Logan strode through their ranks and headed towards the entrance to the settlement. Then at last he was challenged and his path blocked by a few Brigantes. From his vantage point Corbulo could see that a conversation was taking place but, he was too far away to hear what was being said. Then abruptly Logan pushed on through the group of men and continued on his way towards the cluster of round houses. Corbulo sucked in his breath. The warriors were letting him go. He grunted with growing amazement as he watched Logan vanish in between the earthen embankment that protected the Briton settlement.

A few minutes later he re-appeared and started back towards the wood in which Corbulo was hiding. Tensely Corbulo watched him approach. The Brigantes resting in the fields seemed unconcerned and no one made any effort to stop him. As Logan entered the wood Corbulo rose and stomped towards him with a mixture of irritation and admiration.

"What the hell was that all about?" Corbulo hissed as he caught up with his brother in law.

Logan turned and gave Corbulo a triumphant grin.

"I saw them," he exclaimed hastily, "Efa and Dylis, they are being held in the round house closest to the watch tower with all the other slaves and prisoners. They looked alright and I think Efa recognized me."

Corbulo stared at Logan in bewilderment. Then he looked away into the forest.

"How did you get inside?" he snapped, "What did you tell those men?"

"Ah Corbulo," Logan sighed shaking his head, "You forget, I am a Briton, I am no different to these Brigantes. I am a free man. So I told them that I wanted to join the uprising. I told them I had heard the druids were paying men in gold to join the rebellion against Rome. These rebels are not like the Roman army, Corbulo. If a man wants to join or leave, that is his business and his alone. So they let me into the settlement and I kept my eyes open, that's all."

Corbulo opened his mouth and then closed it again and for a moment he was lost for words. Then a little colour shot into his cheeks.

"So you saw Efa and Dylis," he said hurriedly. "You said they looked well?"

Logan grinned with sudden hope and as he did Corbulo's face too cracked into a smile.

"Don't worry. We will get them back Corbulo," the younger man said gripping Corbulo's shoulder. "They looked alright, perhaps a little tired and unhappy, that's all. Now tell me about your plan. You do realise that the Britons are not planning to remain here forever."

\*\*\*

The cave was cool and provided a welcome shelter from the midday heat. Aidan sat propped up against a large, jagged rock. The stump of his leg had been bound in fresh bandages and he was awake but he looked pale and his face seemed to have shrunk like a victim of starvation. In his hand he clutched the bloody remains of his ankle and foot. He'd refused to let go of the limb or say a word since Corbulo and Logan had cut it off, a day ago.

"Are you going to stare at it all day," Corbulo growled as he noticed Aidan staring fixedly at his amputated limb.

Aidan did not reply. He seemed to have retreated into a sullen angry silence. Corbulo caught Logan's eye as his brother-in-law prepared the mid-day meal. Logan shrugged and looked away.

"Alright," Corbulo muttered as he got up and arranged a few loose stones on the rocky floor and drew a rough circle in the dust with the tip of his sword. "This is how we are going to get them back."

Logan stopped what he was doing and turned to look at the cave floor.

"This here is the enemy encampment," Corbulo said gesturing at the crude map in the dust. "Logan, you will enter the camp under cover of darkness and you will set fire to their three wagons. Then you get the hell out of there and meet us back at this cave." Corbulo turned to look at Aidan who was still staring at his amputated limb. "Growler over there will remain close to the cave. Once you see the wagons are on fire," Corbulo said producing the long straight Roman army trumpet he'd purchased, "You will blow this old army trumpet for all you are worth. With a bit of luck the enemy will believe that they are about to be attacked by Romans. Once all is confusion, I will use the diversion to sneak into the camp, free Efa and Dylis and meet you both back here."

"That's it?" Logan muttered with a frown.

"What do you want, a fucking detailed battle plan," Corbulo retorted. "There are only two and half of us and over two hundred rebels. That's the best I can come up with."

Logan sighed despairingly and closed his eyes but against his rock Aidan did not rise to the baited comment.

"When do we go?" Logan said, tiredly glancing quickly at his father.

"Tonight, after dark," Corbulo muttered as he placed the bronze trumpet on the ground beside Aidan, "so get some rest, it's going to be a long night."

Wearily Corbulo clambered out of the cave and emerged into the bright sunlight. The two horses stood tethered to a tree munching on some grass. Corbulo walked over to a large boulder and clambered up onto it and sat down. The forest around him was largely quiet and in the blue sky the summer sun shimmered, radiating heat and bathing everything in bright light. A few birds were chirping away but there was no wind and the stale heat was oppressive. Corbulo sighed and wiped the sweat from his forehead as he looked down at his feet. Their long journey was coming to an end. Suddenly he chuckled to himself. In all his long army career he'd been involved in many hair razing and dangerous moments but none was more important than the one he was about to face tonight. None more critical for this was not about him anymore; this was not about his own survival; this was about his family's survival. The decisions he was going to make were going to determine their fate. If he cocked things up now their lives would be effectively over.

"Don't fuck it up," Corbulo muttered fiercely to himself, "for the god's sake don't cock it up old man."

For a long moment he was silent staring down at his feet. Then he looked up as he suddenly sensed movement in the trees and his mouth opened and he gasped in shock. Sitting perched on a branch in one of the trees half a dozen paces away, was an eagle. The large, magnificent bird was staring straight at him; its wings tucked away in its body; its sharp intelligent eyes watching him; its curved beak motionless; its talons tightly gripping the branch. Corbulo slithered backwards in shock and fright and nearly fell off the large boulder. The eagle was calmly staring straight at him. Corbulo felt his heart thumping away as a sudden terror seized him. "No, he groaned in a frightened voice, "What do you want from me? What do you want me to do?" The beautiful, hunting bird was silent as it stared at him without moving a feather and for a moment, Corbulo seemed mesmerized by the animal's sharp, watchful eyes. Then with a startled cry Corbulo tumbled from the boulder and onto the ground. When he staggered painfully to his feet and turned to stare at the tree, the eagle had vanished.

## Chapter Forty One - Family

It was dark and in the night sky the moon and stars were clearly visible. Corbulo crouched in the open field close to the rebel camp. Entering Stanwick had been easy for the earthen ramparts were too vast to be defended or easily patrolled and it had not been difficult to clamber over them. The Brigantes had not lit any fires, at least not any that he could see, but he could hear the men. The rebels were talking and laughing and from somewhere in the darkness he could hear singing. The Brigantes seemed in good spirits. Tensely Corbulo strained to see in the darkness. The small Briton settlement up on the low hill was no more than a hundred paces away. Earlier during the day he'd seen no guards patrolling the ditch and earth embankment that surrounded the inner core of Stanwick but that was hours ago. The rebels could have changed their routine. In his mind he went over his plan for the hundredth time. He tried to calm himself. It would be alright. He had a good plan. Quietly he exhaled and turned to stare in the direction in which he had last seen the three rebel wagons. Logan should be on his way by now. How was he going to light up the wagons without any camp fires from which to borrow a burning branch? Softly Corbulo groaned. Logan had said nothing about that when they had discussed the plan. He must have devised a way.

As he waited tensely in the darkness Corbulo saw a faint light appear in the darkness. The light grew and Corbulo gasped in surprise. One of the wagons was on fire. The flames were growing stronger and stronger. Moments later the second wagon also began to burn. Corbulo clenched his hand into a fist as the night was suddenly rent with cries and shouts of alarm. Logan had done it. As flames began to lick greedily around the third wagon Corbulo rose stiffly to his feet. The Brigantian camp was in uproar as he could hear more and more voices in the darkness. Sharply Corbulo turned to look in the direction of the cave. A moment later a furious trumpet blast cut through the night. The blast continued, furious, angry and resentful. In the rebel encampment the cries of alarm grew.

Corbulo started moving towards the small settlement of thatched, round houses. In the light of the burning wagons he could make out the outline of the ditch and earthen embankment. The rebels were calling out to each other as some of them tried desperately to save the wagons, whilst the rest seemed to be milling about in confusion. The trumpet continued to blast way, its terrible tone death sound rippling away across the vast, empty fortress. Aidan was giving it everything he had. Corbulo reached the ditch and slithered down into the dried mud and quickly, on all fours, he started to clamber up the grass-covered embankment. As he reached the top he heard a voice close by shout out and in the darkness he sensed movement down amongst the cluster of round houses. Without pausing he slid down the other side of the ramparts and came to a halt beside the wicker wall of one of the round houses. Close by a man was shouting but no one was answering him. The Brigantian camp seemed to be in utter confusion.

Quickly Corbulo glanced about. Where was the tall, watch tower he had seen earlier that day? It had to be close. Then in the moonlight he caught sight of it. A man rushed passed him only a few yards away. The warrior was cursing as Aidan's trumpet continued to blast away bathing the night in noise. Corbulo rose and half bent over scuttled around the back of the round house and came to a stop as he reached the watch tower. With a thumping heart and sweat pouring down his face he crouched in the darkness.

"What can you see?" a Briton close by shouted.

"Nothing," a voice from the watch tower cried out, "Someone has set fire to the wagons and that sounds like a Roman trumpet but I can't see anything. Are we under attack?"

The rebel on the ground did not answer. Wildly Corbulo stared around him. The diversion was not going to fool the Brigantes for long. He had to hurry. Where was the damned hut that Logan had said the slaves were being kept? He'd said they were being held close to the watchtower. With growing desperation Corbulo searched the darkness willing himself to see in the dark. Then he groaned. There were two round houses that could fit Logan's description. There was no time to ponder the issue. He would have to choose and hope he was lucky. Swiftly he rose and ran towards the nearest round house. As he blundered towards the entrance Corbulo suddenly caught sight of a warrior standing guard beside the doorway. It was too late to stop. With a startled yelp Corbulo crashed straight into the guard thrusting his Pugio, knife into the man's chest as the two of them went tumbling to the ground. His opponent cried out but desperation lent Corbulo strength and his hand found the man's mouth and clamped over it muffling the man's groans until he no longer moved. Unsteadily Corbulo got to his feet and glanced around him. No one seemed to have noticed the fight.

Without hesitating he turned and barged through the leather sheet that hung across the doorway of the round house. Inside, he found himself in a smoky and spacious circular room. An old, dying fire was glowing and crackling at the centre and sitting around the edges of the walls, with their legs drawn up against their bodies, were twenty or thirty silent men, women and children. All the occupants were staring at him. Corbulo's breathing came in ragged gasps as he stared back at the people. Some of the men were clad in Roman army uniforms, their faces unshaven and haggard looking and their legs and arms were chained together in slavers irons. No one spoke or made a noise. Wildly Corbulo turned and searched the bewildered looking faces. Then one of the slaves stirred and cried out. It was Dylis. The girl rose to her feet as a flush spread across her face. Corbulo gasped in sudden emotion as he stumbled towards his daughter. As he reached her another person rose to her feet and came towards him and thrust her arms around him. It was Efa and she was sobbing. Corbulo paused, unable to move, as Efa and Dylis clung to him and he fought back against his own tears.

"I knew you would come back for us," Dylis sobbed, "I knew you would come back."

Corbulo's hand trembled as he stroked her hair whilst with his other hand he gripped Efa's shoulder and for a moment he was incapable of doing anything.

"We have to go," he muttered at last, "We have to go now."

"I can't walk," Dylis replied as he felt her whole body shake. Corbulo looked down at his daughter and groaned. Her captors had clasped her legs in iron chains.

"I tried to escape too often," Dylis wept, "They called me a trouble maker and they put me in chains like some animal. Emogene was horrible to me. She said she would feed me to her dogs if I didn't behave."

"You need to be strong," Corbulo muttered trying to give her a reassuring smile. Then he glanced at Efa. She was looking up at him with sudden hope.

"I am alright," she gasped as she wiped the tears from her eyes. "But there is something else...Corbulo."

Corbulo did not let her finish as he stooped and boldly lifted Dylis up and flung her over his shoulder. The chains binding her legs together banged into his shin but he did not feel the pain. Then grasping his wife by the arm he turned for the doorway. "I will carry her," he said turning to Efa, "Stay close to me. Aidan and Logan are here too. Stay close."

As they reached the doorway Efa caught his arm and forced him to a halt. Her eyes were red and her face was streaked with tears but she seemed determined to say something.

"Please Corbulo," she gasped, "look," she said pointing at the people who were sitting around the edge of the round house. "Look."

Corbulo turned to look in the direction in which she was pointing and as he did his eyes bulged and he staggered back in shock and dismay. Sitting quietly amongst the other Roman prisoners, with their legs and hands bound together in a long iron slavers slave chain, was Marcus. His son was barely recognisable beneath his wild un-kept beard and pale malnourished face. Marcus was staring at Corbulo in stunned disbelieving silence.

"Marcus," Corbulo groaned as his face paled and he swayed unsteadily on his feet. "Oh Gods what fate is this. What fate has brought you here, now?"

"Go," Marcus blurted out as he rediscovered his voice," you can't save me father, not whilst I am in these chains. I will get out. I will find you. Go, get them out of here. You have to go now."

Corbulo stared at his son, caught and torn by a terrible indecision.

"What happened to you?" Corbulo said hurriedly.

"It's a long unfortunate story," Marcus gasped, "There was a battle and I think I was betrayed by my second in command."

Corbulo groaned. Then a brief hopeful smile appeared on his lips as his eyes moistened as he made his decision.

"I will come back for you, son," Corbulo said with a nod, "I won't leave you here to die. Not after everything that we have been through. Stay alive Marcus. Stay alive son, we will come for you."

Then he was out through the doorway and into the night with Dylis slung over his shoulder and his fingers clutching Efa's hand. Aidan was still blowing on his trumpet as if his life depended on it and in the night the flames from the burning wagons leapt and roared away into the darkness.

"This way," Corbulo hissed as his eyes adjusted to the darkness. He could feel the tension in Dylis's body as she clung to him but he could not remember her being so heavy and his breath was coming in ragged gasps as he stumbled towards the earthen embankment that enclosed the settlement. Efa too was silent as she clutched his sweaty hand. As they blundered towards the perimeter a crazy image of him carrying Efa on his back and leaping into the Thames after their escape from the Governor's Mansion in Londinium came to him. Corbulo groaned as they made it to the earthen embankment. Marcus, Marcus, Gods, he had never expected to see his son here. What had happened to him? What foul fate had led to his capture? He paused gasping for breath. He had promised to come back for Marcus. He had promised him but keeping that promise was going to be very difficult. There would be little chance of rescuing Marcus once Emogene realised that her two female slaves had escaped. He was going to be too busy running for his life.

Grimly he started to clamber up the steep earthen embankment with Efa scrambling up at his side. His wife's hand-grip was firm and tight and for a moment he was reminded of the time she had refused to let go of his hand, when he and Quintus had rescued her and Dylis from the crannog in the Caledonian lake. The night was still being rent by Aidan's furious trumpet blasts. His father- in-law did not sound like he was about to stop. He was blasting away for all he was worth even though the noise was no longer necessary. Corbulo was panting and puffing as he reached the top. Sweat was streaming down his back. Surely by now the Britons would have realised that the trumpet was just a decoy and that they were not being attacked. In the darkness he could still hear the men's shouts. As he crawled across the top of the rampart and was just about to slither down the other side into the ditch, a shape suddenly loomed up above him. Dylis cried out in panic as a rebel came barging into them, tripped over Corbulo and with a startled cry went tumbling down the side of the embankment and into the ditch. With a roar Corbulo shoved his daughter down the side of the earthen rampart, wrenched his hand from Efa and drew his sword and leapt down into the darkness. He landed a yard away from the man. The rebel however had recovered from his surprise and acted fast. In the light from the burning wagons Corbulo heard a metallic noise and caught the glint of a blade. Then with a grunt the rebel was on him, bowling him backwards into the dried mud. Corbulo cried out in shock and fear as the man crashed down on top of him. Frantically he grasped the man's knife-arm as they struggled and thrashed around at the bottom of the ditch. But the rebel was younger and stronger and with sudden terrifying clarity Corbulo knew he was going to lose the fight. Desperately he cried out again as he felt his strength start to fade.

Then with a thud something struck his attacker in the back and Corbulo heard laboured breathing in the darkness. The rebel groaned and gurgled up some blood and Corbulo felt the pressure on him relax. With the last of his strength he pushed the man off him and using his elbows he backed away. A shape appeared over him looking down at him. The man was armed with a knife and in the faint light Corbulo could see a bow strapped to his back. It was Logan.

Logan was breathing heavily as he offered Corbulo his hand. Gratefully Corbulo glasped it and the younger man hauled him up onto his feet. Close by Efa came stumbling towards him and not far away he could hear Dylis sobbing. Logan's face was impossible to read in the darkness.

"What are you doing here," Corbulo panted gasping for breath, "I told you to go back to the cave and wait for us there."

Logan steadied his breathing as he stooped and grasped hold of Dylis and lifted her up over his shoulder.

"Well I don't always do what you tell me to do," he said unable to hide the excitement and adrenaline coursing through his voice.

"Well thank fuck for that," Corbulo hissed in delight as Efa silently flung her arms around her brother.

## Chapter Forty Two - Destiny

Corbulo stumbled up the slope and through the darkened forest as he tried to find his bearings. Where was the fucking cave? In the darkness it was hard to see where he was going. At his side Efa clutched his hand with such firmness that it nearly hurt and behind him he could hear Logan's laboured breathing as he followed with Dylis slung over his shoulder. Corbulo came to a sudden halt and looked around. Despite the cool night air his face was covered in sweat. Off in the distance in the direction of the fortress the fire consuming the wagons was dying down and so was the noise. Aidan too had finally ceased blowing his trumpet and the night was growing eerily quiet.

"Aidan," Corbulo called out in a soft voice, "Aidan are you there? It's me Corbulo. We've done it. We have got Efa and Dylis with us."

The night remained silent. Impatiently Corbulo growled in frustration. This was the spot where they'd left Aidan and the two horses. It had to be. Was he wrong? In the darkness everything was hard to identify.

"I am over here," a voice suddenly replied from the darkness close by. Corbulo swung round in the direction from which the voice had come and in the dim, moon light he made out a dark, motionless shape sitting on a boulder. With a little cry Efa broke free and ran towards the figure. Corbulo stumbled after her and as he reached Aidan he heard Efa weeping softly and Aidan's soothing, comforting voice. Quietly Efa's family hugged each other in fierce elation, hissing and growling in delight and emotion and as he stood watching them Corbulo felt a sudden strange sense of being apart.

"That's twice now that I have saved your life in recent days Corbulo," Logan whispered with fierce pride. "Don't you forget that, you old fart."

Corbulo looked away and nodded but did not reply. Then he felt a hand tugging urgently at his tunic.

"Corbulo," Efa whispered hurriedly, "It's about Marcus. I only saw him when they put us all together in that house but we managed to talk briefly. He was captured during a fight in the mountains. He was in charge of a whole Cohort and he told me that he thinks Lucius, his second in command betrayed him. Something about Lucius, on purpose, not doing what he was supposed to do."

"Why would this man betray Marcus?" Corbulo asked with a frown.

"Marcus said it was to do with that man, Bestia, the one whom you killed in Viroconium a few years ago, the man who was hunting us and the Christian children. Apparently this Lucius was his brother and he's out for your head."

"Isn't everyone," Corbulo growled sourly.

In the darkness Corbulo did not see the startled look on Efa's face.

"There's more," she whispered, "The King, Faelan, he's here. He's been talking to Emogene, they seem to know each other well. The King, he's promised to give Marcus to her. She remembers him from his time in Caledonia. At first she wanted to kill him there and then but Faelan forbade it. He said that Marcus was valuable. That's why he is being kept alive. He said that Marcus was going to be useful..."

Efa's voice trailed off.

In the darkness Corbulo stared at Efa.

"What do you mean?" Corbulo replied quietly," What do you mean...useful?"

"The King, Faelan," Efa stammered, "He believes that Marcus will lead him to you. He remembers you. He remembers what you did in Hibernia. He is out for your head, husband. He and Emogene want you dead. I saw the blood lust in their eyes. They are not going to let us get away so easily."

Corbulo was silent as he turned to look down at the ground and as the silence lengthened the others too fell silent.

"We've got to go," Corbulo whispered at last, looking up at the shapes in the darkness, "Logan bring the horses. Aidan will ride on the brown one and Efa and Dylis will take the black one. You will look after your father and I will take Efa and Dylis. We're going to head northwest into the mountains."

"Northwest?" Logan muttered in a confused voice, "But that is straight into the fighting. Should we not head south?"

"It's the last thing they will expect," Corbulo replied. "Now move your arses, we've got to get out of here before they realise what has happened."

"You cut my leg off," Aidan snarled in sudden fury.

"Oh do shut the fuck up," Corbulo snapped rounding on the dark figure sitting on the rock.

\*\*\*

As dawn broke, the small party found themselves picking their way slowly across the colourful, open heath land and rolling hills in exhausted silence. To the north and south the barren treeless mountains stretched away towards the horizon and in the western sky dark-grey storm clouds were building up but the summer heat remained, humid, still and oppressive like a friend who had overstayed his welcome. Tiredly Corbulo glanced up at the sky as on foot he led the horse carrying Dylis and Efa across the field. A storm was coming. He could feel it drawing closer. A storm was coming to clear the heat from the land.

Wearily he turned and looked over his shoulder at Logan, who was following on foot leading the horse on which sat his disgruntled-looking father. Aidan had his eyes open and there was a sullen and stubborn expression on his face as he clutched his amputated leg in one hand and the Roman trumpet in the other. Logan plodded along and ignored Corbulo's glance and went on staring vacantly into the distance. The party's progress had been painfully slow since they had left the Brigantian fort for they simply did not have enough horses to make a quick escape and in the darkness it had been hard to see where they were going.

As he trudged along Corbulo caught sight of a strange shape in the distance. As they drew closer he suddenly recognised the building for what it was, an abandoned hill fort shaped like a pear, with an unusually long and narrow entrance passage made of dry stones that tapered away to the ground the further it got from the fort. Curiously he peered at the construction. It was old and it looked deserted for he could see no sign of any people or farm animals. Beyond the hill-fort the open, treeless, moorland descended steeply into a valley. Corbulo studied the stone walls of the fort as he trudged towards it. The place did not look like it had been lived in for a very long time and the long entrance tunnel enclosed on both sides by a parallel dry-stone wall was like nothing he had ever seen before.

"It's the old lead miner's fort," Logan called out as if reading his mind, "The people around here mine the hills for lead and silver."

Corbulo nodded as he led his horse straight towards the fort.

"So where are the miners?" he called out. "I can't see anyone about and why have they abandoned their fort?"

Behind him Logan sighed and shrugged. "The rebellion, the fighting, they must be staying away because they fear for their lives. I don't know. All I know is that they used the fort to honour the gods. On the summer solstice the druids would walk down that long processional passageway on their way to offer a sacrifice to the immortals so that the gods would keep the precious lead from coming out of the earth. The place is old, older than the memory of men."

Corbulo grunted in disgust as for a moment he imagined the white-robed druids walking into the fort to execute Roman prisoners of war. There was nothing holy or sacred about that. It was just plain murder.

They were a hundred paces from the stone walls when Corbulo froze. From somewhere behind him across the deserted moorland, he suddenly heard the barking of dogs. The sound sent a shiver of terror coursing down his spine and the blood drained from his face as slowly and disbelievingly he turned in the direction from which the sound had come. The others too had heard it and had turned to stare in the direction, from which they had just come. Corbulo groaned in despair as he heard the barking and baying dogs again. Someone had picked up their trail. Someone who possessed hunting dogs and knew how to handle them. Desperately he turned to look at his companions. Efa and Dylis had turned pale with fear and Logan was nervously gripping the pommel of his knife. Only Aidan refused to turn and look behind him as he stared moodily ahead at the fort.

"Fuck," Corbulo hissed as he yanked his horse forwards, "They have picked up our trail. We need to move, hurry, hurry now!"

"It's no use," Logan cried out, "I see them, Corbulo. They are on horseback. We'll never manage to out run them."

"Then let's get into that fort," Corbulo bellowed, "If we can't out-run them we will have to stand and fight. Move. Move. Damn it."

Pulling his horse on behind him, Corbulo broke towards the stone-entrance passageway as behind him Logan cried out and did the same. As they ran towards the old hill-fort, dragging the horses on behind them, the sound of the dogs seemed to draw closer.

"Logan, how many of them are there?" Corbulo shouted as he stumbled into the entrance of the long, enclosed passageway.

"I can't see them all but they are closing fast," Logan cried out in alarm. "Maybe four men of horseback and a pack of dogs. Gods, they are closing fast."

There was no time to look over his shoulder. Grimly Corbulo stormed down the long entrance tunnel into the fort. The parallel walls grew in height the deeper he went and the passage itself was six yards or so wide. Here and there the dry-stone walls had collapsed into a natural heap but in other places some of the stones had been deliberately removed. As he emerged into the circular fort Corbulo let go of the horse and hastily drew his Pugio, knife from his belt and handed it to Efa. There was a weary resigned and a defeated look in his eyes as he looked up at his wife.

"I am sorry," he muttered, "I thought we would get away. I didn't think it would end like this. You know how to use this knife, Efa."

Efa looked down at him, her chest heaving and her face suddenly flush and alive.

"This is not how it's going to end," she whispered fiercely. "You are the finest man I have ever known Corbulo. This is not how it's going to end. We are going to get out of here. I know we will."

There was no time to argue with his wife. Corbulo drew his sword and turned to Logan, as the younger man came running into the empty, circular fort pulling his horse along with him.

"Cover the entrance passage," Corbulo shouted as he ran towards the perimeter wall, "If they try to enter the fort shoot them with that bow of yours. They will be easy pickings in that confined space. I will take the outer wall."

"How are we going to hold them, Corbulo" Logan cried out as his voice cracked in despair, "There are just two of us."

Corbulo had no answer to that. As he reached the outer wall and started to climb up the weed-invested ramparts he caught sight of Aidan still sitting on his horse clutching the old Roman army trumpet.

"Why don't you make yourself useful for a change," he roared at Aidan. "For God's sake man, snap out of that stupid self-pitying mood. We need you!"

As he reached the top of the stone ramparts, Corbulo crouched with the blade of his sword touching the ancient stone work and turned to stare at their pursuers. The men and dogs were close now, a few hundred yards away and as they galloped towards the abandoned hill fort Corbulo counted eight riders and several baying dogs. As the horsemen drew closer he groaned in dismay. Leading the pursuit was Emogene, her long unmistakeable black hair, streaming behind her and running alongside her, with a rope attached to his neck was Marcus. He was naked from the waist up and his hands were tied behind his back and he was struggling to keep up with the pace. One of the horsemen was clutching the other end of the rope and threatening to drag Marcus along the ground, if he stumbled and fell. From behind him a furious trumpet suddenly blasted away and the noise nearly sent Corbulo tumbling from the wall in shock.

"What the fuck do you think you are doing?" he roared at Aidan. "I told you to make yourself useful, you prick."

"Well what do you want me to do?" Aidan screamed back, "You cut off my leg, how am I supposed to fight with just one leg? I told you not to cut it off and you went ahead anyway so now you deal with the consequences. This whole mess, it's all your fault. Your fucking fault Corbulo, again!"

"You can still use a sword you moron," Corbulo shouted back as fear and adrenaline added power and fury to his voice but his words were cut off as Aidan defiantly blew on his trumpet sending a furious blast of noise echoing away across the hills. Corbulo turned away in disgust. His father in law had finally lost it. The man was beyond useless. Beyond the ramparts Emogene and the riders were slowing their pace as they trotted towards the hill-fort. Corbulo bared his teeth in a little sign of defiance as he stared at the young woman and as he did so memories of his and Marcus's flight from Caledonia came back to him. They had escaped her then, but it seemed unlikely that they would be able to do the same now. He was outnumbered and there was nowhere to run to and besides, Emogene had Marcus. As he stared at his son a lump appeared in Corbulo's throat. What was the druid bitch planning to do with his son? Why had she brought him out here?

As the riders closed in on the fort, two of them veered away and galloped towards the long entrance passage. As they charged up the corridor an arrow thudded into the chest of one the riders, sending him tumbling from his horse. His companion rapidly reined in his horse and, as another of Logan's arrow smacked into the wall beside him, he cried out and fled back down the way he'd come, leaving his comrade groaning and rolling on the ground.

"That's far enough," Corbulo roared as he stared at Emogene, "I have enough men here with me to hold you at bay all day, all week."

The young woman slowed her horse to a walk until she was no more than fifteen yards away and from that distance he could see her face clearly. At her side on the ground, Marcus, his hands tied behind his back and his torso covered in dust and sweat, sank to his knees in utter exhaustion. The remaining riders turned to stare at Corbulo up on the stone wall, as they came to a halt in a spread-out line behind their mistress.

"We both know that is a lie," Emogene cried out and her voice was filled with fury, "Do you remember who I am, Roman. Do you remember the last time we met?"

"Oh I know your face alright," Corbulo cried out angrily, "You chased me and my son half way across Caledonia and for what? What did I ever do to you? All I wanted was to get my son back. You can keep all your precious amber. I am not interested in your wealth and treasure. Stick it up your arse. Just give me back my son and we will be on our way and you will never have to see me again."

"No, I am not going to do that," Emogene shouted as her face too darkened in rage, "I have waited a long time for this little reunion. But now my gods have finally granted me my wish. You are mine, Corbulo. Your soul belongs to me. You are going to belong to me for all eternity, once I am done with you. Do you remember the last thing I told you in that fort all those years ago? Well do you, Corbulo?"

"Sorry, I can't hear you, can you speak up," Corbulo sneered, cupping his hand to his ear.

"I told you that we would meet again one day," Emogene yelled, "I told you that I would find you and now I have."

"Well good for you, bitch," Corbulo retorted. "So come and get me. I am right here."

Behind him Aidan sent another long trumpet blast echoing away across the hills.

"I have a better idea," Emogene cried as sudden emotion crept into her voice, "I want you to understand something Roman. I want to share something with you." Her voice trailed off as the emotion suddenly seemed to get the better of her. Bitterly she raised her head and glared at Corbulo.

"Six summers ago when Rome invaded my homeland I lost my husband in battle," Emogene shouted in a hoarse voice. "And of all the people in my village I kept my promise to my father. I obeyed his rule and I did my sworn duty. I broke into a slavers tent and murdered my friend. He was just a boy of fourteen but he was going to betray us and for that he had to die. I murdered him with my own hand. I had known this boy all my life. He was my friend! He trusted me but I chose to kill my friend to stop you Roman beasts from learning about my village!"

Emogene's face was flush with rage and pain and her hands shook. "So now you, Corbulo, are going to make the same choice that I had to make. You are going to know the pain and guilt that I have endured these past six summers. I am going to make you choose which one of your children is going to live and die."

Emogene fell silent as she slipped from her saddle, landed on the ground and strode towards Marcus. Grasping him roughly by his hair, she yanked his head back and with her other hand pressed a knife against his soft exposed throat before turning to stare at Corbulo.

"Choose, Roman," Emogene screamed, "Will it be your son or your daughter? Either way one of them is going to die here today. The choice is yours. Now choose. Choose!"

Up on his wall Corbulo recoiled in horror and his face went pale. For a long moment he stared at Marcus who was down on his knees in the grass with a knife pressed to his throat. His son did not move as he calmly looked up at the sky. How could he choose between his children? What monstrous fate had brought him to this point?

"Choose, Roman," Emogene screamed pressing the knife against Marcus's throat. "Make your choice now. Your daughter or your son. Who is going to die?"

With a strangled, panicked cry, Corbulo turned to look at Efa and Dylis standing close by inside the fort. Both of them had heard Emogene loud and clear and both of them were looking up at him with horror and disbelief in their eyes. Corbulo felt the lump in his throat growing until he could barely breathe. On his horse Aidan had lowered his trumpet and was staring at Corbulo in dismay. Corbulo opened his mouth and gasped as he turned to look back down at Marcus. He'd expected Emogene to be cruel but not like this, not in this way. She was asking him to choose between Marcus and Dylis. How could he possibly choose between them? What monstrous choice was this? A ragged gasp escaped from his mouth as he tried to speak but the words would not come.

From high above him he suddenly heard a piercing, high pitched cry. As he looked up an eagle came gliding over the fort; its wings spread out as it circled the ancient construction; its sharp eyes staring at the ground; its talons extended as if they were about to snatch a mouse from the grass. And as the magnificent eagle circled high above them, Corbulo suddenly knew what he had to do. The gods had come to show him a way out.

"Alright," he muttered quietly as he stared up at the beautiful hunter in the sky, "I get it now. I know what you want from me. I am ready."

Stiffly he rose to his feet and turned to look at Emogene and her men.

"A trade," he cried, "You don't want to waste your time with my children. If you let my son and my family go, I will give you something better. I will give you myself, to do with what you like. Come on, I am the one you have wanted all along? I will make a fine sacrifice to your gods."

Emogene did not immediately reply as she stood over Marcus, pressing her knife into his throat and as the silence lengthened the eagle emitted another high-pitched cry as it circled high above on the air currents. Then abruptly Emogene released the pressure on Marcus's throat and tucked her knife back into her belt.

From inside the abandoned fort Aidan sent another furious trumpet blast echoing away across the mountains and suddenly on a ridge, about a mile away, a troop of horsemen appeared, their metal armour, reflecting the sunlight. In alarm one of Emogene's men called out to her and pointed at the distant Roman patrol who seemed to have come to investigate the noise.

"We have an agreement," Emogene cried, "you for your boy here and hurry if you want him to live."

And as she spoke the words behind him Dylis broke out into a terrified scream. Corbulo nodded at Emogene as down below in the fort Efa tried to restrain a hysterical Dylis. Corbulo turned and calmly clambered down the inside of the walls and with a thud he landed on the ground and as he did so Dylis broke free from her mother's embrace and rushed towards him flinging her arms around his waist as the tears streamed down her face. Gently Corbulo stroked her hair as he caught Efa's eye. His wife's face was ashen and her lower lip was trembling. Corbulo dragging Dylis along with him strode towards Efa and clasped her by her shoulders and touched his forehead against hers.

"Look after our daughter, look after yourself," he whispered hoarsely. "May the gods protect you both."

Then without another word he broke away from both of them. Aidan gave him a little respectful nod as he passed by but the two of them did not say anything. As Corbulo entered the long walled passageway he caught sight of Marcus at the other end. Emogene and her horsemen stood clustered around the narrow entrance glaring at him.

Calmly Corbulo started to walk down the passageway towards them and as he did so Marcus started out towards him. His hands were still bound behind his back and he was accompanied by two of Emogene's warrior's. As he strode towards his son Corbulo glanced up at the sky but the eagle had vanished and suddenly he chuckled. In Caledonia he had prayed and asked the gods for help. He had asked them to give Efa and Dylis back to him and they had done so but, in exchange he should have realised that they would demand a great sacrifice. That was the price he would have to pay for his wife and daughter's safe return. He chuckled again. Fortuna and her games! What could a man do but smile and do as the gods commanded. Marcus was lathered in sweat and one of his eyes was bruised and swollen and his face was as white as a sheet as the two of them approached each other along the ceremonial passageway.

"I am sorry father," Marcus groaned rolling his eyes in guilty despair. "This is my fault."

Gently Corbulo smiled at him and shook his head. "It's alright," he muttered, "It's alright, son. You will go on, I know you will."

Then Corbulo drew his sword from its scabbard and flung it onto the ground. The warrior's accompanying Marcus gave the younger man a shove forwards and grasped hold of Corbulo and began to push him down the passageway towards Emogene.

Marcus watched them drag his father away. For a long moment he stood rooted to the ground in the middle of the passage way as his breathing came in ragged gasps and his legs refused to move. Then, wrenching his eyes away from Corbulo, he stooped and picked up his father's sword and started towards Logan who was crouching along the passageway with his bow drawn and pointed at the horsemen and their dogs.

Marcus said nothing as ignoring Dylis' hysterical screams, he clambered up onto the wall and turned to stare at the small party of horsemen milling about at the entrance to the fort. Then he lowered his head and closed his eyes as he saw Emogene force Corbulo down onto his knees in the grass and with a single swift movement of her hand cut his throat. Marcus did not see his father's body flop sideways onto the ground or the blood spilling out into the grass, but he did hear Emogene's triumphant scream and as he heard it he suddenly knew deep down in his heart that Corbulo, for all his past faults, imperfections and mistakes had finally managed to make something of himself. His father was at last truly forgiven and as he opened his eyes Marcus felt a surge of unstoppable pride.

## Author's notes

Britannia is a work of fiction but I have tried to use historical fact where possible. The period between the battle of Mons Graupius in 83 AD, and the building of Hadrian's Wall in 122 AD, is not very well documented and is dominated by the question; why did Rome withdraw from Scotland after they had just conquered it? There are many suggested answers but I think the most likely explanation is a combination of factors.

With the withdrawal of one of the four Legions from Britain, the Romans would simply not have had enough troops to hold down the newly conquered northern territories.

Secondly, and this is what my book Caledonia is based on, Roman expansion policy was always guided by a cost/benefit analysis and it's likely that Scotland was simply not wealthy, developed or lucrative enough to justify the military occupation cost.

Thirdly, I am fairly certain that the Caledonians would have continued to resist the Romans, maybe in an asymmetric manner, long after they had lost the battle of Mons Graupius.

Finally and this is the basis for "Britannia" I think the Brigantes, living in northern England, were never fully pacified. The rapid Roman advance northwards in the 60's and 70's and the conquest and occupation of Brigantia, (the dark red on the cover map), was not completed before Agricola moved on into Caledonia. The Romans did not properly consolidate their hold on northern England, just like they failed to consolidate their hold on Illyria, which led to a local uprising in 6-9 AD. The military ambition of individual Roman commanders may also have played a part in this.

In the source material on the Roman occupation of Britain there are constant references to trouble in the north, of repeated rebellions put down amongst the Brigantes, who must not have taken to Roman civilization like the southern tribes did.

Arvirargus, a possible rebel leader, is a name that is mentioned in one of the source texts that we have, although we know virtually nothing about him. The Roman strategic dilemma in Britain came down to either consolidating their hold on Scotland or Northern England. I don't think they would have had the resources to do both.

This brings us to Hadrian's Wall. Why was it built? To my mind, at some point the Romans made the strategic decision to hold onto Brigantia and built the wall to divide the Brigantes from their Caledonian allies to the north. The wall was not necessarily meant to keep people out but more to keep people in! It was also a powerful, enduring statement, telling us that the land south of the wall, was Roman. This fits with the Roman policy of 'Divide and Rule,' a good example of which is the Legionary base at Deva (Chester); so situated in order to keep the Brigantes and the rebellious tribes in northern Wales from helping each other. That these forts and roads were so placed and built without the aid of satellite maps or a comprehensive understanding of the geography of the UK, is a remarkable Roman achievement.

In writing Britannia, the book "Romans and Britons in North West England" by the excellent author, David Shotter, my old tutor at Lancaster University, was very useful and a brilliant read.

http://www.williamkelso.co.uk/

William Kelso

London

August 2015

Printed in Great Britain
by Amazon